LETTiNG GO

Also by Deborah Wallis

Sweet Dreams and Flying Machines/
Murder at Cherry Point

Child's Play

LETTiNG GO

A Novel by

DEBORAH WALLIS

Deborah Wallis (signature)

McBryde Publishing

NEW BERN, NORTH CAROLINA USA

McBryde Publishing

905 HAMPTON WAY
NEW BERN, NORTH CAROLINA USA
252-349-8146

This book is a work of fiction. Names, characters, places, and incidents either are products of the author's imagination or are used fictitiously. Any resemblance to actual events or locales or persons living or dead is entirely coincidental.

For information, contact:
McBryde Publishing, LLC
Subsidiary Rights Department
905 Hampton Way
New Bern, NC 28562

Paperback ISBN   9780984039159
eBook   ISBN   9780984039166

Cover design and layout by Bill Benners

Manufactured in the United States of America

First Edition: July 1, 2015

In memory of my mother, Vera McBride Haddock.
I miss you, Mom. I have always missed you.

And my brother, Clovis Curtis Haddock, Jr.
This world is a very dull place without you in it.

ACKNOWLEDGEMENTS

*W*HILE I SPENT many hours hibernating with my laptop to write this book, I could never have completed it without the help of a great many people. I owe more than I can repay to those generous souls who helped with research, brainstorming, editing, rewriting, computer problems, cover art, publishing, marketing and the ever-necessary encouragement.

Thanks to Brenda McKeel and Sandy Blackburn for sharing their knowledge and love of Wilmington, N.C. with me. While I might not have used the information in a historical context, it definitely gave my work local color and flavor from "back in the day."

Jason Frye of Teakettle Junction, Inc. worked magic with his editing. He understood the characters and helped me bring them to life. His ideas and suggestions made the story stronger and more believable. He gave me specific criticisms and praised in broad strokes. I'm so very grateful for his help.

Clovis and Dianne Haddock read the manuscript and responded with emotion and encouragement. Melanie Martin offered medical details and caught more punctuation and grammatical errors than I care to admit. Brenda McKeel gave her insights and caught mistakes. Sue Wehner's suggestions encouraged me. Who knew I'd be so happy to say, "I made y'all cry!"? Scott Martin and Scott Capoot went above and beyond to help with my many computer issues. Thank you all.

Skip Crayton read my long-winded first draft and told me how to slice and dice my wordiness into something more readable. As always,

I thank you for your patience, knowledge and love of writing. Your suggestions always make the story better! Thank you for giving me the chance to be a writer. I'm forever grateful.

Bill Benners turned my vague vision into an amazing book cover filled with emotion and symbolism. Your art helps tell my story. You also use your keen eye for detail to get the manuscript ready for the printer. Thank you for being so generous with your talent.

Eryn Kawecki stepped in and used her knowledge and expertise on the final line edit. I appreciate your willingness and effort more than you know. Thank you.

Skip Crayton, Bill Benners and Eryn Kawecki offered criticism and praise for the manuscript. Thank you for pushing me to make the story better. Thank you for sharing your knowledge, experience and talent. I'm delighted that you publish my books and thankful that you've become my friends.

I am fortunate to be surrounded by so many people who never stop chasing their dreams or encouraging one another to do the same. The Monday Night Tennis Ladies are a constant source of inspiration and are a huge blessing in my life. Brenda McKeel, Jackie Gooch, Carol Wagner, Carole Russo, Sue Wehner, Sue Cause, Karyn Soltis, Heather McLauren, Shirley Bolden, Leslie Gaylord, Joanie Theisen, and Jelena Kovrlija have led the way into new adventures and I'm just following along. Many years ago, Leslie Averitt accepted my submission to *The Good Life*. You continue to be an inspiration and a friend. Skip and Theresa Cutting have shown me what it means to follow your passion and I love you both for it.

I am blessed with an enormous family of children, grandchildren, parents, sisters (both step and in-law), nieces, nephews, cousins, my aunt and all the in-laws who show me every day how to set goals, meet them and move on to new ones. I love you all.

Cancer wrecks pain and destruction throughout this book. I've lost family and friends to that damn disease and I hope that what I've written honors them all. Clovis Curtis Haddock, Jr., Susan Watson Dorman, Jim Watson, Zelda Harmon, and Nancy Armbruster all walked through hell with dignity and grace. There are no words to tell you how much I miss you. And I thank God every day for those in my life who survived their battle. Clovis Haddock, Sr., Mary Frances Chapmon, Elly Haddock, Lynn Kline, Martie Davey, Leslie Averitt, Janie Raub and my husband, Pete Wallis – keep up the fight.

Alcoholism, too, leaves its indelible mark on several characters. To all those I have known over the years who are in recovery, I offer you my thanks and gratitude. In keeping with the spirit of anonymity, your names are listed only in my heart. To those who didn't survive the illness, I remember you with great sorrow and regret.

As always, my husband, retired Marine Colonel, Pete Wallis, gets a huge thank you for his encouragement and patience. You believe in me and my stories. You understand when I'm trying to bring a make-believe world in my head to life. You put up with late meals, or none at all, pajama days with a computer in my lap and rampant enthusiasm or frustration, in equal parts. And you do it with love. Without you, nothing that I do is possible. I love you more…

Last, but never least, I offer thanks and gratitude to booksellers and book readers everywhere. You are the final exclamation point of every story. It doesn't feel finished until you've read it. *Thank you!*

November 29, 2011
1:00 PM

Dear Mom,

$\mathcal{I}$ FINALLY FOUND your bathrobe in the back of the closet. Any other time, I probably would have spotted it right away, but this afternoon, everything I saw, touched or smelled distracted me. I ran my fingers over blouses and sweaters, imagining you standing in the same spot, doing the same thing. I pictured you tossing a scarf or a handbag to the top shelf or snatching a jacket off the hanger on your way out the door. A whiff of Beautiful drifted into my nostrils and I thought I could actually see the faint scent of your perfume layering everything with a fragrant mist. Who knew a closet could be so intimate? Surrounded by all your favorite things, I wanted only to pull up a chair and sit with my memories. But you had asked for your favorite bathrobe, so I set aside my yearnings to search for it.

The threadbare sleeve stuck out from behind your winter coat. I jerked the robe down and clutched it to my chest. The smell of your soap and shampoo lingered over the fabric, triggering emotions that I didn't want to explore. Until then, I had managed to control my fear. But when I buried my face in the worn terrycloth, I sank to the floor, unable to stop or even slow the sobs heaving through my body.

I have no idea how long I sat—definitely long enough for my legs to grow numb. When I tried to stand, a tingling sensation spread from my feet to my calves. I stretched while I wiggled my toes to get some feeling back into them. Then I looked around for something to use to push myself off the floor.

That's when I saw it. A crocheted throw covered it so completely that I almost missed the old-fashioned hat box. It sat on the floor in the far corner of your closet, directly beneath the hanger that had held your robe. The covering over the box made it look almost like you had tucked it in for the night. I pulled the afghan away and lifted the lid.

Inside lay dozens of envelopes bundled together in faded hair ribbons. I felt a twinge of guilt, thinking I'd stumbled onto old love letters or something equally private that you had worked so hard to keep hidden. But then I saw the yellowed newspaper clipping lying on top. Grandma's obituary. I picked it up, despite fearing that it would crumble in my hands. That's when I noticed that you had addressed every envelope to *Momma*. My grandmother, CiCi Dolan, *Momma* had been gone for forty years and if you had kept these letters secret from me for all that time, you must have had your reasons.

Guilt pricked me again. I put everything back, just as I had found them, and decided to ask you about the letters when I gave you your robe.

But when I got to the hospital, the nurse caught me at your door with a sympathetic hand on my arm. She tried to look me in the face as she spoke, but had difficulty maintaining the eye contact. I didn't think my guts could possibly knot any tighter, and yet they did. I fought the urge to stick my fingers in my ears and yell, "La, la, la, la, la, la, la!" while I retreated to the security of your closet. I watched the woman's lips move, but willed myself not to hear a word she said. It didn't work.

"I wanted to let you know before you saw your mom. She had a bad couple of hours. We increased her meds. She'll be a lot groggier."

I nodded. "I understand," I said. "But this is just temporary, right? Once her pain eases up, you'll be able to cut the medication back, right?"

For a moment, her eyes met mine before she glanced at the floor. It took no more time than that for me to see the pity. "I'm sorry. It's not temporary. We'll continue to increase the drugs as her pain escalates." She rubbed my arm again. "Take advantage of every moment."

Tears stung my eyes and my breath came in short puffs. As a nurse, I understood what she'd just explained to me. As a daughter, I didn't want to comprehend it at all.

I turned away and opened the door to your room. In spite of everything, I hoped to see you sitting up in bed, waiting for me to return with your robe. Instead, you lay propped against a couple of pillows. When I stepped closer, your glazed eyes opened a little and I swore you looked at something over my shoulder. I glanced behind me expecting to see that the nurse had followed me, but I saw no one there.

As I leaned down to kiss your forehead, I said, "I found your bathrobe, Mom." My fingers stroked your cheek. "I found the letters you wrote to Grandma, too." You looked puzzled. "The letters?" Then you sighed and smiled for just a moment. "Oh, the letters," you added so softly I almost missed it. Your eyes closed and your breathing became more regular.

I laid your robe over the top of your sheet and pulled one sleeve up to your cheek so it could soothe you when you woke up.

"Mom," I whispered. "I hoped to tell you about the hatbox full of letters that I found in your closet this afternoon. They're addressed to Grandma CiCi. It's almost like I was meant to find them. I wanted to ask your permission first, but when I got back, the nurse told me they've had to increase your meds." I lifted your hand to my lips. "Please forgive me. I'm going to read them."

I love you,

Alex

Obituary

Cecilia Cathleen Hewett Dolan

Wilmington, N.C. - Cecilia Cathleen Hewett Dolan, age 48, passed away on April 16, 1972 after a lengthy battle with breast cancer. The Wilmington native was employed as a nurse at Babies Hospital.

She was preceded in death by her father, Nathanial Alton Hewett and her mother, Lucinda May Hewett.

Cecilia (CiCi) Dolan is survived by her daughter, Olivia Marie Dolan Abbott, her son-in-law, Boyd (Sonny) James Abbott and her grand-daughter, Alexandra Madison Abbott.

Funeral services will be held at St. Paul's Episcopal Church on Market Street on Thursday, April 20th at 10:00 AM.

May 14, 1972
Mother's Day

Dear Momma,

IT'S MOTHER'S DAY, and I missed you so much from the time my feet touched the floor this morning that if it hadn't been for Alex, I wouldn't have bothered to get out of bed at all. I wanted to let the day slide by in a pain-numbing cocktail of memories and Boone's Farm. But for my daughter's sake, I functioned, if you consider moving like a depressed slug functioning. Alex kept asking, "What's wrong, Mommy?" And every time I said, "Nothing, Sweetie," and hugged her close, I thought I caught a glimpse of you over her shoulder, standing barefoot in the corner, wearing your favorite T-shirt and peasant skirt. I strained my eyes, afraid to blink, knowing that you'd vanish.

Only a month since your death, but the details of your perfect face dim a little more every day. During your illness, every feature etched itself into my mind and I hoped that one day I could flip the light switch of recollection and you would still be there. But the memory sketch started too late. The cancer had already destroyed the breath-taking mother of my childhood and left a withered shell in her place. That image had rooted in my mind and taken up permanent residence. It seems that eighteen months of watching you die had painted over every memory like an old black-and-white television rerun had replaced the big bold color of your life. I had to make it stop. So I put Alex to bed and grabbed pen and paper, hoping that I could somehow connect to you, refresh the vision of a healthy, vibrant you.

Flashbacks of your illness haunt my days, and one endless, looping nightmare torments my sleep. It never changes, never varies. It ends the same damn way every time.

It started the night before your funeral. With that vivid clarity known only in dreams, I saw myself in the chair next to your bed, watching your chest rise and fall in rhythm with your shallow breathing. I tucked the worn floral bedspread around your shoulders.

I heard a loud snap, almost like an electrical pop and dreamtime jumped into *Star Trek* hyperspeed. Your body shriveled. I grabbed your arm, clinging to you in this world while death pulled you closer to the next. In seconds, the boney lump that had been my Momma shrunk to half its size.

"No! Don't leave me," I screamed. Your panicked eyes sunk further into their sockets. I jumped onto the bed and shook your shoulders, desperate to jar life back into you. Nothing. No spark of recognition. Your lips tightened and pulled back in a horror-movie grin. My hands trembled and I jerked away. Your fingers flew to your face, rubbing at your distorted features. Your skin pulled tighter and the skull beneath became more pronounced until I couldn't distinguish flesh from bone. With every passing second, you looked less human and more skeletal.

My blood pounded in my ears. Th-thump. Th-thump. Th-thump. "Momma," I pleaded. The lump in my throat choked off my words. Another pop, much louder this time, and I screamed as your head imploded. The mattress seemed to have swallowed you whole. My fists pummeled the last place I saw you in that now empty bed. You couldn't be gone. Not yet. God, please. Not yet. I threw the covers back and tossed them to the floor. My palms smoothed every fold of the sheets while I searched for some sign that you had been there. A few strands of your hair lay curled on the pillow and I lunged for them. A soft whoosh and they, too, vanished.

My eyes popped open. I woke from my nightmare to the reality that I had to bury my mother that day. Burning tears slipped from the corners of my eyes and trickled down my temples dampening my already sweat-soaked pillowcase. I forced myself to get out of bed, shower and step into my dress. I bought that black dress especially for your good-bye, knowing I'd probably burn it the next day.

You would have smiled at the crammed church pews. It looked like half of Wilmington showed up. The men prayed for your resurrection while every woman in the room looked for a chance to slap a padlock on your coffin. Slumped shoulders and clasped hands added funeral-appropriate mourning. But relief sparkled behind the veil of grief on more than a few faces.

I don't have to give you names. You already know. You could always spot ally or enemy before the introduction had been completed. You embraced the trusted friend and scraped the backstabbing gossip from the sole of your shoe like day-old dog shit. I, on the other hand, trusted the untrustworthy and couldn't understand why my life periodically exploded like a hand grenade in a fish tank.

Sonny and I sat in the front row and I felt a thousand eyeballs searing holes in the back of my head. But I never turned around. I couldn't let my private heartbreak be passed on in hushed whispers through the small town grapevine.

Your coffin, the focal point of the sanctuary, sat directly in front of the altar. It hovered over the gigantic floral arrangements like a Chinese sampan floating on a sea of color. I couldn't stop thinking that within that polished wood lay my mother, an unseen, but still powerful participant in the drama playing out around me.

My loneliness welled up like a geyser. "Don't go," I whispered.

Sonny glanced down at me and just as quickly, turned back toward Reverend Holland who stood at the lectern ready to begin his eulogy.

The reverend coughed twice before he spoke. Maybe he started all his eulogies that way, but I suspected he hawked up his nerves that morning because he had heard stories of the real CiCi Dolan and couldn't connect the dots from that woman to the one he wanted to describe.

"Cecilia Cathleen Hewett Dolan left us too soon. She lived her life with adventure, passion and joy. Those who loved her never dreamed that vibrancy could be wiped out by illness, that cancer would be the one thing she couldn't strong-arm her way around. The grief left in the wake of her life and her death is almost unbearable."

Reverend Holland looked at me, and when I saw the pity in his eyes, every emotional barrier I had in my arsenal sprung into position. The good reverend yammered on. I heard only, "Blah. Blah. Blah." Music hummed in the background. I couldn't name even one of the hymns.

Sonny elbowed me and we followed the swarming crowd to the parking lot. I imagined I heard, "Gentlemen, start your engines," while dozens of keys turned in their ignitions at once. But even the hurried fanfare couldn't rush the procession as it inched toward the cemetery.

I hunched in one corner of the limousine. Sonny slumped in the other. He picked at the lint on his pants and I stared out the window at the cloud-dotted blue sky. Would it have been too much to ask for a gray day to bury my mother?

My stomach rolled, threatening to spew coffee all over the leather seat. We pulled into the cemetery and I scooted closer to Sonny to lay my head on his shoulder. Just for a moment, I needed to lean on my husband, to let his strength carry me when I felt none of my own.

He opened the door before the limo even came to a full stop and swept me away with a flick of his fingers. He might as well have been swiping at a bug that had mistakenly landed on his jacket.

"Let's get this done, Livvy. People are waiting and I want to get out of this monkey suit sometime today."

He stepped out of the car without a glance behind him. But he left the door open for me. Such a gentleman. I wished I had the energy to slap him, but my grief held me down like a tent peg and I doubted that I could have raised my arm high enough to land a blow.

I stepped out of the car into the sunlight and squinted. Even though I borrowed your Jackie O sunglasses for the occasion, the avalanche of color assaulted my eyes. Azalea bushes blazed in white, coral and red. The pink blossoms of Chinese cherry trees dotted the landscape and drifted in the breeze. Only the crowd clustered near the coffin looked like an oasis of misery. Their shades of black and gray gave off a grim glow that blotted out those irritating blushes of spring. I craved their darkness and wanted them to absorb me into their bleak flock.

When the graveside service ended, people slipped away to their cars. I tried to stand, but my rubbery legs wouldn't hold. I sank back into the chair.

Your flower-draped coffin loomed in front of me. I reached toward it. "I can't do this, Momma."

Three men in work clothes stood off to one side waiting to lower the casket and fill the grave. One of them must have heard me. He stepped closer. "Are you okay, ma'am? Do you want me to get someone to help you?"

I shook my head and waved him off. This time I used the chair back to push up. "Good-bye, Momma." I turned away from you for the last time and staggered toward the limousine.

I miss you,

Livvy

August 12, 1972
Happy Birthday

Dear Momma,

TODAY'S YOUR BIRTHDAY and I've felt you tugging at me all day. Sonny and Alex went to bed a little while ago, so I can talk to you now, in private, through another letter.

Several weeks after your funeral, I worked up the courage to step through the front door of your house. I had tried several times. Got all the way to your driveway once, but couldn't force myself out of the car. I pictured you in the lawn chair on the porch lifting your beer in the air, waving it at me as I walked toward you. That empty chair mocked me. My fingers gripped the steering wheel like a life preserver and my breath caught in my throat until I choked. I threw the stick in reverse, backed up and drove away. My head told me I'd feel closer to you in your home, but my heart said the echo in every uninhabited room would slice my raw wounds open like a scalpel. So, I listened to my heart and let your house sit, undisturbed, until Sonny badgered me into beginning the process of packing you away.

"Have you lost your damn mind, Livvy?" Sonny shook his pudgy, greasy finger in my face. "You're every bit as crazy as your dead momma. You can't leave the house sittin' with nobody living there. You need to pack that shit up and get rid of it so you can sell the place."

My chest tightened and I felt my anger ignite. "I'm not selling Momma's home," I announced through locked jaws.

Sonny shook his head. "You've got no money to make the payment, Livvy." He tickled his fingers up and down my arm. "Besides, baby, we need the money. We could pay off bills; buy that boat we've been wanting."

I shoved him away. "No. I'm not selling it." He pushed back and I fell into the cabinet behind me. "I don't care what you say," I screamed. "I'm not selling Momma's house."

"Do whatever you want, Livvy. Just don't expect me to take care of the yard or pay the damn mortgage for you." He walked to the refrigerator and pulled out a beer. After he popped the top, he pitched the metal ring to me. "Throw that away, will you?"

I threw it back at him and it bounced off his head.

He yelled, "Damn it!" so loud the glasses in the cabinet behind me rattled.

We'd both gotten so lost in our all-important argument that we'd completely forgotten that Alex sat at the kitchen table watching us. Her lower lip quivered and she let out a wail that I'm sure the neighbors could hear. She picked up her plastic Winnie the Pooh bowl and tossed it, Lucky Charms and all, at the refrigerator door. Cereal and milk flew everywhere, including all over Sonny and his beer. A hysterical giggle started in my gut and worked its way up. I held my hand over my mouth to control it but couldn't stifle the laughter. Sonny stared down at his milk-drenched shirt and muttered, "Son of a bitch," before he marched toward the bedroom to change clothes.

I grabbed a paper towel and stooped to wipe the mess off the floor. A faint breath grazed the back of my neck. It might sound crazy, but I could have sworn I heard you whisper, "If he doesn't like you keeping my house, tough titties." I shivered and kept wiping at the floor until my knees gave way and I plopped down, right there on the linoleum while tears streamed down my cheeks. You used to say that all the time. Until you got sick. You never used those words again after they told us you had breast cancer.

Everything changed after that day in the doctor's office. I can still hear his medical monotone. "Ms. Dolan, we got your biopsy results back. You have cancer and it's spreading." I felt like I'd been riding the Tilt-A-Whirl at the county fair, spinning in that metal cup, around and around, except this time, the bolts had broken loose and the seat spun off the platform, airborne and out of control. After the crash landing, I came to in a new world, one filled with disease and pain and fear and suffering. A world filled with words like radical mastectomy and chemotherapy. I looked at you, sitting next to me in front of the doctor's desk and watched terror grow in your eyes, darkening them from the bottom up, like coffee filling a clear glass mug. Emotions had always danced over your face, coming and going with your moods, but from that God-awful morning until the day you died, the fear never left you again. Audacious to terror stricken in the span of that one terrible sentence. "You have cancer, and it's spreading."

In your final weeks, Alex and I stayed at your house. Keeping vigil at your bedside became my life. I watched your strength slip away and your spirit fade. You had always told me that the key to life was knowing when to hang on and when to let go. And you hung on so tight that some days I thought surely your fingernails would pop right off. You gripped your sheets until your knuckles turned white, as though if you let go, for even a moment, your life would slip from your fingers with the fabric. You hung on for me. You clung to your suffering for me.

The helplessness I had felt for weeks vanished that last day when I realized that I had the power to free you. When I finally understood that only through my strength could you let go.

I kissed your cheek and stroked the last wisps of hair that chemo had left you. I whispered in your ear, "It's okay, Momma. You don't have to fight any more. Alex and I will be fine. You can let go now. I love you." I held your hand and felt you slip away. I wanted to call you back, to say, "Wait! It's a mistake. Don't leave yet." But I bit my tongue until I tasted blood. The words, *I still need you,* choked in my throat and tears flooded my eyes until I couldn't see.

I really do still need you.

P.S. Sonny pressured me into making a decision about your house though he hated what I decided to do. The renters moved in a couple of weeks ago. Sonny stormed out of the house and didn't come back until dawn.

Momma, you pegged Sonny way back in high school. You said, "Sonny Boyd is white trash that'll never amount to nothing." Then after we got married you shook your head and said, "Olivia Marie Dolan, don't you ever forget, I told you so."

I hear you now, Momma. I hear you.

Dear Momma,

I SURVIVED my first Thanksgiving and Christmas without you. Barely. But I didn't slap anybody senseless and that felt like a miracle.

Sonny, Alex and I went to Daddy's for Thanksgiving dinner. The Bleached Bimbo asked me—make that told me—"I want you to bring cornbread dressing, green bean casserole, and pumpkin pie." I had never made cornbread dressing in my life, and I suspect she knew that and wanted to embarrass me. It didn't work.

Instead, her demand triggered the urge I'd been ignoring to sort through some of your boxes. It took me an hour of opening, resealing and rearranging, but I found the ones filled with your old cookbooks.

Do you remember when I told you that BB had a great big helping of your cornbread dressing at the reception after Granddaddy's funeral? She had taken tiny dollops of every casserole and when she tasted yours, she closed her eyes and moaned. Then she strutted back to the buffet table and scooped two heaping portions onto her plate. I waited till she had shoveled a huge bite into her mouth before I said, "Good, isn't it? My momma made that." The woman choked. She coughed and sputtered and spat it back onto her plate. When she looked at me like she might smash the whole thing into my face, I stared her down with my best I-dare-you glare. She held her plate between the thumb and forefinger of each hand and marched toward the trashcan where she held the offending dish over the opening and dropped it in. Then she walked back to the buffet and began the process all over again, taking little bitty portions of everything. Everything except your cornbread dressing.

That memory planted the seed of an idea that germinated into a truly great plan. I sorted through every cookbook you had trying to find that same recipe. Four looked like strong possibilities and you had written "Good!" beside each of them. So, about a week before Thanksgiving I made them all, on the same day.

Sonny came home from work that night to find fried chicken and four cornbread dressings for dinner. He grabbed a beer from the fridge and gulped a swig. "You're crazy as a bedbug, Livvy," he complained, but then he sat down and ate every bite of everything. After a huge swallow of one of the dressings, he said, "Man, this tastes just like your momma's."

My helpful husband cocked his head and arched a brow at me when I leaned over, kissed his cheek and said, "Thank you, honey."

So that's the one I made for Thanksgiving. I suspect that BB recognized it from the smell before I even took the tinfoil off the top of the pan. She wrinkled her nose like something foul had crawled in the door behind us and she actually gagged when she took the pan from my hands.

Her voice dripped that nasty sarcasm of hers when she asked, "What did you make, Sweetie?"

"I made the dressing you wanted, Nora Jean. Don't you remember telling me to make it?" I smiled and batted my eyelashes. Her big blue eyes turned black and she stretched her lips so tight over her teeth that she reminded me of a lizard sucking in a fly.

Daddy and Sonny took Alex and a couple of beers into the family room to watch football. Alex curled up in Daddy's lap and yelled for every play like she understood the game.

Daddy adored Alex, but my baby girl didn't do a thing for Nora Jean except gnaw on her last nerve. BB seldom paid any attention to Alex at all, but that day, the longer Daddy and Alex watched television together, the more irritated the Bimbo got. And by the time we put dinner on the table, smoke billowed from her nostrils.

Nora Jean placed a chair between Sonny and me for Alex, but before we sat down, Alex dragged it to Daddy's end of the table.

"No, Sweetie, you need to sit with your parents," Nora Jean ordered.

"I want to sit with Granddaddy."

"You sit there, Alex," Nora Jean commanded.

Alex put her little hands on her hips and said, "No." She tugged on the chair again.

Daddy grabbed it for her and set it right next to his. "Well, of course, she can sit by me, Nora Jean." He reached toward me. "Hand me Lady Bug's plate, Livvy."

About that time, Nora Jean's nostril smoke darkened and thickened until I thought she'd burst into flames. She looked at Alex like she'd rather shoot her than give her a slice of turkey. BB slammed the carving knife on the table in front of Daddy and marched to the kitchen. She came back to the table with an open bottle of wine and made quite the ceremony of pouring it into all our glasses. Then, she turned to Alex and said, "Would you like a glass of wine, Sweetie?"

Every head at the table snapped in Nora Jean's direction. I sat in shocked silence watching BB stare at my daughter. Alex furrowed her little forehead and glanced at me.

"I asked you a question."

"I can't drink wine, Nora Jean. I'm only four."

"That's right. You can't drink wine because you're a child." Nora Jean leaned down until her nose almost touched Alex's. "A child who needs to learn some manners and do what she's told."

"That's enough, Nora Jean," Daddy said. "I don't know what set you off, but Alex didn't do anything."

"Really? Well, I think that little monster knows exactly what she did."

I jumped up, knocking my chair over backwards behind me. Even Sonny looked ready to deck BB.

"Don't you ever talk to my daughter like that again, you gold-digging bimbo!" The words tumbled from my mouth like I spoke to her that way every day.

"Who are you calling a bimbo?"

"That's it," Daddy yelled. "No more."

I picked up Alex and marched out of the house toward the car. Sonny snatched the dressing and pie from the table and followed me.

You would have loved it, Momma. We reached a new low in the Dolan household.

Livvy

P.S. We didn't go to Daddy's for Christmas. The family Super Bowl get-together required a phony truce, but everything had changed. Daddy wouldn't let Alex sit in his lap for more than a few minutes at a time which hurt her feelings and pissed me off. BB smirked like she had just laid down the winning hand in a poker game, but I'll find a way to get even with her.

November 30, 2011
5:00 AM

Dear Mom,

OH. MY. GOSH. I remember that Thanksgiving. Nora Jean had been especially angry. I didn't understand it then and still don't. Was she jealous of me? Because Granddaddy loved me? Could she really have been that shallow? I don't remember her offering me wine. No wonder you hated her.

Do you know what else I remember? When we got home, you walked to the hall closet and took out an old blanket that you spread on the floor in front of the television. You added pillows for each of us, and then grabbed forks and spoons from the kitchen and tossed them into the center of the indoor picnic. You bowed your head and said, "Thank you, Lord, for cornbread dressing and pumpkin pie." Then you picked up a spoon and shoveled a huge scoop of dressing into your mouth.

Dad grinned and dropped down cross-legged on the floor. He pulled me onto his lap, snagged a fork and handed it to me. "Dig in," he said.

I had never eaten anything right out of the pan, except for cleaning the cookie dough remnants from the bowl. While both of you ate like a couple of famished hogs, I picked at the dressing and chewed tiny little bites. Until you took my fork from me, filled it to overflowing and aimed it at my face.

"This is how a fun-feast is done, kiddo. Open up," you ordered.

I did and you popped the fork between my lips, leaving a trail of dressing across the blanket and all over my face. When I tried to chew, more tumbled down my chin and I started to giggle. You and Dad laughed right along with me.

We ate most of the cornbread dressing and all of the pumpkin pie. The filling anyway. We left an awful lot of the crust in the pan. And we had so much fun. More than I ever remember the three of us having, before or after that day. It's my favorite family memory. You, Dad and me – happy at the same time.

Do you even realize how special you made that day? We had no turkey or festive table, but your pretend feast made it my fondest Thanksgiving.

You know, I never thought about it before, but now, I'd love to know how Granddaddy and Nora Jean spent the rest of their day. I don't see fun anywhere in that picture.

Why didn't I ever ask you about all that before? God knows I wish I could now. I want to hear your stories and all the details I missed. I need to hear your laughter. But it's too late. The meds make you sleep a lot and even awake, you're groggy. You talk in circles and I'm not sure from one minute to the next if what you're saying is real or drug-induced.

Will you ever be able to read what I've written? Or be alert enough that I can read it to you? Please find your way back to me, Mom. I'm afraid. I don't want to lose you.

Dear Momma,

REMEMBER Dwayne Montgomery? I saw him. It was only for a few minutes, but I'd have been satisfied with less. It reminded me that I'm not the only one having trouble accepting your death.

Several months ago, Dwayne's Service Repair offered Sonny more money than his last job. He jumped at it. Yesterday, Alex and I stopped by to drop off his lunch. We walked into the garage through one of the huge open doors. Dwayne must have seen us. He stepped out of the office. "Can I…" The man stared at me until the hair on my arms stood up. I swear I saw his breath hitch and his jaw drop. He stepped closer. His eyes narrowed.

I remember when you dated him. I remember him being tall and handsome with the most beautiful hair I had ever seen. The man I saw yesterday bore little resemblance to the Dwayne Montgomery of your past. No hair. Not thinning, not balding. Gone, leaving only a shiny scalp pockmarked with half a dozen giant scars. And his paunchy gut looked at least a week or two past his due date, like somebody stuck a hose down his throat and turned on the water, full force, bloating him almost beyond recognition.

He walked toward me, stuck his hand out and slid his palm over my cheek. I shivered. Handsome Dwayne Montgomery looked like a creepy, old leach. I backed up and jerked my head away.

Dwayne muttered, "You're the spitting image of CiCi." He stepped closer and reached for my face again. I retreated until I hit the wall and couldn't go any further.

Without knowing it, Alex diffused the whole situation. She stepped in front of me and looked up at Dwayne. "Hi. I'm Alex Abbott and that's my daddy." She pointed at Sonny and her eyes lit up like Elvis Presley had just stepped through the door.

Dwayne stared down at her, but his hand stayed stretched out toward me until another man, the man I remembered Dwayne Montgomery to be, stepped out of the office into the garage.

Momma, did you know Dwayne had a son? A son who looked like an improved version of the young Dwayne Montgomery. Taller, more handsome, more hair, no hose down his throat. My heart stopped. Did you feel that way the first time you saw Montgomery Sr.?

Sonny jerked me back into the present when he popped out from under the hood where he'd been working. He slapped the wrench in his hand against his thigh. I grabbed Alex by the shoulders, pulled her closer to me and we both slid down the wall toward Sonny.

Montgomery Jr. strode to his father like he would toward a disobedient child. He patted Dwayne's back. "Come on, Pop. We've got work to do."

Sr. shrugged him off. "Look at her." His head swung back and forth from me to his son. "So much like CiCi Dolan that I'd swear I hadn't watched them lay that woman in the grave."

My chin shook like it had some kind of palsy. Tears ran down my cheeks and when I felt the snot stream from my nose, I picked up Alex and headed back out the garage door.

Behind me, I heard Montgomery Jr. say, "For God's sake, Pop. She looks like CiCi because that's her daughter and you just tore the poor woman slam up." He turned to Sonny. "Go after her to make sure she's all right."

"Nah. She's got to get over her Momma's death sometime," my adoring husband answered. "Can't expect folks to walk on eggshells around her the rest of their lives. She'll be fine."

My cheeks burned with shame. I longed for my husband to embrace me, cherish me, protect me. Instead, I embarrassed him. My pain embarrassed him.

Alex squirmed to get down. I held onto her with one hand and used the other to wipe a tissue under my nose. We trudged through the August heat and humidity and by the time we got home, I had to peel my daughter's drenched clothes from her body so she could get into something dry. Before I'd gotten her shorts pulled all the way up, she skipped into the living room, turned on cartoons and lay down on the floor in front of the window unit air conditioner.

I dropped my sweaty clothes on the bathroom floor and stared in the mirror. Dwayne said I looked like you. I couldn't see it. Your hair glistened like a spotlight followed you around all day. Mine hung limp. Daddy used to say you had sleepy, sexy doe eyes. I leaned closer to the mirror. Mine looked more…well, deer-in-headlights. Startled and definitely not sexy. Your skin shimmered like flawless porcelain. At almost twenty-six, I still fought the occasional acne outbreak. And your curves had a life of their own. Every male head in the room spun 180 degrees to catch just a glimpse of you walking away. I'm sure no man ever followed my exit that way.

I craned my neck over my shoulder to view my own hiney in the mirror. At first, I giggled. Within seconds, my laughter came faster and harder until I doubled over in hysterics. I clutched a stitch in my side and gasped for air. When I could breathe again, I wriggled into shorts and an old T-shirt before I pranced into the kitchen and poured a bourbon and coke.

Guess what, Momma. A man had, indeed, snapped his head around to gape at me. Unfortunately, that man had to be old, bald, fat, creepy Dwayne Montgomery and even he hadn't really reacted to me. He thought I looked like you.

I thought I'd begun to forget. I thought I'd begun to heal. But Montgomery Sr. ripped the scab off my wound and reminded me that even in death, you left me standing in your enormous damn shadow.

I love you anyway.

Livvy

November 30, 2011
6:30 AM

Dear Mom,

IT'S HARD for me to believe that you didn't see yourself measuring up to Grandma CiCi's looks? Do you honestly not know how beautiful you were then and are now? You cast a mighty big shadow yourself.

Love you,

Alex

Dear Momma,

DADDY AND ALEX sat on the dock at his house, their legs hanging off the edge. Alex swung hers back and forth. Daddy's bare feet dangled over the rippling wake from boats passing by on the Intracoastal Waterway. I dropped into a lawn chair behind them, beer in hand, and watched Daddy teach my daughter to fish.

"If you want to fish, Lady Bug, you need to learn how to hook the worms," he explained.

"But they're yucky, Granddaddy. I don't want to touch 'em." Alex's nose scrunched up when she yanked her hand back from the three-inch monster Daddy held out to her.

"Don't be such a prissy butt. Even your mother learned how to hook a worm." He threw a nod in my direction emphasizing that if I could do it, any other moron could, too.

I wanted to stick my foot in his back and shove him into the water, fishing pole and all.

"Here. Get used to holding it in your hand and then we'll practice hooking it."

Alex laid her pole down and held out a shaky palm. Daddy dropped the worm and it squirmed before it hit her skin. She giggled and cupped both hands around the squiggling creature to keep it from getting away.

"I'm going to name him Twister 'cuz he wiggles so much," Alex said.

Daddy shook his head. "You don't name worms, Alex. Now, let's get him on the hook and catch us some dinner."

When he took Alex's hands in his and moved the hook toward that worm, you'd have thought he rammed it through her thumb. She screamed, "No! I'm not putting a hook in Twister!" She jumped up and ran toward the vegetable garden at the back of the yard. Alex bent over and used one finger to push the worm off her hand into the dirt. She glanced back toward the dock like she thought Satan himself might be behind her. "Run, Twister. Hurry."

I heard his sigh before Daddy turned and stared at me. "She's got a lot of you in her, Livvy." Then he actually smiled and the years melted away to the days when he taught me to fish. Nothing mattered to me back then except my father's approval and pride, so instead of standing up for the rights of worms everywhere like Alex had just done, I did the opposite. I skewered them, over and over, until my fingers bled and I could hook a night-crawler every bit as good as Daddy. "She's a stubborn little thing," he said.

"She is that." I swigged my beer. "When did Momma go back to school? How old was I?"

"You weren't out of the crib yet; must have been about a year or so. CiCi had gone to James Walker Nursing School for a while, but then quit when we got married. After you were born she finished school, got on at Babies Hospital and stayed there until…well, you know." He cast his line into the rippling water. "What brought that up?"

"I wondered how she did it all: school, work, child, marriage, home. Alex starts kindergarten in the fall, and I feel like I need to start thinking about a job or training for a job or something."

"Deadbeat you married doesn't make enough money. And drinks up what he does make, right?"

"Daddy, don't." I swigged again and glanced at Alex. She had her fingers stuck in the dirt, building a cave for her new pet worm.

"I'm not saying anything you don't already know, Livvy." He snorted. "And by the way, CiCi didn't do it all. She didn't give a damn about the house, our marriage fell apart, and we could certainly debate her mothering skills, couldn't we?"

I didn't want Daddy's words to be true, but pictures of the past fast-forwarded through my mind. Flash – seven-year-old Livvy couldn't find any clean panties in the drawer. Mommy snagged a pair from the growing dirty clothes pile on the garage floor in front of the washer. "Just put these on and go." Flash – Livvy pulled the covers over her head but couldn't block out her parents yelling. Flash – Mommy tiptoed in to kiss Livvy goodnight, bent down and spilled her gin and tonic all over the blanket. She stumbled back out the door without even noticing. Livvy pulled the wet blanket away and dropped it on the floor.

The knots in my stomach rose to my chest and fluttered before they lodged in my throat and choked off my breath. I wanted to argue with Daddy, but only one thought filled my head: *No wonder I have no idea how to do this.*

I asked anyway because I needed to know. "I seriously want to know how she did it."

"Fine," he grunted. "The whole time CiCi was in school or studying or working, for that matter, your grandmother took care of you like you were her own. And if the house ever got cleaned, more than likely she did that, too." He picked up his beer and chugged the last of it before he crushed the can in his fist. "By all accounts, your mother was a fine nurse, but besides that, the only other things she truly enjoyed were flirting and drinking." He stood up and stared down at me. "And if you're not careful, you'll find yourself headed down that same road."

"What are you talking about?"

"You're drinking too much, Livvy. Not sure if that's because of your Momma or the deadbeat." He shook his head. "But you damn sure better get a grip on it." He picked up both fishing poles and walked back toward the house. Before he got to the end of the dock, he turned back around. "Alex deserves better. Don't do to her what CiCi did to you."

The fluttering knots in my stomach tightened. *Don't compare me to her,* I thought. *I'm not her!*

"Do you ever wonder why Momma left you?" I snapped.

"Nope. She made that perfectly clear when she moved out." Daddy turned back to the house, but I watched his shoulders sag a little bit and I knew I'd hit him, probably harder than I wanted. No matter how many years had passed since little Livvy sat on the dock with her father, the grown woman still wanted nothing more than her daddy's approval and pride.

The sun set at my back while I stared at the water. My hands moved to swipe at a stray tear.

"By the way," I yelled. "If anybody cares, I have an interview tomorrow for a job at Cape Fear Textiles. Good pay and benefits. Maybe your daughter won't turn out to be so worthless after all."

I chugged the rest of my beer and walked to the house.

Livvy

August 12, 1974
Happy Birthday

Dear Momma,

THE CALL CAME on a Tuesday in June at about three in the afternoon. That day the sun shimmered like a huge lump of hot coal and the temperature soared over a hundred degrees. Combined with nearly matching humidity, it made anything outdoors miserable, even for a born-and-raised southern girl. The clanking window-unit air conditioner blew from the living room through the opening into the kitchen like a wind tunnel. I wore torn, cut-off jeans and a tube top. My hair looked great in its ponytail that morning, but by the time the phone rang in the afternoon, most of it had slipped free and frizzed around my face.

Do you wonder why I remember every silly detail surrounding that phone call? Because that one call held the potential to change my life.

Alex lay sprawled on the carpet in front of the TV watching cartoons. When the phone rang I hollered, "Turn that dad-gum thing down! I can't hear anything." My usually well-behaved child ignored me. I grabbed the phone and held it hard against one ear while I mashed my palm into the other. Still, I couldn't make out the garbled words on the other end.

"Can you hang on just a minute?" I asked while I trotted toward the television stretching the cord as far as it would go behind me. I must have looked like an impaired contortionist, gripping the phone in one hand, arms spread as far apart as I could get them, straining to get that last inch that would let me grab the volume knob and twist it, all while I squatted so low that I doubted that I'd be able to stand again on my own without dropping the phone and pushing up on the arm of the sofa. Alex paid no attention to me until she found herself watching a soundless television set.

Tom and Jerry's animated bickering definitely lacked sparkle without the noisy commotion that accompanied it.

"I can't hear it! Turn it back up!" Alex squealed before she jumped up and turned the volume even louder than it had been before.

I backed into the kitchen, glanced around the room and spotted what I hoped would be a sanctuary of silence—the pantry. I opened the door, stepped inside the claustrophobic space and pulled the phone cord under the door while I closed it.

My feet tapped out a little jig right there in the dark when I heard, "Livvy, this is Wilbur Walker down at the plant. I've got good news. If you still want the job, it's yours."

"Yes!" I screeched loud enough to have pierced the man's ears. "Yes, I still want it! When do I start? What do I need to do?"

"Your training starts July eighth. Be at the plant by seven thirty that morning. Nothing you need to bring. We provide everything. If you have any questions between now and then, you've got my number. Call me."

"Thank you, Mr. Walker. Thank you so much."

"Congratulations, Livvy. I'll see you in July."

The click that echoed in my ear when he hung up sounded an awful lot like *cha-ching*. I flew out of the pantry like my pants had caught fire and sang, "I got the job! I got the job!"

Alex sat up on the floor and stared at me. I ran over, picked her up and spun her around in circles until we both landed in a heap on the couch. "What job?" she asked when she stopped laughing.

"I got a job at the textile plant! Isn't that wonderful?" I tickled her tummy and she giggled again. "Let's go tell Daddy."

We slipped into our sandals and danced out the door and down the street.

I saw Sonny working in an open garage bay and I waved. Alex yelled, "Hi, Daddy!" He threw up a hand in return and stuck his head back under the hood of a beat-up Chevy Nova.

Montgomery Jr. stepped out of his office and nodded a greeting to Alex and me before he yelled, "Hey, Abbott, your girls are here."

Sonny kept working so Jr. walked out to meet us.

I ran my fingers through Alex's hair struggling to make it look like I had actually brushed it that morning. Then I realized I hadn't changed out of my cut-offs and tube top, so Alex's hair might be the least of my concerns. "We stopped by to talk to Sonny for a minute. I hope that's not a problem."

Russ Montgomery smiled the most beautiful smile I think I've ever seen. He flashed white teeth and one lone dimple sunk into his left cheek. "No problem at all." When his eyes smiled he looked like he actually meant what he said. "My wife comes in all the time. You and Alex are certainly welcome to visit." He tussled Alex's hair and, with a single swipe, destroyed my efforts to neaten it. "Besides," he said. "I hoped I'd get the chance to apologize to you."

"You don't owe me an apology."

"No, but my pop does."

My temples throbbed. Today, I didn't want to think about you, Momma, or Dwayne Montgomery or anything sad or depressing. I had good news to tell my husband and that's all I wanted to do. But now I stood there, listening to Russ Montgomery bring up the very subjects that made me feel like digging my own grave and jumping in. *Why did I come here in the first place?* I wondered. I could always leave and tell Sonny about the plant when he got home. I backed up a couple of steps and shook my head. "No apology necessary."

Oblivious, Jr. didn't seem to notice me drifting away from him and he never missed a beat. "Pop spends a lot of time in his head, in the past. Your mother was a big part of that for him and I don't think he ever got over her." The smile plastered on his face while he spoke turned down at the corners and showed the sadness behind it. "So, when a beautiful woman walks in the door, he doesn't know how to behave any more. I'm sure bringing up your mother hurt you and I'm sorry for that."

"No, it's fine."

"Well, Pop's not here much these days, so don't let him keep you from stopping by." Russ flicked his thumb out and nodded his head in Sonny's direction. "Sonny's in there."

Alex ran inside and grabbed Sonny mid-thigh in a bear hug. He bent down and patted her back with the inside of his forearm, keeping his greasy hand splayed out away from her clothes. The entire time he rubbed Alex, his eyes remained locked with mine, his lip curled in annoyance.

"I got the job," I announced and even Sonny's visible irritation couldn't contain the grin that spread across my face.

"Huh?"

"The job at the plant." I spoke the words slowly and distinctly like I might be speaking to someone teetering on the edge of imbecilic incompetence. "I got the job. I start in July."

"July? What the hell are you gonna do with Alex?"

No congratulations. No acknowledgement that we needed the money, that this job would help us out. A lot. I knew I had done good and I wanted more than anything else to hear my husband admit that. He didn't. He probably never would.

My joy deflated like an undercooked soufflé. The familiar ache in my heart felt like it would never heal. I wanted to feel angry. I wanted to yell at Sonny, to tell him he could pick his shit up out of the front yard when he got home from work. I wanted to stand up and say, "I deserve better than this, better than you!" I straightened my spine and opened my mouth, but nothing came out. That's when I realized that I didn't believe the words I wanted to say. I didn't believe that I deserved any better at all.

I grabbed Alex's hand and pulled her toward the door. She jerked away.

"I don't want to go yet." Her whine jumped up and down on the seesaw of my patience. "I want to stay with Daddy."

"Now see what you've done," Sonny said in a tone that matched the maturity of his five-year-old daughter's whine.

Before I could snap back at him, I heard Russ Montgomery say, "Congratulations, Livvy. That's a heck of an accomplishment. I know several people who tried for positions out there and never even got a response." He knelt down to Alex and said, "Why don't you and I go into the office and let Mommy and Daddy talk for a minute. I think there's a candy bar waiting for you in the top drawer of my desk."

"Can I, Mommy? Please?"

I nodded and mouthed "Thank you" to Montgomery Jr. He took Alex's hand and led her toward the candy.

As soon as the office door closed, Sonny snatched up the rag next to him and wiped at his hands like he could remove what little emotion he felt toward me with that dirty, greasy cloth.

"Did you come down here to cause trouble for me, Livvy? What the hell were you thinking?"

"I thought my husband would be happy about my good news and I wanted to tell him about it. I thought you'd be thrilled that I got a job. My bringing home some extra money will help us out. You know that." I truly hadn't meant to point out how tight things had been the last few months, but when his eyes narrowed, I knew that he'd picked up on it.

"Now you're complaining that I don't make enough money?"

"That's not what I said. But you know we've been in a little bit of a jam for a while now. I want to help."

"You want to help? Why don't you just do the job you already have? Try taking care of the house and managing the money better."

"Sonny, can't you just be proud of me?"

"Proud of you? You'll never get through the damn training. You don't finish nothing, Livvy. You want me to get excited about something that's never gonna happen? Fine. Congratulations, honey. Good job."

Sonny stuck that sarcastic knife in my back and twisted it. The searing pain that followed the jagged gash brought hot tears to my eyes. I spun toward the wall so he couldn't see me wipe them away.

In defeated silence, I swallowed another round of Sonny's cruelty before I turned away and walked to the office. "Time for us to go home, Alex," I called out.

"Can I take my candy bar?"

"Sure you can," Montgomery Jr. told her.

"Thanks," I said to him.

"Congratulations again, Livvy."

Alex and I walked home. She complained the whole way about her chocolate melting in the heat, while I assured her that we could fix it good as new in the freezer when we got home. Between assurances, I mumbled to myself, giving Sonny the hell I should have piled on him at the garage. Every step strengthened my resolve not only to make it through the training, but also to turn the job at the plant into a career. I had no choice. The only options I could see for my life came through that job. And I couldn't think of anything I wanted more at that moment than options.

Livvy

P.S.   Didn't you used to date Wilbur Walker, Jr.? You called him WWII. I have a foggy recollection of walking in on you two in the middle of the night. I had to be eight or nine. Not sure that's a memory I really want to bring in to focus.

Dear Momma,

FOR MONTHS Sonny had been drinking worse than usual and picking fights with me. Once or twice a week, he came home from work, chugged a couple of beers and started in on me about something stupid. He bitched when I didn't have a job and complained when I did. He didn't like what I fixed for dinner. The TV repairman didn't show up on time or how the television broke in the first place. After he ginned up enough self-righteous anger, he'd storm out the door for a well-deserved night on the town. At least, he thought he deserved it.

In typical schizophrenic fashion, I either cried myself to sleep or paced the floor until dawn, drinking beer while I practiced the angry monologue I planned to deliver right before I shot him between the eyes. He usually reappeared sometime the next day, carrying a flower or a pizza, his face a mask of little-boy guilt. I'm ashamed to tell you how many times I fell for it.

I finally took a page out of your playbook and formulated a plan for what some might consider stalking, but I thought of as fact checking.

Sonny pulled the angry routine one evening after Daddy had picked up Alex to spend the night at his house. The beer I'd already polished off enhanced my bravery and I followed him. I grabbed my keys, purse and the rest of my six-pack before I jumped in my clunker, a gray '64 VW Bug. Sonny peeled out of the driveway, and I burned rubber hoping to catch up.

By the time I got to Carolina Beach Road, I saw two sets of taillights in the distance, one headed toward the beach and the other downtown. Something in my gut screamed that if Sonny had a sideline floozy she had to be a beach broad, so I sped in that direction. I crossed Snow's Cut

Bridge and stayed a few car lengths behind until he pulled in to his favorite pool hall.

I'd been there with him once or twice. He'd rack 'em up with the boys while I sat in a booth, alone with my beer. I hated it. But now I suspected that he'd found someone who didn't mind the place so much. I had visions of her skin-tight blue jeans bent over the edge of the pool table. You have no idea what will power it took not to walk in the front door, announce my presence and ram a freshly chalked cue up her butt.

I backed into a spot across the street and nursed a couple of Budweisers while I watched the front door. My patience paid off when Sonny stepped outside, his arm around a platinum blonde. She wore Levi's and had the bottom part of her button-front shirt tied in a knot under D-cup boobs. My heart raced, my palms oozed sweat that smelled like beer and I actually tasted my anger, bitter bile rolling on my tongue. Before I realized it, I had turned the key in the ignition, revved the engine and shifted into first gear. I figured with my headlights on bright, they'd never know who ran their adulterous asses down in that seedy parking lot. But when Sonny put up his hand to shield his eyes from the glare I saw only Alex's father instead of the drunken whore-hound who'd stood there moments before. I slammed my foot down on the brake.

Sonny opened her door and helped her into the driver's seat. Then he leaned down to kiss her through the open window. I couldn't remember the last time my husband opened my car door and, in spite of everything, that hurt me more that I dreamed it could. Blood oozed down my throat when I bit the inside of my cheek. He stumbled to his own car, our car. The blonde drove away first. Sonny followed her. I slipped onto the street behind them and the three of us looked like the new guys in NASCAR struggling to keep up with the big boys through every turn.

The tramp-driven pace car led the way up Carolina Beach Road to Monkey Junction where it hung a left and kept going until it took another left. I slowed down and drove past them, made a U-turn and pulled onto the same road. The homes looked small but new, certainly newer than my house, and that made me wish I had run over them when I had the chance.

Not far down the road, I spotted her car and Sonny's parked one behind the other in a narrow driveway.

Black shutters accented the red brick of the tiny house. Grass covered the front yard, but the shrubbery looked small enough to have just been planted. I saw no garage, no fence and most importantly, no lights. The two horny toads must have headed straight for the boxy little bedroom.

I U-turned again and sped home, wishing I'd planned a little better. When I jumped out of the car in front of my house, I left it running, driver's door open, waiting for me to dash back inside. I snatched the camera from the top shelf of the hall closet. The metallic feel of my little Kodak brought reality to my plan. Tears filled my eyes, but only for a moment because in my mind, I saw Sonny lean in through her car window and kiss that home wrecking broad all over again. My fury eclipsed my anguish and I raced for the Bug.

When I got back to the tacky love nest, I parked on the street, a couple of houses away. With my camera and lighter in tow, I tiptoed toward the steel trashcans I had noticed earlier. They sat beside the house and when I opened the lids, I saw beautiful, dry, delightfully flammable leaves. Two metal containers full of them. I flicked my Bic and jumped away when the yard debris flamed three feet higher than the can. The leaves would burn quickly so I knew I didn't have much time.

I yelled, "Fire! Fire!" before I ran for the neighbor's house and hid behind their car.

In seconds, Sonny and the tramp streaked out of the house half naked; him in boxer shorts and an unbuttoned shirt and her in a short, flimsy, robe. She screamed, "Put it out, Sonny! Hurry!"

He yelled, "I'm getting it, Terri-Lynn! I'm getting it!"

Neighbors ran out of a couple of houses asking if they should call the fire department. Sonny picked up the trash can lid and said, "I think we're okay."

About that time, I jumped out from the car I'd hidden behind and shot a couple of divorce-court adultery photos. "You're nowhere near okay, dumb ass. Not you or your little cheesecake whore." I snapped one more shot of Sonny's stunned face before I ran for my car.

Sonny's eyes widened to the size of dinner plates. "Livvy, wh-wh-what are you doing here? Babe, it's not what it looks like. This was nothing, baby, nothing at all." He held out a hand and walked toward me like he thought I'd kiss him and make it all better.

Terri-the-D-Cup didn't seem to like that. She yelled, "Nothing? You said you loved me, you lying…" She didn't finish her sentence before she grabbed the hot trash can lid in both hands, swung it around and smashed it into Sonny's backside. "I'll show you nothing." About that time the belt to her silky robe gave way and both boobs spilled out, giving Sonny and several of her neighbors a vision they wouldn't soon forget. But that didn't stop her. She hoisted the lid one more time and brought it straight down on his head, knocking him to the ground.

As the Bug hummed its way down the street, I glanced in the rearview mirror and watched Terri-Lynn shove Sonny's pants into the burning leaves. Sonny grabbed one leg and she had the other in a slapstick tug-of-war. Something in a seam must have given way because they both flew, in opposite directions, landing on their fannies in the dirt with one pant leg lying next to each of them. Terri-Lynn's bellowing sounded like a wounded sow, a very loud wounded sow, even after I turned the corner and headed home.

I love you, Momma,

Livvy

P.S. I hid the pictures to keep Sonny in line. Maybe blackmail can save my marriage. Nothing else has worked.

November 30, 2011
1:00 PM

Dear Mom,

I'M LAUGHING and crying at the same time. My mother, the stalker! I never saw that in you. I remember the fights and hiding under my bed as soon as one started. More than the arguments, I remember the silence every time Dad stormed out of the house. You sat in the living room with your bourbon. And I had long since given up trying to talk to you while you stewed in your anger and your booze.

Back then, I blamed you, for nagging and drinking too much and, most of all, for running Dad off. I wanted so desperately for his absence to be your failing so that I didn't have to face the fact that I really believed it to be mine. I thought that if I had been prettier or smarter or better behaved that Dad would love me enough to stay. I see now that you believed the same thing, that if you could have made him love you more, he would have changed. I also see that neither one of us held him responsible for his own choices. He chose to be a drunk, to abandon his wife and daughter for a good time and, God knows, he made the choice to cheat on you.

Though I didn't know that then. Because you never told me. Not once did you even hint at how badly he'd hurt you. And in spite of your pain, apparently, you turned into a feisty bitch when necessary. The thought of you tailing Dad and staking out the bar makes me giggle out loud. But setting the fire and photographing them in their half-naked glory is classic retribution, Livvy Dolan Abbott style.

I'm laughing, Mom. So hard my damn tears won't stop.

Alex

Dear Momma,

SONNY CAME HOME from work the other day and said that the police came to the garage to talk to Russ. Just before lunch, two Wilmington police officers pulled into the parking lot. They walked into the first open bay and one of them asked Sonny where they could find Russell Montgomery. Sonny pointed toward the office door just as Russ stepped out.

"Something I can do for y'all this morning?"

"Mister Montgomery, is there someplace where we could speak to you in private?"

"Right in here." He directed them into the office. "Is something wrong, officers?"

They said nothing, just closed the door behind them. After a minute, Sonny heard Russ wail. "No! You're wrong! No! There's a mistake. There has to be a mistake."

When the door opened and the police officers stepped back out, Russ stood between them, leaning heavily against the larger of the two. He made no effort to stand on his own. All color had drained from his face. His dazed eyes registered nothing around him.

One of the officers said, "There's been an accident. Mr. Montgomery's wife was badly injured." He shook his head and took a deep breath. Much softer, he added, "I'm afraid she didn't make it."

Russ's knees buckled and the officer who had spoken caught him at the waist before he hit the ground. He hung limp in the other man's arms, but he raised his head to look at Sonny. Russ's hair stood up on his head in wild tufts. His blanched skin accented his swollen, crimson nose. Tears spilled from his red-rimmed eyes.

Sonny moved toward Russ. "I'm so sorry. What can I do? What do you need?"

A low moan rolled from Russ's lips. Sonny saw the shiver start in Russ's head and work its way down. By the time the shaking got to his legs it had built to full, head-to-toe tremors. His moan turned to a high-pitched keen that sounded more like a desperate animal than anything human. Sonny cringed and started to turn away from his boss's public grief, but Russ's lips moved, and Sonny had to lean closer to hear him.

"She was…" His head slumped forward again.

"I can't hear you. What are you trying to say?"

"Jenny was pregnant," he whispered. He raised his head and jerked away from the men trying to hold him up. He breathed in huge sobbing gasps of air and screamed, "Jenny was pregnant!"

Sonny said he had never heard the garage so quiet. No clanking tools, no ringing phone, no chuckles or curses. Only Russ Montgomery's sobs echoed off the walls.

One of the officers shifted his weight and grabbed a now limp Russ. "We don't want him driving, so we'll take Mr. Montgomery home."

Sonny closed up the garage and drove straight home. I knew when he walked in the door that something terrible had happened. Sonny Abbott looked like he'd been crying. He held me tight in his arms while he told me the terrible story. He kissed my forehead and said, "I love you." He sat down on the floor in front of the television next to Alex and lifted her into his lap. He pulled her close and rocked, more to soothe himself than his daughter. Yes, something terrible happened that day, but it reminded me that the tender Sonny I used to know still existed.

I barely knew Russ and never met his wife, but her death rocked me. Beyond the heart-breaking loss, the accident shattered my sense of security, of invincibility. If Jenny Montgomery could be alive, healthy and pregnant one minute and dead the next, the world couldn't hold out a lot of hope for the rest of us.

Some people lived fairytale lives from start to finish. I'm sure those lucky few took for granted their happy families, successful careers, beautiful homes. Most of the folks around me plodded through life, between the hills and the valleys. But the Russes and Livvys seemed to be tragedy magnets, our lives periodically set ablaze by horrific catastrophe, like napalm scorching giant holes in our souls. Every time I heard someone say, "God never gives us more than we can handle," I wondered if that person spoke from some iconic picture perfectness or if they had actually stood on the same island of painful isolation that I knew so well.

At the funeral, Russ's hair looked tinged with new gray, his eyes radiated fatigue and despair. He looked like he died in the car with his wife and child, but his body hadn't quite given in to that yet. Somehow he made it through that awful day, but Sonny told me that he didn't show up at work for a couple of weeks. When he finally did, he walked in the door at ten o'clock in the morning, commode-hugging drunk. I can't say I blame him.

I miss you, Momma.

Livvy

Dear Momma,

A FTER ONLY a few weeks of the happy-hubby routine, Sonny returned to his vanishing act and full-time drinking. Every lying, evasive technique he'd ever used came back in full force. But truthfully, I couldn't muster up enough jealousy to give a crap. I had a job I loved, my daughter all to myself and no one monitoring my daily liquor intake. Sonny's very presence in the house disturbed that delicate balance and I found myself picking fights with him to have an excuse to throw him out. Do I still love him? I'll always care for Alex's father, but beyond that, I don't know any more.

As soon as I put those words on paper I heard you whisper, "So, why do you stay?" I hate my answer. Words like fear, desperation, and neediness make me feel weak. You had a parade of men, in and out of your life, like a turnstile. You allowed each one to stay until he annoyed you with something trivial like leaving his shoes in the living room for you to trip over in the dark. One fatal error and you threw him out with the empty beer cans.

I put up with endless bullshit from one man. You tolerated absolutely nothing from dozens, but never stopped trying. Which one of us looks more pathetic?

You showed me how to let go. I wish I had learned that lesson.

Daddy and Nora Jean invited us for Easter dinner. I took painted eggs so we could hide them for Alex. Azaleas bloomed all over Daddy's back yard and waved in the breeze like a sea of pink whitecaps. The solid sheet of Carolina blue sky met the deeper blue-green of the waterway. The spring backdrop made everything and everyone in front of it appear warmer and even happier. At least for a little while.

Alex wore her brand new dress, pale green taffeta covered with tiny daisies. Every few minutes she set her basket down and spun in circles until she got dizzy watching the ruffles and lace swirl around her legs. "I look like a princess," she cooed with dramatic flourish right before she dropped to the ground next to her basket.

"Alexandra, stop that," the Bimbo hollered from the deck. "You'll get your new dress filthy."

"Leave her alone, Nora Jean. She's having fun," Daddy said.

BB marched down the steps toward Alex. She grabbed her arm and pointed to Alex's white tights. "Look at the grass stains. We bought this dress, Luther, and I don't want it ruined." She dropped Alex's arm and wiped her fingers on her own skirt like she had touched something vile.

I set my beer on the deck railing. "Come on, baby. Let's go change into your play clothes."

"No," she whined. "I want to look like a princess."

"Then don't roll around the grass," BB ordered.

Daddy sighed and took Alex's hand. "Come on, Lady Bug. I'll help you find your eggs."

While they headed toward the water, I chugged the rest of my Bud and wandered to the cooler for another one.

BB started in on me. "You're drinking too much, Livvy."

I shrugged.

"She's not drinking enough to make her any fun," Sonny argued. He threw his head back and poured the rest of his beer down his throat before he pitched the empty can into the trash by the sliding glass door. "Get me one while you're there, Livvy."

"You want it so bad." I picked one out of the icy water and threw it overhand, straight for his head. "Catch it, jackass." Sonny's hand shot out and he grabbed it right in front of his face. *Too bad*, I thought.

"What is wrong with you two? Behaving like a couple of spoiled teenagers." BB pointed at Alex. "You've got a kid. Act like it." She flung the sliding door open and stormed inside.

A few minutes later Nora Jean reappeared and hollered for Daddy and Alex who now stood on the dock. "Dinner's ready! Now!" She glared at Sonny and me. We followed her inside and helped carry the serving platters from the kitchen to the dining room table.

Sonny carried the potato salad in one hand and the ham in the other. The bowl slipped and his thumb slid knuckle-deep into the goop. He set both dishes down and stuck the mayonnaise covered appendage into his mouth. With a loud slurp, he sucked everything off and popped his thumb out from between his lips.

BB's forehead creased and her lips puckered. The Bimbo pounced like a starving tigress on a newborn doe. "For God's sakes, Sonny, wash your damn hands. And keep your greasy fingers out of the food," she snarled.

Before Sonny could retort, Nora Jean turned her back and retreated to the kitchen. Daddy held the sliding door open and Alex skipped past him carrying her overflowing egg basket.

Nora Jean spun toward her and barked, "Put that in the kitchen and sit down."

Alex stood very still, staring at BB like she couldn't figure out what she had done wrong and feared she might do it again if she moved.

"Don't take it out on my kid, Nora Jean," Sonny barked.

Nora Jean turned her back on Sonny, but said nothing.

"Take what out on Alex?" Daddy asked.

I shook my head at Daddy, silently begging him to drop it. He raised his shoulders and eyebrows in matching question marks, but took the hint and led Alex into the kitchen.

When we sat down around the table I thought disaster had been averted, but I let my guard down way too soon. Sonny's darkened eyes and slurred words should have been glaring red flags, but I ignored them.

Nora Jean handed out platter after platter of homemade goodies, but refused to pass the potato salad until she made a big production of spooning out the spot Sonny's thumb had contaminated. She ran the serving spoon through it and plopped the heap on her empty roll plate.

In that moment, I couldn't take my eyes off the slice of ham under my knife. I heard Sonny's breaths coming deeper and louder, in and out, in and out. The ham seemed to grow larger, and I kept right on cutting. I hoped that if I didn't meet his angry gaze, nothing bad would happen. Wrong again.

"You never thought I was good enough for this family and I'm damn tired of it." He threw his knife down on his plate and it bounced onto the white lace tablecloth sending the butter glob on the end of it flying into Alex's lap.

Alex scooped the butter off her dress and slid her finger along the edge her plate to get it off. BB jumped out of her chair, her napkin held out in front of her like she had just witnessed a shooting and she needed to sacrifice the family linens to stop the blood loss.

"You've ruined her dress, just ruined it. And it was a gift from us." BB berated him while she scrubbed at the small blotch like Cinderella frantically scouring her way to the ball.

Alex looked at the offensive spot and burst into tears. "You messed up my princess dress."

Sonny snarled at Alex, "Don't you ever talk to me like that." He jumped up from the table and stuck his trembling finger in Nora Jean's face. "And don't you ever make my daughter think she can treat me that way. Do you understand?" His slurred speech sounded more like "Do you unnerstan?"

Daddy stood up and shoved Sonny away from Nora Jean. "That's enough. Go cool off."

Throughout the entire exchange, I kept my head bowed down to my plate, fearful that if I so much as exhaled, the situation would escalate beyond repair. When I finally lifted my eyes to Sonny's I said, "Please, Sonny, not today."

"Please, Sonny, not today," he mimicked in a high-pitched whine. "Not today." He picked up his glass and sloshed the water into my face. "You're as bad as the damn bimbo." He staggered from the dining room to the front door and slammed it behind him. The car engine raced and we all heard gravel fly out from under the tires when he sped out of the driveway.

Sonny's behavior paralyzed all of us until I moved to dab my napkin against my face.

Daddy asked, "You all right?"

I nodded.

"You and Alex'll stay here tonight," he said.

And we picked up our knives and forks and ate dinner, completely ignoring the ugly scene and Sonny's empty seat at the table.

Momma, I don't understand why I've hung on to my sham of a marriage or the hateful relationship with Nora Jean and even Daddy. I hear you in my head, "The key to life is knowing when to hang on and when to let go." BUT I DON'T KNOW HOW!

Livvy

November 30, 2011
9:00 PM

Dear Mom,

DAD USED to tell me stories like the one in your letter. A lot. Stories about Granddaddy and Nora Jean and how much they hated him. He said they tried to make him look bad in your eyes. He made it sound like they conspired to end your marriage, to save the delicate Livvy Dolan from the evil Sonny Abbot.

One time, I couldn't have been more than seven or eight, and even then, I recognized that Dad had had way too much to drink. Still, I hung on every word. I hurt for him and felt sorry for him and, most of all, I believed him. I mean, my dad would never lie to me. Right?

I'd been lying on the floor watching television. Dad walked in with a beer in his hand. He threw himself down on the couch before he popped the top and chugged about half of it.

"Your granddaddy's been filling your mommy's head with lies about me, Alex. You need to tell her that none of it's true. Can you do that? Help your old man out?"

He propped his feet up on the coffee table and used the heel of his work boots to sweep my coloring book and crayons off onto the floor. I moved to pick them up, but the way he kept staring at me sent chills up my back. So I sat very still and waited for him to finish his story. He crossed one foot over the other and took another swig.

"Luther doesn't think I'm good enough for his little girl. 'Cuz I'm a working man. And what the hell's wrong with that, I ask you?

Work my ass off to take care of you and Livvy. Oughta mean something. But no. Nora Jean acts like I'm a failure 'cuz I don't make a lot of money."

He chugged again and looked down at me. "Do you think your dad's a failure?"

When I looked up at him, a tiny little piece of my heart chipped away. I thought Dad could do anything. He could build things and fix cars and put my toys together. I knew that he didn't come home a lot and I knew that when he drank too much I'd be smart to avoid him, but I had no idea what any of that really meant. At the time, I didn't even understand the word failure. I just knew that when Dad hurt, I did, too.

I ran over to him and threw my arms around his neck. "I love you, Daddy."

"That's my girl," he said.

I felt so connected to him that day. But now as I reread what I've written and try to meld your version of life with Dad into my remembrance of it, I feel like he manipulated me every step of the way. It hurt me then and it hurts me now. Just for different reasons.

Love you, Mom,

August 12, 1976
Happy Birthday

Dear Momma,

THINGS have been strained between Sonny and me for a long time, but it seems like I woke up one morning to find my marriage had slipped from comedic tragedy to humiliating disgrace overnight. My husband and I live separate lives, barely speaking to one another. I drop Alex off at school on my way to work and pick her up at daycare on my way home. I help her with homework and fix dinner. I put her to bed, have a few drinks, fall asleep, get up and start all over again. Most days I have no idea what Sonny does, where he sleeps or who shares his bed. And I don't care.

On July Fourth Sonny, Alex and I enjoyed the only happy day we'd had together in months. We packed up the car and headed to Wrightsville Beach late that afternoon. Alex and Sonny jumped through the waves for a couple of hours before they ran from the surf to our towels.

"I'm really hungry," Alex said. "What did we bring for dinner?"

I opened the picnic basket and pulled out sandwiches, chips, pasta salad and deviled eggs. Sonny got a root beer from the cooler, poured some in to a plastic glass and handed it to Alex before he popped the top on a beer for himself. We ate and laughed and ate some more before we all lay back on the towels to watch the fireworks display that danced in the sky over our heads. For those few short hours, we acted like a real family and I hoped, once more, that we might work things out.

The fireworks on the beach lasted thirty minutes. The ones at home exploded for a bit longer.

By the time we carried a sleeping Alex into the house and set the now empty picnic basket on the kitchen table, Sonny had already picked a fight, grabbed a change of clothes, stormed out the door and sped away, taking all my hopes with him.

He didn't come back until the next night and when he did, he arrived pissed off and unemployed.

I had already tucked Alex into bed and polished off a couple of bourbon and cokes before Sonny stumbled in the front door, reeking of stale beer.

"The son-of-a-bitch fired me." He dropped into his recliner and picked at the tear on the arm of the chair. "Get me a beer, will you."

I ignored the command. "What happened, Sonny? What did you do?"

He leaned so far forward that his stench gagged me. If I'd had a match I could have tossed it into his mouth and watched him blow up like an alcoholic grenade.

"You know what your problem is?" He swayed in the chair while he tried to hold out his arm to point at me. "You always assume the worst about me. You think I'm the problem. You know what? That makes you one lousy excuse for a wife." He threw up his hands and they practically said, *What the hell?* all by themselves. "Where's your support? Huh?"

"Tell me what happened, Sonny."

"I walked into the garage and started working on the Camaro I'd started on Friday. Russ Montgomery walks over to me, tells me to get my stuff and get out. Just like that." He snapped his fingers, but they slipped and made no sound. "Just like that and I'm out of a job."

"That doesn't make sense, Sonny. Something else must have happened."

"I'm telling you, I was doing my job and he fired me."

"What time did you get to work?"

"What difference does that make? People make way too much of this early bird crap. I get more done in a couple of hours than other people do all day. Montgomery knows that. I'm the best mechanic he's got and when he's begging me to come back it'll be too late." He raised his forefinger in the air and waggled it around. "The answer is no, Mr. My-Shit-Don't-Stink Montgomery. Acts like he owns the damn place."

I mumbled, "Shut up, Sonny."

"What did you say?" His head fell back against the chair.

"Shut up, Sonny," I yelled. "He does own the place, you moron."

He never heard me. He had passed out, sitting up. I picked up my glass, went to the bedroom and closed the door.

Momma, what kind of person does it make me that before I closed my eyes, my last thought had been that with any luck at all, I might wake up the next morning and find my husband choked to death on his own vomit?

Livvy

November 31, 2011
4:00 AM

Dear Mom,

WHEN I set your letter back in the hatbox, I glanced over at you before I picked up the next one. You slumped against your pillow and stared at me. I jumped out of my chair.

"Hey, how are you feeling? Do you need anything?"

You shook your head, but when you licked your parched lips, I spooned a few ice chips into your mouth. Your eyes closed again and you moaned a little bit like I had just given you a bite of some rare delicacy.

"Mom, I've been reading the letters I found in the hatbox in your closet." I brushed a few strands of hair back from your face. "I never knew. I lived right there in the same house with you, but I never saw or understood what your life was like with Dad."

My chin quivered. "I'm so sorry. I knew how bad Dad's drinking got after the divorce. How did I not see it sooner?"

You opened your eyes and reached for my hand.

"Once in a while, I can still hear the two of you shouting at each other. I feel my fear as though it's happening now. Some days it seems so fresh that I have to fight the urge to hide from it.

I blamed you for all of it, the arguments, the divorce. Why? I remember being so frightened by your drinking, not his. Do you think that's because I needed you so much? Because I didn't see his as much as I did yours?"

I bit my lower lip. "I'm so sorry."

You squeezed my fingers just enough to let me know that you had heard me. Your touch felt more encouraging than critical so I kept talking.

"I don't remember Dad being home much. Do you think that's why his drinking isn't as vivid in my mind?"

You didn't respond.

"Please forgive me for not seeing it. I'm so sorry you had to live that way, Mom."

This time you squeezed my hand with more power.

"You shouldn't have known about any of it." You hadn't said a word in hours, so when you spoke with such force, it surprised me. It gave me hope that you might be stronger than the doctors led us to believe. "You were a child. We were the adults who should have protected you from all of that."

I tucked your bathrobe around your shoulders. "Somehow I memorized your every flaw and erased his like they never happened. I'm sorry for that, too."

When your breathing became more regular, your mouth fell open in a soft snore. Your temporary spurt of energy had given me false hope. I swallowed my disappointment with my tears and picked up the next letter.

I hope you heard me, Mom.

Alex

P.S. At first, I felt a little bit crazy, writing to you while you're lying in the hospital bed right next to my chair. But the more I read your letters to Grandma CiCi, the saner I feel. By the way, I read what I've written, out loud to you, every time we get a few minutes alone. Sometimes you react. Sometimes you don't. But it makes me feel like we're talking. So, I'll keep writing.

Dear Momma,

AFTER ALL the years of Sonny's laziness, moodiness, irresponsibility, drunkenness, and screwing around, the final blow to our marriage came from Alex's little red record player.

Sonny got a job at another garage in town and, at first, he put everything he had into his work. He still spent little time with Alex or me, but his drinking slowed down so life seemed a bit more peaceful. By Thanksgiving the old Sonny came roaring back. He'd come home from work, have a few drinks, pick a fight and disappear. If he didn't start the argument, I did. And neither of us glanced at Alex or gave a thought to what we put her through. A couple of days after Christmas she decided to let us know.

I took the week between Christmas and New Year's off so I could be home with Alex during her school vacation. One day Sonny came home for lunch and raised hell because I hadn't made the bed yet. He paused from his yelling, grabbed a beer from the refrigerator and popped the top. After he chugged the whole thing he picked right back up with his hollering like he had never stopped.

"You're off work and you still can't manage to get a damn thing done around this house. Before I get home tonight, why don't you turn off Donahue and drag your lazy ass in to make the bed. I don't ask for much, Livvy. Just make the damn bed."

He threw a piece of bologna between two slices of bread and shoved half of it in his mouth. I stood by the kitchen sink and watched him leave the bread bag open, lying on the counter beside the package of bologna.

He said nothing to Alex or me before he slithered back out the door while he swallowed the rest of his sandwich whole.

I put away everything my husband left behind before I stepped into my bedroom to make the bed. I hoped that single act might give us an argument-free evening later. Silly me. As I tucked the last pillow under the bedspread, I yelled for Alex. She didn't answer. I yelled again. Still no response.

I checked her room, but saw no sign of her. Same thing in the living room and the kitchen. I yelled again and felt more than heard the echo of the empty house. "She's in the back yard," I told myself, though the gnawing in my gut said otherwise. The locked sliding glass door validated my gut. I dashed out the front door screaming Alex's name.

My next-door neighbor stopped sweeping her front porch and walked toward me. "Everything all right?" she asked.

"I can't find Alex anywhere." My voice cracked and I felt my panic gaining ground.

My neighbor, an older widow, grabbed my shoulders and shook me. "We'll find her. She can't have been gone long. I'll go down the street this way." She pointed. "You go that way." She pointed the other direction. "We'll meet back here in 10 minutes." She shoved me. "Go!"

I took the first few tentative steps, afraid my wobbly legs might give out beneath me. "Alex!" My legs felt stronger. "Alex!" Stronger still. I picked up my pace and jogged down the street, zigzagging back and forth, searching every yard for any sign of my little girl. By the time I got to the end of our block I had seen nothing to help me find Alex. I knew I needed to cover more ground faster, so I headed home to get my car.

When I turned around, I saw two tiny specks in the distance. "Please, God, let it be Alex," I prayed aloud. My shoes pounded against the pavement and vibrated in my ears. With each step, the specks grew larger, clearer. An adult and a child. Clomp! Clomp! My neighbor and Alex. Clomp! Clomp! My neighbor holding Alex's hand. Clomp! Clomp! Alex carrying her little red record player, tears streaming down her face.

My neighbor held out a hand to me, warning me to calm down. I slowed my pace.

"Alex is all right," the woman said. "She said she just wanted to go to her Granddaddy's house for a while because Mommy and Daddy won't stop fighting."

I looked at Alex and my heart hurt so bad I thought my chest would split open from the ache. How could I have let things get so bad that my daughter ran away? How could I have done this to Alex? The look in the old woman's eyes and the tone of her voice left no doubt that she, too, had already judged me and found me guilty of the crime of shameful mothering. I reached for Alex. My baby girl hid behind my neighbor's skirt.

Tears spilled down my cheeks and I sunk to the ground. "I'm so sorry, Alex. It won't happen again, honey. Mommy and Daddy won't fight any more. I promise."

Alex bent over, set her record player down on the ground and ran to me. She threw her arms around my neck and relief washed over me like a spring shower. "Don't cry, Mommy. I love you past the sky," she said.

Sonny came home late that night, after Alex had gone to bed. I waited for him at the kitchen table. In the corner sat two large suitcases that I had packed with all of Sonny's belongings that I could cram into them. He saw them before he noticed me.

"What the hell?"

"I want you out." He startled and turned toward me. "Tonight. You can get the rest of your stuff later."

"You can't throw me out of my own house. I'm not leaving."

Earlier I had placed Sonny's revolver on the table in front of me and covered it with the newspaper. I put my hand under the paper and pulled the gun out.

"Yes, I can." I aimed for his chest. "There's nothing left between you and me, Sonny, and I'm not going to let us destroy our daughter in this sick marriage. Pick up your bags and get out."

He didn't move. "You crazy bitch. You can't do this."

I waved the gun and aimed lower. He grabbed both bags and shoved them outside ahead of him, tearing the screen door off one hinge in the process. The door slammed shut and hung at a catawampus angle, swinging back and forth, threatening to fall off the door completely.

I locked the door behind him and sat back down at the table. The vision of Alex trying to walk to Granddaddy's with her little red record player wouldn't leave me alone. I had clung to my marriage for all the wrong reasons. My little girl showed me that I needed to let it go.

Wish me luck, Momma,

Livvy

November 31, 2011
9:00 AM

Dear Mom,

HOW STUPID could I have been that I never saw it? You stayed
with Dad for me and you left for me, too.
    Forgive me,

Alex

August 12, 1977
Happy Birthday

Dear Momma,

*W*HAT WERE you like as a nurse? As a professional? I never saw that side of you. I saw the occasional housekeeper, cook and even party girl. But I don't remember the professional CiCi Dolan. Did you compartmentalize your life that much? So much that CiCi Dolan, the wicked temptress never slipped into your nurse's uniform with the previous night's hangover? Memories of more than a few doctors sneaking out of your bedroom before dawn thread my teenage memories. Did you bat your eyelashes at them the next day? Or pretend nothing of importance had happened?

All those years, I tried to ignore the legacy of flirtation you left behind. And then, one day at work, Wilbur Walker threw it back in my face with a reminder I'll never forget. The dubious distinction of being your daughter left me permanently stigmatized. Do you think the huge scarlet C on my forehead will ever fade?

I'd been a damn good employee at the plant for three years and Wilbur Walker had been my supervisor the entire time. I noticed him staring at me from time to time on the walk-away, but other than that, he had been completely appropriate. Strictly professional. Until Sonny and I split up. The occasional stare became outright ass gazing. He whispered all his work-related questions in my ear. Any instruction on new procedures meant he'd find a reason to touch me. Touch me! The man gave me the willies so bad, my nose crinkled up and my mouth turned into a giant pucker any time he stood next to me.

Not long ago, WWII walked across the factory floor, stood next to my chair and stared down at me so long that it forced to look up at him. "Do you need something, Mr. Walker?"

"There's been a change in safety standards. I want you to demonstrate the changes at the meeting in the morning. So I need to cover the information with you in advance."

Warning prickles tingled all the way down to my toes when he said the word "demonstrate," but did I heed them? No. I told myself that he wanted to prepare for the meeting. Wrong. That he singled me out because I'm an exemplary employee. Wrong again.

He leaned down so close that I felt his breath on my neck, but I didn't move. First to flinch showed weakness. Right? Meant he had won the war of wills. Could I have been any more stupid?

"Why don't you come into my office so we can talk about it?"

I shivered and the warning bells clanged in my head so loud I thought a three-alarm fire must have started down the road. WWII pulled my chair out and spun it toward him.

I followed him into his office and felt every eye on the floor fixed on me as I walked past. I'm not sure if they stared with pity or disgust, but I am certain they suspected what would happen behind his closed door. WWII turned to lower the blinds which set off red flags waving in front of my face like the arms on that annoying *Lost In Space* robot, who rolled around screaming, "Danger, Will Robinson! Danger!"

His cramped, little office made me feel like I'd been trapped in a prison cell. And if he'd tried to stand between my chair and the door I would probably have clawed my way out.

Instead, he sat on the corner of his desk in front of me, keeping one leg propped up so that his zipper and the baggage behind it aimed straight at my face. I pushed my chair back.

"Livvy, you've been a real asset to the team. You probably have a bright future at the plant."

"Probably?"

He crossed his arms over his chest. "There's room for improvement."

The shiver returned.

"You look so much like your mother. Some days it feels like she's sitting right next to me." He reached down and touched my hair.

I jerked my head back and scooted the chair farther away. "Mr. Walker, we need to discuss the safety changes. What did you want to explain?"

He grinned and shook his head. "We're here to discuss something a little more personal."

I stood up. "That isn't going to happen. We have nothing personal to talk about."

WWII put his hand on my shoulder and shoved me back into the chair. Before I could move, he stepped behind me, leaned over and stuck his hand down the front of my blouse and into my bra. He squeezed my nipple between his fingers and clasped his other hand over my mouth. "You make me feel young again, Livvy. Relax and imagine what I can do for you in return."

My stomach churned. I thought I might throw up in his hand. At first, my fear paralyzed me; fear that WWII might hurt me, fear of him being in control of my job, fear that if I complained about this, no one would believe me.

And then you danced through my mind, Momma. You dated Wilbur Walker. You slept with that sweaty, half-witted bully. And you left me to deal with the rumors that swirled long after you died. That's when I got seriously pissed; at you, at WWII and at everybody in Wilmington who thought, "Like mother, like daughter."

My rage swelled up like a balloon, lifting me out of the muck where you stranded me. I decided I didn't have to live up to your legacy. I could do it my own way. And I did. I opened my mouth wide and bit down on WWII's fingers. I bit until I tasted blood and heard him howl like a wolf caught in a steel trap.

He jerked both hands away, pulled his handkerchief out of his pocket and wrapped it around his bleeding fingers. "What the hell did you do that for? We were just having a little fun!"

"No, Mr. Walker. I wasn't having fun." I stood up and shoved him away from me. "I'm going back to work now and you are never going to lay a hand on me again. You won't touch me, or whisper to me or stare at my ass when I walk by."

"You've made a big mistake here, little girl. You don't tell me what to do. I tell you. And you'll pay hell for this." He threw back his head and laughed.

I had no idea where it came from, but I had never felt so brazen and powerful in all my life. I walked back toward Wilbur Walker and stood inches from him. He towers over me, but he looked like a skittish weasel as all the intimidation he tried to muster evaporated.

"There will be no hell to pay unless you're paying it," I said. "If you try to make trouble for me, I'll schedule a meeting with your wife."

"Don't threaten me, little girl." He sneered.

I smiled. "Did you know that my mother had quite a photo collection?" My words hung in the silence like unexploded missiles. "I bet your wife would enjoy seeing some of them."

Color rose in his cheeks. "You bitch."

I opened the door. "By the way, Mr. Walker, if you ever touch me again, I'll kill you." I spoke loud enough that everyone working on the line stared at me, and I never looked back for his reaction.

Momma, I've experienced your legacy for years, in the sideways glances or flat out stares I still get from men who knew you. I've even gotten the passing suggestive remark. Always a double entendre, never blatant.

Dr. Marshall walked up behind me at the post office a couple of months ago and said, "Well, Livvy Dolan, I swear, from behind, you could be your mother's twin." Compliment? Could have been. But when he whispered it in my ear he definitely added an element of sleaze that made his intentions pretty clear.

And how about Jason Birkwood who owned the Piggly Wiggy? I had to stop shopping there because he'd follow me through the entire store. And he could say, with complete impunity, "All I ever did was ask her what she needed." Of course, he asked it, blocking the aisle, while he scratched his balls.

Yeah, Momma. For a while there, your shadow kept getting bigger. But maybe, I deflated it a little with my quick jab, right hook threat to Wilbur Walker. It felt like I finally stood up and said, "No more. I'm not her."

Livvy

P.S. I know you didn't have any pictures, but WWII will never know that.

May 14, 1978
Mother's Day

Dear Momma,

ALEX AND I spent the day at Wrightsville Beach. We laughed, splashed in the water, ate gritty sandwiches and got way too much sun. In spite of being tired and burned, I had a perfect Mother's Day with my daughter. I know I mess up with Alex a lot, but today I did it right.

Love,

Livvy

P.S. You had a lot of days that you did it right, too, Momma. I'm sorry if I don't tell you that enough. I do love you. I always did.

Dear Momma,

YOU WOULD be 53 years old today. That sounds so old. I can't imagine it. Are you gray or do color your hair? Have your jowls drooped while laugh lines appeared around your eyes? Do you skip meals so you can still enjoy a beer without adding an inch to your tiny waist? Do you spend every Saturday night at the Shag Club dancing to The Embers and flirting with every man in the room? Do you dote on Alex or did you lose interest as she got more independent? Who would you be today? Who would I be with you still here?

Can you still drink every guy at the bar under the table or did you wake up one morning and realize that the booze made you a little bit crazier every day?

I feel that way, like I've lost my mind in the bourbon. Sometimes I imagine the real me has been locked inside a bottle of Jim Beam and I have to guzzle it down to escape. On saner days, I suspected that the woman in the bottle needed to stay locked up forever. Livvy, the evil bourbon genie, should never be let loose in the world again.

A while back, Daddy and the Bimbo kept Alex for the weekend. I had a gen-u-ine, finalized divorce and not one man had asked me out, so I had planned an evening of bar hopping to remedy that. I headed to Jimbo's to see if I could pick up a contender, hopefully an attractive, gainfully employed one. Heck, at that point, any guy who could fog a mirror and didn't have puke running down the front of his shirt would have sufficed.

I planned to meet Gina Morano, one of the girls from work. Her name states the obvious, But yes, the Catholic, Italian princess moved here from New Jersey to work at the plant. In spite of the Yankee accent, I like her brash humor and kick-ass attitude.

When I pushed open the door and stepped inside, it felt like I had to bulldoze my way through a wall of thick, dense smoke and throbbing country music to get to a table. I gave a quick glance around the room to make sure Sonny hadn't claimed that bar as his hangout for the night. I saw no sign of my ex and knew the dating gods had given me a thumbs-up for the night. That's when I took another peek around the room, and this time I noticed the men; men in booths, at the bar, clustered around the pool tables in the back. A few had women hanging around their necks, but most sat alone or in groups of other guys. I grinned.

I slipped into the first available booth and ordered a drink before I pulled a pack of Kool cigarettes out of the side pocket of my handbag and dropped it on the table. My purse snagged on the torn plastic upholstery when I shoved it down the bench seat into the corner. I tapped the cigarette pack on the table and pulled one out. When I flicked the lighter it sputtered and went out. Before I flicked it a second time, another lighter, cupped by large masculine hands, appeared in front of my face. I jerked back and looked up, straight into the deep green eyes of a very handsome, very drunk Russ Montgomery. Trying not to look like an amateur in the dating world, I leaned forward until the tip of my cigarette touched the flame. I inhaled, hoping to look like Ava Gardner, but I probably came across more like Lucille Ball.

The last time butterflies invaded my stomach at the sight of a man I must have been about fourteen and they felt like a gentle flutter. These announced their presence like an acre of giant flags, snapping in a gale-force wind. They strangled my greeting into a stuttered "Hel-lo."

Russ dropped into the seat across from me. "I wondered how long it'd be before I saw you here." He lit his own cigarette, took a long, slow drag and blew out a stream of smoke aimed at the ceiling. "You shouldn't be here, Mrs. Abbott."

"I'm not Mrs. Abbott anymore. And why shouldn't I be here?" My ringless hand trembled when I brought my cigarette to my mouth. I hoped he wouldn't notice my quivering all the while praying for him to take note of my changed marital status.

"Heard about that." He shook a finger in my face. "Man's a fool. And you shouldn't be here 'cuz you're better than all this." Russ waved that same finger around the room. "You don't want to let the drinking take over your life, Pretty Lady."

That handsome man had to go and rile me up. "Oh yeah. Pot," I pointed at my face. "Meet Kettle." I pointed at Russ before I glanced at my watch. "It's only 8 and you're smashed." I leaned forward and smiled. "And I'm just getting started."

He sat back and stared at me. "You're right. But I've got a reason." He put the cigarette to his mouth and inhaled again.

In a terrible flash of clarity I remembered the accident, the funeral, his devastation and I felt like the biggest jackass that ever walked the planet. My hand went straight to his and electricity shot through me all the way to my elbow when we touched. He jerked away like I'd burned him. "I'm sorry. I shouldn't have said anything. I didn't think."

Russ stood up and walked away. Without looking back he said, "You need to go home while you're ahead, Pretty Lady."

Gina slipped in where Russ had been. "Who is that gorgeous man?"

"Nobody," I mumbled.

We hadn't finished our first drink when two guys from the bar sauntered over and asked if they could join us. We drank and talked and laughed and danced and drank some more before the one I referred to as mine asked if he could drive me home because he thought I'd had too much to drink. I agreed since every time I looked at him, his chiseled jawline got fuzzier and I couldn't, for the life of me, remember his name. So, getting another drunk to drive me home seemed like a solid plan.

The next morning, in the light of day I realized I probably should have chosen door number two. I woke up in my bed, naked, lying next to a passed out man who looked vaguely familiar. He reeked of stale beer, cigarette smoke and something I couldn't quite place. And then he farted, the loudest I'd ever heard in my life. The sheets trembled and the mattress shook. I sat straight up in bed. *That's what woke me up. Oh, my God!* The movement of the covers had been just enough to allow the ambush on my nostrils. I gagged and jumped out of bed. The lump under the blanket rolled over and a snort rolled from his lips that echoed his earlier wind.

I grabbed my pink chenille robe off the floor and ran for the bathroom. Crazed, hung-over thoughts tormented me while I showered. *Does it get worse than this? There's a man I don't know passed out in my bed, snoring and farting. It can't get worse.* I leaned my forehead against the tile under the showerhead. *Yes, it can. I think I had sex with that.* Tears ran down my cheeks even as the water spray washed them away.

I heard Russ Montgomery, in my mind, as clearly as if he stood right there in the tub next to me. "You need to go home while you're ahead, Pretty Lady."

I wish I had, Momma.

Livvy

Dear Momma,

M Y HOUSE and everything in it feels so hollow it echoes: the television, the alarm clock, the telephone. The doorbell might as well chime in an empty house. Even the tinkle of the ice in my glass alternately sets off a parade of shivers up my spine or a cascade of tears down my face. Nothing sounds whole or complete since they took Alex.

You heard me right. They took my baby girl. Who? My own damn father and his Bleached Bimbo. That day branded its imprint on me like a movie I'd seen a hundred times until my lips mouthed the words in perfect time with the dialogue on the screen.

I admit I'd been partying more than usual. But for God's sakes, who doesn't imbibe too much over the holidays? Office parties and celebrations with friends had never caused me to miss a day of work and I shielded Alex from the brunt of it. In fact, I usually tried to make sure she stayed at Daddy's when I had a... date. But that night, Daddy and Nora Jean had plans of their own, so they wouldn't keep her. THEY WOULDN'T KEEP HER! How's that for irony? Daddy said I drank too much, but he wouldn't keep my kid because he had to go to a party himself. There's the Luther Dolan double standard for you.

I had a date. Some guy I met at a party at Gina's. Since Alex would be home, I made dinner for him at my place figuring we could still have a private get-together there.

After I put Alex to bed, Brian and I listened to Billy Joel on the record player. We danced in the dark while Brian whispered the lyrics in my ear and nuzzled my neck. We drank wine and champagne and made out like a couple of sex-starved teenagers. His stomach-jolting, knee-melting kisses melded with the champagne to give me the sexiest night I'd had in years.

Our make-out session sparked frantic groping while we stumbled down the hall to my bedroom. I grabbed his ass and hung on for the ride while he caressed my breast with one hand and gripped the champagne bottle in the other. Somehow, in all our fumbling, we managed to tear off half our clothes and leave a trail behind us as we moved. We fell into the bed without bothering to slip between the sheets. A mindless, sexual frenzy mounted and peaked in an orgasm unlike anything I'd ever known. I clawed Brian's back until my fingers went numb. When he finally rolled off me, we both lay gasping for breath as we stared at the ceiling. My head lolled to one side and I looked at Brian across my floral bedspread. "You have to leave before Alex wakes up in the morning."

A giant black hole swallowed everything after that and I remember nothing until I heard Daddy yell, "What the hell do you think you're doing?"

His deep, booming voice startled me so bad I almost fell off the bed. My eyelids felt thick and swollen, hard to open. When I did, I wished I hadn't. Brian and I never made it under the covers. We both sprawled on the bedspread, stark naked. I tried to cover myself with a blanket that had fallen to the floor. Brian grabbed his pants and wobbled into them.

"What are you doing here, Daddy?"

"Daddy?" Brian asked. He shook his head. "I'm gone."

Daddy balled up Brian's shirt and shoved it into his stomach as Brian skittered past him in the doorway. "I don't know who the hell you are, but don't ever come back here." He raised his fist like he wanted to follow up the shirt shove with a right hook.

"You have no right to throw him out of my house," I screamed. "Why are you even here?"

Daddy punched the bedroom door instead of Brian. "Alex called me. She woke up and found empty wine bottles all over the living room and your clothes strewn down the hall. She followed them into the bedroom." He threw his hands in the air, palms up. "That's where your daughter saw you and that coward you were sleeping with in all your finest glory. And when she couldn't wake you up, she got scared and called me. Your daughter thought you were dead, Livvy." He punched the door again. "That's why I'm here."

He turned away. "Get dressed and get in the kitchen. We're going to talk."

I threw on shorts and a T-shirt and stormed into the kitchen ready to tell Daddy that he had crossed the line, that I had a right to my privacy. But I stood in the doorway and saw the look on his face. I had never seen him so angry. His eyes narrowed and his cheeks flushed. He slammed a coffee mug on the counter and filled it almost to overflowing before he held it out to me. My outrage drained away and I reached for the cup like a cowering puppy with her tail between her legs. I pulled out a chair and sat down at the table, waiting for the lecture.

"I'm ashamed of what you've turned into, Livvy. I've told you time and again that you're drinking too much." He folded his arms across his chest and stared out the window. "You're getting more like your momma every day."

I flinched. Whether from the truth of his words or in defense of you, I still don't know. Maybe, I'd taken root under your shadow more than I ever suspected.

He pointed toward the living room where Alex watched cartoons and ate a bowl of Rice Krispies. "Until now, you at least had the decency to make sure your daughter didn't see your mess, but now you've got her waking up in it." He stared out the kitchen window and gripped the rim of the sink. "I won't let Alex live this way. You're going to pack some things for her and she's coming home with me for a while."

I jumped up and my coffee sloshed over the side of the mug. "No! Alex is my daughter! You have no right. I'll fight you on this and Sonny will help me!"

"Now you're thinking you can rely on the deadbeat to help you? Your ex-husband spends most of his days so drunk he can't find his own ass with both hands. Good luck getting his help."

"You can't just take her! And I won't let that bleached bitch you call a wife raise my daughter! She hates me and she hates Alex and you know it! You can't take her!"

Before I finished yelling at him, I heard Alex sniffle in the other room. Within seconds her sniffles turned to sobs. I ran in and pulled her onto my lap. She pushed away and curled into a ball in the corner of the couch.

"I couldn't wake you up." She ran her finger under her dripping nose. "What was wrong with you? I was so scared."

My heart splintered. It had to have cracked loud enough for Daddy to hear it from across the room, where he stood with that horrible I-told-you-so look on his face. I swallowed the tears that wanted to flow and I walked into Alex's room to pack her bag.

Daddy took the suitcase, grabbed Alex's favorite stuffed teddy bear from her bed and headed to the front door. "Let's go, Lady Bug." Alex put her hand in his and they walked to his car. I watched the damn BB get out of the front seat to let my daughter climb in between her and Daddy. She looked at me and I swear the bitch smirked. I took a step forward, but stopped when Daddy turned back to me. This time he looked like he wanted to cry every bit as much as I did. "Get your shit together, Livvy. Alex needs you."

I stood in the grass and watched them drive away. I didn't move, even long after they had disappeared down the street and around the corner. Chill bumps tingling up and down my bare legs brought me back to the present. I went back inside, opened the last bottle of wine and sat down to ease the pain. It didn't help.

November 31, 2011
4:00 PM

Dear Mom,

THE HATBOX sits in a corner of your hospital room, hidden under my overnight bag. I'm too embarrassed to tell anyone that I'm reading your secret letters to Grandma CiCi. I feel like I've stumbled upon your diary and am shredding any semblance of privacy that you have left.

Whenever you doze off, I pull out another envelope and lose myself in your thoughts. Long buried emotions come roaring back. Your last letter ripped me right out of this room and put me back into 1979. My tears flowed before I finished the second page because I knew how it ended. I remembered that day too well. I lived it.

I woke up early and made my Saturday morning dash to the television set to watch cartoons. When I flopped down on the carpet with my pillow, a terrible stench billowed all around me. Musty, stale cigarette smoke and liquor. I looked around and saw the empty bottles and overflowing ashtrays. Your pants dangled over the arm of the couch.

The tight knot in the pit of my stomach announced its presence with a dull throb. I jumped up and followed your discarded clothes down the hall to your bedroom. My heart pounded and I could barely breathe as I stood outside your closed door. I raised my fist and rapped softly on the wood. "Mommy?" The lack of response fueled my fear and I knocked harder. "Mommy?" I yelled. Still nothing. I turned the knob and pushed the door open a crack, peeking into the room.

I saw you and that man lying on the bed. Neither one of you moved when I tiptoed over to you. Your mouth hung open and I couldn't see you breathing. I tapped your shoulder. "Mommy?" My eyes misted. "Mommy!" I grabbed your shoulder and shook it. Your arm slipped off the side of the bed and hung limp. I screamed and ran back down the hall toward the kitchen. I could barely see the numbers on the phone through my streaming tears when I called Granddaddy.

"I'm on my way, Lady Bug," he said and since I knew that my Granddaddy could fix anything, I believed everything would be all right.

Except he didn't fix it and nothing was all right for a very long time. You woke up. The strange man never came back. But Granddaddy and Nora Jean took me away. For months, I had nightmares of that day, of what I saw, of losing you and my home. I'd wake up screaming for you, aching for you. But you never came. I loved you and needed you. I missed you and blamed you. And I didn't understand why you didn't come for me and take me home.

I look at you now, lying in your hospital bed and all the drama seems so long ago. So much time has passed. We've both grown and changed. But I read your words and my pain comes back like it happened yesterday. The difference is that today, I do understand.

August 12, 1979
Happy Birthday

Dear Momma,

I LOOK in the mirror and can't see me anymore. Only you stare back at me. What the hell have I done?

Livvy

Dear Momma,

FOR MONTHS Daddy said, "I won't let Alex go home with you until you get your drinking under control."

I said, "I'll sue you."

"Go ahead," he challenged. Back and forth.

"I'll never speak to you again."

"I can live with that as long as Alex stays safe."

"I'll get her out of your house, leave town and make sure you never see her again." He had enough and installed an alarm system.

I couldn't afford an attorney, couldn't get past Daddy's alarm and couldn't stand my life without Alex. I despised the person I had become. As much as I hated it, my desperation forced me to reach out to Sonny.

"Daddy took Alex away from me. He only lets me see her if he or the bimbo are there." I choked down wrenching sobs and swiped at a continuous flow of tears. "Help me get her back, Sonny. You're her father. You have a right to her. Daddy doesn't. We can split the cost of an attorney…"

Sonny chuckled so low I almost missed it. "You won't let me spend time with her 'cuz of my drinking, but you don't like it when your daddy does the same thing to you. Now, you wanna say she's my kid and I've got rights. Bullshit. You want money, Livvy. That's all you want. And when you get it you'll go right back to the same old crap. 'If you want to see your daughter, Sonny, you better sober up.' You're a hypocrite, Sweetheart." He put the bottle to his lips and gulped his beer. "You'll have to figure out what to do about Alex on your own 'cuz I don't care if you've got her or not." He chugged the rest of his drink, stood up and walked out of the bar, leaving me with the bill and a sinking desperation.

My final option? Control my drinking. So, I stopped going out. I only let myself drink on weekends. I drank slower, limited myself to three drinks, wouldn't start until five o'clock, stored it in out-of-the-way places, watered down the booze or wouldn't keep it in the house at all.

Nothing worked. I lied to myself, cheated on the count or the time, started a binge on Friday and didn't draw a sober breath until Monday. Visited all my hard-partying friends who wouldn't notice how much I'd swiped of their stash. I spent very little time around nondrinkers. Couldn't handle their judgmental stares.

Even my friend, Gina started in on me. "I know your dad's on your back about this and I don't want to pile on or anything, but it seems like you're drinking a lot more lately. My cousin goes to meetings that helped him quit. Maybe you should think about that."

"Meetings? I don't think so. I just need to slow down a little."

The day I didn't show up for work, Gina came by on her lunch break. Found me passed out from the night before. That night she stopped back by with a couple of burgers. She forced me to eat, ordered me into the shower and announced that she had found an open Alcoholics Anonymous meeting for us to attend. When I started to argue, she stopped me. "You can go willingly or I'll dress you myself and drag your ass to the car. Your choice." She folded her arms across her chest and waited.

She showed no sign of leaving so I went to the bedroom and changed clothes. I stuck my head in the hall and yelled toward the kitchen, "What the hell is an open AA meeting?"

"I called my cousin this afternoon. He said an open meeting means that anyone can go. Like it or not. Listen or leave. Check it out and see if it might work for you. They have closed ones for just the alcoholics. He said they're pretty damn serious about the anonymous stuff, no last names and no talking about people you see at the meetings."

I buttoned up my blouse and glanced up to see Gina standing in the door. "Get a move on, honey. I'm going with you."

"To the meeting? No. You don't have to do that." I fumbled with the button on my jeans. "Just tell me where it is and I'll check it out."

Gina laughed. "Not a chance. I'm taking you to the meeting, sitting next to you through the whole damn thing and driving you back home. You're not getting out of this."

Crap. I figured Gina would leave me to dash out the door alone and I'd fix a drink and go back to bed. Instead, she waved her car keys at me. "Let's go. It starts at eight." I saw no way out. It looked like I'd be going to an AA meeting that night.

Gina drove to the Episcopal church on Market Street and pulled into a space. My heart pounded like hurricane-swollen waves pummeling the beach. Blood thumped in my ears as we walked across the parking lot. My mouth felt like I'd crammed a hundred pork rinds in at once and forgotten to take even a sip of water to wash them down. Sticky sweat dribbled down my spine. Throwing up might actually have felt better than the queasiness in my gut.

Gina pulled the door open and pushed me through it ahead of her. Blue, hazy smoke hung so thick in the air that my arms moved in a modified breast stroke to clear the way inside. But almost immediately I welcomed it, like a familiar old blanket on a frosty night. At least if I had to give up alcohol, I didn't have to sacrifice nicotine in the process.

A podium stood at the front of the room. Probably fifty chairs, lined in neat rows, faced it. People mingled around the room. Some clustered together by an enormous coffee pot, others stood near a long table piled with books. A few sat alone on chairs, staring straight ahead, hands clasped in their laps. Their expressions said they hoped to go unnoticed and I suspected they might be first timers, too. I wanted to say, "My friend dragged me to this ridiculous meeting. How did you get here?"

Gina pointed to the coffee pot and walked that way. I followed. She poured two cups and handed me one. "Let's sit down." I insisted on the back row. She arched an eyebrow and might as well have said, "I'm on to you. There is no getaway." I shrugged and took an end seat on the last row. Tiny aluminum ashtrays waited on every other chair and I grabbed the one next to me. My skin itched and prickled so bad I wanted to shed it and bolt from the room, leaving the sweaty Livvy husk in a pile next to Gina.

Instead, I lit a cigarette, inhaled the first puff and clung to my little ash tray like a lifeline.

I heard a gavel rap against the podium and a deep male voice bellowed, "It's time to get started. Everybody take a seat, please."

One look at the man belonging to the voice and my tingling skin shifted into overdrive. Staring straight into my eyes stood none other than Russ Montgomery. I slumped low in my chair even though I knew he had seen me. If I had worn a ball cap, I would have jerked the bill down over my face, but I had nothing to hide behind. "What is he doing here?" I whispered.

As if in answer to my frantic question, Russ leaned toward the microphone in front of him and said, "Welcome to this open meeting of the Wilmington Group of Alcoholics Anonymous. My name is Russ and I'm an alcoholic."

Almost everyone in the room chorused, "Hi, Russ."

I wanted to disappear and willed my body to get up and walk out. I didn't belong there. Russ Montgomery's personal hell had to have driven him almost out of his mind, to the point that he needed that help. I hurt for him and always had, but I didn't need meetings. I just needed to slow my drinking down a little.

My fuzzy, hung over brain heard nothing anyone said that night and when the meeting finally broke up I grabbed Gina's arm and pulled her out of her chair. "Let's get out of here."

She looked at me and I saw pity in her eyes for the first time. "Okay, but we're coming to the next open meeting together day after tomorrow."

"Whatever. Can we just go, please?"

I had no idea how he got to the exit ahead of us, but he did. The only way for me to leave that building meant walking past Russ so I lowered my head, stared at my feet and plowed my way through the door.

He caught me by the arm and stopped me. "I wondered how long it would be before I saw you here." When I didn't look up he let go of my arm. Much more gently, he added, "Keep coming back. It works."

I walked out the door. It felt like I'd glimpsed a secret part of Russ Montgomery's world, and I hated seeing him there. I sure as hell didn't want him to think I belonged there.

Livvy

P.S. Gina went with me to half a dozen meetings before I got up the courage to pick up a beginner's white chip. The next day I went to Daddy's, told him I had changed and I wanted Alex back home with me. "I'm proud of you, Livvy. You're doing what you need to do." I got my hopes up and then he added, "Let's just give it a little time and see what happens, okay?" I went home that night and got very drunk. Turns out that acknowledging my alcoholism took all the fun out of drinking. I found my way back to the program quickly. When I picked up my first white chip I felt embarrassed. The second one brought shame. I don't want to know what the next might bring.

Dear Momma,

THE FIRST six months of my sobriety, I craved a drink so bad I didn't think I could make it from morning coffee to sweet tea at lunch. "One day at a time," they told me in AA. So, I gritted my teeth and white-knuckled my way through minutes, hours, days, weeks, and months. The time increments added up until I woke up one day, two months sober. My newly de-fogged mind saw changes in my body, my health and my life; loss of guilt, clear eyes, energy, reliability, money in my pocket at the end of the week. Best of all, Alex now ran to meet me when I visited, instead of pouting because she had to spend time with me.

Your words rang true once more, Momma. "The key to life is knowing when to hang on and when to let go." I saw the smile on my baby girl's face and knew I would do whatever I had to do to hang on to sobriety and let go of the past.

Daddy asked questions about the AA program and went to a couple of open meetings with me. "I want to see what all this fuss is about," he explained.

"The open meetings are speaker meetings where somebody stands up and tells their story; what they were like as drunks, how they got to AA and what life is like now," I explained.

After his first meeting Daddy said, "I don't understand people airing their dirty laundry for all the world to hear." He reached out and hugged me. "But if that's what it takes to keep doing what you're doing, then air your mess with the best of them."

I saw love and pride in his eyes that I thought had never been there before. But then I wondered if maybe I'd finally just been sober long enough to finally recognize it.

A few days after I picked up my six-month chip, Daddy called me. "Alex wants to come home." His voice cracked. "She's right. It's time. You're ready, Livvy."

I must have sounded like a sobbing, babbling fool. I cried and sniffled and blubbered and blew my nose and even with all of that ringing in my ears, I could have sworn I heard Daddy doing the same thing. He denied it. But I know what I heard.

"There's nothing I want more than having Alex with me. I'll be there right after work." I sniffled again and whispered, "Thank you, Daddy."

"She'll be packed by the time you get here. If she forgets something, I'll get it to you this weekend. And Livvy…" I heard him swallow. "I love you, and I know you can do this."

I clung to the phone even after it clicked in my ear and his words echoed long after the dial tone hummed in the background.

When the five o'clock whistle blew, I don't think my feet touched the ground from the time I clocked out until I turned the key in my car door. *My baby girl is coming home,* I thought. Even the summer thunderstorm couldn't dampen my spirits. By the time I climbed in behind the wheel, the rain had soaked my jacket all the way through and my hair hung down past my shoulders and dripped onto my lap. I shook my head like a wet Terrier and laughed.

The storm drifted off the coast before I pulled into Daddy's drive. It left thick, white clouds hanging in the blue sky behind it. Alex stood on the front porch watching for me and she looked like my very own pot of gold waiting at the end of the rainbow. I left my keys in the ignition and the driver's door standing open when I jumped out and raced to pull her into my arms.

"You're so wet," she complained though her arms held tight around my neck.

"Oh, for God's sakes. You'll ruin her clothes," Nora Jean whined. She pulled at Alex's hands, trying to drag her away from me.

Nora Jean had taken care of my little girl when I couldn't. My gratitude for that dwarfed any irritation I felt right then.

"It's okay, Nora Jean," Alex said. "It's not a big deal."

Daddy pushed open the screen door. "Leave them alone, Nora Jean."

Over Alex's shoulder I watched Nora Jean snort her dissatisfaction with Daddy's interference before she marched into the house. "Alex's bags are on the porch. No need for Livvy to drag her wet butt into my clean house." The screen door slammed behind her.

"She's sad to see you leave, Lady Bug." Daddy shook his head. "She doesn't know how to show it."

Alex looked at me and rolled her eyes. We both doubled over in waves of giggles.

My baby girl had lived with my father and BB for over a year and a half. And Alex's simple eye-roll showed me how very much I had missed of her growth and change. She had just celebrated her 11th birthday. She stood only a couple of inches shorter than me and I couldn't help but notice that breasts budded where her little flat chest should still be. She had developed her own sense of humor. She knew what she liked and what she didn't. In spite of my weekly visits, I had missed her entire transition from sweet child to sassy preteen. In front of me I saw a confident, funny young girl that I couldn't wait to get to know.

I turned to Daddy and held my arms out to embrace him. "Thank you, Daddy, for everything."

He cupped my face in his hands and leaned toward me until his forehead touched mine. "You're a strong woman, Livvy," he whispered. "Don't ever forget that."

I responded with a grin. "Alex, what do you say we go home?"

She jumped in the air. "Yeah!" Then she turned to Daddy and ran into his arms. "I love you Granddaddy. I'm gonna miss you so much." She kissed him on each cheek.

Alex grabbed one of the suitcases sitting nearby and I snatched the other. We threw them in the trunk and climbed in the front seat.

I rolled down the window and waved. "I'll call you, Daddy."

Alex didn't speak a word from the time she got in the car until she saw her grandfather walk into the house. Then she turned in her seat and stared at me, making no effort to hide the mischief dancing in her eyes. "I still love you past the sky, Mom, but if you ever leave me with Nora Jean again I swear I'll shave your head in your sleep."

My laughter choked me until tears trickled down my cheeks. I reached over and grabbed her hand. "I'm so sorry. And I swear to you, I'll never let that happen again."

Love you Momma,

Livvy

November 31, 2011
9:00 PM

Dear Mom,

*Y*OU DID it. You got sober. Back then, I didn't recognize that as a huge accomplishment. I knew nothing of our family history of alcoholism or the dismal rate of recovery. You took control of your life, and in the process, you changed mine.

"Please wake up so I can tell you," I said aloud.

Your eyelids fluttered. "Tell me what?"

I scooted my chair closer to your bed. "I'm so proud of you."

A small smile escaped your lips even as you furrowed your brow. "What on earth for?"

"For everything. But right this minute, for getting sober."

"What brought that on?"

"I guess I just realized what it took for you to do that and it makes me proud."

Your head nodded up and down. "Okay," you said before your eyes closed again.

And I've realized how very little time I have left to tell you that, I thought.

Panic tightened around my heart making it almost impossible to inhale more than a slight gasp. I laid my head on the edge of your bed, clutching your hand while you slept.

Please don't leave me.

Dear Momma,

THE RENTERS who lived in your old house gave their notice. I hope you'll be happy to know that Alex and I moved into it. I dreaded stirring up the ghost of CiCi past, but after we got settled, I found comfort instead of grief, peace instead of anxiety. Sober memories of you in my childhood superimposed themselves over all the intoxicated ones. I had come home.

Alex took over my old room, insisting that it would look perfect painted in a bizarre shade of neon green. I saw no possibility for sleep inside a glow-in-the-dark cocoon, but she remained adamant. So, we painted her room before we unpacked the first box.

Alex bought a new cassette tape by The Stray Cats and I liked it. Right up until she made me listen to "Rock This Town" fourteen times that day. At one point, after we slathered a first coat on about half the room, Alex held the paintbrush up to her mouth like a microphone and sang so loud her bedroom window vibrated in the wood frame. When I laughed at her, she flicked neon green paint at me and laid down the challenge. "You can't do any better." I arched an eyebrow at her, cleared my throat and jerked my own paintbrush to my lips. It took less than sixty seconds of my tone-deaf shriek to have both of us laughing so hard, it looked like we might be having convulsions. Alex snorted, covered her mouth in embarrassment, laughed harder and snorted some more. I teetered on the edge of gleeful hysteria and bounced back and forth from one foot to the other trying desperately not to wet my pants.

I swiped the back of my hand across my face to staunch the flow of giggle-tears. That's when I noticed Russ Montgomery leaning against

Alex's doorframe. He held two over-stuffed McDonald's bags in front of him. I gasped, jumped a foot off the floor, and smashed my paintbrush microphone into my T-shirt in auto-response to being scared witless.

"Sorry. I didn't mean to scare you." He held the bags out like a peace offering or a shield. "At the meeting last night somebody said you were in the middle of moving. Thought you might need some help. I tried the doorbell, but y'all were singing so loudly…" He grinned. "I guess you didn't hear it." His shrug made his grin look even more playful. "The door was unlocked."

The Stray Cats blared in the background. My face flushed and I looked down hoping Russ wouldn't notice his effect on me. A neon-green paint glob glowed on one nipple. Could it get any more embarrassing? Why yes, it could. That's when I remembered my torn cutoffs, way too short to wear outside my own house, my bare feet, no makeup and hair stuck on top of my head in a Pebbles Flintstone ponytail that probably had paint flecks in it. I winced.

"That was nice of you," I mumbled.

"Say it again like you mean it, and I'll give you a burger," Russ replied.

Alex looked from Russ to me and back again. "I think it was nice of you, and I'm starving."

She laid her brush across the top of the paint can and led the three of us into the kitchen where we cleared a spot at the table so we could sit down and eat. By the time we polished off burgers, fries and milkshakes, our banter felt unforced and comfortable.

Russ stayed through the afternoon, painting the trim while we put a second coat on the walls.

"It's perfect." Alex surveyed the final touches. "I can't wait to put my posters up."

"And cover up this…" Russ searched for the right word. "Elegant paint job?"

Alex punched him in the arm.

As soon as Russ pulled out of the driveway, Alex and I dumped our paint-spattered clothes on the deck, showered and collapsed into my bed. We talked about bedspreads and school clothes.

After a couple of minutes, Alex scooted closer to me and buried her face in my shoulder. I could barely hear her when she asked, "Mom, is there something wrong with me?"

I leaned back and cupped her face in my hands. "Of course not. What's going on?"

"Then how come Daddy acts like he doesn't want to see me?"

Memories of my own longings pricked my heart. I remembered craving my father's attention and approval. I knew exactly what my daughter felt.

"Of course, he wants to see you." I stroked her hair.

She shook her head. "He never shows up on time to pick me up and sometimes on his weekends he doesn't come at all. He always acts like he's so busy, but I know he's not." Alex's eyes welled with tears. "He'd rather be at the bar than be with his own daughter."

I knew then that my covering up for Sonny's drinking, in a misguided effort to spare Alex's feelings, had only hurt her more. "Look at me," I said as I tilted her face up to mine. "You are perfect. There is absolutely nothing wrong with you. The brokenness is in your father." I chewed my lip and wondered how much to say to my little girl who had already been through more than any child should. The truth won out. "You know that Mommy's a recovering alcoholic." Alex nodded. "Well, Daddy has a drinking problem, too."

"I know," Alex said with a certainty she shouldn't have at her age. "But I don't understand why he can't get better, too." She stared at me. "You quit drinking. Why can't he?"

I pulled her hair away from her face and tucked it behind her ear. "Alcoholism is a disease, honey. And not everybody recovers from it. But we won't give up on him. We'll keep praying that he'll find the strength to quit." I kissed her forehead. "And while we're praying for that, don't you ever forget that he had this problem before you were even born. His drinking isn't about you or me or anyone else. You can love him and still realize that he's an alcoholic. Does that make sense?"

"I guess." Alex nodded, but her sadness never left her eyes. She turned into my shoulder again. "I didn't tell you after I came home, but

Granddaddy and Nora Jean are fighting a lot. I'm scared that the same thing will happen to them that happened to you and Daddy."

I froze. For so long I had been drowning in my own troubles and hadn't noticed anyone else's. Suddenly, I felt terribly selfish.

"What?"

"They argue all the time, Mom, about you and me, Nora Jean's drinking and Granddaddy working too much. Even what restaurant to go to for dinner. They fight about everything. Sometimes, it's so bad that Granddaddy sleeps in the other room. I never told them that I know that. They tried to keep it a secret."

"Oh, Alex. I'm sorry you had to see that. I'm sorry you had to live with them through that, especially after everything with your Dad and me. You shouldn't have had to go through it again."

"I'm worried about Granddaddy."

I cradled Alex in my arms. "You don't have to worry about him anymore." She looked up at me. "I'll take over the worrying from here on out, okay?"

I took back the parenting reins from my daughter and felt like the adult in our relationship for the first time in a very long while.

Love you,

Livvy

Dear Momma,

WHEN RUSS helped us paint, we laughed and talked and got to know one another. My heart still fluttered at the sight of the man, but the nerve twinges I'd felt around him before vanished. I caught him staring at me a couple times that day and could have sworn I saw interest, desire. Okay, maybe it was just temporary lust, but I saw it and I hoped he'd ask me out. He didn't. We crossed paths at AA meetings, but we had no date, no romance. My old insecurities returned ten-fold: unattractive, boring, undesirable, unlovable, not worth the effort.

Then I happened to drive past his house on my way to the grocery store. The passenger door to Russ's pickup stood open and I saw Russ carry his daddy in his arms down the driveway. He bent at the waist and slid the older man onto the bench seat. Dwayne Montgomery looked like a withered sliver of his old self. He'd lost so much weight that Russ lifted and carried him with ease. Even from a distance, I could see his sagging skin and pinched face. The intimidating bear of a man looked so frail that if he hadn't been with Russ, I would never have recognized him. Russ moved with slow, deliberate steps like he feared that any sudden movement would either cause his father pain or break him completely in half.

I'd witnessed a private moment, never meant for anyone else to see. I shivered, looked the other way and kept driving.

Within days, I heard that Dwayne Montgomery had lung cancer. Russ had taken his father into his home and cared for him until Dwayne died a few weeks after I saw him. Chalk another one up to the damn disease.

I attended the funeral. Sat in the back of the church and hoped to go unnoticed. Russ hadn't let me know that his father died and I had no way of knowing if he would even want me there. I didn't want him to think I'd try to use his pain and grief to get closer to him.

Several weeks later, at an AA meeting, I helped set up eight or ten tables in the center of the room and surrounded them with standard issue church potluck metal folding chairs.

The counter top dividing the fellowship hall from the kitchen area looked like a coffee buffet. Beaming red lights on two enormous metal pots signaled fresh, hot coffee. Mountains of Styrofoam cups stood alongside the pots. A light dusting of powdery Coffee-mate covered the plastic red stirrers next to them. A metal spoon stood straight up in the center of a Tupperware container of sugar. Small woven baskets waited on each end of the coffee buffet for donations.

I sat down at one of the tables, laid my cigarette pack and lighter in front of me and reached for an ashtray. As soon as I popped a cigarette in my mouth, familiar masculine hands picked up my Bic and flicked it. I let my cigarette tip touch the flame and inhaled before I looked into Russ Montgomery's eyes. My heart quivered the same way it had the first time I saw him in his garage all those years ago when Sonny worked for him. I could have sworn I heard his heart pounding, too. He pulled out the chair next to me and sat down.

"I'm so sorry about your daddy," I said.

He nodded. "I saw you at the funeral. Thanks for coming."

I shrugged. "No problem. I know how hard it is."

"You do know, don't you?"

"Yeah." The word came out scratchy, colored with more emotion than I thought would be left after all these years.

Russ reached over and laid his hand on mine. His touch took my breath away. If the group leader hadn't called the meeting to order right then, I'd like to think the moment might have progressed to a flirtatious kiss. Instead, Russ moved his hand and I stared at the cigarette glowing in the tray. After a minute or two my pulse slowed and my breathing kicked in again. I hadn't even realized that I'd been holding my breath.

The meeting progressed all around me, but I couldn't tell you who spoke or what they said. That night, I knew only that I sat next to Russ Montgomery and he touched me.

At the end, when we all stood in a circle and said the Lord's Prayer, the trembling started again as soon as Russ reached for my hand. Everyone holds hands during the closing, so I had the perfect excuse. I took his hand and prayed I wouldn't faint.

After we chanted the last "It works, if you work it," I looked up at him. "It's nice to see you again, Russ."

I started toward the trashcan to pitch my cup. Russ's hand on my shoulder stopped me.

"Would you like to have dinner with me sometime?"

I had feared swooning, but when he actually asked, all my nerves evaporated. "I'd like that."

"I wanted to ask sooner, but they say not to get involved during your first year in the program and I didn't want to screw you up. Then Pop got sick." His last sentence hung in the air like a bridge connecting us. "Can I call you?"

I grinned and nodded.

Oh, Momma! He did call and since then, we've gone to dinners and movies and meetings. With every date, Russ gets kinder, gentler and even sexier. How did I get so lucky?

Loving my life,

Livvy

Dear Momma,

RUSS TOOK Alex and me to the Azalea Festival. We meandered from booth to booth, zigzagging from one side of Water Street to the other, through throngs of people. I'd never seen Wilmington so crowded. We studied jewelry, handbags and wood carvings. Alex dashed ahead of us, pausing to talk to friends she spotted along the way. They clustered together, whispering and giggling as Russ and I approached. Then Alex dashed away, maintaining the gap between us.

I looked up at Russ. "I think the teenage years everybody warned me about are here."

"She's not so bad." Russ laughed. "It'll get worse." He pulled me into the line waiting for a hot funnel cake. "If we wave one of these at her, she might decide she can tolerate our company for a little while."

Russ carried the plate-sized treat, and I grabbed a handful of napkins. We walked to an empty bench facing the river and sat down. I tore off a hunk and shoved it in my mouth. Russ did the same. Neither of us had even begun to chew when I heard a familiar voice. I swallowed hard as I looked up into the face of my drunken ex-husband.

Sonny leaned down, glaring at Russ and me. "Well, if it ain't my two exes. Ex-boss screwing my ex-wife. When did that shit start? So, this is why you threw me out."

"I'm not going to fight with you here, Sonny. I'm not even going to have this conversation with you, ever. Who I date is none of your business. Leave me alone."

"It's my business if you were sleeping with him before we split up!" Sonny turned toward Russ. "You fired me so you could move in on my wife."

Russ handed me the plate and stood up, towering over Sonny. "The lady doesn't want to talk to you right now, and she asked you nicely to leave."

Sonny snorted his laughter through his nose. "The lady?"

Russ grabbed him by the T-shirt and backed Sonny into the railing by the river. He spoke through gritted teeth. "Livvy asked you to leave her alone. Now, I'm telling you to go before your daughter comes back and sees you making a fool of yourself."

"What the hell you gonna do when I don't leave? Huh?"

Russ said nothing but pushed harder until Sonny's feet left the ground and was barely balancing on the rail along his lower back.

Russ didn't move until Sonny conceded. "Fine. I'll go."

When Russ set Sonny back down on the cobblestones, he gave Sonny a little shove in the direction of Market Street and watched as he walked away.

Sonny turned back and yelled, "This ain't over. Not by a long shot."

Russ sat next to me and reached for the plate.

"I'm sorry," I said, feeling all the joy of the morning drain away with my words.

Russ cupped his hand under my chin and tilted my head up. "Nothing for you to be sorry for."

Alex ran toward us and plopped down next to Russ while she reached for the plate. Russ grinned and pulled it away from her. "Hurts my feelings that you only come see us for the food." He closed his eyes and chewed.

"Can I have some? Pleeeease." Alex delivered her best starving child face.

Russ didn't fall for it. He moved the plate closer, but still out of her reach. "Will you sit with us for a few minutes?"

"Do I have to?"

Russ presented the plate to her and Alex tore off a giant piece. I marveled that Russ had transitioned from roadhouse bouncer to teenage sparring opponent without effort.

Alex chewed in silence until she remembered a necklace she'd seen earlier. She described it and pleaded with me to buy it for her while she munched.

"How about if it's a present from me?" Russ intervened before I could respond.

Alex's eyes widened and she nodded.

I shook my head. "No. You don't have to buy things for Alex."

"I know I don't have to. I want to." He looked over at me. "I'd like to do all kinds of things for Alex, because I'm in love with her mother."

A stray piece of dough lodged itself in my throat. I sputtered so bad I couldn't be sure if my face flushed from shock or choking. "What?"

"I love you, Livvy." Russ dabbed my sugarcoated lips with his wadded up napkin.

I slid across the bench until we sat so close that a feather couldn't have slipped between us. When I looked up at him I didn't care if I had powdered sugar on my lips or funnel cake stuck in my teeth. "I love you, too."

"Gross," Alex whined. "Really gross, you guys." She grabbed the plate from Russ and skittered as far from the embarrassing adults as possible.

Russ licked one side of my mouth. "Sugar," he explained. He licked the other side. "More sugar." Then he kissed me and everything in that kiss verified that he really loved me.

I know you knew his daddy, but I so wish you could meet Russ, Momma.

Livvy

Dear Momma,

I THOUGHT Wilbur Walker, Jr. threw sexual advances my way because of his unrequited love for you. Turned out old WWII had more horny-dog in him than lovesick puppy.

Apparently, he picked on many single women at work and found divorced mothers especially attractive. I guess that made them more vulnerable to his job loss threats. A couple of the gals I worked with got caught in his trap and did the daytime-dirty with him for months. But the man seriously misjudged the susceptibility of my friend, Gina Morano. And her brass cojones.

Both of us worked on the line and since we always sat near one another, I heard Wilbur holler to Gina that he needed to talk to her in his office. Not unusual. WWII wore his supervisory position like a weapon that he used to bully people. He loved to sit behind his desk and berate his prey of the day for some trivial infraction of Wilbur's rules. I assumed Gina to be the sacrificial lamb that morning. I should have known better.

Wilbur Walker and Gina Morano had been in his office for only a few minutes when I heard a loud thud like something had hit the wall. Half a dozen heads turned at the same time to stare at the closed door.

Every one of us heard Gina's voice loud and clear when she said, "What the hell do you think you're going to do with that? I've seen miniature poodles hung better, you perverted prick!"

That day we all learned something we had long suspected. Nothing beats a Jersey girl to knock the stuffing out of an over-inflated, southern, male ego.

The office door flew open so hard, the knob smashed into the wall behind it and stuck. WWII tumbled out and bounced against the railing outside his office. His pants drooped around his ankles. Wilbur's office perched on a kind of partial second floor that looked out over the line. Usually, when he stood on it, he looked like a controlling monarch surveying his kingdom. But that morning, the roles reversed and his kingdom surveyed the monarch in all his fully aroused glory. Fully aroused, until his penis got smashed between two hundred pounds of Wilbur and a metal rail. OUCH. It died, right there in front of all of us, like an overripe cucumber withering in the scorching heat of a Carolina August.

We gasped and the sound must have risen to the second floor like a symphony crescendo. I knew it reached Wilbur's ears when his red face changed from flustered to outraged.

"Get back to work! What do you all think you're doing? Get back to work!"

Gina stood behind him, leaning against the doorjamb, her arms folded across her chest. "What do they think they're doing? They're witnessing the downfall of a pompous dick-tator."

And then I felt like a participant in a play where someone behind the curtain whispered, "Cue the plant manager." He appeared on the line next to me and I held my breath for fear that my slightest exhale could blow the apparition away. His mouth gaped with the rest of us, though now most of the line workers stared slack-jawed at the plant manager instead of Wilbur.

"Walker!" He bellowed out the name with an authority I had never heard.

WWII jerked his pants to his waist, fumbling with his zipper and belt. Gina never moved.

"It's not what it looks like, sir." Wilbur's face flushed so red I suspected he might have a stroke and topple over the railing. "There's been a misunderstanding."

"My office! Now!" In a gentler voice, the manager added, "Miss Morano, I'd like to see you there as well."

Gina smiled, stepped around Wilbur without a glance and pranced down the stairs.

An hour later, she sashayed back onto the line with a grin that said she had swallowed the canary whole. The happy spectators stood and gave Gina the rousing ovation she'd earned.

The rumor mill kept us updated on the consequences of that day's events. The plant fired Wilbur Walker. They interviewed everyone he supervised and learned he had made unsuccessful passes at six different women. Three others had been sexually tormented for months, constantly fearful of losing their jobs if they didn't do what he wanted.

The plant manager called me into his office a few months after Wilbur's termination and offered me the jerk's old job! I snatched the opportunity with both hands. With the promotion came a big raise and Wilbur's old office, after I had it disinfected, of course.

I hope you'd be proud of me.

Livvy

P.S. Wilbur Walker left town. I heard they gave him partial retirement to disappear without a fuss. If his wife knows about his reign of terror, I sure hope she makes him pay for it the rest of his life.

December 1, 2011
11:00 AM

Dear Mom,

A FEW YEARS ago you told me that this happened to you. But at the time, I had no idea.

You came home from work that day so excited and even took me out to dinner to celebrate. You said you'd get a raise and things would be easier for us. You promised to get me the new stereo I'd been wanting. That's when I got excited for you. Selfish? Yes. But then teenagers are nothing but great big growing globs of selfishness.

When I stayed with Dad that weekend, I told him about your raise and promotion. He got so angry it scared me. He poured his beer down his throat and threw the can across the room. It bounced off a lamp and knocked over my Coke. He yelled, "Clean that up!"

I ran into the kitchen and brought the roll of paper towels back. Dad stood at the window drinking another beer while I wiped everything up. After I'd thrown the mess away, I stood next to him. "Is everything okay?"

"Oh, yeah, everything's great. Just great." Guzzle. "Your damn mother will really be on her high horse now." He scrunched up his face and forced his voice to go a couple of octaves higher. "You're not good enough, Sonny. You don't make enough money. If you'd just get a decent job and quit drinking..." He twirled in a circle. "But look at me! I got a promotion and a raise. And if I try to hold my nose any higher in the air, I'll fall flat on my ass." He walked away from me.

My shoulders slumped. "I'm sorry, Dad. I didn't mean to hurt your feelings."

"You didn't hurt my feelings. I know the only reason Livvy got that promotion is because she slept with her boss. Just like she did with my old boss. Your mother always gets what she wants and that's how she does it. Worked for your Grandma CiCi and I guess it does for Livvy, too." Dad laughed, sauntered back over to me and slapped me on the back like he'd just let me in on some terrific joke.

Except I didn't laugh. I wanted to cry. After all, my dad wouldn't lie to me. Right?

I didn't want to believe him back then, But I have to admit that a big part of me did. When you told me the story of what really happened to you and how Wilbur Walker was fired and you got his job, I finally did let myself cry. For all the wasted time I spent believing that you could do what Dad told me you'd done.

Dad became so bitter and paranoid. I want to believe the booze did that to him instead of it just being his nature. I'll probably never know what caused it or if anything could have changed it. Even so, I wish it could have been different.

I love you, Mom. And I really am proud of you.

Dear Momma,

I FELL in love with handsome, faithful, gentle, sexy Russ Montgomery. And, even more astounding, he loved me, too. Still, I wouldn't risk losing my independence, not even to keep Russ in my life. I fought so hard to break away from Sonny and stand on my own. And I feared losing myself all over again in this relationship. I felt myself being sucked back into the relationship black hole. According to my recovery literature, that behavior has a name: Co-dependency. It's a big-ass word for desperate to have a man in my life. And that made me feel pathetic all over again. Pathetic and weak.

So, I clung to my freedom like a crutch, in spite of you constantly whispering your damn secret to life in my ear. "When to hang on, when to let go." Nag. Nag. Nag.

Psycho-Livvy, who needed a man, but had to have her independence, ran right smack into the brick wall of love about a week ago and I came away from that encounter bloodied, but maybe a little wiser. Russ Montgomery asked me to marry him.

We spent so much time together that most days I already felt like half of an old married couple, even if we kept our own homes to withdraw from time to time. Boxers needed separate corners between rounds, didn't they? Not that I'm comparing marriage to a boxing match.

That particular day, I walked in the front door after work and heard Willie Nelson crooning from the stereo. I smelled a mixture of fresh-cut flowers and burning charcoal before I saw the most beautiful red roses beckoning to me from the dining room table. Your old wedding china sparkled around the vase. The smell of sautéed onions and garlic drifted in from the kitchen.

Russ had cooked dinners for me before, even special ones, but nothing like this. A grin spread across my face. He walked out of the kitchen and leaned against the doorframe. His white, button-down shirt tucked into his faded blue jeans accentuated his lean hips. The shirtsleeves rolled midway up his forearms absolutely made my mouth water. My heart pounded until the throbbing dropped somewhere south of my waist. His smirk told me he knew full well the effect he had on me. I had always reacted that way to the sight of Russ Montgomery in Levi's. Made me want to see him out of them.

"Dinner's cooking, but you have time to shower and change, if you want." He walked toward me, leaned down and our lips touched; tender and searing at the same time. Russ spun me toward the bedroom and swatted my rear.

I kicked my shoes into the closet, dropped my slacks and shirt in a pile by the bed and headed for the bathroom. Candles burned around the edge of the tub. More roses sat on top of the small table I use for toiletries. A folded towel lay on the closed toilet lid. Steam rose from the already full bathtub and bubbles floated across the surface almost touching the bottom of the candles.

I smiled again and turned, feeling Russ's presence behind me. He took me in his arms, holding me like he would never let go. Somewhere in that embrace, he unhooked my bra and slipped it off my shoulders. It dropped to the floor right before I stepped out of my panties. He took a slow breath and said, "If you don't get in the tub now, dinner will burn."

I kissed him again. "Let it burn."

"Get in the tub." He turned me away from him and groaned. "God, your ass is beautiful."

I stepped into the water and sank down through the bubbles. "You could always join me." I crooked my finger at him. "You don't know what you're missing."

"I know exactly what I'm missing." He sighed as he closed the door behind him.

All the stress of the week drained from my body and I knew that when I dragged myself out and pulled the plug, every problem would swirl down the drain with the water and vanish. Until it poured back out the showerhead on Monday morning to pee all over my week. But for that moment, I felt as light as dandelion fuzz in a summer breeze.

After I stepped out of the tub and dried off, I used one corner of the towel to wipe the steam from the mirror over the sink. It occurred to me to slip on my robe and slippers and pad into the dining room in relaxed comfort, but I thought about all the effort Russ had put into our evening and decided on Plan B. I freshened my lipstick and sprayed Chanel No. 5 in a few out-of-the-way places for Russ to discover later. Then I put on my sexiest black bra and matching panties, my shortest shorts and tightest blouse, unbuttoned to show the black lace beneath it.

When I walked into the kitchen Russ rolled his eyes. "You're determined to ruin our meal."

"Think of it as an enhancement." I smiled and kissed him.

Russ turned off every burner, eyed the steaks marinating in teriyaki sauce while they waited to be grilled and shrugged. "They can wait." He picked me up and carried me to the bedroom.

An hour later, we looked exhausted, but content in the afterglow. Russ had thrown new charcoal on the grill and we sat on the sofa waiting for the coals to be steak-ready.

"This didn't go as I'd planned," Russ said. He kissed the tip of my nose. "Though I must admit your way was better." He slid off the couch, bent down on one knee and reached under the nearest cushion. When he pulled his hand back out, he opened his palm to reveal a small black velvet jewelry box.

Alarm bells wailed in my head like a siren. Dread clawed up my throat. "What are you doing?" I tried to pull him up next to me, to make it stop before he said the words I knew would follow. He wouldn't budge.

"Olivia Maria Dolan Abbott, you are the most amazing woman I have ever known. I don't want to live another day of my life without you in it. Will you make me the happiest man in the world and marry me?"

I choked, literally, choked on my own fear. The most romantic moment of my entire life ended with Russ pounding on my back until I could breathe again.

I could still feel my heart thudding against my chest when I took his hands in mine. "I love you with all my heart and things are so wonderful between us. I don't want that to change. And, I'm so afraid that it will. Can't we please stay the way we are?"

I might as well have slapped him. The pain in his eyes said I had done exactly that. Without a word he stood and walked into the bedroom. I followed.

"Please talk to me."

He dressed and threw a few of his things into a bag.

"Russ, don't leave," I begged. My fear of commitment turned into paralyzing terror at the thought of being abandoned and alone again. "Please don't leave me."

He walked out the front door.

How could I have been so stupid? I know when to let go now and when to hang on. I hope to God it's not too late.

Livvy

P.S. Two days later when Russ agreed to speak to me again, he listened to my lame excuses with an arched eyebrow and clenched jaw. But after watching me squirm for what felt like hours, he accepted my apology, which we followed with a lengthy chaser of the best make up sex ever. Then, right there, snuggled up in the afterglow in our bed, we planned our wedding.

Dear Momma,

O N JULY ninth, temperatures retreated from triple digits to the high eighties. The sun burned off every morning cloud and I believed it did that as a gift to me on my wedding day.

When I met Russ at the altar, I wore an above the knee, royal-blue silk dress. Enormous shoulder pads and a large matching belt accented my curves in all the right places. Russ wore a deep gray suit. Together, we looked like we had stepped straight off the set of *Dynasty*. My hair hung down my back in big waves. I felt truly beautiful for the first time in years. One look in Russ's eyes told me he thought so, too.

We invited only thirty people to the ceremony and their joy pulsated in the small chapel. Love surrounded all of us that day.

Alex seemed excited about our wedding one minute, sullen the next. I hoped hormones caused the shifts in her mood instead of any reservations she might have about Russ. At times, she confided every embarrassing secret to him, trusting him completely. The next day, she could just as easily snap at him and snarl, "Don't tell me what to do. You're not my dad."

Eventually, with a little bit of pleading, Alex agreed to be my maid of honor. Rich, chocolate-brown hair framed her face and her electric smile lit up the room. The thirteen-year-old with hormonal attitude refused to let her excitement show, but traces of it emanated from her huge doe eyes. I saw in my baby girl a glimpse of the lovely young woman she will soon be.

We stood in one of the small reception areas near the chapel. I smoothed her hair and puffed the capped sleeve of her coral-colored dress. "You are so beautiful. I feel like I've lost my baby. You're all grown up."

She rolled her eyes, clicked her tongue and said, "As if." Her maturity dimmed and the awkward teenager returned. I smiled, realizing that Alex still needed her mom for a while yet.

Russ stepped into the room. "The two most beautiful women I've ever known," he said. He crooked both arms and Alex and I moved to his side. Each of us gripped an elbow. We moved down the hall to the door of the chapel. Then the three of us walked in together.

Instead of bridal attendants, Russ and I wanted Alex to be the only person with us at the altar. She handed us our wedding rings and held my roses while Russ and I exchanged those rings.

We said, "I do" at the standard "will you take this man and woman" questions, but then, the pastor said, "Russ and Livvy have written their own vows. They will exchange them now."

I turned to face Russ. He pulled a piece of paper from his breast pocket and unfolded it. Then he looked at me over the top of the paper and mouthed, "I love you" before he read.

"Olivia, you came into my life at my darkest time, like a gift of light. You were so full of love and joy that, at first, I had no idea what to do with you. Now, you are such a part of me, I don't know what I'd do without you. I know things in the past left you wounded, but I promise I will never add to that pain. I promise to love you, be faithful to you, cherish and care for you in all times, in all places and under all circumstances. For the rest of our lives I will show you that you are the most important person in my world, that you are my best friend and my life. I love you, Livvy. I always will."

I fought the tears because I knew, once they started, I would never be able to speak. Throughout the ceremony, I'd kept my hand-written vows wadded in a death grip around my flowers. My shaking fingers fumbled to open the paper and I took a deep breath.

"Russell Montgomery, I am so grateful that you asked me to be your wife. You are the man I always hoped to meet and fall in love with. You are kind and honest, faithful and loving. And so darned handsome."

I heard chuckles all around me and I smiled up at Russ.

"You're more than a good man. You're my hero. I love you. I need you. Now and always."

The pastor stood a little straighter and said, "Russ and Livvy have also written a few words that they would like to share with Alex." He turned to her and smiled. "Alex, why don't you hand the flowers to your grandfather and step up here to join your mom and step-dad."

Alex blushed beet-red and shook her head. I thought for a moment that we should have warned her about what we planned to do. But then, she took a deep breath before she shoved my bouquet and her own in Daddy's direction. He jumped up and managed to catch them before they fell. Alex stepped closer to me and I pulled her in between Russ and myself. Out of the corner of her mouth, she whispered, "What are you doing?"

"You'll see."

The pastor said, "Today's ceremony doesn't just unite two people in a marriage. Russ and Livvy are very well aware that they are joining three lives, in a family. That new family is so important to both of them that they have written vows to Alex as well."

Alex smiled through her crimson cheeks, so I knew we hadn't gone too far with what she referred to as our "mushy stuff."

We stood in a circle. The three of us held hands, joined together in front of everyone we cared about. I said, "Alex, I know I haven't always been the best mother to you, but I have tried to change because I love you more than you can possibly understand. I promise you that this marriage only makes me even stronger in that love. I promise you that the three of us will become a true family. You are a vital part of that. I promise you that with Russ and me, you will always be loved and you will always be home."

I watched tears drift down Alex's eyelashes. While Russ spoke they slipped to her cheeks.

"Alex, when I fell in love with your mother, she made it very clear that if I loved her, I had to love you as well. The amazing thing was that she never had to say those words, because I already did. I loved your spunk and your humor and that sassy mouth. I will never replace your father and would never try, but I promise you that I will always be there for you. I will always love you. We're a family now, Alex. And I promise that I will never do anything to make you doubt that."

We clung to one another, no one wanting that moment to end. The pastor grinned. "You may now kiss your bride."

With no visible shift in our group, Russ leaned over Alex's head and kissed me. Then he tilted his head and kissed Alex's cheek. The streaming tears couldn't camouflage our wide grins.

I miss you, Momma, on my wedding day and always.

Livvy

December 1, 2011
2:00 PM

Dear Mom,

TEARS SLIPPED down my face while I read your last letter. Once again, I'd gotten so lost in the past that I hadn't noticed you watching me.

"Which letter got to you?" you asked.

Seems so foolish, but it embarrassed me for you to catch me crying. I wanted to be strong for you, to be the rock you leaned on when your pain or fear overwhelmed you. Instead, I sat by your bed and cried over our shared history. And you wanted to help me through it.

"This one talks about your wedding to Russ."

You closed your eyes and smiled. "I can still see myself in that dress and if I try really hard I can smell Russ's cologne."

"I remember that, too." I laughed. "A little bit of his Chaps went a long way."

"What made you cry? I remember us all being happy that day."

I leaned back and wondered how much to tell you. Cancer had erased so much of our time. Time to talk and explain, time to laugh or cry, time to hug you and share my love. Time itself seemed to shrink over the last few months. Days dwindled to hours, hours to minutes and seconds disappeared completely. I realized that I might never get another chance and I didn't want to leave anything unsaid.

"Mom, I wanted to be excited about your wedding. I liked Russ back then and I wanted us to be a family." I took a deep breath. "And I felt so guilty for that."

"Why, babe? You had nothing to feel guilty for."

"Dad," I said.

When I heard your soft, "Oh," I knew that you had had discerned, in the time it took you to inhale, the full range of emotions encompassed in that one word.

"When I compared your life to Dad's and his always came up short, I blamed you. I guess that was natural, since he blamed you for everything, too."

"I don't understand, Alex. I mean, I know you thought the divorce was my fault, but why was your Dad's life my fault?"

"You left him. More than that, you moved on. You had a good career, a new marriage, a home. You were sober and enjoying life. But Dad had lost almost everything. He'd lost jobs and money. Friends turned away. Even a couple of bars asked him not to come back. How bad is that?" Tears slipped down my cheeks. "He lived all alone, in that broken down trailer. And Dad always said you left him for Russ. And that's why Russ fired him."

"That's not true." You tried to sit up in bed, but fell back against your pillows, exhausted from the effort. "That's not true. I never even went out with Russ until after I got sober. And you know that was a long time after Sonny and I split up."

"I always thought I knew that, Mom. But Dad sounded so convincing and so sure that you were cheating on him." I remembered your letter about catching him in the act and grinned. "He sure never admitted his own indiscretions or your finding out about it."

You ignored my joke. "I wish I had known this then. Alex, your Dad had a serious drinking problem and he wouldn't get help. And one of the things that alcoholics do so that they can keep drinking without taking responsibility for it is to blame everyone and everything for their problems. Everyone except themselves. Alcoholics are master manipulators."

"Alex, your mother never cheated on Sonny with me."

You and I both jumped like we'd been caught doing something we shouldn't. Russ stood at the door. His jaw set like it does when he's angry, but his eyes showed his hurt.

"Livvy had been divorced for at least a couple of years before we dated. And the only reason I fired Sonny was because he kept coming to work late. And drunk. And your parents were still together when I let him go."

I stood up and walked toward Russ. We met at the foot of your bed and hugged until my tears soaked through his shirt.

"Deep down, I know that. You and Mom have always been straight with me. It's just that sometimes it gets all jumbled up with Dad and my guilt."

"God knows, you saw me at my lowest, Alex. You lived with me through the worst of it. You also saw what it took for me to climb out of that damn rabbit hole." Tears welled up in your eyes. "I wanted Sonny to be successful and happy because he was your father. I wanted good things for him because I wanted good things for you. I left him, Alex, but I would never have hurt him."

You leaned back and closed your eyes. Within minutes I heard your ragged snores. I clung to Russ and let my tears fall.

May 13, 1984
Mother's Day

Dear Momma,

ALEX HAD avoided visiting Daddy and Nora Jean whenever possible. She had the occasional overnight with them, but complained about their bickering the minute she walked back in our door. I smelled trouble, but when Nora Jean actually moved out, Daddy would only say that they had decided to separate. Though I wanted far more detail than he offered, when I saw the pain in his eyes, I stifled the questions and wisecracks perched on my lips.

Since I couldn't get what I wanted from Daddy, I went to the next best source—his secretary at the dealership. And she gave me more than I ever wanted to know.

Delores told me that all hell broke loose one day when Daddy came back from a Kiwanis luncheon and walked into his manager's office. When he opened Stan Weatherington's door, it looked like Stan sat at his desk alone, but the look on the man's face made it pretty darn clear something was up...so to speak.

Stan froze. "Luther, what are you doing here?"

Daddy crossed his arms over his chest. "Better question is what the hell are you doing?"

A squeal erupted from beneath the desk, but the woman behind the sound remained crouched out of sight. Stan jumped out of his chair so fast he kneed her in the face and almost knocked out one of her teeth. She squawked again.

"For God's sake, man! Pull your pants up!" Daddy shook his head in disgust.

Stan reached for his belt to yank it and the pants up. He didn't bother to tuck anything in, just jerked the zipper and glanced back at Daddy. "I'm sorry, Luther. It won't happen again."

"Damn straight," Daddy said. "Clear your desk. Take whoever's hiding behind it with you."

Daddy's secretary said Stan sniveled like a whiny girl, so loud she could hear him from the next room. "Wait a minute. Let's talk about this, Luther. We can work something out."

"Get out before I throw you out."

Daddy slammed Stan's door and marched to Delores's desk. "Did you know what was going on in there?"

She stuttered. "When I saw Nora Jean go into Stan's office, I assumed she had business with him like always."

"Nora Jean?" Daddy stuttered her name out while his face reddened and his hands balled into fists. "'Like always'?" He turned back just as the worm tried to slip through the door. Daddy decked Stan on the spot, punching him right in the nose. Before Stan hit the floor, Daddy saw Nora Jean, fluffing her hair with one hand and smoothing lipstick smears with the other.

She held a hand out in front of her. "Stop right there, Luther. This isn't what it looks like."

Daddy's rage vibrated his body from his head to his feet. "What it looks like is that my wife's a cheating whore."

Nora Jean stomped over to Daddy with all the ginned-up indignation she could muster. "How dare you talk to me like that!"

Daddy squared his shoulders and raised up his head, looking as angry as a hooded cobra.

"You better move your ass, Nora Jean." He looked at his watch. "You've got five hours to get your shit out of my house before I get home from work. Don't be there when I get back."

Momma, I know it hurt Daddy terribly and I'm sorry for that. Really. But as I retold it for you, I smiled at the fairy-tale ending to the story of how Daddy got rid of the Bleached Bimbo.

Love you,

Dear Momma,

OVER A year and the honeymoon rolled on. I don't know how I bumbled my way into this wonderful man, but like Daddy always says, "Even a blind hog finds an acorn now and again."

Alex had problems adjusting to the marriage. But then, what rebellious, hormone-ridden, boy-crazy, continually-PMS-ing, fourteen-year-old girl doesn't have issues? With everything.

My daughter treated me like an ignorant hick, relegated me to the lonely, dismal world of the embarrassing parent. No matter what I said, Alex rolled her eyes and clucked her tongue as though she found even speaking to me to be beneath her.

My thoughts just flashed to you and me. You reared your hand back, open palmed and slapped the crap out of me before you screamed, "Don't you ever roll your eyes at me again, young lady!" So, maybe Alex comes from a long line of eye rollers.

While I played the part of the dimwitted dork in my daughter's life, it seemed she placed Sonny on the pedestal of fatherly perfection. To quote Alex, "As if!"

A while back, Russ and I had worked in the yard all day, but planned a cookout and family dinner for the evening.

Alex spent the afternoon at the beach with a girl friend's family. She pranced into the house barefoot, her flip-flops dangling from her fingers. Very short blue jean cut-offs barely covered her bikini bottom and the skimpy top left little to the imagination. A huge, sandy beach towel hung over her shoulders. Her cheeks looked bronzed after a day in the sun, but as soon as she stepped past me in the kitchen, I saw her flaming red shoulders.

"Oh, my goodness, Alex. You got way too much sun!" I touched a fingertip to her skin and watched it go from red to white and back to blood-red again in seconds. "Doesn't that hurt?"

She jerked away from me. "It wouldn't hurt if you'd quit poking it," she complained.

"Fine. Why don't you take a shower and get ready for dinner. It'll be ready soon."

"I'm going over to Denise's house for dinner."

"Excuse me?"

"They invited me."

Her high-pitched whine grated on every cranky nerve in my body. The eye roll started. I took a calming breath.

"This is the first I've heard about this. You didn't ask me if you could go and I didn't agree to it. We have dinner plans at home tonight so you're staying here."

"That's not fair! You and Russ are all kissy face all the time." She pursed her lips in distaste. "Dad says I shouldn't have to be around it all the time. I want to be with a normal family."

I lost it. I raised my arm and pointed down the hall. "Get in the shower. Put on some clothes and help me set the picnic table." My heart pound punctuated every sentence. "We are going to have a nice family dinner and we are all going to have fun." I made the last decree through gritted teeth, which made it sound insane, even to me.

Alex's chin quivered. "I am not and you can't make me." She trudged out of the kitchen. "I wish I lived with Dad. He lets me be with my friends and have dinner at Denise's if I want." She threw one last glare over her shoulder. "You act like a prison warden!"

My first outburst looked like the warning rumble before Mount Saint Helen's blew and took half the mountain top with it. I followed her down the hall, stomp for stomp. "You get in that shower before I blister your fanny to match your sunburn. The only reason your father lets you have dinner at other people's houses whenever you want is because he doesn't want to have to feed you and you know it. He probably doesn't have anything but beer in his refrigerator anyway." My voice grew louder and shriller. I made no effort to rein it in. "And he lets you be with your friends because he has no idea where you are and you know that, too."

Things I yearned to say about Sonny filled my mind, begging to be unleashed. The mother in me maintained enough control to stuff it all back down before I did real damage to my daughter.

"Don't you say anything about my dad!" Alex threw her beach towel at me, but it fluttered to the floor at her feet, which seemed to make her even angrier. She kicked at it. "I hate you!"

"That's fine. You're allowed to hate me, Alex, but you darned well better do it politely."

I recoiled. That line sounded idiotic to me as a teen and time hadn't improved it at all.

Alex slammed her door in my face, but I didn't have sense enough to let that stop me.

"You get dressed, get back in the kitchen and act like part of this family, Alexandra Madison Abbott. We are going to have a good time," I screamed.

How did something so trivial escalate to a shouting match just shy of a fistfight? Teenage hormones, hostility and rebellion. Oh my.

Livvy

Dear Momma,

RUSS AND I barely survived Alex's freshmen year at New Hanover High. For months, her mood fluctuated from semi-polite to drama-queen in the time it took to ask, "How was school, Hon?" Whoever coined the term split personality must have had a teenager in mind. Russ and I never knew which persona to expect in any situation.

Alex took clarinet lessons and played in the marching band. The day they gave out the uniforms, she wore hers to the dinner table in August. She wiped sweat from her brow throughout the meal, but refused to even unbutton her wool jacket.

In this football-loving town everyone turned out on Friday nights to cheer the players to victory. Russ and I attended every game, but we screamed for the band instead of the team.

Sonny showed up at Homecoming. I don't know if his alcoholism brought out the worst in him or if Alex being in high school rekindled bitter memories of his own glory days. Either way, he acted like an ass.

The full moon and bright lights made even the players look ghostly, so when Sonny staggered up the bleachers at halftime, I thought nothing of the fact that he looked blanched and tired. But when he stumbled and grabbed the nearest shoulder to stay upright, I knew. Not quite nine o'clock on the Friday night of his daughter's homecoming and Sonny had arrived, snockered.

Russ saw him the same time I did. He elbowed me in the side and cocked his head in Sonny's direction. I nodded. We both sighed and looked toward the band gathering on the far side of the field, taking their positions to perform. I hoped that Alex hadn't noticed her father.

Sonny sat near the top, leaning back with his elbows propped on the seat back. He wore a ball cap pulled low over his face, but I recognized the glazed look.

Periodically, I glanced over my shoulder to make sure he hadn't fallen through the slats. Or maybe I hoped he had. He remained motionless and silent for about ten minutes. His head slumped forward like he might have fallen asleep and I prayed he would stay that way until the game ended. No such luck.

The band marched out to the field, took their places and raised their instruments. Trumpets blew. I cringed and checked on Sonny. He hadn't moved. Then the bass drum pounded, and the band kicked in to the theme from *Rocky*. And they played it with gusto and volume.

Sonny startled awake and looked confused. But that didn't last nearly long enough, because he stood up, cupped his hands around his mouth and yelled, "Go Wildcats!" Then he looked around and screamed, "Where's the damn football team?"

I hung my head and closed my eyes hoping to block out the image of my daughter's father making a complete fool of himself. I heard people around him tell him to sit down and shut up. I heard him tell most of them to go to hell.

And the band played on.

Russ stood up and turned in the direction of the fuss. I grabbed his arm and pulled him back down. "Please don't," I begged. "Maybe he'll just go away."

He patted my hand. "I have to do something before Alex hears him, Livvy. I can't let him embarrass her like that."

Russ stood again, excused himself and made his way up the bleachers toward Sonny. Sonny, on the other hand, shoved the crowd out of his way as he lurched toward the ground. He almost made it, but five or six steps too soon he tumbled off the edge and landed with a thud on his butt.

I heard the disgusted murmurs of those nearby and even a few snickers. One guy yelled out, "If you're too drunk for the bleachers, then stay home!" I wanted to pretend that I had nothing to do with the annoying lush in the dirt. But when Russ jumped down to help him, I knew I had to do something, too.

By the time I got there, Russ had led Sonny toward the restroom. They didn't make it in time. Sonny doubled over at the corner of the building and chunked his cookies all over the brick wall.

I didn't wait for him to finish vomiting before I started in on him. "What the hell is wrong with you? Why would you embarrass your daughter like this?"

Sonny swiped the back of his hand across his mouth and wiped that on his pants. "My daughter? What are you talking about? Alex ain't here. I came to watch football."

"You didn't know Alex was supposed to play in the marching band during halftime tonight?"

"Hell no, I didn't know that. What do I know about marching band shit?"

That's when I heard Alex's quiet sobs behind me. She looked like a little girl playing dress up in her uniform while she clutched her clarinet to her chest, a protective buffer that might keep her heart from breaking.

"I told you, Daddy. I told you about tonight. I wanted you to see me."

"I forgot, baby. I'll see you next time."

Alex turned and ran toward the gates that opened onto the parking lot, her thick brown ponytail flying out behind her.

"You bastard," I yelled. "How could you do that to her?"

I didn't wait for an answer before I ran to catch up to Alex. Russ followed close behind me for a couple of steps, but passed me quickly. By the time I got to our car I could see him holding Alex close as he wiped the tears from her cheeks. Russ Montgomery meant the world to me, but that night, I loved him more than I thought possible. The three of us climbed into the car in silence and drove home.

P.S. Alex stayed angry at Sonny for a long time, but started talking to him again a couple of months ago. I worry that he tries to fill her with his vitriolic hate because every time she visits him, when she comes home, she's a little more distant from Russ and me.

Last time, I made the mistake of asking her, "So, have you and your dad worked things out from Homecoming?"

She snapped her head around and glared at me. "Maybe if his wife hadn't left him, Daddy wouldn't have to numb his loneliness by drinking."

Since Alex doesn't use phrases like, *numb his loneliness*, in everyday conversation, I'm pretty sure her snippy comments are courtesy of parental brainwashing.

December 1, 2011
4:00 PM

Dear Mom,

STILL feel the shame that sent me running to the car. I'll never understand why drunks do what they do. Or why seeing the anguish they cause isn't enough to make them stop. Or why I believed Dad's words when his behavior never matched his empty promises.

"I swear to you, Alex, I'll be there. I'm gonna cut back on my drinking, Darlin'. I'll get another job and things will be better. If your damn mother hadn't thrown our marriage away, I wouldn't be livin' in this dump. Hell, I'd probably have my own shop by now."

Like Peter Pan said, "If you believe, clap your hands." I clapped and clapped and clapped. But Dad kept drinking, getting fired, not showing up and blaming you for all of it. Sometimes, I think I heard his excuses and accusations so often that they became a part of me.

That night, though, I remember thinking Russ did everything for me that I wished Dad would do. He showed up, cheered for me, protected me. That's the first time that I realized how much I could count on Russ Montgomery.

And I've counted on him ever since. All of us have these last few weeks. He's been our rock. While you've been in the hospital, he hasn't left you except to grab a bite in the cafeteria. He showers here and sleeps in the chair beside you. He watches over you, second-guessing your every need. You never had any doubt of Russ's love, but his devotion has now touched us all.

I don't know how you drummed up the courage to take another chance on love and marriage after Dad, but I'm glad you did. Our lives would never have been the same without Russ Montgomery. I know that now.

Alex

Dear Momma,

DADDY AND BB had been married so long that I'd almost gotten used to her, like adjusting to chronic eczema or daily diarrhea. Though I never understood why he loved her, I tolerated her for him.

Months of legal separation, desperate pleas for reconciliation, angry arguments and dueling attorneys still came down to one final day in court. Within a matter of hours, every negative aspect of their marriage—from drunkenness to infidelity—had been laid bare and made public.

I can still see her on the witness stand squeezed into a black pencil skirt that looked a couple of sizes too small. Her breasts spilled out of a push-up bra under a V-neck satin blouse. She batted her eyes in Daddy's direction, so I knew she'd worn the ensemble to remind him of what he'd be losing. But Daddy never took the Double-D bait Nora Jean bobbed in front of him. However, the judge's raised platform perched him above the rest of the courtroom and meant that he received the brunt of the display. One glance at the witness box told me that the poor man would be staring at BB's crotch through her cleavage for the entire proceeding.

I sat in a chair behind Daddy and listened to his attorney set the scene, asking questions about that pivotal day in Stan Weatherington's office. Then, he moved in for the kill.

He leaned closer. "Let me get this straight. Your husband walked into Stan Weatherington's office, stood in the doorway and spoke to Stan, but couldn't see you. Why was that?"

"Well, I was under Stan's desk," Nora Jean stated as though that should have been obvious.

I heard soft chuckles around the room. Daddy lowered his head and rubbed his temples.

"Why were you under his desk?"

"I'd lost an earring. When I stood up, I tried to tell Luther that it wasn't what it looked like, but he wouldn't give me a chance."

"Isn't it true that Stan Weatherington had his pants down around his ankles while you were searching for your earring? Is that where you thought you dropped it?"

Uncomfortable laughter increased.

Nora Jean's cheeks reddened. "Of course not. I don't know why his pants were down."

The attorney looked out at the people seated in the courtroom. He arched his brows and rolled his eyes. "You don't know why his pants were down? Do you know why your hair was tousled or your lipstick smudged? Do you want to explain the semen on your neck?"

Daddy sunk lower in his chair. Nora Jean, on the other hand, sat straighter and squared her shoulders. Her chest heaved. "No, I do not," she answered.

Nora Jean's sexual antics cost her dollars in the settlement and her lies in the courtroom almost meant jail time. And while Daddy had to pay a fraction of what he would have if his wife hadn't been the town slut, the breakup cost him so much more than money.

Daddy withdrew from almost everything after the humiliation of that day. He spent more time at work with less enthusiasm. Where I used to see pride in Daddy's eyes, I now saw shame. I hated the bimbo for that. Letting go of that resentment would be a long time coming.

When you and Daddy split up, I didn't understand how much it had to have hurt him. He intimidated me back then and maybe that kept me from seeing that he had feelings. While I watched him go through this breakup, my mind made comparisons to you. Nora Jean hurt him, shamed him. You, on the other hand, destroyed him and made him vulnerable to someone like her. I wish I'd understood that then.

Dear Momma,

*L*ORD HELP us! Alex got her driver's license! I failed miserably as her reluctant licensed adult during the learner's permit phase. It seemed that every time Alex got behind the wheel, my steely nerves melted.

The first time I rode with her, I folded my arms across my chest so she wouldn't notice my shaking hands. I said things like, "Please don't move into the left lane before you make a right turn. The car really doesn't need the extra space." Under my breathe I added, "Did you even see the car that had to swerve around you?"

The second time, before she had even pulled out of the driveway, I screamed, "Don't back up so fast! You're going into the ditch!"

By the fourth time, I slapped on my seat belt and snarled, "Do not touch that radio and if you so much as glance in the rearview mirror to check your hair, I will get out of this car and I won't be back." We both knew we needed another man for the job. Alex jumped out of the car, slammed the door and ran into the house, red-faced and sobbing.

Russ heard the commotion from the master bedroom shower and ran out in his bathrobe thinking something terrible had happened. He tried to look annoyed when he found out the situation involved more nervous Nellie mom than fender bender, but it didn't work. He stood on the wooden floor in the hall with water droplets pooling at his feet, his navy-blue terrycloth robe hanging off his dripping body and his shampoo-laden hair spiked all over his head. His eyes danced.

"You, Livvy Montgomery, are officially relieved of learner's-permit duty." He turned to Alex. "Give me 10 minutes and I'll go with you."

Alex yelped, threw her arms around his neck and kissed his cheek. "You're the best." She cut her eyes sideways at me and pranced into her room.

"You're only encouraging her," I griped. "You know that, right?"

Russ laughed. "Of course, I'm encouraging her…to learn to drive." He turned back toward the shower.

I didn't ride with Alex again until her birthday when she took the driver's test. Russ had taught her well and she made no life-threatening mistakes, though she spent more time looking at me for approval than she did the road in front of her.

Alex drove my car to the Department of Motor Vehicles and had no idea that Russ planned to deliver a Mustang to the house and have it parked in the driveway when she got home. He found it as a clunker, did some engine work on it at the shop and repainted it. It gleamed like new.

When we got back to the house, the Mustang blocked the driveway. I told Alex to pull into the grass and park along the street.

"Who's here?" She handed me the keys as she asked the question.

"I don't know."

Alex spotted the giant note taped to the driver's side window. In bold red marker Russ had written, "Happy 16th Birthday. We love you. Mom & Russ."

Alex turned to me, her brow furrowed. "What?"

I grinned. "Happy Birthday, babe."

"You got me a car?" She screamed, shoved her purse into my stomach and jerked the car door open. A loud squeal pierced my ears as she dove into it.

Her head swiveled from side to side. She sighed as she ran her fingers over the seats and the dashboard. Her hands hit the gearshift and she looked up at me. "A stick shift?"

We hadn't noticed Russ sitting on the front porch. He held a camera to his face and clicked off pictures of Alex's reaction. "Yep, it is," he said.

"But I can't drive a stick shift," she whined.

"Don't worry about it. You'll drive it fine when I get through teaching you."

"Now? Can we start now?"

"Can't do it. Your mom and I have to get to work, so we'll do it when I get home tonight."

"Pleeease. I want to drive my car."

"You will as soon as I get home tonight." He smirked. "You know, you can always wash and wax it while I'm gone. That way you can get to know it, up close and personal."

"That's not funny, Russ."

"Yeah, it is." He turned to me and said, "Since my car's blocked in, why don't you drop me off at the shop on your way to the plant?"

I kissed his cheek. "That's the least I can do."

Russ and I rode home together about six. That evening, when we pulled onto our street, he noticed it first. "What the heck?"

The house looked normal to me and I almost asked him what he'd seen. Then I realized that the house shouldn't look normal. It should have a white Mustang with two navy blue stripes down its middle sitting in the driveway. Instead, I pulled my little brown Ford Taurus in and parked it right where the Mustang had been when we left.

Russ and I stared at one another.

"Maybe one of her friends came over and took her for a ride," I suggested.

"Then where's their car?"

I scratched my head. My chest felt heavy and my stomach flip-flopped.

About that time, we heard a high-pitched screeching, metal on metal. Our heads spun around and I'm sure Russ's eyes bugged out worse than mine when we watched the white Mustang chug-a-lug around the corner and down our street.

The setting sun glinted on the windshield, but I saw Alex in the driver's seat. She gripped the steering wheel at the ten and two positions so hard I'm surprised it didn't pop off and land in her lap. I saw no one else in the car with her. But then, who would be brave enough to do that? Stupid enough to do that? Insane enough to do that? The girl couldn't drive a stick shift.

The car lurched ahead a few feet, rocked back and forth, moved forward a little and then stopped. It rocked again, moved a bit more and paused. The process repeated at least half a dozen times before Alex rolled her window down and yelled, "What do I put it in to turn it off?"

Alex's hair hung in thick waves around her face accenting her sparkling eyes. She radiated complete joy when she jumped out of the car. "I called Kristy a little while ago and told her to wait in her yard and I'd drive it past for her to see. That way I could go around the block and not have to stop. I'm so excited! I can drive this thing!"

Russ closed his eyes and beat the side of his head against the car window.

Love you, Momma,

Livvy

August 12, 1986
Happy Birthday

Dear Momma,

A FTER ALEX got her driver's license, something strange happened to me. I paced the living room until she got home. I wondered how many kids she'd piled into her car, where they'd gone, if the traffic had been bad, if she'd buckled her seat belt. I waited and worried. Not unusual for a mom. But my reaction surprised me, more than a little bit. I prayed. I prayed for her safety and her judgment. I prayed for her to walk through the front door, happy and safe. I even found myself praying for Sonny. For him to get sober. To be the father that my daughter deserved.

As I prayed, I felt peace. And at the same time I noticed a longing, a gnawing in my gut that I couldn't quite pinpoint. I'd been going to AA meetings a couple of times a week for years and it changed me. I quit drinking, found happiness and love. Now, AA didn't feel like enough anymore. I began to suspect that the hole in my heart might be spiritual and that to get to the next level of joy in my life, it might be time for me to find God.

Please don't laugh. I remember you mocking your own parent's faith. Because they'd been so extreme in their beliefs or because you had run so far in the opposite direction? Did you believe? Or did you think you didn't need it? Did you pray for me to get home safe? Or were you so drunk yourself that you didn't notice?

I've decided to believe that you would tell me to go for it. Whether that's because you would encourage my faith itself or my self-exploration. I love you, Momma. And I'll let you know what I find in the search.

Livvy

Dear Momma,

TURNED OUT that Russ had been struggling with an emotional journey of his own. When I explained my feelings and suggested that we try to find a church home, he gaped at me like he'd just pulled a real diamond out of the Cracker Jack box. "I've been thinking the same thing."

My turn to look surprised. "Really? What got you thinking about it?"

"Alex," he answered. "Every time I'm making a breakthrough, she pulls back. I know she feels like she's betraying her father, so it's hard to be close to me. But I don't know what to do."

"I know. Lately, her mood swings are so bad, and she's angry at me all the time. Now that she's driving, I sit up worrying about her until she gets home. The other night I ended up praying about it. That's when I realized that through everything, I haven't really let God come into my life. I'm not sure how I really feel about that, but I think I'd like to try."

Russ gazed out the kitchen window. "As a kid I went to church with my mother all the time. Then Jenny and I went once in a while. But after she died, I turned my back on it. I couldn't find comfort in church or anywhere else."

Russ stirred his coffee. I waited.

"Or maybe I didn't want to find any." He put the mug to his lips and sipped slowly. "I can't crack the code with Alex. Do you think it's too late to go back through those doors?"

I reached across the table and took his hand. "Let's try it and see what happens." I smiled. "A little divine intervention with that kid couldn't hurt."

Looks like we'll find out answer together.

Livvy

Dear Momma,

SONNY'S DRINKING destroyed our marriage, his career and his health. He spiraled out of control and the whirling dervish of destruction seemed to be picking up speed.

My Jersey friend, Gina, had been sitting in a bar downtown when Sonny strutted in like he owned the place. She said he reminded her of a peacock on the prowl, even getting in a little slap-ass with one of the waitresses who passed by carrying a loaded tray. He dropped down onto a stool, reached for a handful of peanuts and tossed them in his mouth. "How 'bout a beer?"

The bartender slammed a frosty mug down in front of Sonny. Then he leaned across the bar and said something through thin, tight lips. Between what she actually heard and what she interpreted, Gina thought it sounded a lot like, "I told you last time to keep your hands off my waitresses. We ain't having this conversation again." He shoved the bowl toward Sonny, spilling a trail of peanuts across the bar top.

Sonny hunkered over his drink and stared at it for a minute before he chugged the whole thing. "I need another one." He looked up at the grizzled bartender. "Please."

Every few minutes the front door opened, allowing enough of a breeze to stir the smoke drifting up from cigarettes scattered around the room. Sonny turned each time as though he might be interested in the latest arrival. Then, he grunted and spun back toward the bar while people around him flirted and joked. Beer spilled. Waitresses wandered from table to table. The jukebox blared from the corner and a few brave souls hit the dance floor. But Sonny and the smoke didn't move, except when the front door opened just right. He didn't even get up once to go to the bathroom, and Gina gave up trying to figure out how many pints of bloated he had to be.

At eight thirty, Sonny pushed himself up, grabbed a couple of dollar bills from his pants pocket and tossed them into the empty peanut bowl. He staggered out the door. At eight forty-five, Sonny crashed through the front wall of Floyd's Garage. Police found him passed out in the front seat of the car. He suffered only a few cuts and bruises. But the totaled vehicle would never see another interstate and the garage would be shut down for weeks to repair the damage.

Floyd fired him. The police took his driver's license away for God only knows how long. And Sonny blamed everyone for his current mess but himself.

He decided to take it out on Russ and me by showing up at our house, in the wee hours of the morning, liquored up and pissed off. He stood in the yard, screaming obscenities in the dark.

Russ jumped up and glanced out the window. "What the hell?" He grabbed his pants from the bedpost and stumbled into them.

I rolled over. "What's going on?"

"Sonny's out there." Russ didn't bother to slip into his shoes or put on a shirt. He wore only his jeans when he threw open the front door and stepped onto the front porch. "Sonny, shut up before you wake up the whole damn neighborhood. What the hell is wrong with you?"

"Whatsa matter, Boss man? You afraid the neighbors'll hear that you stole my wife? What are they gonna think when they found out what you really are?"

I had slipped into my bathrobe and followed behind Russ. As soon as Sonny started, I stepped around my husband. "Stop it! You'll wake Alex up and you don't want her to see you like this."

"No, no, no, no, no." He shook his finger at me and laughed. "She needs to wake up and hear everything I have to say. She needs to hear about how her whore of a mother left me for this jackass." He pointed at Russ. "And she needs to hear how her step-father got her daddy fired."

Russ shook his head and folded his arms across his bare chest. "What are you talking about?"

"You think I haven't figured it out? You and Floyd are friends, right? You talked to him and got him to let me go. You took everything from me, you son of a bitch."

"Your drunkenness got you fired! Your attitude got you fired! Your driving a car through the garage wall got you fired!" Russ stepped off the front steps and walked toward Sonny. "Now, get out of here before I call the police."

Sonny backed out of Russ's way. That's when he tripped over a tree root and fell, cursing God and Russ the whole way down.

Alex shoved me aside and ran to her father. "Leave him alone! Don't hurt him!" She knelt beside Sonny and helped him sit up. "You two have everything and he has nothing! Leave him alone!" Tears streamed down my daughter's face while she glared at me and pushed Russ away.

Sonny turned his head my direction, arched one eyebrow and grinned at me. "I win," he mouthed, patting Alex's back the whole time.

My fists tightened at my sides and my breath came in short, rapid bursts. I wanted to throw my arms around Russ to protect him from my insane past, kick Sonny to the gutter and drag Alex back into the house by the scruff of her rebellious little neck. All at the same time.

Instead, Russ and I stood in silent shock as Alex stormed back inside for her purse and keys. She buckled Sonny into the back seat as gently as she would an errant toddler. Wearing only her nightgown and slippers, she got behind the wheel and backed her car out of the driveway.

When I couldn't see even a faint glimmer of her taillights anymore, I started to shiver and my tears ran like overflowing creeks down both cheeks. Russ led me into the kitchen.

My precious, guilt-ridden daughter took her father's drunken tirade seriously. More than that, she believed it.

I wanted her high school experience to be full of football games and dances, girlfriends and sleepovers, band concerts and boys. I wanted it to be carefree. Instead, she had to live with the consequences of my decision to marry Sonny Abbott. Alex carries all the guilt, sadness, longing, embarrassment and humiliation that every other child of an alcoholic bears. And it's my fault. I did that to her. I hung the drunken father around my daughter's neck like an albatross.

If the key to life is knowing when to hang on and when to let go, then how do I teach my daughter that it's okay to love the man and let go of his illness? How do I show her that real love is letting Sonny be responsible for his behavior and choices? How do I convince her that every minute she spends cleaning up her father's life means a minute she doesn't spend living her own? How do I teach her not to be me? Or him? Or you?

Livvy

December 1, 2011
9:00 PM

Dear Mom,

I CAN STILL see Dad lying in the grass screaming at you and Russ. I hear him calling you a whore and accusing Russ of almost every bad thing that ever happened to him. I didn't want to believe him, and, at the same time, every word gave him an alibi of sorts. And me, just enough hope to hang on to the idea of a real dad. If someone else had cursed his life and caused his problems, then none of it was his fault. If he could do it differently, he would. And he loved me enough to change, but he couldn't. Because you and Russ and everyone else plotted against him.

Now, I wonder how I could have given any credence to the things Dad said about you and Russ. The only answer I can come up with is that I knew he was sick. I knew he couldn't control his drinking, much less his life. And you could. You proved it every day. You'd gotten better, stronger. You worked your ass off to get sober and when you succeeded, I held you to a higher standard. And while Dad wallowed in his alcoholism, I held him to no standard at all. I regret that, with him and with you. Please forgive me.

Just so you know, I do remember you trying to teach me that I could love my father without getting caught in the cesspool of his disease.

I have no idea if this happened before or after yard-drunk night, but I can still see myself slumped at the kitchen table. Must have been a Saturday morning because I wore cut-offs and a torn T-shirt. I dumped Fruit Loops into a bowl, drowned them with milk and spooned huge, drippy bites into my mouth.

"What are you doing up so early?" you asked.

"Going to Daddy's," I answered, maintaining a death stare on my cereal.

The phone rang, granting me a pardon from your questions. You picked it up, grinned and handed it to me. I knew from the look on your face that it had to be a guy and I felt the blush start at my neck and work its way up. I snatched the phone and stretched the cord, but it didn't make it to the next room. I gave you my best pleading face, begging you to give me some privacy. You poured another cup of coffee and sat down. I sighed.

I mumbled through most of the conversation, but your ears actually twitched when I said, "I can't. I have plans with my dad tonight." I hung up and stared out the kitchen window.

"Did you just turn down a date?"

I couldn't respond for fear I'd cry.

"Honey, you're going to Sonny's this morning. You can do what you want tonight."

More silence.

"Alex, Sonny needs to take care of his own problems. It's not your job to parent him."

My anger flashed. "He's my dad. I'm all he's got."

"That's because of his drinking. And that's his choice, Alex. He knows where to get help. He doesn't want it."

I threw my spoon. It clattered across the table. "He's sick! Isn't that what you always said? He's sick and it's okay to still love him."

"Yes, he's sick, but this isn't like cancer or diabetes. And, of course, it's okay to love him." You reached out to me, but I jerked away. "Alex, taking care of everything for him isn't love and it doesn't help him. Sonny has to hit bottom to want to get better. I know that's hard for you, but he has to clean up his own mess and pay the consequences of his drinking to be able to recognize that he has a problem."

"He said he's going to quit. He just needs my help for a little while." I recognized the shame that physically knotted my stomach, but I couldn't understand why I felt that way.

"Honey, Sonny's an alcoholic. He tells you what he thinks you want to hear so you'll keep doing what he wants. And as long as you do that, he never has to face his problem. Because you're dealing with it for him. You have to let him fall so he pick himself back up."

I couldn't control my tears or my rage. "HE'S MY FATHER! I can't leave him in that filth all alone! Maybe you could do that, but I can't! I won't!" I ran from the kitchen, grabbed my keys and barreled out the front door to be the rescuer one more time.

I wasn't ready then to learn what you needed to teach me.

Alex

Dear Momma,

I'M WORRIED about Daddy. I don't want to hear you say, "I told you so." And I really don't want your bossy voice in my head telling me what to do. Still, I wish I could talk to you about it.

Daddy's loneliness blankets him like a death shroud. He seems content in it, but I can't stop trying to rip it to shreds so he can come back to life.

I drove to his house the other day. Took leftover beef stew and cornbread as my excuse to check on him. Before I stopped the car, I spotted him on the dock in a beat-up lawn chair. One butt cheek sagged well below the other because half the seat strings gave up their job years ago and dangled from the aluminum frame like ribbons in the wind. He cast a line and tilted his face toward the sun.

"Hey, Daddy," I yelled as soon as I stepped from the car. I held up my Tupperware and pointed toward the house.

He nodded and turned back toward the waterway.

I walked in the front door and headed for the kitchen. When I opened the refrigerator, I muttered, "You can't survive on this." A half-empty gallon of expired milk sat between a couple of pounds of coffee and a six-pack of beer. Several plastic bottles of condiments nestled together in the door made me wonder, "Why condiments and no food?" Three cardboard Chinese food containers with little metal handles shared the bottom shelf with a couple of cans of Pepsi. The stale stench told me that everything had been there for a while. I shoved my food offering onto the barren shelf between the soda and the Chinese food.

I grabbed a Pepsi, walked out the sliding glass doors and down the sloping lawn to the dock. Daddy pointed at one of the sturdier chairs and I dropped into it. "There's some beef stew in the fridge for you. I made way too much last night."

"Thanks."

"Cornbread, too. On top of the stove."

"You know I like cornbread."

"If I'd known you were out of butter, I'd have brought some from the house."

"Don't start, Livvy."

"I'm worried about you. I miss seeing you." I sipped my drink. "Russ and I are barbequing tomorrow night. Why don't you have dinner with us? Best steaks and baked potatoes in town."

"Thanks, Hon, but I've got plans. Maybe another time."

"That's what I mean, Daddy. What plans? Sitting here alone? You're scaring me. Please come to the house tomorrow."

"Don't start, Livvy," he repeated, using the same words with a lower, softer tone. When Daddy got angry, he always got quieter and, even as a kid, God blessed me with the survival instinct to back off when I noticed it.

So, I sipped again, kicked off my sandals and stretched my legs in the sun. "Catch anything?"

"Naw."

"How's work?"

"Busy."

"Alex got a job for the summer. She'll start when school's out."

"I offered her one at the dealership."

"She told me that. It was sweet of you, Daddy." I reached over to rub his arm, but decided against it and let my hand drop into my lap. "She said your offer meant a lot to her. But she felt like she needed some hospital experience and they had a part-time receptionist opening there."

"She told me."

"Hey, Daddy, I'm starving. Let's go out to breakfast. We haven't done that in ages." I stood up, hoping to kick start the momentum.

"Not today." He turned to look at me and nodded his head. "But soon, okay?"

"Sure." I leaned down and kissed his cheek. "Don't let that stew go to waste, Daddy."

I walked off the dock, but stopped in the nearby grass. "Do you remember Momma saying, the key to life is knowing when to hang on and when to let go?"

He laughed that long, slow chuckle he lets out when he's really more annoyed than amused. "How could I forget? CiCi usually followed it up with, 'So let the hell go, Luther!'"

He turned back toward the water. I'd gotten about halfway up the yard when I yelled, "The bimbo's not worth this, Daddy. Don't let that bitch take any more away from you. Maybe it really is time to let go."

He didn't move and I had no idea what else to do. I wanted to shake him back into the world of the living.

I lost you, Momma. I don't want to lose Daddy, too.

Livvy

December 2, 2011

6:00 AM

Dear Mom,

NEITHER RUSS nor I have gone home since they admitted you to the hospital last week. Every night, one of us catnaps while the other sits with you, on call to help with anything from a sip of water to repositioning your pillows. Last night neither one of us closed our eyes, because you barely closed yours.

Your pain broke through your meds and once it did, it took hours for the nurses to find the narcotic level that controlled it without knocking you out completely.

While they adjusted the drugs, you tried not to aggravate the pain. You lay so still that I checked your breathing, more than once, fearing we had lost you already. Several times, you drifted into a drugged sleep, but the beeping machines around you startled you awake. In your best moments, you let out a low moan and leaned your head back against the pillow. Worst case, you screamed as if a jagged dagger had been plunged into your gut.

Two nurses rushed through the door, taking positions on either side of your bed. One checked your IV lines. The other took your pulse as she asked about your pain.

"On a scale of one to ten, what is your pain?"

Your fingers clutched the sheets. Trembling that started in your fists inched up your arms. You gasped for a shallow breath. "Ten," you whispered. Tears trickled down your cheeks. You screamed, "Ten! Ten!"

Russ and I stood at the foot of your bed. I hadn't realized that we had our arms around one another until my knees buckled and only his strength kept me from hitting the floor. I grabbed him tighter and felt the sobs that wracked him until he doubled over and had to grab the foot rail with one hand while he held me with the other.

The nurse near the machines plunged a hypodermic needle into your IV. "This will give you some relief, Mrs. Montgomery."

She said it with an assurance I no longer believe. I don't know how much more I can watch you suffer, and God knows, I don't know how much more you can withstand.

Sometimes, I think I can actually see the cancer eating away at you from the inside out. And I can't do a damn thing to stop it or to help you. I've begged God to heal you, to give us more time with you. How the hell do I bring myself to pray for Him to let you go?

I love you, Mom.

Dear Momma,

I'D GIVE anything for you to have seen your granddaughter on her graduation day.

All afternoon, Alex and her friends clustered in her room, venturing out only for snacks or a bathroom break.

Russ zipped his Dockers and I slipped my dress over my head while teen-age giggles entertained us through the walls.

"It'll never be the same," I whined.

"Sure it will," Russ assured me. "It's not like she's heading across the country. She's just going to UNCW." A fresh round of laughter interrupted him. "There will still be plenty of this…" he cocked his head toward the sound. "For years to come."

I stared into the bathroom mirror. All the eyeliner in the world couldn't change the fact that I looked like a woman ready to padlock her daughter's bedroom door for another decade.

"My head agrees. But my heart says you're wrong. It's all changing, way too fast."

Russ walked up behind me and slipped his arms around my waist. He nuzzled his nose into my hair and kissed my neck. "We'll get through it. Together."

I spun to face him and kissed him so long that I felt his response. "I love you." I grinned. "How about we take care of that later when Alex goes to her party?" I pointed to his pants.

He sighed. "I guess it'll have to do."

He opened the closet door and stepped into his loafers while I put on my earrings. Russ threw open the bedroom door, bowed at the waist and gave his arm a grand sweep while I sauntered around him. He rapped his knuckles on Alex's door as we passed.

We'd barely gotten to the front door when three beautiful young women pranced down the hall and through the foyer. Russ and I watched all of them teetering on the brink of adulthood, one foot in the house as adolescents, the other stepping out the door into maturity. Alex said something I couldn't quite hear and they all laughed again. Relief washed over me realizing that childhood hadn't been completely left behind.

Each girl wore a brand new spaghetti strap sundress under flowing black polyester graduation gowns. Wispy strands of hair framed their overly made up faces. Orange and black fingernail polish, alternated on every other finger and toe, displayed child-like school spirit.

When we pulled into the parking lot, the girls threw open the back doors and jumped out of the car before Russ pulled the keys out of the ignition.

"See you later," Alex yelled over her shoulder. She pulled her gown up to her knees and ran toward her classmates.

"See you later," I yelled before I added a whispered, "I love you."

Russ and I joined Daddy in the stands along with hundreds of other parents, grandparents, siblings, and friends of the graduating class. I glanced around the crowd, looking for Sonny. We listened to speeches and award presentations, and then came the diplomas. By the time they called Alex's name, we would have used any excuse to jump out of our seats to give our numb fannies a much-needed break. But truthfully, only pride fueled our screaming, fist-pumping hoorays. I looked again for Sonny, praying that he hadn't forgotten his daughter's big day.

Alex walked across that platform and shook the principal's hand with the poise of an adult. After they handed her the diploma, she looked for us in the crowd, threw both her hands in the air and yelled, "Whoo-Hoo!"

Russ, Daddy and I laughed along with most of the audience. But I cried, too. I cried at the thought of losing my baby girl. I cried because time and life change even the good things. I cried because Alex's father hadn't bothered to show up for his only child's graduation. I cried for you, Momma. For all you had missed in the past and would still miss in the future. And I cried tears of joy for my daughter's accomplishments.

December 2, 2011
7:00 AM

Dear Mom,

*I*T HURT that Dad didn't come to my graduation. I fought my tears through the whole thing. I scanned the crowd, hoping to find him. When he didn't show up, it felt like he might as well have thrown me away with his empty beer cans.

Whenever you and I quarreled, my last resort, argument-stopping maneuver had always been screaming at you, "Dad loves me so much that he lets me do anything I want! Unlike you, the prison warden!" I cringe when those words echo in my head now.

Truthfully, I wanted parents who enforced rules and boundaries. You did. I wanted parents who encouraged me and showed up. You did. I wanted parents who protected me when I needed it and watched me step into the world when I was ready. You did.

Dad's indifference made me angry. And I stayed that way for years; I thought the anger would shield me from the pain. It didn't. It only pushed you away.

When Russ came into my life, he became the father I wanted Dad to be. I do love him for that, but if I'm really being honest, it never felt like enough. I needed that love and attention to come from my own father. It never did. And I continued to blame you. If you'd forgiven him... If you hadn't left him... If you'd helped him get sober... How sick is that? That I held the person who loved me responsible for the one who didn't?

I'm better now. And yet there's still a tiny part of me that wonders what Dad would have been like, what our lives would have been like, if you hadn't left him. Does that ever go away?

Alex

Dear Momma,

EARLIER THIS afternoon, I pulled out Grandma's antique hatbox. Even as a kid, I hated the ugly black hat she kept inside it, but loved the box. From the first time I wrote to you, it became the perfect place to store the letters, part of the bond that spanned time and space, life and death. Grandma's box filled with my letters to you bound by Alex's old hair ribbons. Four generations linked by so much more than mere genetics.

Years ago, the big round box looked empty. Not so much anymore. Seeing sixteen years of memories ribboned together took my breath away.

I curled up on my four-poster bed and felt the tears that came every Mother's Day. Russ walked in and found me clutching the hatbox. He sat on the edge of the bed and wiped a tear from my cheek.

"You okay?"

I nodded.

"Did you get the letter written?"

"Not yet. I've been debating rereading the old ones first."

"How about you get your letter written and we'll meet Alex for lunch?"

He leaned over and kissed my lips with such tenderness that I melted in his arms.

"Give me thirty minutes," I said.

"Done." He stood up. "What are you going to do with those anyway?"

I looked at him and laughed. "I never thought about it. I had things I wanted to say so I wrote them. Nothing beyond that ever occurred to me."

He tapped the hatbox with his forefinger. "You might want to give them to Alex one day."

"Oh, God, they'd bore her to tears." I looked at the bundles. "And there's stuff in here I'm not sure I want her to know."

"Think about it." Russ grinned. "Your secrets aren't that dark and scary and the letters would probably mean a lot to her. They're part of her heritage, her history."

I waved him off. "Let me write the next piece of her history so we can go eat."

After he closed the door, I decided I really would think about his idea. It might be a good one.

Love you,

Livvy

December 2, 2011
9:00 AM

Dear Mom,

WHEN YOU woke and saw me crying, you reached for my hand. "What is it, Alex?"

I held your palm against my cheek. "It's nothing. It's silly."

You stared and I knew your gaze wouldn't waver until I answered the question.

"I just read one of your letters. The one where Russ suggested that you give the hatbox and letters to me." My breath caught in my throat. "I wish you had."

"I wish I had, too," you admitted. "Maybe if I'd let you see them years ago, I'd have stopped writing them. You'd have told me I was being foolish and wasting my time trying to share my life with a dead woman. Maybe that would have forced me to let Momma go."

I smiled through my tears. "I would never have called you foolish or asked you to stop writing." I grabbed a tissue from the box on your nightstand and swiped it under my nose. "I wish you'd let me see the letters sooner so I could have asked more questions." The flow of tears renewed. "So we could have talked when we had more time."

You leaned against your pillow. "I was afraid that reading the letters back then would have made you run from me and never come back."

I shook my head.

"Alex, mothers and daughters all go through phases of pulling away from one another. It has to be that way so independent daughters can live their own lives and possessive mothers can learn to deal with it. I feared that if you read my letters then, they would have driven a permanent wedge between us."

We sat in silence for several minutes.

"I wish you had trusted me with your secrets, Mom."

"I'm trusting you with all of them now. If you have questions, ask them. If you have something you want to say, say it."

I thought about all that I wanted to say and all that I wanted to ask and, suddenly, it seemed so very trivial. Time had become the only thing that mattered. Time to hold you and tell you how much I loved you and how grateful I felt to be your daughter.

"Maybe you're right," I said. "Maybe I wasn't ready back then. I am now. Your secrets don't scare me and your thoughts can't put a wedge between us. Because you gave me a lifetime of memories. Memories of a mom who was willing to do anything and sacrifice everything for me. Didn't you always try to teach me to trust the behavior and not the words? You showed me, in every possible way, the kind of woman and mom you are. I don't have to question anything. All I have to do is remember."

You closed your eyes and fell asleep even as your tears continued to fall.

I love you, Mom.

Dear Momma,

HOLY CRAP! Daddy had a date. Or, maybe he'd had a lot of them and finally let me in on it. Anyway, he had a date with…drum roll, please. Delores Folsom. His secretary of over 20 years. The woman who gave me the down and dirty on Nora Jean's office antics.

I suspected that Delores had a crush on Daddy. Homemade cookies might have buttered up the boss. Skirts and heels every day could be professional. But the way her eyes lit up when Daddy walked into the room gave it away like a billboard announcing her feelings to the world.

Delores divorced a few years after she started at the dealership. She raised two teenage boys on her own and never remarried. I liked her. More to the point, Daddy liked her.

He called me a couple of months ago. "Livvy, I took your advice."

"What advice is that, Daddy?"

I heard him swallow. "You know. That I needed to get back into life."

I hesitated, struggling to remember saying that. It hit me. "Daddy, are you dating someone?"

His silence answered my question. He cleared his throat. "Yes. Why don't you and Russ join us for dinner Friday night? Oceanic?"

My jaw dropped. I closed it, but it popped right back open and the words tumbled out. "Who is she? Where did you meet her? How long have you been dating? Are you getting serious?"

"We've been seeing each other for a few weeks. Livvy, it's Delores."

I screeched so loud it echoed in my office. "Delores Folsum? You're dating your secretary?"

"Yes. She's a wonderful woman."

"Daddy, Delores is great. Wait. How serious are you? Are you getting married again?"

"Oh, for goodness sakes, Livvy. I just want you to spend time with her, with us." He took a deep breath. "We haven't talked about marriage."

I swear I heard him smile over the phone. "I like her, Livvy. And I want you to get along because I want to include her in some of our family gatherings." I heard the smile again.

In spite of my feelings for Delores, I experienced an attack of nerves on the way to the restaurant. I wondered what I would do if the Delores I liked morphed into the crazy girlfriend from hell. "Tread lightly, Sweet Cheeks," I told myself. "You've seen it before."

We climbed the wooden steps at Oceanic and walked through the front door where the hostess, standing behind her wooden podium, greeted us.

"Reservation for four under the name Dolan," Russ told her.

She pointed to the inside stairs. "Second floor. The rest of your party is already here."

I swallowed, but it stuck in my throat. Russ held my hand as we took the first few steps. He turned to look at me. "Take a deep breath, babe. You'll be fine."

Daddy waved as soon as we rounded the corner into the dining room. The knots in my stomach turned to butterflies when I saw the look on his face. Delores sat next to him wearing a long, flowing skirt and a turquoise T-shirt with a shawl draped around her shoulders. A banana clip held her permed gray hair back from her face. Classic silver jewelry accented her outfit.

I visualized split-screen portraits comparing the Bleached Bimbo to Delores. Delores won.

She gave us a small nervous wave. Then she glanced at Daddy with an adoration I recognized. I see it when Russ looks at me, and Alex groans when she sees that look on my face.

I squeezed my husband's hand and whispered, "You're right. It'll be okay." Even my butterflies flitted away in the face of their joy.

Dear Momma,

SONNY'S DRINKING hit a new level after he lost his job at Floyd's. He'd manage to get hired somewhere for a few months, but eventually everyone fired him. Or he deemed them unworthy of his talent and quit. He sulked around his trailer until the craving for sex or camaraderie compelled him to hit the bars. Usually, even that couldn't drag him out of his booze bubble.

Alex doted on her father, hoping her love could exorcise Sonny's demons. He used that devotion to convince Alex that the primary responsibility of a good daughter involved clean up and cover-up. As much as Russ and I tried to convince her otherwise, Alex fell into line.

She bought his groceries and washed his laundry. And when she couldn't sit down for all the crap on the sofa or walk past the coffee table without knocking empty beer cans off the edge, she cleaned.

Sonny set the guilt-hook in her mouth and pulled it tight. And Alex allowed him to do that. I don't remember taking care of you that way. I remember drunken arguments and slammed doors, but I never had to become your caretaker. But my daughter seemed to need her father like her father needed his liquor. That frightened me.

One Saturday in April, Russ and I spent the entire day raking and weeding. By dinnertime, I didn't have the energy to climb the deck steps. We dropped into the lawn chairs under the big shade tree in the back yard. I slipped out of my tennis shoes, pulled off my filthy socks and propped my feet on Russ's lap. He swatted them away.

"You need a shower. Those things smell like fertilizer." He turned up his nose.

"My feet do not smell like shit. And, just so you know, you'll be in the tub all by yourself tonight." I twitched an eyebrow at him. "Which is too bad for you."

"I'm so tired it won't matter. I'll be surprised if I can lift my arms to scrub my back."

"Poor baby," I whined before I took a long swig of frosty, cold lemonade. The leaves over my head rustled in the breeze. I leaned my head back and watched them. "You know what I think?"

"No telling." Russ gulped his drink like he'd wandered the desert for a week.

"I think we should clean up and throw some steaks on the grill."

Alex opened the kitchen door, stepped out onto the deck and seemed to glide across it. She jumped down the steps and danced across the freshly mowed grass.

"Your timing is perfect, as usual." I shook my finger at her. "The work is done."

She laughed. "If I'd only known you were doing the lawn today, I'd have helped."

"Liar." I offered her a sip of my drink. She shook her head. "Are you eating dinner with us?"

"I can't." Alex tilted her head and grinned. "I have a date."

Russ and I leaned forward at the same time. If Alex had dated anyone during her freshman year at UNCW she hadn't brought him home or introduced him or even mentioned his name. So the giddy girl who stood in front of us looked like a stranger. "Who is he?"

"A guy I met at school," she answered. "Will Crenshaw."

"Never heard of him," Russ said. "Who are his people?"

Alex giggled. "Did you really just ask me that, Russ?" She laughed again, harder this time. "I have no idea who his people are." She waved her fingers in the air in quotes. "He's from Burgaw and we met in biology. We've gone to the beach together a couple of times. He called me this morning and asked me out. Dinner at Wrightsville Beach."

"Burgaw, huh? Country boy?"

Alex leaned over and felt Russ's forehead. "I think you've been in the sun too long. You're starting to sound like Granddaddy."

"Not funny. How would you like to be grounded for the night?"

Her eyes widened. "Now, that's not funny."

I interrupted, "He's picking you up and we'll meet him?"

"Yes, at six thirty." She dug at the grass with her flip-flop. "Daddy called me and wanted me to drive him to Carolina Beach tonight. I told him about my date, but he still sounded mad." Alex looked at me, and her eyes pleading us to tell her she had done the right thing. "I feel bad, but I really want to go out with Will."

"Alex, don't think twice about it. You do so much for Sonny all the time." I stood up and kissed her cheek. "Tonight is your night, babe. Enjoy it."

"Thanks, Mom." She took the deck steps two at a time and dashed back into the house.

Russ had just put the steaks on when Alex led Will Crenshaw to the deck. After ten minutes of Russ grilling him, I'm sure the boy felt like another slab of beef on the barbeque. But he held up well, answered every question to Russ's satisfaction and earned the right to date Alex.

When the two of them disappeared around the corner of the house, I heard Alex say, "I'm so sorry. Sometimes they act like such..." She paused.

Will filled in, "Parents?"

Russ and I grinned. After we inhaled our T-bones, we lay back on our padded lounge chairs and stared up at the full moon. I woke to the sound of our doorbell ringing repeatedly. It sounded faint, like an alarm clock jangling in another room. I opened my eyes and realized we had fallen asleep on the deck.

Russ pushed up off his chair and mumbled, "I'll get it."

I rubbed my eyes. "What time is it?"

"I don't know."

I followed Russ inside. The kitchen clock said eleven thirty. *Maybe Alex forgot her key*, I thought.

Russ opened the front door. Brody Waters stood on the porch, running his Wilmington Police Department hat in circles through his fingers. I'd known Brody since high school and he gave me a look that said he wanted to be anywhere but on my porch giving me bad news.

"What's going on?" Russ asked.

My heart stood still. "Alex? Is my baby all right?"

Russ slipped his arm around my waist and held me tight against his side.

Brody shook his head. "It's not Alex. It's Sonny. Something bad's happened, Livvy. Can I come in?"

We nodded and moved aside. I pointed to an armchair. Russ and I took the sofa.

Brody sat and continued to finger his hat. "There's been an accident. We think Sonny's dead."

I heard a gasp. It came from me.

Russ asked, "What do you mean you think? What happened?"

"We got the call a couple of hours ago from someone who'd been following Sonny's old truck down Carolina Beach Road. They said the truck had been slowing down, speeding up, swerving all over the road."

"But Sonny lost his license," I argued. "He can't drive."

"That hadn't stopped him yet, Livvy. I pulled him over myself a couple times." He looked down at his hat like he dreaded what he had to say next. "They said cars honked and flashed their lights, had to pull over to the side of the road to get out of the way." He swallowed and looked up at me. "Livvy, at least a dozen people watched Sonny's truck start over Snow's Cut Bridge, heading toward Carolina Beach. He had to be doing seventy or eighty when he clipped the front bumper against the cement side and the truck flipped. It rolled two or three times before it slammed off the bridge into the water."

"No! No! You're wrong! That's not my daddy!"

Alex stood at the front door. Her skin looked chalky white in spite of the fact that she'd left earlier that night with sunburned cheeks. She breathed in short, shallow puffs. Will stood behind her. He put a hand to her shoulder. She jerked away and marched into the living room.

"Daddy probably loaned his truck to somebody." She shook a finger at Brody. "You'll see. You're wrong." She turned toward the phone. "I'll call him. He's home."

Brody shook his head.

I stood up and pulled her close to me. "Alex, let's listen to what Brody has to say and then we can check things out."

"I'm sorry, Alex. We have boats in the water now, but we can't do much till daylight. We'll know more then." Brody looked at Alex like his heart might break with hers. "Honey, we sent a car to his house right away to check on him. Nobody's home."

"He's sleeping. He didn't hear you. I've got a key. I'll go over there and wake him up and find out who has his truck."

"The front door was unlocked. Sonny's not there."

Alex let out a wail like I've never heard. Russ and I pulled her down onto the couch between us and circled our arms around her. Brody clung to his hat. Will stood at the front door staring at Alex like he wished he had taken her anywhere but home.

I need you, Momma. We all do.

Livvy

P.S. The next day they pulled Sonny's truck and his body from Snow's Cut. We don't know much other than that. We don't know why Sonny got behind the wheel. We don't know where he wanted to go or who he planned to see. We don't know.

As a teenager, Sonny used to say childish things that he thought sounded macho. "When it's my time, I want to go out in a blaze of glory." Sonny died drunk, alone and pitiful. He left our daughter with enough pain and guilt that she could have drowned in it right along with him. That's how he treated the one person who loved him, always and everywhere, no matter what. I find no glory in that.

December 2, 2011
11:00 AM

Dear Mom,

I CAN'T see the page for my tears. Details of that night came back like it happened yesterday. And the guilt sucker punched me all over again.

When I told him I had a date, Dad said, "You can go out with this kid any time. But you don't always get the chance to do your old man a favor."

I didn't even bother to ask him where he wanted to go. Who he wanted to see. I promised I would take him another night, but it turned out he was right. I never got the chance to do that. I never saw him again.

For months after Dad died, I felt like a self-absorbed monster. Over and over, I'd hear him say, "You don't always get the chance to do your old man a favor." I'd play out different scenarios in my head where I'd changed my mind and driven him to Carolina Beach. Once in a while, in those make believe do-overs, Dad decided to stay home that night. But in every scene I rewrote, my father stayed alive. He didn't die that night. And it wasn't my fault.

When I read your letter, I heard his voice and felt the same regrets. God, why didn't I just do what he asked? How do I ever learn to live with that?

Dear Momma,

OTHER THAN classes and her part-time job, Alex seldom left her room. She sat at the dinner table with Russ and me, but only played with the food on her plate. Will invited her out on dates. She said, "No." I couldn't remember the last time I heard her laugh.

We talked her into seeing a counselor for a little while, but saw little improvement. We even went to a few sessions with her.

When I was a child, no one I knew saw a therapist. And a psychiatrist? Please. Loony bin level insanity only. You had problems in life—deal with it. Emotional issues—suck it up and press on. Life came with a side order of problems. Nobody walked away unscathed.

Times have changed. We voice our darkest secrets in AA meetings. We share our emotional pain. Share. Slang for spill your guts. Even people at work admit going to pastors, counselors, or support groups. Alcoholics Anonymous, Narcotics Anonymous, Overeaters Anonymous and even self-help for sex addicts. Yes, you can sit in a group of complete strangers and chronicle your lusty libido. Progress.

My husband never bought into the life-as-public-fodder movement. In AA he talked about not drinking. End of story. No problems, no feelings. "Don't take a drink, one day at a time."

But Russ agreed to go to counseling, for Alex's sake. We met once a week for about a month. He'd lean back in his chair, absorb every word and say very little. After the last session, when we got home, he said, "I think we need to talk. Let's sit down for a minute."

Alex and I looked at each other and back at Russ. I asked, "Is everything okay?"

He nodded. "I want to tell Alex a story that may help her." He reached out and let his fingertips brush my cheek. "It's time you heard this, too."

My stomach rolled. Stable, steady Russ had never acted like this. It scared me, more than a little. I tossed my purse onto the chair in the living room and plopped down on the couch. Alex joined me. Russ sat in the recliner, but perched on the edge instead of his usual sprawl.

He took a deep breath and stared up at the ceiling. "This won't be easy, so let me tell my story, start to finish, or I may not be able to do it."

Alex and I glanced at each other and back at Russ. I nodded.

"You both know about the accident when Jenny died. You know she was pregnant and on her way to a doctor's appointment. You know that I was in my office, the dutiful, hard-working husband and father-to-be when it happened."

He closed his eyes for a second and swallowed so hard I saw his Adam's apple bob up and down from across the room.

"Most of that is true, but part of it is a lie I've lived with all these years. I didn't want to face the truth. At least, not aloud. I saw it in my nightmares every day for years. Even now, once in a while. But I've been a coward and never told anyone what really happened."

Russ ran his fingers over the stubble on his chin. "The night before the crash, Jenny and I had an argument. She was four months pregnant and she wanted me home. She said I spent too much time at the garage. She said that we could afford for me to be away from it more often." He shrugged. "I could handle that. I even agreed with her. But then she said that even when I was at home she felt alone, like she'd been going through the pregnancy without a husband. Because when I wasn't at work I spent most of my time drinking."

He stared off in the distance at something only he could see. When his eyes filled with tears, I suspected he saw his wife and the child he never met.

"It pissed me off. I thought Russ Montgomery was a damn good husband. I worked hard, didn't screw around." He snorted. "I even gave myself points for never hitting her. What was so wrong with a man enjoying a few beers? I actually asked her that question. Jenny looked at me with so much hurt in her eyes. I still see it. She reminded me that I was going to be a father and our child needed me. She needed me. Sober."

Alex drew up closer to me and leaned against my side. I put my arm around her shoulder.

Russ continued, "I'd already had a couple of beers when the argument started so I sure as hell wasn't thinking very clearly. I thought Jenny was calling me a failure. I thought she was saying she wasn't happy and didn't love me anymore. I know now that she really said she loved me enough to want better for me." He rubbed his forehead, hard, willing to wear a hole in his skull if it meant he could erase the memories. "But I didn't hear that then."

"We argued. I drank another beer and we argued some more. I told her I'd been plenty involved, that I'd gone with her to every doctor's appointment, painted the baby's room, put the damn crib together. She said she needed more. She tried to tell me. I didn't want to hear it. I walked out the door. Jenny said, "You can't run away from our problems." I slammed the door, got in my truck and headed for the nearest bar. I sat in a corner booth, drank myself into oblivion and decided that what I needed to do was to teach her a lesson. So, I drove to the garage and passed out on the couch. I have no idea what time any of the guys came into work that morning because I didn't come-to until a few minutes before the police showed up. I remember staring at the clock on my desk until it came into focus and thinking, *Shit, I was supposed to take Jenny to the doctor and she'll be seriously pissed now.*

He leaned back in the recliner. "The police told me about the accident. I'm sure they smelled the booze on me, but they never said a word. They drove me home and I'll never know if they did that because they thought I was in shock or drunk. The guys at the garage assumed I'd gotten to work early. I never told them any different."

My eyes stung as the tears washed away all evidence that I'd worn make-up that day. Alex pulled closer to me and shuddered with silent sobs.

"I was supposed to take Jenny to her appointment that morning. If I'd been there she'd still be alive. And so would my son." He held his palms over his tear-filled eyes. "I never told anyone that the baby was a boy. I found that out after they died. When my wife and son needed me the most, I was passed out, drunk."

Russ took a deep breath. Several.

"For a long time, I figured I might as well have killed them myself. The guilt sat on my shoulder and called me a son of a bitch day and night. So, I jumped into a bottle of Cutty Sark and hoped I'd drown." He shook his head. "No such luck. At some point I decided that staying drunk dishonored their memories more than I had already destroyed their lives. I went to AA as some sort of atonement to the dead. I ended up sober, helping other people recover. Jenny's death was the catalyst that made that happen."

Russ looked at Alex and me for the first time since he had started speaking. He fought the sobs that I heard catch in his throat.

"Alex, please listen to me. I was the drunk that caused the pain and the problems in my past. I was one who set the disaster in motion." He bit the inside of his cheek. "You did nothing wrong. You loved Sonny more than some fathers get in a lifetime. You were there for him. You never, not once, turned your back on him. He had a disease called alcoholism. Very few people survive that disease, much less recover from it. The illness was his, Alex, not yours. I know you've got to grieve, but this guilt isn't yours to carry. Let it go before it drags you down with it."

I heard Alex's whimpers. She stood up. Russ rose to meet her. He reached out and she ran to his arms. He held her and stroked her hair while she leaned against his chest. She clutched at him and I wondered if she offered consolation to him or needed absolution from him. Her shoulders shook as her whimpers turned to sobs. His story had connected with her guilt in a way no therapist could ever reach her.

"The choice is yours. You can stay so hung up in the past that it screws up your future or you can live every single day making the best decisions you know how to make. Your life is what you make it. The people around you make impressions in it, but the big picture is yours to create." Russ kissed her forehead. "You gave up a lot of your life to your Dad's alcoholism. Don't let that God-damned disease take any more from you, Alex."

My heart swelled with so much love for Russ that I clasped my hands to my chest. He carried his pain in secret all those years and opened up about it only to save Alex, not to ease anything for himself. Everything he said that night planted healing seeds that took root. She has good days and bad days, but I know that she will come through it stronger. Something shifted that night. Alex began to lean less on me and more on Russ, like they shared a pain I couldn't understand. At first that hurt me, but the hurt's been replaced with gratitude for the man I married and the strength he gives my daughter.

December 2, 2011
2:00 PM

Dear Mom,

DAD'S DEATH hit me hard. For months, the memories taunted me, daring me to change the past. I felt lost, guilty, angry, used and manipulated. Yes. I said used and manipulated. I think I knew, even then, that Dad needed me more than I did him. He used me to take care of him and even to hurt you, Mom. I guess I suspected it then, but I know it now. No matter what, I loved him and I dreamed that one day I'd wake up to find that Sonny Boyd had become the father I'd always wanted.

You know, maybe that's why I hurt so bad that I didn't want to get out of bed. I hadn't actually lost the world's greatest dad. I'd lost the dream of one. When he died, my hope for a real relationship with my father swept over the bridge and into Snow's Cut with him.

I'd lay in bed at night and imagine what he went through in his final moments. I prayed that he'd been knocked unconscious the first time his truck flipped. Otherwise, it meant he might have been aware of going off the bridge, plunging into the darkness, water seeping in around him through every gap. Did he struggle to get out of the truck? Did he fight for breath? Did he think help was coming? Every night I'd get to that same point in my circular thoughts, and I'd beg God to have knocked him out in the first moments.

Once in a great while, I'd think, "Or did he just pass out and that's why his bumper clipped the bridge in the first place?"

I couldn't get past any of it. Not Dad's alcoholism. Not my part in his death.

And then, when Russ told me what he had done and lived through, it felt like he reached down into the mire of my pain and pulled me free of it. I can see us both, dripping with anguish and shame that we couldn't wash away, no matter how hard we scrubbed.

That day, Russ threw me a lifeline and I clung to it. The nightmares still came. I still wondered if I could have changed things, though I know that it would probably only have delayed the inevitable. To this day, I tell myself that Dad didn't die from a car accident. He died of alcoholism. Some days I believe it.

Mom, you and Russ have been there for me through everything. Have I done that for you? I know I have since you got sick, but sometimes I think that's more for me than for you. I need every minute with you that I can get.

I want more time,

Dear Momma,

IN SPITE of Gina's brash Yankee-ness, her friendship fits me, tailor-made. We have much more in common than our differences suggest. Anyway, my best friend, the ultimate, independent single girl, got hitched. Newly promoted detective, Brody Waters had given her the full-on sparkling diamond and bended knee proposal to which she shrieked, "Oh, yes!" They met at Sonny's funeral and I don't think they took their eyes off one another since that day.

The Catholic wedding of Jersey girl and redneck boy could have been a disaster and I think local bets had ten-to-one odds on that. But not one misstep marred Gina's dream wedding. After they exchanged vows, Brody leaned down and gave Gina a tender, soft smooch on the lips. Since she had asked me to be her matron of honor, I stood near the altar, close enough to see the come-hither smile she responded with as he pulled away. He grinned, threw his arms around her, lifted her off her feet and planted a huge, wet, noisy kiss on his new bride. Family and friends burst into spontaneous applause, raucous enough that the brick, domed ceiling of the church should have come tumbling down.

Brody and Gina's reception at the Blockade Runner Resort at Wrightsville Beach offered the perfect backdrop for the two extended families to meet. In spite of their differences —— think *The Godfather* meets *The Real McCoys*—strong bonds formed that day.

Wine flowed from carafes on each table and beer from the keg on the outdoor dance floor. Non-drinkers downed sweet tea. And, since no self-respecting southern woman would ever reveal exactly how much sugar she used to flavor her tea, the uninitiated Yankees never knew what hit them.

But their eyes lit up like flickering matches all over the room at the first sip of that syrupy southern delight.

The band in the corner played beach music and by the end of the evening, the southerners had taught almost every Yankee in the room to shag. I led Gina's father to the dance floor while Russ did the same with her mother. Gina and Brody glided past us, focused only on each other.

Complete strangers talked, laughed, slapped backs and danced. They traded stories, jokes and phone numbers. By the end of the evening, the North and South had embraced and made this the Wilmington wedding reception of the year.

All in all, a party you would have loved, Momma,

Livvy

P.S. At some point during the festivities, the bachelors lined up to catch the garter and bachelorettes lunged for the bouquet. Will snagged the former and Alex the latter. Good thing we like the boy, huh?

Dear Momma,

THE CRENSHAWS invited us to their family farm in Burgaw for a Fourth of July cookout. I wondered if an announcement loomed over the festivities since Will and Alex had been dating for two years, and the clans had yet to meet.

The farm lay well outside the city limits. We passed a gas station, a mom-and-pop grocery store and a couple of miles of absolutely nothing before Alex said, "Turn right," into what looked to be a gigantic cornfield. Turned out to be a narrow dirt road that snaked between two cornfields for almost a mile before it stopped at an oasis, tucked out of sight from the highway. We pulled up into the grass and parked near several other cars.

A large two-story frame farmhouse sat in the middle of the clearing. The covered porch formed an L-shape across the front and down one side. Nestled among a huge variety of potted plants, several wicker chairs beckoned us to enjoy the afternoon breeze. The Crenshaws burst through the screen door before we had the chance to announce our arrival. Will's parents threw their arms around Alex and welcomed all of us with introductions and hugs.

To see Jeffrey Crenshaw's face, I had to tilt my head so far back I thought my skull might end up touching somewhere between my shoulder blades. Will's father had to be six-four and 220 pounds. His calloused hands and dancing eyes seemed mismatched until his smile blended every feature. He looked like Magnum P.I. in John Deere green.

Jenci Crenshaw stood next to him. Her petite stature and tiny frame only enhanced her husband's masculinity. I suddenly felt like an Amazon.

Her size four hiney next to my size ten emphasized the feeling dramatically.

"Come on in," Jeffrey said. "Let's get y'all something to drink."

Delores and I carried enough potato salad and blueberry cobbler into the kitchen to feed a hungry battalion, but when we saw the herd through the sliding glass doors Delores, gave me an uh-oh look that I felt certain matched my own.

Will opened the glass doors from the screened porch and rushed toward Alex. He picked her up and squeezed until I thought she might pop. When he noticed us behind her, he set her down as gently as a china cup to its saucer and asked, "Did you meet everyone?" He draped an arm over his mother's shoulder. "Mom, this is Alex's mom and dad." I felt Russ's joy swell into a grin at being referred to as Alex's dad.

Jenci patted her son's back. "We've met. Now, introduce these folks to the rest of the family." She swatted him away.

I watched Will walk toward a covered carport in the backyard with the other men. *My heavens, Will's as tall as his daddy*, I thought. How had I not noticed that? Maybe I just thought of him as Alex's boyfriend, a kid. But that day, I saw him, for the first time, as a very grown man. And from the look I saw on my daughter's face, I knew that she saw him the same way.

Delores and I sat down in a couple of empty wicker rockers on the screened porch. Jenci dropped into a rocker across from us. She followed my gaze toward Alex. "I'd say our young'uns might just be in love."

"I'd have to agree."

We watched Will slip away from the guys to be with Alex. That tough, country-boy linebacker turned into a teddy bear with just one glance at my daughter. Alex stared up into his face, stood on her tiptoes and kissed his cheek. Will blushed.

"I've never seen my boy this way," Jenci said.

"Alex, too. She's either with Will or talking about him—all the time."

Fireflies lit up the yard and hovered over the cornfields as the sun set. Their tiny flashes of light gleamed like diamonds sparkling in the dusk. In the growing dark, the younger Crenshaws set off a fireworks display that lit the sky in a blaze of color.

When the first one exploded, Alex flinched. Will's arm tightened around her. Alex eased into his side. Literally and figuratively, she leaned more on Will now than on Russ or me. My head knew that to be a good thing. My heart still needed to catch up.

I can't help wondering if I had just caught a glimpse of my baby girl's future. I like Will, but I don't feel anywhere near ready to let her go.

I love you, Momma. I miss you always.

Livvy

Dear Momma,

ALEX GRADUATED from the University of North Carolina at Wilmington. She did it on the five-year plan, but she did it. Majored in nursing, following in your footsteps.

I couldn't help but contrast the differences between Alex at high school and college graduations. Last time, she spent the day surrounded by giggling, primping girlfriends. This time, she ate breakfast with Russ and me and lingered over a cup of coffee as if she had all day. Last time, my little girl picked up her diploma wearing way too much makeup and multicolor nail polish. This time, my adult daughter looked every bit the sophisticated young woman.

She left the house wearing her black graduation gown over a sundress and sandals. Her thick brown hair hung free and framed her face. I watched from the kitchen as she pulled out of the driveway, parental pride and wistful longing battling for emotional control. I love the woman she has become, but I miss my baby.

That afternoon, Russ and I waited in front of Trask Coliseum on the UNCW campus. Russ looked handsome in his shirt and tie, khakis and deck shoes. He carried a bouquet of roses to give to Alex after the ceremony. I wore a sleeveless black dress, sandals and silver jewelry. I carried a little handbag and a big camera.

I laughed when I saw Delores and Daddy in the distance, an older version of Russ and me. They, too, carried flowers and photography equipment and had even thought to bring binoculars.

We hauled everything up the stairs to the seating area that looked down on the floor of the arena, where hundreds of chairs were lined up facing a makeshift stage, complete with podium and microphones. Though the coliseum holds several thousand, it looked nowhere near full, but even so, the crowd's excited chatter rose to the ceiling, bounced back and echoed around us. Daddy couldn't hear squat on a good day and he had to lean in close when one of us spoke. He finally sat back and played with his camera to get the focus right for his Lady Bug's big day.

After a few minutes, a dozen people walked single file to the stage and stood in front of chairs arranged in a semi-circle behind the lectern. They wore the same black robes as Alex, but had different colored sashes hanging from their necks. A short, heavyset woman walked to the microphone, welcomed family and friends and announced the arrival of the Class of '92. A small band behind the stage played *Pomp and Circumstance* as an army of graduates swarmed through the back doors and down the aisles.

I strained to find Alex in the crowd but had no luck until the entire nursing section stood and cheered while their department head stepped forward to hand out diplomas. Tears filled my eyes when I realized the little girl hadn't outgrown us completely. On the top of her cap, Alex had glued cutout letters that read "Thanks Mom & Russ!" Russ grabbed my hand and squeezed.

The announcer called out, "Alexandra Madison Abbott."

I jumped from my seat, shouting, "Way to go, Alex!" But nothing drowned out the clicking of the camera shutters as Daddy and Russ shot dozens of pictures. I paused to catch a breath and heard a commotion in the distance. The entire mob of Crenshaws stood across the auditorium, giving Alex a standing ovation.

Alex accepted her diploma, shook hands with the UNCW chancellor, walked across the stage and back to her chair, where she turned toward us and yelled, "We did it!"

Within moments, the foot stomping commenced once more as the accounting department handed out their awards and diplomas and Will Crenshaw took center stage. The message on his cap read, "Thanks for your $upport!" The crowd roared.

After applauding the last student, we waited outside in the shade of an old oak tree for Alex to find us. She zeroed in on us, hauling Will and his family behind her. Alex teared up when Russ and Daddy handed over their floral offerings. My eyes had overflowed from the time she walked in the door until I held her in my arms to congratulate her. When Jenci looked up at her oldest boy, the waterworks started there, too.

Russ and Jeffrey looked at each other, nodding silent understanding that the emotion they had to tolerate on a daily basis could curl a bald man's hair. Jeffrey sniffled and, as if on cue, he and Russ wiped away imaginary tears. Alex swatted both of them. Jenci and I linked arms and walked toward the parking lot.

Love you, Momma

Livvy

P.S. The process of letting go of my daughter gets a little easier every day, though I doubt I'll ever complete that transformation. Student, graduate, nurse. Alex's part time job at Cape Fear Memorial Hospital gave her the foot-in-the-door she needed. Full time in intensive care. You'd be proud.

December 2, 2011
4:00 PM

Dear Mom,

YOUR LETTERS capture my own memories from the past, but you do it from such a different perspective.

I see that morning in my mind, breakfast with you and Russ. The coffee mug feels warm in my hands and the aroma makes my mouth water even now.

That day, I never thought about my high school graduation. Your description made me cringe. The nail polish. Yikes! You made me remember.

You said I majored in nursing to follow in Grandma CiCi's footsteps. I don't think I did that consciously. You used to talk about her being a nurse at Babies Hospital, but I don't actually recall that. Makes me wonder how big a part genetics plays in likes and dislikes, interests and professions, vocations and hobbies. Hmmm? Am I like her? Do I want to be?

Since I didn't get to see Granddaddy until after the ceremony I never knew he'd been so excited. I can still see that great big camera strapped around his neck with him muttering to himself while he fiddled with the setting.

And finally, I was crazy about Will in college and thought it only natural to spend so much time with his family. I read nothing more into it. You saw not only the present, but also the potential place he and his family might have in my future.

I'm grateful that you saved all the special memories in your letters. Since, I'm writing to you now, does that mean I'm following in your footsteps? I hope so.

Alex

Dear Momma,

A FEW months ago, Delores called me at work, so frantic I could barely understand her. "Your daddy fell in the parking lot. He hit his head on a trunk bumper. It knocked him out cold and the ambulance took him to the hospital."

"Is he okay? What hospital?" I couldn't hear my words over the blood pounding in my ears.

"Cape Fear Hospital. I'm here, but he's with the doctor and they won't let me see him. Hurry, Livvy. We need you." She sniffled.

I grabbed my purse and raced down the steps from my office to the working floor below it. Gina grabbed my arm. "What happened?"

"It's Daddy. I have to go." Tears blurred my vision. "He fell. He's at Cape Fear Hospital."

The entire day shift surrounded me. One of the guys shoved Gina and I toward the door. "Go with her. I'll tell management."

I don't know what I would have done without Gina that day. She got us to the hospital in record time and while I bulldozed my way in to see Daddy, she hit the pay phone and called Russ. Then she followed the trail I had blazed through the emergency room's swinging doors.

She found our curtained cubicle and threw back the sheer fabric that corralled off the last of our family privacy. Delores, Alex and I clustered around one side of the bed. When Gina saw Daddy sitting up and heard him lecturing us about panic and overreacting, she burst into tears.

"Oh, for God sakes, Gina," Daddy said. "Get in here and close that damn curtain. He shook his head. "You're supposed to be the hard-nosed Jersey kid that keeps the rest of 'em in line."

She looked from me to Daddy, and back to me before she said, "You scared us, Luther." She swiped at a tear, her face reddening in embarrassment. "You shouldn't do that," she snapped.

The hospital staff ran Daddy through every possible test before stating the obvious. "He has a slight concussion from his head/bumper collision. We don't see a problem that could have caused the fall in the first place. If you'll monitor him closely, we'll send him home."

"Like he's coated with Krazy Glue," I replied.

Daddy groaned.

Delores led the parade on the way home. Gina followed with me, wringing my hands, in the passenger seat. Alex held the number three position, and Russ looked like the caboose.

Several months earlier, Russ and I had joined the little Methodist church on South College Road. When we pulled into the driveway, we saw a car we didn't recognize. A couple of women from the congregation opened the doors and stepped out laden with food, home cooked and still warm. Enough to feed the lot of us and then some.

Delores settled Daddy into the bedroom. Gina and I helped the church ladies arrange food on the counter and tuck some away in the refrigerator. My stomach rumbled and my mouth watered.

The woman at the fridge said, "There's an egg casserole and a pan of cinnamon rolls in here for breakfast." She slapped a piece of paper down on the counter top. "This is my phone number so you can let me know if y'all need anything else."

After they drove away, Gina glanced at the mountains of food and said, "Damn, girl. I want to go to your church. I'll call Brody and tell him I won't be home for dinner."

The love of a great friend and the blessing of my church family got all of us through the day.

Livvy

May 9, 1993
Mother's Day

Dear Momma,

WHAT WOULD you think of the changes in me? Would you like the woman I've become? Would we get along or still bicker? Back then, I couldn't envision you being my age, ever. Through my distorted lenses, I saw you as a sexy thirty-something party girl. Always. Born that way. A woman who snatched life by the throat and dangled men on a string at the same time, without ever breaking a sweat. How could you possibly have understood my teenage angst?

I didn't recognize you as an adult until I became one myself. Unfortunately, that psychological pivot came several years after you died. Instead of seeing the partier clinging to her escaping youth like an outgrown pacifier, I saw you as an independent woman who demanded what she wanted and needed, no matter what anyone else thought. I saw a more balanced version of you with flaws and strengths.

Did you have a similar turning point about me? I suspect you died too young to get there. And I know that most of my maturity came long after that.

I've watched Alex grow from a child to an adolescent and the adolescent to a woman and all along the way I've seen hints of what was to come. Did you see bits and pieces of me as a child that predicted who I would be?

I want to believe that you're beaming at my sobriety and Christianity, at my marriage and my life. I want to believe that you're proud to be my momma.

Livvy

December 2, 2011
8:00 PM

Dear Mom,

THE NURSES increased your meds again. You sleep more and more, so I read your letters and write my own back to you.

You woke a little while ago and wanted to talk.

"Have you finished the letters?"

"Not even close, Mom. I read a couple and then write one to you."

"Will you read me one of yours?" You smiled in anticipation.

"How about I read the letter I just finished reading and then I'll tell you what occurred to me as I read?"

You nodded. I read your last letter aloud.

"How can a grown woman still be looking for her mother's approval? I sound a little needy, don't I?" You rubbed your eyes as you slowly shook your head.

I straightened your sheet and blanket, tucking it around you. "No, you don't sound that way at all. Or, if you do, then I do, too. Because I still want your approval."

You smiled and took my hand. "You've always had that."

"Not always." I chuckled. "I've been in and out of some pretty obnoxious behavior, but you always showed me when I earned your respect back." I kissed your cheek.

Your gaze held mine with a longing I had never seen before. "Did I earn yours?"

I sat down and pulled my chair closer to your bed. "Yes. Completely." I hesitated.

"Alex, if there was ever a time to spill your guts and be honest, this is it."

"Mom, when I was a kid you and Dad fought and drank all the time. And then when Dad left, nothing changed for either of you for the longest time. When you got sober, I was too young to realize what that took or to be proud of you for it. I was just happy to have my mom back. But sometimes I wondered if my enjoying one sober parent contributed to the other's illness. I loved you and hated you in rotating shifts. Like a war going on in my head. And then I started growing up. Or maybe I just spent a little time at the pointy end of Dad's blame stick."

You took my hand and held it between both of yours.

"Dad would get fired and blame me because I didn't get to his house and drive him to work on time. If he had no food in the fridge it was because I didn't go to the grocery store. Dirty trailer — I didn't clean it. I wondered if that's how he treated you, too. Blamed you for his failures. That's when I started to think my anger might have been misplaced. That's when I really started to be proud of your sobriety and your career and even for giving me Russ." I pulled my hand away to wipe a tear from your cheek. "And reading about your experiences and struggles has only strengthened that. So, to answer your question, yes, Mom, I approve of you and everything you've ever done, the good and the bad, the drunk and the sober. All of it made you into the mom I cherish."

I leaned over and laid my head on your lap. You ran your fingers through my hair like you used to do when I was a little girl.

"I love you past the sky, Mom."

Dear Momma,

AFTER GRADUATION, Alex got her own apartment. A real job and a regular paycheck did wonders for her independence. She still paid us occasional visits to eat a home-cooked meal or to borrow something. Translation—not very often. And when Alex came by, she always brought Will. So, when Will called and asked if he could stop at the house for a talk, my finely tuned momma radar hummed. I paced the kitchen while Russ sat at the table and stared into his coffee mug. We didn't speak, but every glance said, "This is it."

I dashed toward the ringing doorbell. My heartbeat thumped so loud I figured Will could see my ears throb. Russ stepped up behind me and laid a settling hand on my shoulder.

I reached up and squeezed Russ's hand with gratitude. I needed him to take the lead since I seriously doubted my mouth or tongue could have formed an entire sentence at that point.

Russ dropped his arm to my waist and pulled me away from the door toward the kitchen. "Coffee's on and I think there's still a few biscuits left from breakfast, if you're hungry."

Will swallowed hard. "I don't think I could eat anything, but I'd appreciate a glass of water."

Silence echoed in the kitchen while Russ poured two cups of coffee and a tall glass of ice water. Will and I stood behind our chairs at the table and watched him. "Have a seat," Russ said.

Our chairs scraped across the wood floor at the same time and we both jumped. All three of us looked like our every nerve had been set on high alert. I chuckled. Russ looked at me and laughed. Will swallowed again and dropped into his chair.

I sat down across from him, and the frightened little boy I saw in the strapping young man's body filled me with pity. "The biscuits are homemade. Sure you don't want one?"

Will stared down at his hands in his lap. "No, ma'am. Thanks."

Russ set his mug down. "What's on your mind this morning?"

Will wrapped both his hands around his glass, twisting it back and forth. "I've known both of you for a long time now." He smiled. "On a normal day, you feel like family. And I think you know how much Alex means to me." He pushed his glass toward the center of the table and laced his fingers together. Then he looked at me for a moment before he stared at Russ. "Alex means the world to me and I can't imagine my life without her in it. I wanted to talk to you to..." Tremors started in his hands and he gripped them tighter. "I would like to ask Alex to marry me and I came here to get your blessing."

He looked from Russ to me and back again. It seemed Will had decided Russ to be the decision maker in one of the most important times of my daughter's life. At first, the hair stood up on the back of my neck and I fought the urge to say, "Just a minute, young man. That's my daughter. You need my blessing." But then, I saw Will's love for Alex reflected in Russ's eyes and I knew that we had truly become a family and that, since the day we married, Russ had been the father Alex needed. If I didn't let go of a little bit of control right then, I ran the risk of undoing all that it had taken us years to build. I leaned back in my chair and waited.

"If I could have made the choice for Alex, I would have chosen you." Russ looked at me and smiled. He reached beneath the table to take my hand. I grinned back at him and squeezed his fingers. "Welcome to the family, son." Russ glanced away as his eyes filled with tears.

Will let out the breath he'd been holding. "I did it. I did it. I'm getting married." He beamed.

I patted his hand. "Alex does get a vote in this, honey. You still have to ask her." I laughed when he paled. "But I feel good about her answer."

"Do you think so? Really?" He reached into his pocket and pulled out a small, square jewelry box. "I tried to get one she'd love." He popped the lid open to reveal a three-quarter carat diamond solitaire in a white-gold setting. "Do you think she'll like it? Do you like it?"

I reached out to take it, but pulled my hand back, afraid my slightest touch might somehow diminish the promise of love that sparkled in that velvet-lined box. "It's perfect," I whispered.

Will leaned back in his chair and heaved a sigh of relief like he had survived the worst and could get through anything still to come.

Russ rested his arms on the table in front of him, shifting forward until they propped up most of his upper body weight. He spoke so softly I had to strain to hear him. "You've been part of our family for a long time now, Will. And today, you asked us to give you the most precious thing we have." The two men looked at one another and I had a sense of circling alpha males. "Take good care of her." His last sentence sounded more like an order than casual conversation.

Will hadn't missed that subtle distinction. He sat up. "Yes, sir. I would never do anything to hurt her."

We all stood. Will and Russ shook hands until Russ pulled him into a brief embrace.

I hugged Will and said, "Be good to my baby."

We walked him to the door and watched until he pulled out of the driveway. Russ looked at me. "You okay?"

I leaned against his shoulder. "I think so. He's a good man." I smiled. "But he can't hold a candle to you." I tilted my head up and Russ leaned down to kiss me.

Our baby girl is getting married, Momma.

Livvy

Dear Momma,

THE SUN outshone its very best day while the cool breeze reminded everyone that summer had yet to arrive. Flowers, bushes and even the trees bloomed in honor of Alex's wedding.

Daddy offered Alex full run of his home for the day. He said, "I've got more mirrors and space for all that fussing you ladies do before..." His eyes clouded over. "Lady Bug gets married."

So Alex and half a dozen of her closest friends invaded his house for their pre-bridal primping. Hair, makeup and nail people prepared to give us all some extra pizzazz. A complete array of beauty equipment stood ready to transform morning frump to matrimonial chic. I had never seen Daddy's house look more cluttered. Every possible flat surface held food, mirrors, makeup, hot curlers and blow dryers. Female chatter and laughter completed the chaos. Daddy played host to every person there and the busier he got, the wider his grin spread. Not one woman left his house that day feeling lonely, hungry, thirsty, unattractive or unloved. In fact, not one woman left his house that day feeling anything less than glamorous.

The wedding photographer froze time and captured our memories in classic snapshots. The click of his shutter punctuated every comment and chuckle.

Alex walked into the living room just as Delores said, "It's time." She stood in front of me in a fitted, off-the-shoulder white dress. The pearl-beaded bodice clung to her waist. From there the dress flowed and the train pooled at her feet. I had given her your pearl studs, Momma, and they looked perfect. She wore her long brown hair back, leaving wispy tendrils floating around her face. The veil she hadn't yet pulled forward hung down her back and the beads that dotted it glistened in the sun glowing off the water through the picture window.

Those last few seconds of her being my little girl, Alexandra Madison Abbott, slipped through my fingers faster than water. I couldn't make it stop or slow it down. I wanted to turn back the clock and feel my baby curled up in my lap. But in less than an hour, my daughter would stand in front of all her friends and loved ones, say, "I do" and start her own family.

I did the dainty wedding dab when my eyes filled with tears. Alex fanned her hands in front of her face as if that could stop her own. We reached for one another, but barely touched, fearing a makeup smear or mussed dress.

"Alex Abbott, you're the most stunning bride I've ever seen." I had forgotten that we stood in a roomful of other people until I heard Daddy sniffle. I traced her cheek with one finger. "I love you, baby girl. Will is a very lucky man."

"I love you past the sky," she said, repeating her favorite phrase from childhood.

Daddy threw open his double front door. A convoy of dealership vehicles, straight off the showroom floor, lined the driveway, waiting to deliver us to our little Methodist church.

Alex and a couple of her bridesmaids climbed into the white Ford Explorer in the front. Russ drove. The rest of the wedding party piled into the second car. Daddy drove the third for Delores and me. Several of Alex's other friends took the two cars behind us while the hair and makeup crew escaped in their own vehicles after a very long day.

The church parking lot had already begun to fill up. Thank goodness, for alleyways and backdoors allowed us to sneak in unseen.

Will and his tuxedoed entourage stood at the front of the church. The groomsmen looked calm and relaxed. Will, on the other hand, reached into his pocket, pulled out his handkerchief and swiped it across his forehead. But then, he had more at stake that day than the rest of them.

An usher offered me his arm and led me to my designated seat on the first pew. Daddy and Delores sat next to me.

Alex's bridesmaids filed down the aisle. Each wore a coral silk dress and carried white bouquets. The flower girl pranced in ahead of Alex, dropping fistfuls of coral and white rose petals along the floor. Before she reached the front of the church, she waved half a dozen times, like royalty to an adoring crowd.

A change in music signaled the bride's arrival. Alex and Russ paused in the back doors. He whispered in her ear. She looked up at him and smiled. Russ walked up the aisle, but it looked to me like Alex floated the entire way. She stopped at my pew and surprised me with a rose from the center of her bouquet. This time my dainty wedding dab didn't help at all.

As Alex stepped closer, Will's clenched muscles relaxed. By the time she reached him, he looked like an old pro. No sweat. She smiled up at him and I swear his knees buckled. Mid-ceremony he looked like he would just as soon have scooped her into his arms, waved good-bye, and sped out of town on their honeymoon.

Instead, he turned to her when the time came to share their vows and took both her hands in his. "Alexandra Madison Abbott, you are the most beautiful woman I've ever known. Sometimes, when I'm near you I forget to breathe because I'm so busy memorizing everything about you. The way your eyelids crinkle when you laugh, the way you blush all the way up to your forehead when I embarrass you, the way you talk so fast when you're excited, the way your eyes flash when you're angry, the way you smell. I love your ambition, the way you care about your family, the way you love me." He chuckled. "I even love it when you're so darned stubborn, there's no changing your mind. I want to wake up every single day knowing that you are the most important thing in my life."

Alex sniffled. She pulled out a piece of paper she had wrapped around the stem of her bouquet before she gave the flowers to her maid of honor. When she opened it up, she couldn't read the words through her tears, so she wadded it into a ball and handed it to her friend as well. She looked up at Will.

"I think I fell in love with you on our first date. You were so nervous and sweet. We laughed and talked and then you took me home where I got the worst news I've ever gotten. And you stayed. Through the terrific and the terrible. You make me laugh and you give me strength. You make me think there's nothing I can't do. And it sure doesn't hurt that you're the most handsome man I've ever met. I will always love you, William Jeffrey Crenshaw."

Smiles intended only for one another beamed like rays of sunshine, warming everyone in the sanctuary. Even through misty eyes and sniffles, every person in the room felt uncontrollable grins spreading across their faces.

I treasured every moment of the wedding and the reception. Too soon, Will threw the garter. Alex tossed her bouquet. They toasted one another and cut cake. Alex danced with Russ, and Will with his mother. Tick-tock, tick-tock rang in my ears until it echoed in my heart.

Before I knew it, the bridesmaids had passed out tiny bottles of bubbles and people lined up from the door of the club to the limousine waiting in the parking lot. Will and Alex ran the gauntlet, covering their heads as blown bubbles rained down around them. The limo pulled away and the tin cans attached to the bumper clattered even when I couldn't see the car anymore. Russ held my hand the whole time and squeezed when he knew I needed it.

Our little girl is a married woman now, Momma. Her name is Alex Crenshaw and I'm learning to let go all over again.

December 2, 2011
Midnight

Dear Mom,

RUSS AND I sat on either side of your bed for what seemed like hours while you slept. We talked in whispers at first, but as we realized it didn't disturb you we talked in normal tones.

"Your mom has been writing those letters since before I met her," Russ said.

"How long have you know about them?" I asked.

"She told me about them before we got married. But she's never let me read them or even told me what she writes about."

"Didn't you wonder about them?"

"I asked Livvy about them many times. She said it was her way of staying connected to CiCi and trying to heal the past." Russ reached over and tucked the blanket around your shoulders. "You've been reading the letters for a couple of days now. What is in them?"

I tried to synopsize them in my head before I answered. "Her life story."

Russ watched you sleeping.

I stared out the window behind Russ.

"I just finished reading Mom's letter about my wedding day. Her descriptions are so vivid. I can hear the wedding march and smell my bouquet. I see her dabbing at her eyes and you fighting tears. My heart's actually pounding like it did that day when I saw Will standing at the front of the church."

"I remember. I practically had to hold back to keep you from running down the aisle to him." Russ smiled for the first time in weeks. "You were a beautiful bride, Alex."

"Did I ever thank you for everything you did for me that day, Russ?"

His brow furrowed. "I didn't do anything every other dad on the planet does when his daughter gets married."

"But you didn't have to. You helped decorate the reception hall, drove me to the church, walked me down the aisle. You even helped tie ribbons around the guest's gift bags. And you paid for everything." Tears spilled from the corners of my eyes and trickled down my face. "From the minute you married Mom you've done everything in the world for me. And you didn't have to. Thank you."

"I wanted to, Alex. At first, because I loved your mother, But it didn't take long before I loved you, too."

You looked asleep, but you spoke like you'd heard our entire conversation. "It was a perfect day. I can still see Russ whispering to you in the back of the church. I always meant to ask you what he said."

I leaned over your bed and kissed your cheek. "He said, 'Alex you look as beautiful as your mother did on our wedding day. And I know that you'll be every bit as happy. But I want you to know, that if you ever need me, I'm there. If you ever want to come home, the door is always open."

Your shoulders shook even as you fell back to sleep.

Dear Momma,

SINCE ALEX married Will, I feel like centipede legs on a humpback whale. In the time it took the pastor to say, "I now pronounce you husband and wife," I became expendable, unneeded and unnecessary. No longer do I have to be on high alert, just in case. If my little girl needs anything, her husband will be there. I come in a distant second place, occasional backup.

I had hoped to move seamlessly to the next phase of my life, like every other well-adjusted woman. It hasn't work out that way. Right now, I'd rather curl up in bed and not come out until…well, maybe, until I have grandchildren.

And, by the way, Momma, I hear you nagging me about hanging on and letting go, but I'm leaving fingernail marks all over Alex as I struggle to do that yet again in my life.

Russ moved on with far more grace than I could muster. I find myself watching him, studying him. He seems to know innately when to let go and when to hang on. But even at my lowest, most cantankerous point, he has never ever let go of me, not once.

Love you,

Livvy

Dear Momma,

I WORKED at that damn plant for over twenty years and what the hell good did all my experience do me? I learned the ropes, put up with Wilbur Walker and his disgusting harassment. And still worked my ass off for that place when I could just as easily have sued them. Stupid me took the job WWII had screwed up and fixed it. Increased my team's production and restored their trust in the company. Then, when I stood in line for the promotion I had earned, they stabbed me right between the shoulder blades. The position went to the new kid, the youngest team player who still sported acne and flaunted his arrogant attitude. I earned my stripes with twenty-one years of hard work. At age twenty-seven, he offered four years on the job and a degree in management. He might know how to wipe his own ass, but I suspect the jury's still out on that. In his short time at the plant, he showed little initiative, no people skills, a marginal work ethic and no balls.

Do I sound pissed off? Like I've unleashed my inner bitch? Good. Because that's how I feel and I see no sign of improvement any time soon.

The plant manager called me into his office a while back and explained that the line manager (my boss) would be retiring in a few months. He said, "Your name is on the short list being considered to replace him. You think you're up to the job?"

He caught me totally off guard since I hadn't heard a thing about the retirement or my name in the hopper. A few seconds of stuttering, "Really? Really?" and I pulled it together.

Opportunities like that don't come along every day and I wouldn't squander it. "Thank you for considering me. I am up to the job and I have several ideas I'd like to discuss with you."

He pointed to the chair in front of his desk. "I hoped that would be your attitude. If you've got time, let's discuss some of those ideas now."

Suggestions cascaded from my mouth before I even sat down. "I've implemented a few things with my team that have worked well on morale and production. I think some of those changes, employed on a larger scale could benefit the entire plant. We've become a real team in the last few years. I recognize individual accomplishment, but I try to promote the idea of team success through group effort. The team takes time off when we meet goals ahead of schedule. We have a brief meeting once a week and people feel like they have a say in what works and what doesn't. If someone has an idea, we're open to it and are willing to give it a try. It took a while to eliminate the status-quo-at-all-costs attitude, but I think, for the most part, we've succeeded."

I shared not only what my team had already done, but strategies that I hoped to employ in the future. The manager sat back and rubbed his chin.

"I've seen what your team has accomplished. That's why you're here. And you have innovative ideas. We may call you in for a panel interview. I'll keep you posted." He nodded, ending the conversation and letting me know that I could leave.

I didn't move. "May I ask you who else is under consideration?"

"You and Mark Dockerty are running neck and neck for the position."

I choked. A little coughing sputter, but a choke, all the same. I knew Mark Dockerty. I'd been forced to sit through line supervisor meetings with wet-behind-the-ears Mark Dockerty. I knew several miserable people on his team. Their grumbling hadn't escaped me. In fact, I didn't think anyone at the plant could possibly have missed it.

I sensed a con job and my bullshit meter shifted into overdrive. I had just explained the best I had to offer, handing it to the man who chose Mark shit-for-brains Dockerty as my primary competition. I had screwed up beyond repair. My stomach threatened to hurl when I stood up.

"Thank you for the opportunity. It's a job I'm ready for."

I walked out of his office and locked myself in mine for the rest of the afternoon. I ranted and fumed, berating myself for my naiveté.

The announcement came about a month later in the form of a memo to all line supervisors. "We are proud to announce that Mark Dockerty has been promoted to line manager. Mr. Dockerty's exceptional resume and innovative ideas should prove to be a true asset to the company. Please join me in congratulating him on his new position."

Really? That pimply-faced pipsqueak should be called Little Marky, not Mr. Dockerty. Exceptional resume? What? He finished college, so that deemed him the final authority on all things industrial? And innovative ideas? What the hell? The man couldn't blow a fart in the bathtub without a detailed instruction diagram!

And then there's the double-crossing butt-wipe we call the plant manager. Did he keep me informed? Did he call me in for a panel interview? Of course not. But the jerk sure as hell took my ideas and handed them to Dockerty like a welcome-aboard bonus.

I'd never before begrudged someone their success. Until then. Because *I* earned his success. *My* work, *my* ideas, *my* plans, and he got the credit, the promotion and the raise. If that made me a resentful bitch, I accepted the title with pride.

I accepted it until a little voice in my head said, "I've told you to turn the other cheek. I've told you to forgive seventy times seven."

I actually started to argue, "But you don't understand. I'm being cheated out of something I earned. It's not fair."

The silence might as well have spoken. "So, you only forgive those who haven't hurt you?"

Maybe I imagined it. Maybe I dreamed the whole thing, but the words made an impact.

Hanging on to my resentment only gave the dueling donkeys power in my life. I didn't want to lose sleep over them or let them take one minute of joy away from me.

I looked up and said, "I'll try. But I might need some help with that."

Nothing huge happened, no lightening or thunder or booming voice from the sky. I did feel a little lighter, though, and I knew that no matter what happened, I would be okay.

Even so, I have some doubts. I have to ask, am I a failure because I didn't finish college? Are you ashamed of me for that? Did I let you down, Momma? Because right now, it feels like I let myself down. I wish I had done things differently, but most days, I know I did the very best I could. A lot of the decisions I made in my drunken, stupid years have really come back to bite me in the ass.

Livvy

P.S. On a happier note – Gina showed up in my office waving a positive pregnancy test strip over my desk. I jumped up and did the preggers dance with my best friend.

Dear Momma,

FOR MONTHS Gina looked like she'd topple forward in a slight breeze. Enormous fresh-grown boobs and a bulging baby belly to match made her more than a little front heavy. In spite of all that, the Jersey Princess looked like one of the most beautiful mommies-to-be I'd ever seen.

When I walked into Gina's hospital room and saw her sitting up in bed, cradling her baby girl, I couldn't contain my grin. She gazed down on the tiny, swaddled thing with unmasked awe, and I thanked God for my best friend's beautiful, healthy baby.

Brody couldn't pull his eyes away from his wife and daughter to even glance up at us.

"Look," Gina whispered. "She's perfect, absolutely perfect."

She pulled back the receiving blanket to reveal ten fingers curled into two little palms. All ten toes stretched, enjoying their newfound space. A pert, button nose flared just above pink, heart-shaped lips. Gina licked her first two fingertips and swiped them over the baby's dark, spiky hair, trying in vain to smooth the unruly growth.

"God help her. She got it from my side of the family." Gina had pulled her own thick, dark tresses back into a ponytail earlier, but now they escaped the elastic band and hung around her face and down her neck in sweat-clumped ringlets.

Russ stepped closer to see the baby. For a moment, I wondered what this must be like for him, to share in the joy of a friend's new baby when he never got to have that elation in his own life. That experience in his life ended in such heartbreak that I wondered if he had ever recovered.

Russ concealed any discomfort well. "You got damn lucky, Brody. She looks like her mother." He chuckled. "Even has the same hair style." Gina took a one-armed swat at him.

Brody's contagious smile infected all of us. "She does look like Gina, doesn't she?" He ran his fingers over Gina's cheek. "I am the luckiest man I know." His fingers moved from his wife to the bundle in her arms and those huge hands touched his daughter as tenderly as if she had been a butterfly and he feared damaging its fragile wings. Detective Brody Water's seven-pound baby girl had already reduced him to emotional mush.

"So, what's her name?" Russ asked.

Gina looked up at us. "Let me introduce Mia Elizabeth Waters." She held her out for me to hold. I moved close to the bed and reached for Mia.

It had been years since I'd held a baby, but my arms cradled her like I'd done it yesterday.

And I longed for a grandbaby.

Livvy

Dear Momma,

MARK DOCKERTY got the promotion at the plant and the raise that accompanied it. He strutted around the line floor like his penis had grown three inches since he moved into his new office. I had visions of his toy soldier at half-mast on his best day, but his advancement seemed to have given him delusions of engorged grandeur.

Several months ago Dickerty—sorry—Dockerty announced his first team meeting. At least that's what he called it. I felt certain the plant manager had suggested that approach. Unfortunately, I suspect he neglected to give him a quick overview of how to conduct professional meetings. While several line supervisors used their favorite crass phrase to describe what happened that morning, I'll stick with disaster.

We arrived in the conference room to find no coffee or water, no doughnuts or bagels, and, most noticeably, no Mark Dockerty. The bare credenza and naked table spotlighted the fact that the newly promoted jerk didn't care enough about his own command performance to even bother turning on the lights. Meeting Prep 101. Clearly, Dockerty skipped that class.

Eight of us sat around the oval table and stared at one another while we waited for the emperor to make his appearance. We said nothing, fearing that as soon as we did, the little freak would pop out around the doorframe and scream, "Gotcha!" The tick of the wall clock set the beat for nervous fingers drumming the table.

Dockerty sauntered in fifteen minutes late and dropped into the chair at the head of the table, offering no explanation or apology for keeping us waiting. The emperor clicked his pen, did a quick count around the table and flipped open the notebook in front of him.

"We have a problem. Production levels over the past year are down about twenty percent."

After a quick math review, I realized the time frame corresponded to his promotion. The decline happened on his watch. I couldn't help it; I smiled.

"You see something funny in reduced production levels, Mrs. Montgomery? You do realize that will result in reduced revenue and eventually in pay freezes and layoffs. I like my pay and my job."

"I bet you do," I mumbled.

"What was that?"

"I said, we all like our jobs," I replied.

Dockerty ignored me. "This is a team," he announced to no one in particular. "We fail or succeed as one." He stared out the window. "I don't care what it takes. I want productions levels to surpass anything we've ever done. And I want to see results within the week. The head office will sit up and take notice. If your people don't produce, we don't need them."

Across the table from me, a hand shot into the air. Dockerty didn't bother to address the man by name. He pointed at him to indicate that he could ask his question.

"Does this mean overtime is available to meet our quotas?"

"Absolutely not. Efficiency can accomplish more than overtime." He looked at the supervisor who had posed the question. "If you don't think you can get the job done..." He looked around the table at each of us. "If any of you think this is more than you can do, let me know. We have people in the wings, waiting for a chance to show me that they can."

I held my breath and knew a couple of the other supervisors well enough to know they did, too. Shock wouldn't keep the anger at bay long.

The initial questioner stood up. "Was that a threat, Mr. Dockerty?"

"No threat. A statement of fact. Upper management gives me a hard time and when they come down on me, I pass it on to you. Shit rolls downhill. Bottom line: if you can't do the job, I'll find someone who can."

He picked up his folder and walked out of the room, leaving us frustrated and resentful.

Later that afternoon, I called my team together to brainstorm. We exchanged ideas and by the end of the meeting, we had a plan, only partially formulated, but a plan all the same. We made a conscious decision to ignore Dockerty's attitude and most of his production-strangling directives. We decided to go back to the way we did things when we did them well.

Within one week, our numbers jumped significantly, not to pre-Dockerty levels, but apparently enough for the plant manager to notice. He showed up unannounced in my office.

"Do you have a few minutes?" he asked.

"Of course." I stood up behind my desk and struggled to hide my surprise. "Have a seat."

He sat in one of the fake leather office chairs across from me, laced his fingers together and laid his hands over his stomach. "I need your help."

I said nothing and waited him out.

"As it turns out, Mark Dockerty may have been a little green for a management position."

No shit, Sherlock, sprang to mind, but I kept my mouth shut.

"He has a little bit of tunnel vision in his business ideas and we need to broaden his expertise in that department. And he needs to fine tune his people skills."

I couldn't control the smile threatening to burst into full-blown laughter. "Do I hear you saying he's wet behind the ears and rude?"

His lips curled up in spite of his effort to appear neutral. "He may be a little green."

I nodded.

"Can you help him?"

Here it comes, I thought. *No raise. No promotion. Just a request to turn the guy they want into what they need.*

"I'll make it worth your while if you take him under your wing; teach him some of the nuances of management."

"Why me?"

"You brought your team out of hell after we fired Wilbur Walker and turned it into a highly productive unit. And I've seen your numbers recently. When everyone else's are down, yours are on the way up. You could teach him a lot."

I leaned back in my chair and took a deep breath before I spoke. In those few seconds, anger and compliance fought for top billing in my head. I said a silent prayer, *What I want to say will help no one. Please give me the words.*

"I appreciate the faith you seem to have in my abilities," I said. "Truthfully, though, I don't think I can help you. More specifically, I don't think I can help Mark Dockerty."

"And why is that?" the manager asked, his voice edged with irritation.

I leaned forward and rested my arms on my desk. "Because Mark Dockerty doesn't want help. He doesn't believe he needs it. That may be because of immaturity and inexperience and those things can't be taught. But I believe the man's issues run deeper than that. He has a serious attitude problem, an exaggerated belief in his own importance and an overly developed sense of entitlement. I can't teach Mark Dockerty because he isn't teachable." I leaned back and waited.

The plant manager sighed. "You aren't the first to express that opinion." He stood and walked toward the door. "Thank you for your time." He looked back at me. "And your candor."

After the door closed behind him, I sat in stunned wonder at what I had just done. "Thank you, Lord," I said.

I never felt so bold and in control in my entire life. I didn't have to kick myself for giving in and doing something I didn't feel right about. Saying *no* felt more than cathartic. It felt empowering.

Love you, Momma,

Livvy

P.S. They transferred Dockerty to the plant up north, so he is no longer a boil on my butt. I got the promotion, the raise and the I-have-a-bigger-penis-than-you-do office! I did it, Momma. I did it.

December 3, 2011
9:00 AM

Dear Mom,

YOU SLEPT for almost four straight hours. Which meant that Russ and I did as well. Russ gave me the foldout bed while he took the chair next to you. Every time you snored, moaned or even moved your head on the pillow, he jumped up to help you. I watched him meet your every need with such tenderness. Your love for one another has been a great gift in my life. Your and Dad's fighting all the time frightened me. You and Russ offered me security.

Knowing how much the man has always loved and protected you makes me wonder how he reacted to all of this going on at the plant. I asked him about it a little while ago.

"I just read Mom's letters about her promotion to line manager. I never knew all the behind-the-scenes drama with that. Did you ever meet Mark Dockerty?"

Russ shook his head. "Never had the pleasure."

"That's probably a good thing." I grinned. "I suspect you might have hurt him."

"I wanted to. But your mom said if it ever came to that, she wanted the honor herself." Russ threw his head back laughing. "She would have done it, too."

I nodded. "You're right. You know, I never realized how strong she really is. She always made it look so easy. But she faced down all her demons and beat most of them. Speaking of which, what ever happened to Wilbur Walker?"

"Your mother has run into him a few times. She said he looked pretty rough."

"I can't see Grandma dating him. How could she have fallen for someone so horrible?"

"Maybe he wasn't so bad back then." Russ stared out the window for a moment before he looked back at me. "Then again, sometimes horrible disguises itself pretty well in charming. You've got to cut through the mask to find out what's really underneath."

"Your dad dated Grandma CiCi, too, didn't he?"

Russ nodded.

"Did you know her?"

"I was a kid but I knew who she was. May have met her once or twice, but I never spent any time around her."

"Did you know then about her and your dad?"

He nodded again. "You call it dating, Alex. It was really an affair. He and Mom were still married and she knew about it."

My jaw went slack and my mouth fell open.

"While the affair was going on, Mom dragged me to church with her even more than usual. She prayed about it there and cried herself to sleep at home. She was insecure anyway, and that just about did her in." He sighed. "CiCi was a beautiful woman and she brought out the self-doubt in just about every woman in town."

"After all of that, how could you and Mom have gotten together?"

"I guess it does seem odd. But Livvy is very different from Cici. When I first met your mom, I thought she was one of the most gorgeous women I'd ever seen. And after I got to know her I found out that she also had backbone and character and sass. Your mom has it all, Alex." He smiled at me. "And she passed it on to you."

You do have it all, Mom. And I hope that I got just a little bit. I love you.

Dear Momma,

WHEN THE Myrtle Beach police had trouble finding Nora Jean's next of kin, they contacted the Wilmington Police Department. Brody showed up at our front door, standing on the porch in his uniform exactly the way he did when Sonny died. My heart stopped.

Alex or Daddy? I could have sworn I only thought the question, but maybe I asked it aloud.

"It's about Nora Jean," Brody answered.

I exhaled with relief and pushed the door open. "Come on in. You've got my curiosity up."

We walked into the kitchen. Russ turned from the sink where he had been drying the dinner dishes. He stuck his hand out to shake Brody's.

"I've got some bad news," Brody said. "We got word this afternoon that Nora Jean's dead. She was murdered."

I gasped. "What happened?"

"Neighbors said she and the guy she lived with drank and fought all the time."

"There's a shocker," I muttered with unkind sarcasm, immediately wishing that I had silenced the words before they slipped out my mouth. The bitterness I felt toward Nora Jean, even in death, shamed me. "I shouldn't have said that. What happened?"

"The neighbors called the police last night. Said they heard yelling and screaming next door. While they were on with 911, the front door opened and the guy came running out. He held a towel up to his nose with one hand and carried an open bottle of booze in the other. Nora Jean stumbled down the steps after him, half-naked. The 911 operator could hear her screeching and beating on the hood of a car. Then she picked up a rock and smashed it into the windshield. The boyfriend turned around and swung the bottle into the side of Nora Jean's head before he dragged her by the T-shirt back into the house. The police got there within minutes, but it was too late. He beat her to death."

"Jesus," Russ whispered.

"Oh, my Lord," I said.

"I thought you and Luther would want to know," Brody said. "Came here first hoping you'd go with me out to his place. To help me tell him." His eyes pleaded.

I had no idea how Daddy would take the news of Nora Jean's death. She hurt and humiliated him, but I think he truly loved her once.

I nodded at Brody. "I'll follow you to Daddy's."

Russ still held the damp towel he'd used on the dishes. He pitched it to the countertop next to the sink. "I'm coming with you."

A half-sun hung in the orange glow across the western horizon as we turned in at Daddy's mailbox. Over the water, behind the house, the moon glowed, ready to control the sky within minutes.

Daddy and Delores must have heard the cars. They stepped out onto the front porch before we had opened our doors. Panic filled their eyes and I knew each of them must be wondering if Brody's visit meant terrible news for one of them.

Brody recognized it, too. He turned to Daddy and said, "It's about Nora Jean, Mr. Dolan."

Daddy's mouth tightened into a straight line. He arched an eyebrow, assuming Nora Jean had hatched some crazy new scheme to get more money out of him. He shoved his hands in his pockets, so he couldn't accept whatever court order Brody had to serve him.

Brody stepped to the foot of the stairs leading up to the front porch. "Sir, Nora Jean Dolan was murdered early this morning in Myrtle Beach." He looked from Delores to Daddy. "I know you divorced a long time ago, but it still seemed like I needed to let you know."

Daddy leaned against Delores.

Brody held back the gory details he'd given to Russ and me. He softened the news, saying only, "It seems the man she'd been living with beat her to death, sir."

"Dear God," Daddy said.

"Thank you, Brody," Delores said. She pulled Daddy toward the front door.

Brody looked at me. "Can Gina and I help?"

I shook my head and followed Daddy and Delores inside.

"How the hell could she have ended up like that?" Daddy asked, rubbing his fingertips over his forehead like that might ward off the onslaught of memories. He stared out at the waterway through the sliding doors. "She was a boatload of terrible things, but nobody deserves that."

When I first heard the news, I felt shock and disbelief. Then, a little bit of ugly eased out when I felt relief that none of us had to deal with her again. Then came the guilt. The woman had been murdered, for goodness sake. God nudged my heart that night saying, "Why don't you try forgiving her? She can't hurt you anymore anyway."

Nora Jean's drinking problem had made her vulnerable to something like this. As much as she had pointed her finger at me and my drunkenness, I knew she had done it more as a distraction from her own than as an indictment of mine. Alcoholics are professional smoke and mirror manipulators. There but for the grace of God.

Livvy

December 3, 2011
11:00 AM

Dear Mom,

I FELT like a psycho-monster after Nora Jean's death because of my reaction. Or lack of reaction. I tried to be sad. That's how anyone with any sense would respond, but a dark shadow over my life had been erased. And it had been so many years since I'd seen her that I didn't feel much of anything. Maybe pity that she died the way she did.

Your heartless, heathen daughter felt better about herself after she read your letter. You had conflicted feelings, too. Why didn't we ever talk about that? Maybe we are a lot alike.

Your oncologist came in earlier and said, "You look like you're feeling better." He put his fingers to your wrist and felt your pulse. He flipped your chart open, glancing from the page to Russ. "It looks like the meds have stabilized her pain." Then he looked at you, Mom, and my heart soared when he said, "If you keep this up we may let you go home tomorrow."

"Home?" I asked. "Seriously?"

You nodded your head slowly. I looked at Russ. He hadn't moved. I didn't understand. I thought we had just been given great news and neither of you even smiled. When I looked at your doctor again, I recognized the sadness on his face. My excitement plummeted. Can a beating heart shatter? Yes. Mine did when I realized that if he released you, he would be sending you home to die.

A choked sob clogged my throat. You reached out a hand to me. I sat on the bed next to you, wrapping one arm around your waist.

You stroked my hair. Russ stared out the window.

I love you so much,

Alex

May 11, 1997
Mother's Day

Dear Momma,

HURRICANE FRAN slammed our shores last fall threatening trees, homes, businesses and even roads. It knocked the stuffing out of the locals and blew a few Yankee transplants back up north as well.

Before the worst of it hit, I made a last minute emergency run to Food Lion for storm supplies. The crammed parking lot should have clued me in to keep on driving, but stubborn me snagged a grocery cart and headed inside. Huge bare spots greeted me where the canned goods should be. No Chef Boyardee, no pork and beans, and no Vienna sausage, but the swarming hoard had left me more tomato paste and pickled beets than I needed in my lifetime.

I dashed to the baked goods. Not a stale hot dog bun in sight. The bare shelves mocked me. Somehow, I managed to scrounge up a box of Cheerios, a head of iceberg lettuce, half a dozen bruised apples and a quart of chocolate ice cream. Between the last aisle and the cash register, I guarded my stash from grocery poachers and even considered swiping a bag of Nacho Cheese Doritos that a distracted shopper had left unprotected. I shuddered at the thought of becoming one of the storm plunderers that I so despised and decided against it.

I dashed home, dropped the groceries in the kitchen and headed to the back yard to help Russ. I found him arranging patio furniture in the shed. He slammed the door and threw the bolt, giving the shed a final pat in case it didn't survive the storm.

Daddy's voice boomed from the patio. He held up grocery bags. "Where do you want these?"

Delores walked out the sliding doors and added, "We picked up a pizza on our way, too."

"Y'all are life-saving geniuses," I hollered as large, heavy drops of rain splattered the patio. Lightning flashed in the distance and the thunder chasing it rumbled deep and fierce. The tops of the pine trees in the backyard whipped in the wind. Just over the trees, mountainous clouds so thick they looked like I could walk on them, raced by. I could still see a patch or two of blue sky, but beyond that, it looked like a definitive squall line of tree-snapping storms.

Russ and I shook the rain off like a couple of slow-motion Saint Bernards before we joined Daddy and Delores in the kitchen.

Alex and Will pulled into the driveway and I watched them race for the front door, hauling a grocery bag in each arm. Alex walked in first, drenched. Will stood right behind her, looking even wetter. They dropped their bags on the tile in the foyer. Alex said, "We'll put these away after we change clothes." She looked at me. "Seriously, Mom, please leave them alone."

They headed to Alex's old room to dry off. When they returned, they snatched up the bags they'd left in the foyer and set them on the kitchen counter.

Will sported an enormous grin, but since most days, he looked like a happy teddy bear, that didn't seem unusual. The giveaway should have been Alex's glow, but I hadn't spotted it yet.

Alex reached into the first bag. "We brought a few things to snack on during the storm," she said. She set a bag of baby red potatoes next to the sink. Then came a can of baby corn.

Daddy's brow furrowed. Delores smiled. Russ and I looked confused.

Alex pulled out a tub of vegetable dip and said, "I bet this would be really good with baby carrots." She reached back into the bag and held up the carrots.

"Do any of y'all notice a theme going on here?" Will opened the bag and the dip, grabbed a carrot and popped it in his mouth. Then he added, "What a shame it's too wet to grill these baby-back ribs." He beamed as he held up the huge slab.

My heart pounded, my eyes welled and my throat tightened when I tried to speak.

"What theme?" Russ asked.

Will and Alex pulled out blue and pink bags for each of us. Delores and I squealed. Daddy and Russ finally looked at each other with a flicker of comprehension.

We each pulled an oversized T-Shirt from our bag and unfolded it to reveal "World's Best Grandma" or "World's Best Grandpa" emblazoned on each one.

I grabbed Alex and hugged her so tight I thought she might deliver right there. Then I pulled away, rubbed her still tiny tummy and heard the automatic baby talk roll from my lips like every day conversation. Within seconds everyone else sounded as foolish as I did, cooing to the newest family addition.

An enormous crash disrupted our joy. It boomed so close that the pictures on the walls shook. Daddy and Russ grabbed flashlights.

"Sounded like it came from the front of the house," Russ said.

We huddled on the front porch while the wind pummeled us with horizontal rain.

Daddy scanned his flashlight over the yard. Russ walked toward the side of the house.

"The pine tree between our house and the Warners' is down."

We followed Russ into the yard and trained our lights where the tree should be. It looked like it had snapped in two, missing the garage by inches.

I heard a distorted groan and turned toward the sound. We all watched the huge oak tree across the street lean, slowly at first, until it reached the point that its own weight hurled it to the ground. The leafy top of the tree bounced until it stopped and lay still, like it had just lost a life-and-death struggle. The entire root system came up intact, looking like an eight-foot circle of dirt standing sentinel in the yard.

"Back inside," Russ ordered.

We didn't argue.

By the time the sun came up the next morning, Hurricane Fran had moved on, leaving a shell-shocked community in its wake.

I stepped outside and struggled for breath. The almost visible humidity hung so thick in the air, I thought I could actually drown in it. It felt like a sweat-soaked blanket covered Wilmington, keeping the heat and the moisture hovering over us. The storm took any hint of breeze with it and the temperature skyrocketed, threatening heatstroke to anyone foolish enough to start their clean up. I longed to climb back in bed and lay in air-conditioned comfort on fresh, crisp sheets, but Hurricane Fran had knocked out power all over town, so any hope of relief vanished.

Our neighborhood looked like it had been the victim of a bombing raid. Power lines hung loose, with one lying in the road. Roof shingles dotted every yard. A layer of branches, tree limbs and wet leaves littered the ground. Several pine trees had snapped and come down in the street, looking like someone had used them to play Pick Up Sticks.

It would take days to clean up the mess Fran dropped in our yards and longer than that to get our power restored. In fact, when the electricity finally came back on, everyone on my street ran outside to applaud the heroes from Carolina Power and Light.

But our family came through it better than ever. After all, we might have lost a few trees and shingles, but we gained a grandchild-to-be.

I wish you were here, Momma,

Livvy

August 12, 1997
Happy Birthday

Dear Momma,

A LEX DELIVERED a beautiful baby boy in May. Will swaggered into the waiting room, threw his hands in the air and yelled, "It's a boy!" He puffed up with such pride, I thought his chest might burst. The crowd burst into applause and surrounded Will, peppering him with questions. "When can we see him?" "How is Alex?" "When can we hold him?"

"The doctor says I can take a few of you back there now," he answered. He grinned at Jenci and me. "Grandmas first."

My grandson. Those magical words took flight in my mind and soared. My handsome, amazing, perfect grandson. I couldn't wait to get my hands on him.

Will led the way and opened the door. Jenci and I waltzed into the room, teasing one another about who got first crack at the grandbaby. My joy withered in my gut when I saw Alex's face. Tears rolled down her cheeks and she gripped the sheets so tight, her fists looked like knots. I couldn't see the baby, but two doctors and a nurse huddled in the corner, their backs forming a barrier between tiny Garrett and his family while they examined him.

Will pushed past us into the room. "What's going on?" He ran to Alex's bedside.

"Something's wrong," Alex said. She shook her head. "I don't know."

Will pulled Alex's fingers from the sheet and clutched her hand to his chest. It looked like neither one of them breathed while they stared at the doctors.

Quivering spasms wracked my body. Jenci grabbed my hand and squeezed. It didn't help.

The nurse wrapped the blanket around Garrett and bustled him out of the room. I reached out, hoping to stop her. I wanted to touch my grandson, to see his face. I needed to know that he was okay. She kept walking.

The doctors turned to Will and Alex. One of them spoke. "Garrett's heartbeat is irregular. We need to get him on a monitor and figure out what's going on. We'll know more in a few hours."

Alex sat straight up in bed. "Is my baby all right? He's going to be okay, isn't he?"

"We're going to do everything we can."

It felt like they sucked the oxygen out of the room with their abrupt exit. Jenci's knees buckled. This time I held her up.

"This can't be happening," Alex cried. She looked up at Will. "He has to be okay. He has to."

Will looked like he might pass out as the color drained from his face.

Jenci and I functioned on adrenaline and maternal instinct, moving to our grown children and holding them while they cried. We sobbed with them.

Garrett looked so beautiful through the glass of the incubator that it physically hurt me. I wanted to reach right through it and grab him. I needed to hold him, cuddle him, strengthen him for what he had to face. And if I felt that way, all I had to do was look through the glass to his mother on the other side to see the agony in Alex's eyes.

Garret William Crenshaw came into this world with no hair, a little bud of a nose and a pout to melt every female heart whose path he crossed. He also arrived so frail that he needed surgery to correct a heart defect. But he had to be strong enough to survive it, so hopefully the incubator could give him the time to stabilize. Every day I sat by his side, wishing I could give him my heart. From the moment he took his first breath, it belonged to him anyway.

All that time that I willed Garrett my love, I felt my anger surge as well. I raged at every lousy mother who ever had a healthy child; at myself for being drunk during so much of Alex's childhood; at the basic unfairness that unwanted babies are born every day, but when a functional, loving family hopes and prays for the birth of a healthy baby, they instead face the kind of crisis that threatens to destroy them after ripping their guts out. And most of all, I directed my anger at the God that allowed this to happen.

Day after day, I watched my daughter's anguish and I could do nothing. I watched Garrett fight to live, and I could do nothing. I sobbed. I questioned God. I railed against Him. I raised my fists in fury. Then, when I felt so spent that I no longer had the strength to sit in the chair, I surrendered all of it and fell to my knees next to the little cube that held my precious grandson. And I sobbed all over again. This time, I asked God to forgive me my fear and lack of faith. I asked him to make me what I needed to be to help my daughter and her son. If Garrett could fight to live, then I would fight with him the only way I knew how—prayer.

For the month that Garrett lived in the incubator, his mother never left his side. She catnapped in the chair next to him and moved only to shower or eat. Will had to work, but he came to the hospital several times a day bringing food or a change of clothes for Alex. Jenci, Jeffrey, Russ and I stood vigil in shifts so that someone would always be there for Alex, Will and Garrett.

The day of Garrett William Crenshaw's birth, the Montgomery, Dolan and Crenshaw families had gathered in that waiting room, filled with so much joy that people passing in the hall stopped to give us a thumbs up or a smile. We chatted, joked, laughed, ate doughnuts, and paced.

The day of Garrett's surgery, the same people came together, except this time Alex and Will sat with us. This time I heard no laughter, no chatter. We spoke in hushed whispers, if at all. We fought tears or we let them fall. Everywhere I looked, I saw family members, heads bowed and lips moving, begging God for a miracle, for a healing. Their pleading reverberated in my head like a mantra. "Please, God. Please."

Your words mingled with the prayers, Momma. "The key to life, Livvy, is knowing when to hang on and when to let go." That day, I hung on for dear life. I hung on to Russ and Alex, to God and His healing power. I sat in the corner of that boxy little room and clung to hope, fearing that if I let go of it for one second, I risked losing everything that mattered in my life. I hung on to the assurance that God would do for Garrett what we couldn't. I envisioned His hands cradling that tiny baby, His lips breathing life and strength and healing into that fragile body. I saw those same heavenly hands touch Alex's cheek and thought I heard Him whisper in her ear that everything would be all right.

Alex perched on her chair, ready to jump at a glimpse of Garrett's surgeon. She paced from that chair to the window, from the window to the nurse's station to ask about her son's progress. The young nurse swiped at her own eyes before she responded with, "We don't have any word yet." Alex walked back to the window and her shoulders shook with her sobs.

Will ran to her, slipping an arm around her and cradled her head to his chest. She looked up at him and he leaned down until their foreheads touched. Tears streamed down both their faces.

Alex pulled away and announced to no one in particular, "I need to be closer to Garrett." I heard the determination in her voice and I stared in awe at the mother my daughter had become in that one long month since her son's birth. She walked to the hall outside the operating room.

Will took Alex's hand and walked beside her. I stood up to join them. Jenci matched me step for step. Russ and Jeffrey followed close enough behind us to be our shadows.

We stopped outside the OR and leaned against the far wall. Prayers radiated from every one of us, and I knew that, like some holy, out-of-body experience, our hearts circled the newest, smallest member of our family, strengthening him when he felt too weak to fight.

My remarkable husband stepped out in front of us. "I haven't done much public praying," he said softly. "But there's never been a better time to start."

Russ reached for my hand on his right and Jeffrey's on his left. Each of us took the hands of those nearby. When I looked up, I saw Daddy and Delores, Brody and Gina and all of the Crenshaw clan. We formed a tight circle in the hall exactly as I had just envisioned our hearts around the operating table.

Russ bowed his head. "Lord, I don't bother you often, so you know it's important. Our little Garrett needs your help and since we need that little boy, we're begging you to help him, to make him healthy and whole. Please heal that tiny little heart. Give him your strength. And let him feel how very much he's loved. Guide the doctors. Give them your wisdom. And strengthen us, Lord. Give us everything we'll need to help Garrett get through this. Please help our boy."

For several minutes no one moved. Our families clustered together, holding on to one another, barely breathing. I feared that breaking our connection might weaken the strength that grew from it. When I lifted my head I saw the love and the resolve on every face, and I felt a peace I've never known before. I can't explain how I knew, but I knew, in my heart and in my gut and in my spirit, that Garrett would be okay.

Alex stood on the other side of Russ and when she peeked around him and looked in my eyes, I saw that she felt it, too. Her ashen skin had come back to life, flushed with pink. Her exhausted, heavy-lidded eyes took on a new strength. Her jaw clenched in that familiar way I'd seen and loved since her childhood, as if she'd fought her emotional battle and won. She broke the circle first and threw her arms around Russ's neck.

"He's going to be all right," she whispered in his ear. "Thank you for praying, for being here, for everything you do. I've always been able to count on you, Dad."

I heard Russ's sharp intake of breath. Alex had told him many times that he had been more of a father to her than her own father, but she had never actually called him "Dad."

Thirty minutes later, we remained at our posts outside the swinging doors. When the doctor breezed through them, he stopped short but didn't look too surprised to see the crowd waiting for him. He nodded at Will and Alex.

"Your family got a miracle today. Garrett made it through the surgery. We were able to repair the faulty valve. You've got a tough little guy there. We'll keep him in the neo-natal intensive care unit, so we can monitor him constantly for the next twenty-four to forty-eight hours." He took a deep breath. "But so far, he looks good."

We held our breath while the doctor spoke. But when he said, "He looks good," the collective inhale could have sucked the pictures off the walls. With breath came questions.

Alex asked, "When can we see him?"

"A couple more hours and the nurse will come and get you."

"Does a successful surgery mean Garrett can live a normal life?" Will's eyes showed his fear of the answer even as he asked the question.

The doctor's hand rested on Will's shoulder. "He should be able to live a full, normal life."

"Can I stay with him while he's in intensive care?" Alex pleaded.

The look on the doctor's face said he wanted to say no, but the longer Alex's unwavering gaze fixed on him, the more he eased away from that firm answer. "Not for the first twenty-four hours." He smiled the smile of an understanding parent. "After that, I'll sign off on you staying with him. But if I do that, you have to go home tonight and get some rest yourself."

Alex nodded her acquiescence, but I knew she wouldn't leave the waiting room until she could be with her son.

Garrett William Crenshaw stayed in the hospital for three weeks after his surgery. The day of his release, the families converged once more. Tenuous smiles lit every face. We had ridden the emotional roller coaster from elation to despair and back again. None of us would ever take another day for granted.

Will brought the car to the hospital exit and opened the rear door for Alex to put Garrett in his car seat. Alex handed Garrett to me before she turned to set the diaper bag on the floor and get the straps and buckles situated for the baby. All very normal things. Except I had never held my grandson until that moment and nothing about it felt normal to me. My heart pounded and my shallow breathing made me feel lightheaded. I clasped Garrett to my chest and pulled the receiving blanket away from his face. When I stared into his eyes, he gazed right back at me.

"Hi there," I whispered.

A perfect little hand came up out of the folds of the blanket. It wrapped around my finger and gripped it. Tears spilled down my cheeks.

"I love you, Little Man."

December 3, 2011
3:00 PM

Dear Mom,

MY HANDS trembled so badly as I read your letter, that twice I had to stop and take deep breaths before I could pick up the pages again. It all flooded back. The panic, the dread, the anger and the God-awful fear. I remember that, back then, I acted the part of a mature, functional parent. I listened to the doctors and did what they suggested. I sat by Garrett's side, struggling to stay calm and strong for my son. I maintained a composure that I didn't really feel. I wanted to kick something, anything. And yell. At the doctors, the nurses, strangers on the street, you, Russ, Will, God.

I heard a constant buzz in my ears, like the white noise on TV when a station goes off the air. I watched people's lips move, but I couldn't hear them and never once wondered what they were saying. Because I didn't care and nothing they had to say mattered anyway. I might lose my baby boy and all I wanted to do was open my mouth and let loose with a blood-curdling scream. I wanted to pick Garrett up from the incubator and run. Fast enough to escape the heart problem and the surgery and the fear. I wanted to run from sickness into health, near-death to life. I wanted my love to protect my son from everything. But every moment of every day, I learned that I could protect him from nothing. Could random events really be in control of the crapshoot of life? Who'll be born with a heart valve problem? Spin the wheel. Will a bus full of schoolchildren be in the intersection when the brakes fail on the semi? Pull the slot-machine arm. Who comes out of the fog of their colonoscopy to learn that they have cancer? Roll the dice and see if it's your lucky number that comes up.

I feel all those same things now, Mom. The panic, the anger, the fear. I even hear the buzz. Like a swarm of bees getting closer and closer. What the hell happens when they get here? Will the noise stop or explode in my head? What happens to you? To me? To Russ and our family? What are we without you?

You walked beside me every step of the way with Garrett. Held me up when I couldn't stand. You made me believe in the miracle. There is none to be found this time. You're fading in that bed and none of us can stop it. The best I can hope for is to walk beside you, every step of the way.

I'm here, Mom.

Dear Momma,

AFTER HIS rocky start, Garret thrived. The scar on his chest healed, though it still glowed red after a bath, reminding us all over again to thank God for the miracle child in our lives. Once he recovered, the boy never looked back. But the rest of us did. We watched him constantly for any sign of fatigue or chest pain, anything to indicate a return of his problem. Paranoia gripped our family so tight we held our breath if he sneezed.

It took months for Alex to agree to leave Garrett with me, and when she did, she only stayed away long enough to get her haircut and pick up a few groceries. But in that short time, Garrett and I played and even managed to get in a walk around the block.

I zipped him into the jacket that Brody and Gina gave him as a welcome home gift when the hospital released him. "You're such a handsome boy," I gushed before I kissed his cheek. In bright red, across the front, the hooded windbreaker said *Rookie* and on the back, the words *Wilmington P.D.* practically jumped off the fabric in the same bold hue. My little man truly looked like a little man, and I couldn't help but grin.

I swung the front door open and held it there with my foot until I could push Garrett's stroller through it. As we walked from the front porch to the driveway, I watched a beat up old car drive slowly down the street, so slowly that we could have walked along side it. The passenger side window rolled down and I assumed someone needed directions. I pushed the stroller down the drive. No one spoke, but I did see a hand reach out to wave. I shivered. A man's face popped into view in the window. Wilbur Walker II grinned at me. My heart raced. I turned the stroller so that I stood between it and the car. The car kept rolling.

Garret laughed and I turned to check on him. The neighbor's beagle had escaped his fenced backyard and met us at the driveway. Garrett giggled. The dog stood with his front feet perched on the stroller while he stuck his head as close to Garrett's as possible and licked. Laughter bubbled up from the baby while drool trickled down his chin. Panic stirred in my gut. What if he had an allergy? What if the dog scratched him or bit him? I pushed the dog down and shooed him away. Garrett whined. The beagle returned. I blocked his way. The baby tried to reach around me and the dog just wouldn't give up.

I heard your voice. "Let go of Garret's past problems. He's a little boy with a beagle, for God's sake."

And when I heard you, I remembered the car. I spun around to find an empty street. No beat up car. No WWII. My heart pounded.

Livvy

Dear Momma,

A LEX TOOK an extended leave of absence from the hospital until Garrett had passed every healing milestone. Even then, she decided to work part-time weekend shifts. A few weeks after she returned, I pulled into the driveway after work to find Alex and Garrett already there. I jumped out of the car.

"What a great surprise! How's my boy?" I reached into the back and lifted a sleeping Garrett from his car seat. I brushed his little cheek with a kiss and inhaled the baby scent that still clung to the growing toddler. After I'd satisfied my grandma urges, I glanced up at Alex. My smile disappeared. "Is everything all right, honey?"

"Something happened that I don't want to talk about in front of Will. Do you have time?"

"Of course."

Alex grabbed the diaper bag and followed me up the sidewalk.

I dropped my pocketbook on the end table and sat down on the couch. After I grabbed the closest throw pillow and got it situated under Garrett, I slipped off my shoes and propped my bare feet on the coffee table. My fingers smoothed a few strands of Garrett's hair that stood straight up from his sweaty little head.

Alex dropped down on the other end of the couch and pulled off her sneakers.

She wasted no time in explaining. "When I went back to work, I agreed to a different unit so my hours could be what we needed. I'd done internships in the ER in school, but I knew nothing then about the power struggles or personnel problems in the hospital."

Alex looked small and vulnerable when she tucked her legs up under her.

"There's a basic responsibility structure to each unit in the hospital, but every nurse manager functions a little bit differently as does each team."

She brought her knees up to her chest and wrapped her arms around them. That's when I noticed her trembling fingers. I reached out a hand and rested it on her arm.

"We'll figure it out, Alex, whatever it is."

"I heard rumors when I worked there before about the nurse manager Brian Carney, but I never paid much attention to them." She chewed her bottom lip. "I should have listened."

Garrett squirmed in my arms so I pulled my hand away from Alex and rubbed circles on his tummy until he stilled and I heard his deep, sleepy breathing.

"I overheard a conversation between one of the nurses and Brian. More like an argument. She said it had to stop, that things couldn't keep going the way they were. At first I assumed they'd been having an affair, but she sounded outraged. He told her she had no choice, that things would continue exactly as they had been and she would say nothing to anyone."

Alex looked at me. "The way he said it made my skin crawl. I didn't want them to see me, so I left." She took a deep breath. "Shortly after that, the nurse quit. She didn't transfer to another unit. She quit. And she had eight or nine years of experience. She was one of the best nurses in the ER." Alex shook her head. "The rumors kicked in before lunch. Some people said Brian had broken off an affair and she couldn't handle working with him. Others said she'd been flirting with him and he shot her down. Again, the rejected nurse quit."

She rubbed her hands up and down her legs and hugged them even tighter. "But that's not what it sounded like to me. She was the one who tried to put a stop to something, not him."

Alex's disillusioned eyes brimmed with disgust. But I saw the fear there, too, and got angry.

"What are you not telling me?"

"A couple of days ago, Brian pulled me aside, told me what a wonderful job I'd been doing. He looked me up and down the whole time." She shivered.

"He looked at you sexually?" I asked, louder than I intended. The baby grunted and wiggled telling me to quiet down.

"Exactly. It was so creepy. I thanked him and started to walk away. He grabbed my arm and said that he wanted to take me to dinner to thank me for all my hard work. I told him I appreciated the offer, but I had a husband and baby that I needed to get home to. He said that he could m arrange for dinner during one of my shifts, and I wouldn't have to miss out on my pay or time with my family. I pulled my arm away and said no thanks."

The man touched my daughter. I saw spots in front of my eyes and forced myself to breathe. The incident with Wilbur Walker, Jr. flashed in my mind, with Alex's situation superimposed on top of it. My own helplessness churned up all over again, but the realization that my baby girl faced the same crap sent my blood into a volcanic boil-over. "He made a pass at you? Touched you?"

"I really thought I had handled it, brushed him off. But the next day he cornered me. He held up two pieces of paper and waved them at me. My probationary performance review. One raved about me, calling me a credit to the ER. The other one rated me substandard, bordering on incompetent. I told him he couldn't do that. He smiled and said the choice was mine, good review, bad review. He never actually said I had to do what he wanted, but he did the up-and-down stare and touched his crotch. That shithead had an erection. Threatening me aroused him." Alex showed no sign of tears and the more she described her encounter with Brian Carney, the stronger she looked. She straightened her legs and pounded her fist on her thigh. "He told me I had until the end of next week to give him my decision."

"You're not considering this? Is that why you didn't want to tell Will?"

"Of course not," she sputtered. "I don't want Will to know because he'll beat the crap out of him before I can prove anything. I want to stop this guy. At least three good nurses have quit the ER in the last year, and I suspect it's because of Brian Carney. All of them were single, and one had a young child. They needed their jobs." She stared at me. "Will you help me?"

"Yes, she will. And so will I."

Neither of us had heard Russ come in. He stood in the kitchen door. From the rage on his face, I knew he'd heard the bulk of the conversation. He stood behind his recliner and gripped the top of it. "Tomorrow, the three of us will meet with the CEO of the hospital and…"

Alex interrupted him. "The CEO is Brian's uncle. That's why people are afraid to pursue it."

Russ's hand balled into a fist. "I'll call Brody and have him do some research into our legal options." He turned to Alex. "Get your facts together, write everything down. Names, dates, circumstances. Contact the nurses who left and make sure your suspicions are right. See if they'll join us in a possible lawsuit against Carney and the hospital."

"The hospital?" I asked.

"The hospital allowed the sexual harassment to continue. If the CEO is as bright as he should be, he'll realize that protecting this family member could jeopardize his own job."

I arched an eyebrow, impressed with my husband's quick thinking. I'd been so busy being indignant that options hadn't occurred to me yet. Russ cut straight through to the next step.

Alex followed Russ's logic train and the tiniest smile formed at the edges of her mouth. "You're right. The hospital is culpable. And if the other nurses are willing to testify against Brian, then it's not just my word against his."

"Exactly," Russ said. "By the way, the district attorney is a long-time customer at the garage. As soon as you get your information lined up, I'll run it past him and see if he has any ideas."

Alex ran into Russ's open arms and kissed his cheek.

"You're not going through this alone," Russ assured her. "And we will stop this asshole." Russ pulled back and looked down at Alex. "But you have to tell Will. If you keep this a secret from him, it will blow up in your face."

"Russ is right, babe," I said. "You have to trust Will to control his anger until we've stopped Brian Carney permanently."

Four days later, our ambush meeting went better than we ever could have hoped. All three nurses that Alex contacted insisted on being there. The district attorney sent a letter saying that his office would be interviewing the four women making the complaints and would most certainly look into the allegations against Brian Carney. Alex had managed to sneak into Brian's office on his day off and found both copies of her probationary performance evaluation.

The stunned CEO apparently had no idea that his nephew used his professional position to augment his sex life. He listened to each story, looked over the documentation and made his decision on the spot. He removed Alex's probationary status and rehired all three of the other nurses. After only a little arm-twisting, he gave them well-deserved back pay in return for dropping any possible law suit against the hospital. He also made it very clear that he had no problem with their continued legal action against Brian.

Best of all, Brian Carney lost his job that day. I'll never forget the look on his face when all of us marched into the ER after the meeting like a train headed straight at him.

And I loved watching the wimp cower behind the nurse's station when Will approached him and leaned in close enough to whisper, "If you ever touch my wife again, I'll break your arm."

The good guys won that day, Momma.

Livvy

December 3, 2011
6:00 PM

Dear Mom,

YOU HAVEN'T eaten in a couple of days. Most of the time you reject offers of water or juice. You sleep more, and I have to fight the urge to wake you. I need to see your eyes, to hear your voice. I need to feel your presence.

"I don't know if the good guys could have won that day without you and Russ," I said aloud while I rubbed lotion on your chapped hands.

Your eyelids fluttered. "What good guys?"

I smiled, grateful for your response. "Do you remember when you helped me get Brian Carney fired from the hospital?"

You nodded.

"I wish I could have helped you nail Wilbur Walker." I squeezed more salve into my palms and spread it up your forearm. "It seems so strange to me that we both went through sexual harassment at work. How weird is that?"

"I hate that you went through it, but it's not so unusual. As long as there's power, there will be people who abuse it. Bullies have been around since the beginning of time."

"I remember Russ saying that bullies are just cowards who prey on weakness and fear. He told me that the fastest way to stop one is to punch them in the face." I chuckled. "I'm sure that was a metaphor for 'stand up to them.' Right?"

You shook your finger at me. "Maybe not."

Your breathing slowed and your eyes closed. This time, I let you sleep.

I love you past the sky,

Alex

Dear Momma,

THURSDAY, February eighteenth started out like any other day. Gina and I pulled in to the parking lot at the same time and walked in together. She rambled about dropping Mia off at preschool and how cute she looked bundled up in her coat and mittens.

Once inside, Gina shrugged off her coat and headed for the coffee pot. I closed my office door and booted up my computer before facing the day's paperwork. At about ten thirty, I stretched and headed for the restroom.

I noticed the plant manager standing with two uniformed Wilmington police officers at the end of the hall. The stricken look on the manager's face concerned me. He waved me over to them. Concern blossomed into fear.

He said, "Livvy, you're friends with Gina Waters, aren't you?"

"Yes. What's going on?"

"There was a shooting this morning. These officers need to speak with Gina." His eyes flickered away from mine and I thought I might vomit.

No, please don't say it, I thought.

He said, "Gina's husband has been shot."

"Oh, my God." Stars flashed around the edges of my vision. One of the men grabbed my arm to steady me. "Is he…"

The officer shook his head. "He's at the hospital about to go into surgery. We need to get Mrs. Waters there as quickly as possible."

I ran toward Gina's workstation. The three men followed. I felt the grey walls closing in but continued. I had to get to Gina.

We pushed through the doors and made it halfway across the room before Gina looked up. Her hands froze in front of her. Her eyes didn't blink, but she mouthed, "No."

The man behind me spoke before Gina could say anything.

"Brody's been shot. He's at the hospital and needs surgery. We'll get you to him."

She shoved her chair back and bolted for the swinging doors. The rest of us ran to catch up.

"What happened?" she asked on the run.

"A call went out about an armed robbery at a convenience store. Brody and his partner got there first. The guy held the clerk hostage and Brody tried to talk him down, offering to go in himself unarmed to replace the clerk. Brody took a couple of steps toward the door. The guy fired through the glass and caught Brody in the gut."

Gina grabbed the door handle. Tears welled in her eyes when she turned toward the officer. "How bad is it?"

"I honestly don't know." He pushed the door open.

I grabbed Gina in a bear hug. "I'm taking my car, and I'll meet you at the hospital."

Gina pulled away and asked the officer, "And the robber?"

"He's dead."

"Good," I heard my best friend say, and I knew she meant it.

I called Russ before I ran for the parking lot.

When I burst through the ER doors, the nurse behind the counter asked, "Can I help you?"

"Officer Brody Waters. I'm trying to find his wife."

She flipped through her clipboard. "Officer Waters was taken to surgery a little while ago. His wife is in the waiting room." She looked up at me. "We're all praying for him."

I managed to choke out a "thank you." By the time I found Gina, half a dozen Wilmington police officers, including the chief, surrounded her. Russ sat next to her. She clutched the sleeve of his jacket. A couple of men paced the room, one thumbed through a magazine without looking at it, and Brody's partner stood at the window.

I couldn't believe how different Gina looked from the woman who had arrived at the plant that morning. Dark circles under her eyes stood in stark contrast to her pale complexion. Most of her mascara and all of her blush had vanished in the 45 minutes since I had seen her. Her wild eyes looked like she hadn't decided whether to claw at someone's throat or collapse.

Russ motioned for me to sit next to my friend. I grabbed her hand. She laid her head on my shoulder. "What do I tell Mia?" She sat up. "Mia's at school. I have to get her."

"Alex already picked her up. She can stay with them for as long as you need." I turned Gina's face until she had to look in my eyes. "Brody is strong, and he's a fighter. He's coming back to you, Gina. Do you hear me? When you tell Mia anything, it will be good news."

For over an hour, Gina leaned against me. I heard an occasional sniffle and felt her wipe a tissue under her nose. Then she sat up. "I need to find the chapel. Will you go with me?"

We followed the signs down the hall. Gina almost ran through the door. When she saw the cross covering the entire far wall, she fell to her knees, crossed herself and stared up at it.

Out loud, Gina said, "I need you to know how important Brody is, not just to me but to our daughter." She took a deep breath. "My little girl needs her daddy. Please. Please. Let him come back to us." She never took her eyes off the cross. "We need him."

I knelt beside her. "Protect Brody, Lord. He needs your strength and your healing." I glanced at Gina. "Mia and Gina need you, too. Give them your peace." I don't know how long we stayed on that hard floor praying, but at some point, we both used nearby chairs to push ourselves up.

When we walked back into the waiting area, it was like no one had moved. Those who had been standing still stood. Those who had been sitting occupied the same chairs. They clustered around Gina, as if their presence could get her through whatever happened. I hoped that Brody felt that strength as well and that it could tip the scales in his favor.

Within minutes, a doctor pushed through the swinging doors nearby and pulled the paper mask from his face. His gesture reminded me of every low-budget B-movie doctor who had ever walked out of surgery to meet with the family—a cheap imitation of real life.

"Your husband made it through surgery."

"Thank God," Gina said.

"He has a long way to go, Mrs. Waters. We had to remove his spleen and part of his liver. He had a lot of other damage as well."

The doctor detailed the surgery and the requirements for Brody's body to recover. Gina's face paled until she looked like a wax doll.

I knew Brody had been badly hurt, but hearing the details in cold, clinical terms sent shock waves through me. Everyone standing in that room grimaced in their shared suffering.

Gina clutched at her stomach. "Can he recover from all this? Is it even possible?"

"Yes, but it'll take time," the doctor answered.

Gina nodded. "When can I see him?"

"That'll be hours. You should go home and get some rest. We'll call if there's any change." The doctor placed a hand on Gina's shoulder. "He's going to need you, so you have to take care of yourself to be in this for the long haul."

Gina shrugged him off. "I'm not leaving this hospital until my husband is released."

Color rose back up in her cheeks and the Jersey girl emerged. I had to smile. The surgeon backed away a step or two as if he might be debating the wisdom of telling this woman no. He decided to live to operate another day.

"He'll be in intensive care for at least the next twenty-four hours, but you can see him for a few minutes every hour. I'll make sure he gets a private room after that, so you can stay with him." He took a breath. "Mrs. Waters, please consider getting some rest."

"Thank you, doctor." Gina spoke the words like she had just dismissed a servant.

He shook his head and walked back through the swinging doors. I watched the signs "Hospital Personnel Only," sway with the doors and hoped those three little words could keep the doctor safe from my best friend if he tried to get between her and her husband.

Russ held both of Gina's hands. "He's right, Gina. I'm going to drive you home, just for a couple of hours, so you can at least take a nap. You can't see Brody while he's in recovery, anyway. You can bring an overnight bag back with you."

"I'm not leaving." She turned to me. "Livvy, will you go to my house and throw a few things together for me? You know what I'll need. Could you call my parents, too? Mom'll come down and take care of Mia." Her chin quivered. "For as long as I need her."

I nodded, knowing that arguing would do no good. I would have done exactly the same thing.

I hugged Russ. "Please stay with her until I get back." I whispered.

"I'm not going anywhere." Russ kissed my forehead. He glanced over at Gina and added, "But don't leave me alone with her for too long, okay?"

"Scares you, doesn't she?"

He spun me toward the door.

I returned later, armed with everything Gina might need for a few days. By then, the crowd in the waiting room had dwindled to Russ, the chief and Brody's partner. No sign of Gina.

"They let her go in about ten minutes ago," Russ said before I could ask.

"How is he?"

"Hanging on."

Dawn rose the next morning with the same group still waiting, rumpled, wrinkled and exhausted. Every few minutes, someone's stomach growled. We had long since given up on small talk and found the rhythmic sounds of the hospital to be soothing in a bizarre way. They lulled us to a waking rest.

Sometime that afternoon, they moved Brody to his own room. I helped Gina get her things situated before Russ and I drove home and fell into bed.

The following days blurred in my mind. I sped home long enough to nap, shower and change clothes before I stayed with Brody while Gina grabbed something from the cafeteria.

Brody slept in a drug-induced fog for the first few days, but then the physical therapy began. With it, so did his own personal hell. I cried with

Gina when her husband's pain threatened to overwhelm him every time he tried to get out of bed.

I sobbed with Mia when she hugged her daddy and she heard him moan before he pulled away. She wanted to climb on the bed and settle in with Brody the way she always had. She wanted him to tickle her and toss her in the air. She wanted him to laugh like he used to, to be the same man he was before. She couldn't possibly have understood what her daddy had been through or still had to face. She knew only that she wanted him back.

Russ walked with Brody up and down the hall. He pushed his friend's IV pole and stayed close enough to grab him if his knees folded under the exertion. Each walk lasted a few more steps. Every day, Brody rolled over and pushed out of bed a little bit easier.

Three weeks after an armed robber shot Officer Brody Waters, the hospital released him to go home. Not well, not whole, not painless, but alive.

Eventually, Brody returned to work and life seemed almost normal in the Waters's household, but when I looked deep in Brody's eyes, I knew that something very basic had changed that day. From the way Gina looked at her husband, I knew she saw it, too.

Dear Momma,

DADDY THREW a Fourth of July party at his place and roped all of us into helping. The weather cooperated, providing a canopy of sunshine and blue sky. By noon, we had transformed the back yard into a patriotic sea of red, white and blue. Streamers fluttered in the breeze, and balloons hung from chair backs. A centerpiece of red and white carnations topped with a small American flag adorned each table. Several large blue-and-white party tents shaded the area.

Guests arrived that afternoon wearing Fourth of July beach-chic: flip-flops, shorts and tank tops. Within minutes, the backyard hummed with activity. Children ran to the water while their mothers hollered for them to be careful. Garrett followed Mia and the bigger kids, moving his little legs as fast as they would go, struggling to keep up. His cheeks reddened from the exertion, and Alex, who still worried about everything her son did, hovered nearby.

Brody and Gina sat across from one another staring toward Mia; although it didn't look like they actually saw their daughter.

"Is he okay?" I asked Russ.

"No," Russ answered. "I think physically he's almost at a hundred percent, but emotionally he's not even close. He's negative and bitter. He's convinced something bad is about to happen, all the time. He thinks everyone else has changed." Russ shook his head. "I tried to explain that no one knows how he'll react anymore, so we don't know what to do. And that pissed him off."

"Gina said the same thing. She's having a hard time with it. I get the impression that he takes his frustration out on Gina and even Mia." I glanced at my friends. "I thought Brody had to see the department psychiatrist for approval to go back to work. It's obvious that he's not ready."

"I don't get it either. Either the shrink he saw needs to look for another line of work, or Brody's a top notch actor."

We sat down at their table. They smiled for a moment and turned back toward the water.

About dusk, Daddy walked over, nodding toward the guys. "Could you boys give me a hand?"

They followed him to the end of the dock, about forty feet out over the water. I suspected that Daddy needed help with his fireworks display. Soon light flashed across the darkening sky. Tiny popping noises sounded like a rapid-fire BB gun. An occasional boom set off a hail of colorful exploding stars, intersecting one another over our heads. Their color burned bright at first but faded as the sparks fell over the water. Residual smoke looked fog-like and carried a sulfurous odor like hundreds of matchbooks lit all at once. The crowd's gasps rose to meet the smoky haze.

The last of the fireworks dimmed. As Daddy, Russ and Brody made their way up the sloping lawn, Daddy gave Brody a backslap of appreciation. Brody flinched. The display that had given the rest of us so much joy may have pushed Brody's already sullen mood over the edge.

Russ and Daddy strode up to Delores and me like conquering heroes. Daddy kissed Delores's cheek while Russ picked me up and spun me around until I screamed, "Stop!"

Brody walked past Gina without a glance and yelled at Mia, "Time to go home."

"I don't want to go yet," she whined. "I'm having fun."

"We're leaving," he growled through his clenched jaw.

Russ set me down, stared at his best friend and debated saying something. Gina didn't move.

Brody grabbed Mia's arm and jerked her away from Garrett. "I said let's go. Now."

Mia sniffled and tears rolled down her delicate cheeks.

"Stop crying, or I'll give you something to cry about." Brody still hadn't raised his voice, but the barely controlled anger couldn't be missed.

Mia pulled her arm away and ran toward Gina. "Mommy! Mommy!"

Gina opened her arms and her daughter fell into them. "Daddy's being mean again," Mia cried. Gina rocked her sobbing child. She glared at Brody.

Russ stepped between Brody and Gina. "We need to talk." He crossed the deck and walked though he sliding glass doors without looking back. Brody followed close behind.

I heard Russ's and Brody's raised voices through the closed doors. Apparently, Mia did, too. She nuzzled her face into her mother's neck.

Gina and I said nothing as we waited to see who would emerge unscathed. When both our husbands stepped back outside, Brody's jaw remained clenched. Russ reached over and patted his friend's shoulder.

Brody waved toward Gina signaling that he still wanted to go home. She held Mia close and gave me a one-armed hug. "Tell your dad and Delores thanks for us."

When Russ's arm slipped around me, I knew he needed reassurance as much as I did that everything would be okay for our friends.

"He's angry at the world and thinks everyone's out to get him. I told him he can't keep taking it out on Gina and Mia." Russ watched them walk around the side of the house toward the driveway. "He needs help."

"I hope he gets it."

Livvy

P.S. I think realizing he'd bullied his daughter woke Brody up. He scheduled an appointment with a private counselor—a huge step for a prideful man. Gina told me that she felt real hope for the first time in months, that the man she fell in love with might find his way back to her.

Dear Momma,

CHRISTMAS MORNING our entire clan gathered at Daddy's. Twinkling lights on the Christmas tree in the front window beckoned us inside before we'd even opened the car doors. Daddy and Delores met us on the front porch, wearing matching red caps. I stepped across the threshold and felt like I'd stumbled into a Christmas wonderland. Beside me, Garrett gasped.

Twinkling lights framed every door. Garland graced the mantle and every other flat surface in sight. Delores's collection of nutcrackers rivaled anything the North Pole could possibly offer. Giant ones that stood taller than Garrett greeted us in the foyer. Smaller ones stood sentry amid the greenery and flickering candles. Colorful holiday throws draped the sofa and recliner while an inflatable Santa Claus quivered on the back deck and waved through the sliding glass doors. The Christmas tree glowed in the corner of the family room and dozens of presents spilled from beneath its branches to the hearth of the fireplace, where flames popped and crackled around three huge logs. Christmas carols played softly in the background and the scent of pine, cinnamon and pumpkin filled the air.

Daddy kissed Delores's cheek. "I'm so glad all of us could be together today."

Garrett ran to his great-grandfather and threw his arms around his neck. "Merry Christmas, Great-Grand!" He kissed Daddy's cheek before he whispered, "I made you a present."

I saw Daddy's misty eyes, but he buried his face in Garrett's neck before anyone else noticed. When he looked up again, the tears had evaporated.

We spent that day in a chaotic blur of wrapping paper and ribbon, giggles and gratitude, toys for all ages, apple cider, hot chocolate and mountains of food. More than once, Daddy took up residence in his recliner where he said he just needed to rest his eyes. If I could have gotten away with it, I would have shooed everyone away and staked out the couch for a nap.

After Alex and family left, Russ and I helped scrub away the last reminders of the celebration.

"Anybody want another piece of pie?" Delores asked.

I groaned. "No way, but I'd love some coffee."

Daddy kicked his recliner back and yawned. "What a great day. Worth all the work."

Thirty minutes later, his snores vibrated the hand-made mug Garrett had given him against the table next to him. Russ and I laughed as Delores walked us to the door.

Sunday, December 26, dawned cold and clear. Though temperatures hung in the high thirties, the cloudless blue sky tricked me into thinking a warm breeze might surprise me outside. I dashed out the front door without my jacket to grab the newspaper and realized my mistake before I snatched it from the grass. Even the leafless tree limbs shivered along with me.

I trotted back toward the house and heard the phone ring before I got to the front porch. Once. Twice. Russ answered it, so I headed for the kitchen, poured a mug of coffee and cupped my hands around it, savoring the warmth as much as the aroma. I walked toward the bedroom.

"Are you at the hospital?" Silence as he listened to the response. "What did the doctor say?" Silence.

He glanced up, saw me standing in the door of our bedroom and looked back down at the carpet. My heart hammered in my chest. Something terrible had happened. My hands trembled.

"We're on our way, Delores."

The trembling turned to shaking and coffee sloshed over the rim of the mug onto my hands. Steam rose up. It should have hurt, but I felt nothing. I couldn't take my eyes off Russ even when my tears blurred my vision.

He walked around the bed, took the mug from me and set it on the nightstand. He pulled a tissue from the box nearby and dried my still-damp hands. "We need to go to the hospital, Livvy. It looks like Luther had a stroke."

I sank toward the floor, and Russ grabbed me. He held me tight before we both slid down onto the bed. I grabbed the sleeves of his sweatshirt in my hands and jerked it so tight that the rounded collar pulled away from Russ's neck. "How bad?"

He didn't let go of me. "We need to go to the hospital."

Russ stood up and pulled me to my feet. He took my winter coat out of the closet and held it open while I slipped my arms into it. Then he put on his own coat, picked up my purse from the small corner table and handed it to me. "We'll call Alex when we know more details." He put his hand on the small of my back and pushed me out the front door toward the car.

We made the ten-minute drive without a word. I could smell the suffocating fear that engulfed the car. Even when we stepped into the parking lot, that odor followed us, its tentacles chilling my spine. I stepped faster, desperate to outrun it. Russ sped up, too. I thought it worked, that we had left the terror behind, that we would enter the hospital and find the doctors in control of Daddy's stroke, banishing all his symptoms with an IV or a prescription.

I rushed through the sliding doors to be met by smells and sounds that triggered emotions I didn't want to feel. Alcohol, disinfectant and something else I couldn't quite nail down. I sniffed. *Dear God, it smells like grief.* Tears, used tissues, wilted plants, dying loved ones, and the musky scent of emotional pain sprayed the entryway and halls with a mist I couldn't escape.

Then came the assault on my ears.

Ding. Ding. "Doctor Morton, please pick up on line one."

Seconds later. Ding. Ding. Ding. "Code Blue. ICU. Code Blue. ICU." Flashbacks flooded my mind, of hours waiting with Gina. Desperate to know but dreading the knowledge.

I prayed for hope but found only more fear. I shivered again. Russ spun me around to look at him. "Whatever happens, we'll get through it, Livvy."

We followed the signs to the emergency room and scanned the waiting room for Delores. I spotted her first, sitting in a corner chair, rocking back and forth. The closer I got, the smaller she looked, shrinking under the weight of her anxiety. When she looked up, I saw the puffy lids, chalky cheeks, and tears suspended from her eyelashes like melted icicles. She stared at me, looking, I knew, for comfort.

Delores said, "We had breakfast together. He was still showing off the mug Garrett gave him. He set it in the sink and kissed me. Said he was going to take a shower. I waved him off and kept washing the dishes. I didn't even tell him that I loved him." Her words rushed together faster. Her voice got louder. She grabbed my arm. "Livvy, what if Luther dies and I didn't tell him I loved him? I heard the water in the shower, and then, I heard him fall. I knew it was him. It was so loud. I thought he'd slipped." She took several deep breaths. "It was a stroke."

As Delores spoke, I felt the lump in my throat swell as tears streamed down my face. I needed to hear every detail and, at the same time, I didn't want to hear another word. I pulled Delores close and hugged her. She leaned against my shoulder and sobbed.

Russ sat down on the other side of me. We waited. Every few minutes, one of us bowed our head, and I knew that we offered up a constant stream of prayer. The doctor came out and walked toward us. His fingers picked at the little cap he had just pulled off his head. He held his mouth in a straight line and his eyes offered no reprieve.

He introduced himself before he said, "Mr. Dolan had a major stroke. He's a strong man." He swallowed. "But he's in for a hell of a fight. You need to know that even if he recovers to whatever extent is possible, he won't be the same man. He'll need speech and physical therapy for a very long time. It won't be an easy road for him or for you."

I don't think any of us even blinked while the doctor spoke. Our hope shrunk to a pinpoint, popped and vanished in a puff of dust by the time he finished. "When can we see him?" I asked.

"He's being taken to ICU. You can go in soon, but only one at a time. Try to keep him calm."

"He's awake?"

The doctor nodded. "He's sedated, but awake. You can see him within the next hour or so."

Delores went first. She returned, walking slowly, planting each step like her feet had gone numb, and she needed to be sure they had hit the floor. Her already pale cheeks looked ashen. "You need to go in with her," she said to Russ.

They said Daddy had a major stroke. I learned what that meant when I walked through the curtain of his ICU cubicle. That day I watched my father, that big bull of a man, wither away until he looked like a whispered breath could knock him over. I watched part of his face fall as though his muscles, fully functioning one minute, announced, "I quit" the next. A constant stream of spittle trickled from the corner of his mouth and down his chin, and nothing indicated that he felt it. He made no move to wipe it away. I know it can't be possible, but his muscles atrophied over a matter of hours. An arm and a leg that worked the day before hung uselessly unless someone else moved them for him. That tall masculine body that worked, sweated, hugged, loved, danced and raged, lay in the hospital bed like a deflated balloon. Instead of whistling its way out of him, a little at a time, Daddy's life escaped him that day in one gigantic whoosh.

I'm hurting, Momma, and I really miss you,

Dear Mom,

GRANDDADDY NEVER tried to be flashy or ostentatious in his own life and he certainly never tried to be controlling in mine. But in every memory I have of every major occasion, I see his face. I see his smile. I feel his pride and love. People talk about the background music of their lives. Granddaddy formed a big part of the backbone of mine. He loved me and encouraged me, showed up in good times and bad, even took me in for almost 18 months. He raised me like a dad and spoiled me like a grandfather.

Tall, handsome, strong, smart, capable, successful, and tender. Luther Dolan stood bigger than life. Nothing could diminish him. Until the stroke. Overnight, my imposing granddaddy looked weak and frail, sickly and thin. The strong arms that hoisted me off my feet shrank to stick figures of themselves, incapable of lifting even a coffee mug without assistance. His booming voice dulled to a raspy mumble. His infectious laughter stopped.

And I ached for him, every minute of every day. I hurt for the hurdles he faced just to eat breakfast. I cried more tears than I thought possible.

As a nurse, I grew accustomed to seeing people in the worst of their illness. I went home at night, showered my professional concern for them away, ate dinner, slept without worry and got up to do it again the next day. And then the illness struck someone I loved. The showers didn't help. Dinner brought nausea. Sleep wouldn't come.

Granddaddy's stroke changed my life. Your cancer brought it to a complete halt. God, that damn word changed everything and filled me with terror that grew by the hour. One minute the doctor said he might be able to let you go home, the next your pain refused to submit to the narcotics, and he changed his mind. The cancer roller coaster had bottomed us out again.

I sat on the edge of your bed and wrapped your robe around your shoulders.

"Where are you in the letters?" you asked.

"Granddaddy's stroke, after Christmas."

You closed your eyes. "I hated seeing him that way. He was so independent and vital. For the longest time, I tried to hang on to the memories of him before the stroke, but I see him most vividly after it." You opened your eyes and cupped my cheek. "I don't want that for you." A tear slid down your face. "I don't want you to remember me like this." More tears chased the first. "Promise me you'll hang on to me laughing and dancing and arguing and generally being a pain in the neck." You grabbed my hand. "Promise me."

I wanted to say, "Don't leave me. Please. I still need the arguing mom, the pain-in-the-neck mom. Don't die! I can't get through this."

I actually said, "I promise."

You dozed off. I watched you sleep. When your breathing deepened, I picked another letter from the hatbox and opened it.

I do still need you, Mom.

Dear Momma,

D ADDY SPENT weeks in the hospital followed by months living in a rehab center. I visited him every day and, while I tried not to, I found myself scrutinizing his every move for improvement or decline. In spite of daily speech therapy, I struggled to understand a fraction of what he said. I finally stopped asking him to repeat himself because I couldn't bear to see his angry frustration. He strained and sputtered to get one word out, eventually pounding his good hand on the bed railing and giving up. He fed himself, but couldn't feel the drool on his chin. One leg looked strong and functional, the other dragged behind his walker.

Every night, I dreaded leaving Daddy's room, fearing something awful might happen. When I looked at him in that hospital bed, I knew that it already had. The man I had leaned on for so long had been replaced by a stranger who needed to lean on all of us just to get through a day. And it took all of us. We never set a schedule, but it always worked out that someone showed up in Daddy's room for breakfast, lunch and dinner. We made sure he had on clean pajamas or sweats. We shaved him, helped him brush his teeth and go to the bathroom.

My tough, independent Daddy hated that. The first time I had to help him urinate, I knew we'd crossed a demarcation line in our relationship that marked a permanent change in our lives. Daddy's cheeks flushed with embarrassment. "Alone," he mumbled.

"Daddy, if you want to be alone, then you need to sit down on the toilet, so you won't fall." He shook his head. "I can't leave you if you want to stand up. You need your good hand to hold your, your... so you can aim." I sighed. "And then you can't prop yourself up."

"Get out," he said it as one word. "Get out!"

"Please, Daddy. I can't let you fall. I'll hold you up from the back." My voice cracked.

His wounded pride died a little bit more each day, along with my hope for his recovery. Since Daddy's stroke, the world had tilted on its axis. The parent had regressed into the child, and the child had stepped in as the caretaker/parent. I know that has probably been the cycle of life since the beginning, but that doesn't make it easier or less disturbing.

And even with all of that, we had no idea what lay ahead when the rehab center released Daddy to go home. Delores insisted she didn't need additional help. Her insistence wavered during the first week and crumbled completely in the second. She helped Daddy to bed one night before stepping out to the patio to call me. I recognized her sobs before she said a word.

"I can't do this." She gasped for breath. "By the time I get Luther dressed, we both need a nap. He goes with me to work and sleeps in the recliner in his office. But twice last week we never even made it out our front door." She blew her nose. "His mind is alert. He wants to feel like he's still part of things. And I want him to feel that, but I can't do it all."

Her call came as no surprise to Russ or me. We expected it and had already discussed options. We had one idea in particular we thought might work.

"Russ and I don't expect you to carry the burden of Daddy's care by yourself." I took a quick breath and plunged in. "What if Russ and I moved into the guest bedroom at the house for as long as you need us?"

"No, I don't want you to have to do that," Delores argued.

"We really think it could work for all of us. If we do that, there's always someone available to help get Daddy up or put him in bed at night. If one of us has to run an errand or has an appointment, the others can schedule their day to take up the slack. The three of us can handle whatever needs to be done. And what if the dealership hires an assistant for you and Daddy?"

"An assistant? To do what?"

"To keep an eye on Daddy during the day, help him to the bathroom and keep him mobile. We tell Daddy it's a business assistant, but we actually hire a companion. Since he'd be at the dealership, you could check on him any time. We can try it and see how it works out."

Delores's sniffles slowed until I heard only deep breathing. "I hate for you and Russ to be so inconvenienced, but it could work. At least for a while."

Whoever said, "The only constant in life is change" must have had my life in mind. Russ and I moved to Daddy's.

Doing all this for Daddy reminds me of the months I spent doing it in your last days, Momma. I wish I'd had the maturity back then to know to treasure every minute. I'm grateful that I know that now.

Livvy

December 4, 2011
5:00 AM

Dear Mom,

WITH GARRETT so young, I couldn't visit Granddaddy every day, but I went often. I helped him eat or get out of bed or practice with his walker. And when he needed help in the bathroom the nurse side of me wanted to stride in and assist the patient. Until I looked into my grandfather's eyes and saw his humiliation. I reverted to the mentality of an embarrassed ten-year-old. I buzzed for a nurse's aide and left the room until they finished.

I couldn't imagine your discomfort and Granddaddy's shame. I can now.

Several hours ago, Russ couldn't sleep. He slipped out of your room to get something to drink. Afterward, you tossed and turned and then tried to get out of bed. The IV and its accompanying pole, your meds and tangled sheets made for a daunting combination, almost impossible to escape from alone. By the time I got to you and pulled the covers away so that you could move your legs, the damage had been done. You'd wet the bed. I picked up the call button to ring for the nurse, but you grabbed my hand to stop me. Even in the darkened room, I saw tears glisten in your eyes.

"Please help me clean up and change clothes before Russ comes back." You ran a finger beneath your nose. "I don't want him to see this." This time, you grabbed a tissue from the box and blew. "I don't want him to see me like this."

I opened a drawer in the dresser and pulled out a fresh nightgown. "I'll help you into the bathroom and we'll get you changed. But let me call the nurse so they clean up the bed while we do that, okay?"

You nodded. I could barely hear you, but I know you said, "Thank you."

Once you finished using the toilet, I gave you a quick sponge bath and slid the gown over your head. Your tears never stopped.

"I'm sorry to be so much trouble."

I squeezed you as tight as I dared. "You're not any trouble, Mom. None. You ready to get back in bed?"

You nodded. "I'm tired."

By the time Russ returned, your snores filled the room. While he never knew what happened, the doctor decided you needed to be catheterized.

You're slipping away from us a little more every day.

Dear Momma,

THE SLIGHTEST movement required Daddy's total concentration and focus. Every minute of every day, he looked dour and angry because he had no control of the fallen side of his face. Once in a very great while he laughed. Not his familiar, jubilant guffaw, but a spooky cackle. So much so, that when Garrett heard it, he ran to his mother's side until the frightening noises stopped. I saw the distress in Daddy's eyes every time he realized that the distorted sound of his laughter terrified his only grandson.

Russ, Delores and I thought a family get-together might lift Daddy's spirits, so we planned an Easter party. Even if it did nothing for him, it might do wonders for the rest of us.

Gina, Brody and Mia arrived first and pitched right in with setting things up. Gina and I worked like Siamese twins—the kitchen version—pulling pies and cookies from the oven and rearranging the refrigerator to accommodate pasta salad and dozens of hard-boiled eggs.

"How are things with you and Brody?" I asked.

Gina grinned. "Pretty damn great. The counselor helped him get control of his anger and his fears. The man I married finally came home." She looked out the window and watched her husband race her daughter to the dock, stumbling along the way, so Mia could win.

I hugged her. "I knew he'd find his way back. He loves you too much not to."

Gina grabbed a pile of paper plates and a basket of silverware and carried them out to a table on the deck. Before she stepped back inside for more, she stopped at Daddy's chair and stooped down to talk to him. Feeling like an intruder glimpsing their private moment, I watched my best friend help my father take a sip of his iced tea. She pulled a napkin off the table and gently wiped his mouth. I willed away the tears that came without warning.

I heard a car in the drive and headed to the front door. Alex, Will and Garrett parked behind Brody's car. Will's family from Burgaw pulled in right behind them. I held open the front door while they all slipped past me, laden with Easter baskets filled to overflowing with food, chocolate and plastic eggs.

Once the crowd had filled their plates and found a place to sit, Alex and Will stood up. Will beat his fork against his Michelob can. Alex said, "Can you come up here and help us with something now, Garrett?"

He knocked his chair over when he jumped out of it. "Is it time for our secret, Mommy?"

Alex nodded.

"What secret?" Mia asked, looking peeved that she hadn't been let in on it.

Garrett ignored her and ran toward his parents.

Alex reached under the table and pulled out a beautiful basket filled with plastic eggs. She handed it to her son. "Would you please give one of these to everyone?"

"Yes, ma'am!"

He dashed around the tables handing out little plastic eggs to each person. We held them, unsure of what to do.

Will said, "Having both of our families together today made this the perfect time to make our announcement." He looked around. "Does everybody have an egg?"

"Yes," we all yelled.

Will nodded. "Open them up and check out our surprise."

Russ and I twisted our eggs apart at the same time. A tiny plastic baby tumbled out onto my lap and another one landed on the table in front of Russ. His brow furrowed at first, but we both realized what it meant at the same time. Jenci and Jeff did the same. We shouted, "A baby!" And then we said it again, in an awed whisper. "A baby."

Garrett stood tall, stuck his chest out and announced, "I'm gonna be a big brother." His eyes gleamed while he rubbed his mother's tummy. "We're havin' a baby!"

"Lady Bug's having another baby," Daddy mumbled.

All Garrett's previous fears of Daddy's sounds and movements disappeared and he threw his arms around his grandfather's neck. "Another one just like me, Great-Grand! And we can teach it to fish and crab swim." He grinned. "You and me and the baby."

Daddy choked back a sob and Garrett squeezed tighter.

I swiped away a tear and noticed everyone around me doing the same thing. We all cried with joy for the new addition. But we also cried for our loss, that the vibrant great-grandfather Garrett had known couldn't be the same with this child. And I felt a twinge of fear. I quelled it with a quick prayer. "Please protect this baby." I looked at Garret, healthy now, but so frail in those first days. "Please."

Livvy

August 12, 2001
Happy Birthday

Dear Momma,

I HAD three more years before I could retire from the plant, but for months I'd been feeling like I could do more good at the dealership. *I'm too close to retirement. I can't quit now,* I thought. *You're being selfish, I argued. They need you.* My head throbbed and my heart ached.

On a rare, lazy Saturday morning, the four of us had barely finished our first cup of coffee when I tried to express my jumbled thoughts. As soon as the torrent began, I felt a release like a pent up geyser finally exploding. Delores, Daddy and Russ listened while I spilled my guilt.

Before I'd put the final period on my monologue, Russ said, "I can't believe you brought that up today. I've been toying with an idea for a while now that I think could work." He looked at Daddy without a glance at me. "Luther, you know I've been helping out in your service department a couple of days a week." He smiled. "More cars, more problems, more people, employees and customers and a lot more challenges than my garage. I love it. What would you think if I sold my place to manage the service department fulltime?"

Daddy's head bobbed up and down so fast he looked like an emaciated bobble-head doll. A half-smile broke out on his face. Delores exhaled her relief. I seemed to be the only one at the table with a corncob up her butt.

"You can't sell the garage," I argued. "Your father started it. You put everything you had into that place. You can't give up your family business to help mine. It's not right."

"I've gone as far with the garage as I can unless I build another one. The dealership offers so much more and I'd feel like I was doing something to build a future for Alex and Will, if they want it someday." He reached across the table and took my hand in his. "Livvy, don't blow your pension and benefits when you've only got another couple of years to go," Russ said. "You can come to the dealership when you retire."

Daddy nodded again and pounded his bad arm on the table. "Do it later." Daddy struggled to articulate each word.

I leaned back in my chair and looked around the table. Delores nodded at me before she reached over and grabbed Daddy's strong hand in a display of unity. Russ smirked.

"I'm feeling outnumbered," I whined.

No one responded.

"Fine." I rolled my eyes. "Whatever."

Once again, the Dolan/Montgomery clan came together to make it all work.

Livvy

Dear Momma,

SEPTEMBER 11, 2001. People used to ask, "Where were you when Kennedy was shot?" Now it's "Where were you when the Towers came down?" We all know. We all remember.

I drove to the plant and clocked in like every other day for the last twenty-five years. Nothing looked or felt any different. No omen indicated anything other than a typical day ahead.

I shoved my purse into the bottom drawer of my desk and slammed it shut. Before the backlog of paperwork could ambush me, I headed for the coffee pot in the break room. I poured myself a cup and inhaled, sending a caffeine rush to my brain. Then I trudged back to my office and started at the top of the pile.

The coffee vanished, and I'd only made it through a fraction of what I needed to read when I heard yelling on the plant floor. I ran downstairs and found half a dozen people clustered in a semi-circle around the small television in the corner of the break room.

One guy asked, "How the hell do you fly a plane into the World Trade Center?"

"Maybe the pilot had a heart attack or something. Man, that smoke looks bad."

The clock over the door read eight fifty-five. People crowded into the room, hollering for others to join them. "Get in here! Hurry!"

The twenty-two-inch screen made the unfolding scene look surreal. The stunned voices of Matt Lauer and Katie Couric struggling to maintain some semblance of professionalism made it undeniable. That's when I realized that for so many at the plant, New York City might not be home, but they had grown up as close to that vibrant, now damaged city as I had to Raleigh. Most of them had probably been in the World Trade Center, knew someone who worked there. I looked around and saw the stricken faces. I moved toward Gina and put my arm around her shoulder. She held her hand over her mouth while tears spilled down her cheeks. We watched in disbelief as a huge jetliner crashed into the second tower.

"What the hell was that?" someone asked.

The news anchors sounded as confused as we did. They played the video again. Gasps filled the room as we realized the second tower had been hit. I heard wails echo all over the building.

Another news report broke in, this time from Washington D.C. A jetliner had crashed into the Pentagon.

"My God, we're being attacked."

Not one person moved while we watched the smoke roil and flames billow from the World Trade Center. Choked sobs filled my ears when we saw people jump out of windows from the floors above the flames.

If I hadn't had my arm around Gina, she would have fallen to the floor when Tower Two crashed to the ground in a gut-wrenching scene of falling concrete, smoke and flames. I led her to a chair and helped her sit down. My hand moved in circles around her back while she sobbed, but I could find no words of comfort. I couldn't speak at all.

Moments later, a fourth plane crashed in a field in Pennsylvania and less than thirty minutes after that, the first tower that had been hit collapsed.

More dazed people crammed themselves into the break room. Many held hands. Tears streaked every stunned cheek.

Gina's body stiffened beneath my hand. She whispered, "How many more planes?"

No one responded. We didn't know the answer and we feared the possibilities.

September 11, 2001. No country declared war on us that day. That would have been too easy. This sucker punch came from an ideology. And I don't think we had a clue what to do about it.

Alex gave birth to Darcy Cathleen Crenshaw on September 15, 2001. New life. Innocence, unmarred by evil or hatred or fear. In the midst of such raw pain and grief, our family experienced the greatest joy since Garrett came home from the hospital.

When I stepped into Alex's hospital room, I saw Will first. He hovered near his wife's bed, alternately beaming pride and relief that his little girl had arrived.

Alex cradled the baby in her arms. She looked up at me and said, "Look at her, Mom." Tears filled her eyes while her smile lit up her face. "She's healthy."

All the medical assurances of the miniscule chance that this baby could have the same health issues Garrett had at birth did nothing to assuage Will and Alex's worry. Statistics hadn't helped me or Russ with it either. Prayers for our grandchild's wellbeing crossed our lips first thing in the morning and last thing at night. Alex rarely expressed her fear, but I saw it every time she gave her growing tummy a love pat.

Darcy weighed in at seven pounds, six ounces. She had the most beautiful bald head, blue eyes, dainty fingers and fully formed, fully functioning set of lungs in history. Her ear-piercing wails sounded like a Mozart sonata to me.

I unwrapped her blanket long enough to do the finger and toe count exam known to mothers and grandmothers everywhere. I scanned for birthmarks and moles. With one glance, I saw that she got Alex's smile. Will bragged that she'd gotten his ears. And, Momma, she has your heart-shaped pout. I see flawless perfection in Darcy Cathleen Crenshaw.

You'd be proud of your great-granddaughter, Momma.

Livvy

December 4, 2011
9:30 AM

Dear Mom,

WE NEVER discussed our fears during my second pregnancy. I saw yours. Now, I know you recognized mine, too.

I couldn't imagine another crisis with a newborn. I didn't think I could watch another child suffer. For nine months, I felt suffocated by my own worry. The stress lay on my chest like Darcy sat on my bladder. And then, the doctor said, "You have a healthy baby girl." The worry, the stress, the fear all fluttered away like a flock of starlings, moving in many directions, but somehow ending up traveling together. I felt lighter. Not just baby-weight smaller, but freer.

Now, I sit by your bedside and I'm suffocating all over again. So is Russ. Just a little while ago, I looked at him. His right hand clutched his chest. His mouth hung open and he struggled for breath. I jumped up and ran to his chair.

"Is it chest pain?" I grabbed his arm and put my fingers to his wrist to check his pulse.

He shrugged me off and jerked his hand away. "I'm okay." He looked at me before he turned back to you. "Your mother always took my breath away. Now, I can't breathe because I can't see the future without her." He buried his face in his hands. His shoulders shook.

I knelt beside him and held him while he cried.

How do we go on without you, Mom?

Dear Momma,

DADDY AND I offered Russ part ownership in the dealership. He turned us down saying he needed to earn the respect of the people who had worked there for years. He did exactly that. In a matter of months, he demonstrated his knowledge of engines, cars and customers. Those who felt they deserved the promotion to service manager came around to rally behind Russ.

The dealership continued to grow, so much so that Will and Alex took notice. They showed up at the house one Saturday morning bearing grandbabies and hot Krispy Kreme doughnuts.

Garrett grabbed his Batman fishing pole from the garage and headed to the dock.

"Be careful," Alex yelled as she slipped Darcy into the old wind-up baby swing. Alex gave the seat a gentle push. Darcy cooed and babbled before the swaying soothed her to sleep.

"Will and I would like to spend some time at the dealership." Alex kicked off the conversation. "We'd like to learn the business."

"What brought this on?" I asked.

Alex reached over and rubbed her grandfather's arm. "We want to help." She smiled at Russ. "Russ has been so excited about what he's doing there. Even Mom looks forward to going in every Saturday."

"Even Mom?" I asked. "If Mom can do it, anybody can."

Alex laughed. "That came out wrong. I just meant that Granddaddy always wanted the dealership to be a family business. Now, it really is and I want to be part of that. The dealership is a family legacy and for the first time in my life that means something to me."

She glanced toward the dock and saw Garrett sitting in the oversized white Adirondack that his great-grandfather loved. I had gotten him a *Star Wars* lawn chair, but he far preferred the other. Garrett kicked his feet back and forth while his fishing pole dangled in the water. Alex moved to Darcy and turned the crank on the swing. A slight push started the gentle motion again before her sleeping baby noticed it had stopped.

Alex's world changed course after the births of her children. Her self-revolving universe shifted to child-centered.

Daddy grinned the lopsided smile we'd all grown accustomed to and beat his good fist on the table. "I knew she would come around," he mumbled.

I asked the obvious questions. "What about nursing? And Will's accounting firm?"

"I can stay part time at the hospital and add a couple of days a week at the dealership. Will's offering to do the bills, the books, the taxes, whatever will help. He'll stay with his firm and do all of that on the side."

"You've thought this through."

"I have, Mom. I want to do this."

The swing stopped and this time Darcy fisted her little hands and let out a high-pitched screech that scattered the seagulls who hovered nearby.

Delores reached into the swing and cradled the screaming baby in her arms. "I'd say we have a real family business here."

Alex picked up her coffee and raised it in a toast. We clinked our mugs to hers.

"To family," she said.

"To family," we agreed.

Livvy

Dear Momma,

I'VE RUN into Wilbur Walker II maybe half a dozen times since the plant fired him. Every time, he looks wilder, crazier, angrier. And every time, if he speaks at all, he mentions you.

This time, I'd just stepped out of a convenience store, and I saw him sitting in his car. He didn't wave or acknowledge me at all.

I took a deep breath. "How are you, Wilbur?"

He stared at me. "You look more like your damn mother all the time."

The imprint of your life remains, Momma, even after all these years.

I got in my car and locked the doors.

After your death, I wrote to you when my grief threatened to explode. The letters seemed cathartic, easing the pressure off an emotional valve. Not only did they give me an outlet, they helped me maintain a connection to you that I didn't want to lose.

Over time, I learned to live without you. Once in a while, you flash through my mind like a comet, fading quickly. But two days a year, you latch on and won't let go. Mother's Day and your birthday, I can't escape your memory, no matter how hard I try to outrun it. You wake me in the morning and harass me until I put pen to paper.

I still love you more than you could ever know, but the letter writing has evolved now. It feels more like an exorcism that brings me peace.

I miss you,

Livvy

Dear Mom,

EVERY TIME I think I can't do this anymore—I can't watch your pain, I can't stay in this hospital room one more minute, I CAN'T LET YOU DIE—I see what you are actually going through. You face your death. I face my life without you in it. You live the pain. I only see it. Then I realize that I can do whatever you need, for as long as you need it.

I continued to cling to my hope that you would beat this and that our family would get another healing miracle. Until last night.

Your pain brought Russ to his knees beside your bed. He whispered, "Livvy, I love you. You don't have to fight anymore. I'll make sure Alex and the kids are okay. I promise you. You can let go now, baby."

On the other side of your bed, I reached out to hold your hand, but pulled back, afraid that the slightest sensation would only add to your agony.

"Mom, don't do this for me." I couldn't control my sobs. My words came out garbled and choked. "Please don't hang on for me. You taught me to be independent. You showed me how to be strong. You can rest now."

Russ knelt on that hard hospital tile for over an hour, stroking your arm and hand. He laid his head on your bed until I thought he might have fallen asleep. When he stood up, his eyes had swollen so much from the constant flow of tears that he could barely see through the slits.

When he moved, you startled and struggled to sit up. The fear I saw in your eyes terrified me. Russ dropped back down to soothe you.

"Why is he here?" you screamed. "Make him go away!"

"Who?" I asked.

You pointed to the corner of the room. "He won't stop staring at me." You grabbed Russ's arm and screeched, "Make him stop."

Before Russ or I could respond, your nurse stepped into the room. She turned to where you had been pointing and said, "She asked you to leave. Now." She escorted the figment of your delusion out the door before she closed it. Then she turned to Russ and me and said, "Hallucinations can be a combination of the pain medication and oxygen deprivation. They're fairly common. Arguing with her or trying to convince her that what she sees isn't real will probably only upset her more."

She checked your chart and IV line. "How's your pain level, Mrs. Montgomery?"

You just stared at her so Russ answered for you. "It's been bad. She moans and cries."

"We'll increase the dosage right away." She looked at Russ and me. "We'll be giving her enough medication that she'll probably be unconscious most of the time now, but she won't be in pain."

I couldn't move. Russ nodded through his tears.

You can't take much more, Mom. I know that. It's okay for you to let go.

Dear Momma,

ON JULY 8, the alarm jangled at six thirty AM. Delores rolled out of bed and walked Daddy to the bathroom like always. She helped him shower and shave. Together, they dressed him in khaki pants and a polo shirt. He slipped his feet into deck shoes.

I got to the kitchen first, filled the pot with water and scooped coffee into the machine's filter. I hit the start button, pulled four mugs from the cabinet and set them on the counter.

Daddy used his walker to get to the family room where he plopped down in his recliner. I fixed him a mug and set it on the table next to him. "Good morning, Daddy." I kissed his cheek and dashed toward my room to get ready for work.

"Mornin'," he answered to my backside.

I jumped in and out of the shower, applied a little lipstick and dried my hair. Then I threw on clothes, kissed Russ good-bye and headed back to the family room.

"Love you," Daddy said when I walked through the room.

I turned back to him, bent down and kissed the top of his head. "I love you so much, Daddy. Have a good day."

I remember sunshine, blue sky, and billowing clouds. A light breeze made it feel cooler than the thermostat claimed. I turned my radio up, rolled my window down and sang at the top of my lungs. Only once during the twenty-minute drive to the plant did anyone in a nearby car give me the give-it-a-rest glare. And I ignored him. I remember being happy that morning.

When I pulled into a parking space at work, my cell phone rang. I shifted the car into park and grabbed my tote bag off the passenger seat.

"It's always at the bottom of the bag," I grumbled, shoving tissues and my wallet out of the way. I hit talk. "Helloooooo."

Russ said, "Where are you, Livvy?"

"At the plant." His tone set off alarms in my heart. "What's wrong?" My voice carried no trace of the singsong giddiness that had been there moments before.

"Are you still driving?"

"I'm in the parking lot. You're scaring me, Russ. What's wrong?"

"It's Luther, babe. You need to come back home, right away." His voice cracked.

Stars floated across my vision and a loud ringing echoed in my ears. My heartbeat drummed over the vibrations. I leaned against the headrest. My arms grew so heavy, I didn't think I could hold the phone up. I didn't want to anyway. I didn't want to hear any more.

"Livvy, are you there? Are you all right?"

"I'm here," I said. "What happened?"

"Your Daddy had another stroke."

I wanted to ask if the ambulance took him to Cape Fear Hospital or New Hanover. I wanted to ask where I should go. I wanted to ask if Russ had called Alex because she'd been scheduled to work that day and she would take care of her granddaddy. I wanted to ask when I could see him. I wanted to ask why Russ told me to come home when clearly I needed to get to the hospital. I wanted to, but I didn't, because his meaning exploded in my head like a nuclear weapon.

"Luther's gone, Livvy. He just slumped over in his chair. It happened so fast."

"No. That can't be," I argued. "I just kissed him good-bye." My heart sped up, faster and faster with my words. "I just saw him. I just kissed him." I screamed, "He can't be gone!"

Gina must have pulled into the parking space next to me. She stood beside my car and heard every word. Her hands shook and her face looked as ashen as mine felt. Tears rolled down her cheeks. Sobbing, she reached through the window and touched my shoulder. I jerked away. I didn't need her comfort. I needed my daddy.

Russ kept talking. "Don't try to drive," he insisted. "Stay there. I'll come get you." I wanted to take that damn phone and throw it out the car window. I wanted to watch it bounce and shatter on the pavement before I stomped on every piece until those God-awful words stopped flowing out of it. "Livvy? Are you all right?"

Gina stuck her arm back through the window and turned her hand palm up in front of me. "Give me the phone, Livvy."

I turned to look at her. Her lips moved. I thought she said something, but I had no idea what. Her lips moved again, but I couldn't hear anything over the incessant ringing in my ears.

She took hold of the phone and pried my fingers loose. "I'll give it right back," she promised.

"Russ? It's Gina." She listened. "I'll drive her home." She nodded her head as though Russ could see her. "We're on our way."

Gina opened the car door. "Let's put you in the other seat and I'll take you home."

I stared up at her and got out of the car. I walked to the passenger side and opened that door. My purse sat on the seat so I grabbed it and threw it into the back. Old receipts and loose change spilled out and scattered on the floor. A tube of lipstick rolled all the way to the other side of the car. I felt the ground tremble. Was it an earthquake or my world crumbling around me? I would rather have faced an earthquake.

Gina slid into the car and opened her arms to me. I leaned on her and cried until my tears soaked through her shirt. When I pulled back and tried to wipe away the stream, it wouldn't stop.

Gina grabbed my hand and squeezed. "I'm so sorry, Livvy. I hope you know how much Luther meant to me." Her voice cracked and her own tears flowed. "I'll miss him with you."

She drove in silence. I didn't open my eyes until I heard Gina say, "We're here."

I lifted my head, looked at the house my father had called home for decades and burst into tears all over again. They say your life flashes in front of you when you're drowning. I sure as hell felt like I was going under as memories flooded my mind. Torturous rapid-fire machine-gun bursts to the brain, filled with joy and pain, love and regret. I begged them to stop, but they kept coming. I saw Daddy on the porch, in the yard, on the dock and slumped over in his recliner. I saw him teaching me how to fish and drive a stick shift. I saw him driving away with Alex when he knew I couldn't take care of her and I saw him crying on the day he gave her back to me. I saw flashes of him with you, Momma, and with Nora Jean and Delores. I remembered adoring him, hating him, rebelling against him, and begging for his forgiveness. I saw the times I needed him and the final days, when he needed me. I saw him strong and weak, healthy and sick, loving and angry. I banged my head against the headrest over and over, trying to make it stop.

"Are you okay?" Gina asked.

Russ opened the car door and pulled me out and into his arms. I clung to him and sobbed. My rubbery legs wouldn't hold me up, and if I let go of my husband, I would have collapsed. He helped me walk to the house. Gina followed us.

Delores sat on the sofa next to Daddy's chair. Even after I walked in, she didn't stop staring at it, like she hadn't even realized that I'd stepped into the room.

Gina spoke first. "Did you get hold of Alex?"

Russ nodded. "I called her after the EMTs took him. She's on her way."

Delores finally looked up at me. "I tried to take care of him," she said, her face contorted by grief and guilt. "I tried, Livvy."

I dropped down on the couch beside her, and we fell into one another's arms. Our choked sobs lasted several minutes, maybe longer. I don't know. "You did take care of him, Delores," I said. "And you loved him. We all know that." I sobbed again. "And he loved you. He came back to life when he found you."

Cars came and went that day. People offered condolences and help. They brought food and flowers. Finally, they left us alone with our pain. You know, people who grieve feel their loss every second of every day. Those around them tire of the high-RPM-emotion quickly. They want to be happy. I'd like to feel that way again, too. I'd like this ache to go away, but I can't leave the pain, Momma, so I have to wait, once more, for it to leave me.

Livvy

P.S. Have I told you how much I hate being an only child? How much I always hated it? I'm the only survivor of the original Dolan threesome. The last woman standing. Childhood memories descend in my mind like a fog and I need to remember it all. I want to ask someone if I remembered it right. But I'm alone. I have no one to validate my memories. No one to say, "You're not crazy. That really happened."

No one to ask, "Do you remember when Daddy said…", "when Momma did…", "when this happened" or "when we did that"? I'm fifty-five years old and no matter how ridiculously childish it sounds, I still want my Momma and Daddy. I don't want to feel so terribly alone.

Dear Mom,

M Y TEAR-filled eyes blur the words I'm trying to write.
You and Granddaddy had always been the foundation of
my life, for as long as I could remember. We had all
watched his strength and vitality diminish more every day after his
stroke. But then he died. And the gaping hole left by his life seemed
like a crater. Nothing filled the loss. Nothing calmed the ache.

Garrett insisted on going to the funeral. At first, I fought it. I
feared he would be left with memories that are the stuff of
nightmares. Instead, he comforted us. Do you remember?

He looked so grown-up in his new suit although the way he
fiddled with the clip-on tie gave it away that he had never been in
one before. He sat still and somber, moving only to scoot closer to
me. The coffin, draped in floral arrangements, sat in the front of the
church. Garrett stared. "Is Great-Grand in there?" he asked. I
nodded. He swallowed hard.

The pastor offered us biblical comfort, spiritual hope, and
amusing anecdotes. I fought tears while my six-year-old son held
my hand. I glanced down at him thinking that he looked like the
perfect combination of Will and Granddaddy. He even possessed a
great deal of their strength. Right up until the pastor said, "Luther
Dolan loved his family. And he didn't just give lip service to that
love. He worked hard for them, spent time with them, treasured his
family like something precious in his life. I remember him telling
me about his great-grandson, Garrett." Shocked to hear his name,
Garrett sat up a little bit straighter. "Luther told me about teaching
Garrett to fish. He said Garrett soaked up everything he said, like a

sponge, that he watched Luther bait a hook once and did it perfectly all by himself every time after that. Luther said that to him there was nothing better than time with Garrett."

My son looked up at me with tears running down his face. He crawled into my lap and buried his head in my shoulder. He'd been strong for as long as he could. Then he was just a little boy who missed his great-grandfather.

I missed him, too. I still do.

May 9, 2004
Happy Mother's Day

Dear Momma,

I NEVER got to the point that I could drive by Babies Hospital and not think of you working there. I wanted to see your car in the parking lot and stop by for a quick visit. The building reminded me of you without it having to hurt, but then they started talking about tearing the old building down and the pain came roaring back.

I followed the news reports like a fanatic. A dedicated group fought the demolition. They tried to have the building designated as a historic site. When they lost the battle, it felt like destroying a piece of my family history just to make way for some tacky new construction. On that blustery day in January, they might as well have torn a chunk of my heart right out of my chest and let it tumble to the ground with the other discarded bricks.

The morning started out overcast and chilly and when the clouds parted and the sun glowed, it somehow felt even colder. I wrapped a scarf around my neck and pulled gloves out of my coat pocket as I walked toward the people standing in the parking lot across the street. A few held homemade protest signs. Most just watched, as bricks and mortar fell, sporadically at first, then crashing down in heaps. No one spoke, which suited me. I had come to say good-bye.

I hid my red-rimmed eyes behind my favorite Audrey Hepburn-style sunglasses. Salty grit from the Intracoastal spray coated the lenses. The cold breeze dried my tears before they traveled halfway down my cheeks and their salt combined with the ocean's leavings until I felt my face stiffen and crack with every movement.

I felt you there, Momma. I caught a glimpse of your long brown hair blowing in the wind. The scent of your Shalimar lingered in the air. I heard you whisper so softly that no one else could have heard, "The key to life, Livvy, is knowing when to hang on and when to let go."

The previous six months taught me that I had still a lot to learn about letting go. Truth be told, I sucked at it. I hung on until my fingernails ripped off.

In a matter of hours, a mountain of rubble lay where Babies Hospital once stood. Nurse CiCi Dolan could no longer wander those empty halls. The building took those memories with it like a black hole sucking up everything in its path.

I felt the sting of loss. From the faces around me, I knew many others did, too.

When the noise of the machinery died down and the dust settled, a couple of hardy souls ventured across Eastwood Road and picked up bricks to take home. I joined them, scanning the mess in front of me in search of a few perfect mementoes. I found half a dozen whole, unbroken bricks that would find a place of reverence in my home and Alex's.

One brick in particular reminded me of you, Momma. When I held it up to the sunlight, the variation of color swirled and swayed, dancing in my hand. I imagined that it held music locked inside it, throbbing to be released. And when I turned it over, I noticed a jagged hairline crack on the backside. I knew if I hit that crazy crack just right, the brick would fracture and come apart in my hands. I also knew that if I treated it gently and held it with kid gloves, no one else would ever see the potential for destruction that lay hidden inside that beautifully formed rectangle.

I named that brick CiCi. Its flaw will remain our secret. It's probably best that way. Your secrets have always been safe with me.

I love you, Momma,

Dear Momma,

DARCY AND Garrett spent the weekend with Russ and me. They entertained us, made us laugh and helped us forget. Right up until Russ walked into the backyard and needed to have his heart jump-started as he watched Darcy, lying flat in Garrett's red wagon, hanging on to the sides as it raced down the hill toward the drainage ditch.

Darcy looked exactly like you, Momma. Her thick, wavy brown hair flowed halfway down her back. Her eyes sparkled with humor and mischief, and she had learned that she could use the adorable pout she'd been born with to get just about anything she wanted. Two major differences between you and her: she seldom used her pouty powers for evil and the tiny daredevil didn't have a girly bone in her almost three-year-old body.

Oh, and one of the things that Garrett loved best about his little sister—if Darcy had fear, she never, ever showed it.

That Saturday afternoon, Garrett and his neighborhood buddy built a makeshift ramp with plywood and bricks they nabbed out of the garage. As usual, once they finished their construction project and chose the perfect vehicle to try it out, they still needed a test pilot.

"I can do it," Darcy announced when the boys showed her their design. She climbed into the wagon and yelled, "Push me, Garrett."

Garrett looked at his friend. "I'll push her and you stand at the bottom of the hill to stop the wagon before it goes into the ditch."

The other little boy ran down the hill while Garrett showed Darcy where to grip the sides of the wagon. Then he grabbed the handle and lined the wheels up with the ramp.

He yelled, "Ready! Set! Go!" One shove and within seconds the wagon hit the plywood, rolled up the ramp and flew several feet before it slammed back to the ground and sped down the hill. Garrett's friend moved to block the wagon, but as it aimed right for him, his wide eyes said Darcy might well be on her own long before she hit the ditch.

That's when Russ walked out the sliding glass doors, sprinted across the deck, and bolted down the hill in time to grab the long black handle dragging behind the wagon. He jerked it to a stop and stared back and forth from Garrett to Darcy, too shocked to even voice his anger.

Garrett had sense enough to look sheepish while he kicked at the grass with the toe of his tennis shoe.

Darcy, on the other hand, jumped up, breathless, and yelled, "I wanna do it again!"

Beautiful and reckless. Remind you of anyone, Momma?

Livvy

Dear Momma,

THE DEALERSHIP couldn't have been better. Alex worked every chance she got and Will settled into his role as our on-call financial advisor. Russ loved the service department and I hadn't missed a Saturday since I started working there. Sales and profits increased.

But while Delores loved the office, she no longer felt the same way about Daddy's house.

Daddy left the house to me, but gave Delores the option of living there for as long as she liked. As it turned out, she liked it only while Daddy lived there, too. She said being alone in that big isolated house scared her. I bet she saw Daddy in every corner and felt him on the morning breeze. She told me she could still smell him on his side of the bed. More than once, she'd hollered for him to bring her a clean towel when she turned off the shower. And then she'd remember and her tears merged with the water running off her body.

When I went to his house, I expected to see the active, vibrant man I'd known all my life stride up the dock. I'd see him sweaty and smiling, hauling in an overflowing crab trap. I'd blink and the vision would disappear. The sliding glass doors remained closed and the smell of fresh crab faded. It hurt me and must have haunted Delores.

So, Russ and I spent one entire weekend helping her move back into her old house. That Sunday night, after Russ and I collapsed into bed, I felt him staring at me in the dark.

"What?" I asked.

"What you want to do with the house?"

"What house?" I asked, stalling in an effort to avoid the emotion that came with the question.

Russ said nothing, just kept staring.

"I don't know, and I don't want to think about it." I rolled over and slapped my pillow down over my head.

Russ wiggled closer and snuck his face under the fabric. "Can I come in?"

"Only if you agree not to talk about Daddy's house," I pleaded.

"Can't do that, Livvy. You know you can't leave it sitting there empty for too long."

I snorted. "Damned if I do. Damned if I don't."

"You have options."

"Like what?"

"Move in, rent it, sell the place, let Alex and Will live there."

I grabbed the pillow and tucked it under my head. Then I rolled onto my side.

"I don't know if I can live there. It makes me so sad."

He nodded. "It does me, too. That will probably get better over time. We could try it for a couple of days. See how it goes. Come back here if it gets to be too much."

"Why does that sound so reasonable and feel so hard?"

Russ tucked a strand of hair behind my ear. "It'll be hard at first." He ran his fingers down my arm. "How did you feel when you moved in here to your momma's house?"

"No comparison," I said. "Daddy's house looks like he walked out the door to go fishing, and he'll be right back. Momma had been gone for years. The renters had painted and changed things up, so a lot of the house didn't even look the same." I glanced around the bedroom. "This was the only room that gave me problems. I used to sleep on the couch to keep from seeing her in here."

Russ leaned over and kissed me, slow and deep. "Is she gone now?"

"Mostly," I answered before I pulled his face even closer to mine.

The next Friday, Russ convinced me to pack a bag. We drove to Daddy's and pulled into the long circular driveway. Russ got out of the car, walked around to the trunk and jerked our luggage out. My fingers picked at my jeans, but my legs wouldn't move. Even though I'd been back in

Daddy's house many times since he died, I'd never thought about living there. My stomach lurched, just a little, in revolt.

Russ walked back and opened my door. He offered me his hand and waited until I took it. I stepped out and leaned into him.

When Daddy and Delores lived there, the house drew me in like an embrace. Now, it felt like the warmth had died with him. No welcoming light glowed from the windows. It looked like an abandoned shell. I shivered.

"You okay?" Russ asked.

"I don't know if I can do this." I looked up at him. "It feels like all my memories, good and bad, are waiting inside that door."

"They are," Russ agreed. "But you need to confront them because the memories are trapped in your head, not that house." He put his arm around my shoulder. "When I gave the keys to my daddy's house to the new owners, I didn't hand over the memories, too. I had to deal with them. Sometimes, I still do." He kissed the top of my head. "It'll take a while, but I promise that you'll wake up one morning and remember something from the past that you'd rather forget, but it won't bowl you over. You'll realize how far you've come."

"You sound like AA. Can't promise exactly when, but God will remove your desire for alcohol. You'll wake up one day and not remember the last time you wanted a drink."

He nodded. "Same principle. Time heals all wounds kind of thing."

"Does it?" I looked up into his face and saw his eyes cloud over with sadness.

"Sometimes."

I kissed his cheek.

Russ stepped inside first and turned on every light he could reach. It worked, at first. My ghosts scattered in the glow. I sensed a few clustered in dark corners, but as long as I moved from circle to circle of lamp light, they kept their distance.

I thought I caught a glimpse of Daddy sitting on the deck in the dark, but then Russ closed the shades on the sliding glass doors, and he was gone.

Russ headed to the guest room and tossed our bags on the queen-sized bed. I stood on the other side of the family room by the door to the master bedroom. I remembered that last day when we moved the things Delores wanted to her house. She finished in that bedroom, looked back once and closed the door. I found it symbolic at the time. Just as significant now that I would have to reopen it at some point to move forward in my life.

"Let's cross that bridge another day," Russ suggested.

He snatched up the television remote, found an episode of *Wheel of Fortune* and clicked the volume up until it vibrated even in the kitchen. I guess he thought light and sound would drive out my goblins. Once again, Russ knew exactly what to do. When to leave me alone and when to stand by my side. When to let me cry in the dark and when to turn on the light. I never did anything to deserve this man, but I'm so grateful that he's mine.

We've stayed at Daddy's house four times now. Each time gets a little bit easier. I still don't know if I can live there, but I don't have to make that decision right away. I won't decide anything until I know whether to hang on or let go.

Dear Momma,

THIRTY-one years I put into the plant. I felt so inadequate when I started, but they gave me a chance. With that chance, came opportunity, hard work and freedom. I grew up there, professionally and emotionally. Even in my sobriety. Maybe that would have happened no matter what, but I'll always be grateful.

Company retirement policy included only a framed Certificate of Appreciation complete with an eight-by-ten color glossy photo of the moment you received it in the middle of a mind-numbing "you'll be missed" speech. In spite of the no-party policy, co-workers typically planned a grand farewell. Mine would be a beach day at Carolina Yacht Club.

Russ and I arrived, as ordered, wearing shorts and T-shirts, toting only a beach bag loaded with towels and swimsuits. I felt like a tourist at my own retirement party.

When I got out of the car, my flip-flops stuck to the asphalt. Waves of July heat rolled over the surface of the parking lot. "I think my shoes are melting," I complained.

Russ nodded. "The whole damn parking lot's melting. Let's go before it sucks us in."

He jogged toward the wood-shingled building without looking back, his shoes slapping against his heels. When he reached the bottom of the wooden steps, he leaned against the railing to wait for me. Together we walked up the wide steps leading to an enormous front porch.

When I got to the top, I saw you, Momma, sitting in one of the rockers lining the front of the building. Your flowing cotton skirt billowed around you in the breeze. You stretched your legs displaying perfect cherry-red toenails. Your fingernails matched while your lips looked slightly less dramatic in a more muted shade of berry. With your long brown hair pulled back in a ponytail, you looked young and healthy—CiCi Dolan, pre-cancer. You gave a lazy wave of your hand and said, "All of this served its purpose, Livvy. It's time to let go and move on."

"I am, Momma," I whispered.

Russ held the screen door open for me. "Did you say something?"

I shook my head, and when I looked over again, you had vanished. The same waves of heat that I had seen in the parking lot rose above your rocker. A lump formed in my throat, but I swallowed it down, put a smile on my face and walked inside.

About a hundred people hit the beach in my honor that day, and from the noise rising from the back porch, I knew most of them had arrived early and started the party without us. People filled the chairs and clustered in groups talking and laughing. Folks wandered the back deck, and up and down the dock. Smoke from the enormous charcoal grills drifted in on an occasional gust of wind that carried a hint of beer on it as well. On the opposite side of the deck from the grills, a swarm of people parted, revealing the keg.

Gina yelled, "The guest of honor's here!" She hugged me tight and cocked her head in the direction of the beer. "Ignore it," she ordered. "Too many drunks to ever win that vote."

I smiled that day until my cheeks hurt, mingled till my legs turned to rubber bands and my feet felt like anvils. Russ and Brody flipped burgers and hot dogs. Every time I saw Russ, he had sweat running from his hairline down his neck. When his T-shirt looked soaked beyond any possibility of drying, he caught my eye across the room with a "Ready to go?" look.

That's when I noticed the man on the other side of the deck. Though I'd seen him recently, the changes time had scarred into his face shocked me. He made his way through the crowd and moved toward the door. Most of the people there that day hadn't been with the plant long enough to remember him. The few who did moved out of his way without a word.

He'd been an asshole back then and if twenty-three years of bitterness had changed him at all, it had only made it worse. The pudgy, red-faced, bulbous-nosed man stumbled through the screen door, heading straight for me. Russ recognized his rage and stepped between us like a Secret Service agent blocking a bullet intended for the president.

I stepped out from behind my husband. "How are you, Wilbur?"

"Heard you were retiring," he growled. "My invitation must have got lost."

Gina shoved her way through the growing crowd. "What are you doing here?"

He smiled and the gaping holes between his yellowed teeth made him look like a rabid animal. "A dream come true," he mumbled. "A return engagement of the bitch twins."

Russ's jaw clenched. "Let me walk you outside, buddy." He grabbed Wilbur's arm.

Wilbur jerked back and fell against the wall. "Don't touch me," he snarled as he stuck his hand in his pocket.

I hadn't noticed Brody come up beside Gina. He leaped across a small table and knocked Wilbur to the ground. Hand to pocket—I thought cigarette or lighter. I guess a cop who'd been shot thought gun.

Brody grabbed Wilbur's hands and held them firm above his head. "Russ, check his pockets. Make sure he doesn't have a weapon."

Wilbur squirmed. "What the hell? You assaulted me. I'll sue, you son of a bitch."

Russ pulled a few quarters and a pocketknife from Wilbur's pocket. Brody helped Wilbur get up. Russ held the knife in front of his face.

Wilbur's thin lips curled into a sneer. He pulled away from Brody and stepped closer to me. Close enough that I smelled stale beer, cigarette smoke and urine. I gagged and backed away.

"What the hell do you want?" Gina asked.

"Just wanted to congratulate the backstabber on retiring from my job."

"Call 911," Brody said to Gina.

I put a hand on his arm. "Let him go, Brody. I don't want any trouble." I looked over at Wilbur and felt a wave of pity. "He's just a bitter, old man. Please let it go."

The look on Brody's face told me he wanted nothing more than to see Wilbur Walker, bitter, old man or not, behind bars. But he stepped back and watched Wilbur walk through the screen door. "If you come near either one of these ladies again, I'll see to it that you go to jail. If I had my way, you'd be there today."

Wilbur smirked. "Ladies? Real comedian you are." He reached for the knife that Brody still held in his hand.

Brody curled his fingers around it. "You can pick this up at the police station. I'll leave it at the front desk."

I saw something in Wilbur's eyes in that moment that scared the crap out of me. A shiver wriggled across my shoulders and down my spine. I hoped we'd seen the last of Wilbur Walker, but a nasty, nagging feeling gripped my gut and twisted.

"You want to talk about it?" Russ asked on the way home.

I shook my head. "I've told you the story, and you've met the man behind it. 'Nuff said."

Russ nodded slowly. "That's not just bitterness and old age. The man's nuts. If you ever see him again, get the hell away from him."

I saw evil in Wilbur back in the day, Momma, but now it oozes out his pores.

Livvy

December 4, 2011
10:00 PM

Dear Mom,

I DIDN'T know that Wilbur Walker continued to be an irritant, heck, a full-on threat in your life. He ruined your retirement party and you never told me!

Your eyelids didn't even flutter when I sat on the edge of your bed and tucked the blanket around you. "I would have been there for you, Mom. I would have let you vent and listened to you rant. About Wilbur Walker, or the plant, or the dealership, or an argument with Russ. You always listened to me, and you never judged. I wish I could have done that for you."

The familiar tightening started in my chest. For days, that sudden pressure bloomed, followed by panic and tears. I grabbed a couple of tissues.

"Did I make you feel like you couldn't talk to me? That I wouldn't understand? That I'd blame you?" My tears ran rivers of damp condemnation down my cheeks. "Oh, God. For years, I did blame you for Daddy's problems. I know I was wrong. Please forgive me. Please just open your eyes enough that I know you hear me."

I didn't hear Russ come back in the room. "I'm sure she hears you. And there's nothing to forgive. She didn't keep secrets because of you. She thought that's what a good mother did. Livvy had been the adult in the relationship with her own mother and she didn't want that for you. She wanted you to be the kid. Even long after you'd grown up."

I stood up and put my arms around Russ's neck. "What are we going to do without her?"

He shook his head. "I don't know, Alex. I don't know."

I love you, Mom. Past the sky.

Dear Momma,

DID YOU know that I had a fantasy retirement? Lazy mornings, reading an entire book in a single sitting, lunch with the girls, world travel. Guess what? I get bored with down time, can't sit still long enough to read a whole chapter, have a hard time organizing a trip to Myrtle Beach (so Europe seems out of the question), and I already have lunch with the girls I care about, at work. I like my life. And I may never retire from the dealership.

A couple of months ago, Delores and I met for a status update. She showed me her chart, showing a strong increase in sales. Our family-owned-and-operated business had grown. We both looked up at the portrait of Daddy that hung on the far wall of what we still called "Luther's office."

"You'd be proud, Daddy," I said.

"I wish Luther had lived long enough to see his whole family working here. That was his dream." She looked at him again and sighed.

She snapped her fingers and turned back to me. "I meant to tell you that I saw Wilbur Walker last night."

Worry lines furrowed between my eyebrows. "Where on earth did you run into him?"

"I stopped for gas on the way home, went into the store and he walked in behind me. He carried a six-pack up to the counter. Stood right next to me, so close I smelled the wad of tobacco in his mouth." She grimaced. "I know it sounds silly, but I felt like he followed me there. That's the first time I've seen him in years. But something seemed off about it."

"Why would he follow you? It's me and Gina that he hates."

"He made that pretty clear. Said to give you his best. "

I gasped.

"His exact words, 'Give CiCi's daughter my best.' Then he slapped a ten dollar bill on the counter and walked out."

"That man gives me the creeps, Delores." I shook my head. "He's got to be in his late seventies. How can he still be so nasty?"

"He always was a vile thing, Livvy. I remember him when I was growing up, even though he was four or five years older than me. Mean as a snake if he didn't get his way. He scared me then and doesn't look like he's changed."

I picked at a cuticle. "Did you know that Momma went out with him for a while?"

"I didn't know it, but I gathered that when he mentioned her. Sounded like he's got it in for you and your momma. Be careful, Livvy. He might be old, but the man is still hateful as hell."

Hateful and more than a little bit scary.

Livvy

Dear Momma,

THE GOOD news—work gives me lots of family time. The bad news—work gives me lots of family time. And sometimes, I see things I probably shouldn't and hear things I wish I hadn't.

Steve Richards, one of the bankers the dealership uses, pays way too much attention to Alex to suit me. He used to stop by a couple times a month, but since he met Alex, he heads straight for her office every time he walks in the door. Tall, dark, handsome, divorced and on the prowl means trouble to me, but my daughter seems intrigued. And the spark in her eyes when she seems him scares me.

She met him at the door the other day and the look that passed between them sent shivers down my spine. Alex has always resembled you, Momma. But what I saw that morning made me wonder if she had more in common with you than doe eyes and thick brown hair.

My stomach nosedived when he put a hand to her face and stroked her hair. Instead of pulling away from his touch, she smiled and leaned into it. My gut lurched again and bottomed out as she cocked her head toward her office. The banker followed her like a leg-humping puppy.

I've kept what I saw to myself and feel guilty for not sharing it with Russ. I want to talk to Alex, but have opted for the see-no-evil, speak-no-evil route instead. Prayer helps, but some days, I think minding my own business might just kill me.

Livvy

December 5, 2011
3:00 AM

Dear Mom,

EVERYTHING the nurse said turned out to be true. You had several more episodes of seeing things Russ and I didn't. I wanted to reason with you, explain the hallucinations away. Instead, I tried to live them with you and dispel them for you with a brush of my hand.

You startled awake a couple of hours ago, shrieking and swiping your hands over your blanket. You looked at me with a combination of terror and confusion. "Get them off of me!"

"What is it, Mom?" I ran to your side.

"Spiders! Can't you see them?" Your hands swatted at the bed, your forearms and even your face.

I debated for only a second. Your eyes begged me to help you. I jerked the blanket off the bed and shook it several times. Then I laid it across the back of my chair while I brushed imaginary spiders from your nightgown and your hair. "We got 'em, Mom." I straightened your sheets and put the blanket back on your legs.

You grabbed my hand. "Thank you," you said.

Not long after that, you palmed your hands over your ears. "How can you read with all that noise in the bathroom? They're too loud."

"What's too loud?"

This time you looked at me like you didn't believe it possible that I could be so deaf. "The band." When I didn't get an answer out fast enough, you threw your hands up in frustration. "That damn marching band in the bathroom." You yelled like you had to in order to be heard over the din. "They're too loud!"

I walked into the bathroom and glanced around the empty room. "The party's over. It's time for you to leave." I escorted all of them, including the tuba player and the drum major, out the door. You pointed at what I assumed to be a lone straggler. "You, too. Out," I ordered.

The meds kicked in, you closed your eyes and went back to sleep. Tears slid down my cheeks as you slipped further away.

I pulled out more letters. They made me cringe. You saw me flirt with Steve. You had every right to think the worst of me. You saw Grandma CiCi in my behavior and that makes me ashamed. I know I look like her. I've seen the pictures. The resemblance is a little unnerving. But I never wanted to be like her.

I hurt and I wanted to be comforted. I felt unloved and I wanted to be adored. I felt used up and tossed aside. I wanted someone, anyone to see the value in me. And I turned to Steve Richards for that.

I regret it.

Dear Momma,

I SPENT months inching my way into Daddy's house and even longer making it my home. With every box, I wondered if we had done the right thing. By the time we put up curtains, I knew that we had. The chill I first met in every corner warmed to an embrace. Tears followed my memory flashes until those memories became treasures that brought smiles. Daddy's home, my home and someday, Alex's. Daddy's business passed on to me, and eventually it will be handed down to Alex.

Continuity. It felt right. And speaking of feeling right—I decided to sell your house, Momma. At first, I thought I'd rent it again, but Alex suggested that selling it might be a better option.

"Mom, you and Russ are so busy with the dealership and the grandkids and church. Do you really want to take care of a rental?"

"That was our home for so many years and Momma's before that. How could I let it go?"

Alex gave me the wise smile she uses when she's about to make me feel childish. "For me, home is being with the people I love, whether it's in Granddaddy's, Grandma CiCi's, Will's family farm, or my own house." She thought for a moment. "In fact, I don't remember Grandma CiCi in that house at all." She grinned. "I have great memories of you and me there. And I'll still have those memories, even if you sell the house. Don't hang on to it for me, Mom."

I kissed her cheek. "I'll think about it," I promised her.

I did think about it and took her advice. A young couple fell in love with the house within days of the For Sale sign going up. A tiny twinge of loss pricked my heart when we signed the papers. But their bright faces and big plans reassured me. After thirty-five years, handing over the keys and moving on didn't seem like such a hard thing at all. Letting go felt peaceful, fitting.

In the spirit of letting go and hanging on, Russ and I decided to host the first official Russ and Livvy cookout in our new home. Food, fireworks and barefoot line dancing kept the partygoers enjoying themselves for hours.

By midnight, most had vanished, leaving only a few stranglers behind. I walked toward the dock carrying a huge plastic trash bag. Every few steps I picked up a cup or a stray paper plate and shoved it in with the other garbage. I saw a couple standing on the far end of the dock but couldn't make out the faces in the dark. I should have walked away, but I didn't. As my cleanup drew me closer, I heard bits and pieces of conversation, snippets of an argument. And while I couldn't see the faces, I recognized the voices.

Will said, "I'm sick and tired of your attitude."

"I don't give a damn what you're sick and tired of. You have no right to judge me or tell me what to do. If you don't like my attitude, I can sure as hell find someone who does."

Alex's voice shook with a rage that shocked me. The Alex I knew maintained levelheaded reason no matter what. The Alex I knew displayed calm in the face of chaos and peace in the midst of turmoil. At that moment, she sounded nothing like her usual self, but more like me in the days of bourbon and beer.

I closed my eyes, trying to block the images of Alex and Steve Richards that flooded my brain. Flashes of you, Momma, and a dozen different men replaced them only to be chased away by visions of my own promiscuity. Behaviors and traits handed down from generation to generation. I thought that some of the terrible ones stopped with me. I guess maybe you can't fight genes after all.

"Looks to me like you already did that," Will snarled. "How long has it been going on?"

My stomach knotted. Will knew. I panicked as though I'd been caught having an affair myself. *I saw this coming and I should have talked to her, reasoned with her, stopped her. Why didn't I do something?*

Alex didn't respond.

"You left me emotionally months ago." The anger dwindled from Will's voice. He sounded tired, deflated. "There's been no us for a long time. You acted bored with everything I said or did, like it disgusted you to even be in the same room with me. And to be in bed with me! Christ, I couldn't even touch you. What the hell did you think would happen? You pushed me away!"

Alex shoved Will away from her. "Don't you dare blame me for what you did! I didn't push you away. You ran. And anything that happened after that is your own fucking fault!"

I backed away, stumbling across the grass toward the house. Gina caught my arm. "Are you okay? You look terrible."

I shook my head. "I'm fine. Just tired."

"Are you getting sick? You look a little flushed." Gina put her palm to my forehead.

I jerked back. "I'm fine."

I pointed to a table still covered in napkins and silverware and headed that direction. When I walked away, Gina's stare bore a hole in my back that I felt long after she'd gone home. I couldn't share my suspicions about Steve and Alex with anyone. My fears for my daughter's marriage and my grandchildren's future had to stay with me. I couldn't risk doing any more damage.

December 5, 2011
6:00 AM

Dear Mom,

WHY DIDN'T you ever tell me what Grandma CiCi had really been like? Did you think silence would protect me from passing on the patterns of behavior?

I've sat in this chair, beside your bed, for days thinking about my life and my decisions, wondering what makes me who I am. Genetics or environment? Nature or nurture?

While Will and I struggled to keep our marriage together, I felt like a drunken party girl lived inside me, waiting for a flashing moment of weakness so she could take over. Does that sound crazy? I didn't like her. I didn't want her in control. But that party girl offered me quick fixes, pain-numbing infusions of flattery, self-esteem through meaningless hook-ups.

So I tried it her way. Flirted with Steve Richards to feel desirable again. And, if I'm being honest, I did it to hurt Will. Except, I couldn't actually tell Will about my extracurricular flirtation, so who did it really hurt? I woke up in the morning feeling unloved and unwanted and went to bed at night the same way. I just wanted the pain to stop. And I wanted Will to know that other men could still find me desirable. No price seemed too much to pay for a quick hit of a fleeting feeling.

After reading your letters, I know that the women in our family used to take that sick, twisted road. I also know that I had the potential to go that old route, too. But you had already shown me another way. I hate that you saw me capable of behaving like Grandma CiCi.

I wish you had trusted everything you taught me to win out in the end.

Dear Momma,

FOR MONTHS I watched Alex and Will's marriage crumble to dust, trickling through their fingers. The damage in the Crenshaw household seemed irreparable. Alex grew more and more distant. When I couldn't take it anymore, I stepped into her office and invited her out to dinner.

"That's sweet, Mom, but I need to get home."

"How about we just grab an appetizer? We haven't had any time together in months."

Alex sighed. I heard adolescence in the sound. It surprised me that she didn't rolled her eyes at me as well.

"I'll call Will and tell him he's got the kids." She picked up the phone and pounded in the number. "Yeah. I'm going out with Mom after work." She paused. "Not long." A longer pause. "There's leftovers. I'll be home when I get home." She dropped the phone back onto its base.

We drove separate cars to Dockside, pulled into an almost empty parking lot and had our choice of tables inside. We chose a window booth. Though we couldn't see the waterway in the dark, the spot still gave us some privacy.

Alex ordered calamari and I requested clams. The waitress set a platter in front of each of us.

We munched without speaking. Alex stared at her reflection in the window. When I snatched a bite from Alex's plate, she smiled, but said nothing.

After another sip of wine, Alex asked, "So, what's this about, Mom?"

"I'm worried, Alex. About you and Will."

She stiffened and her fingers tightened on the stem of her glass. "Please stay out of it." She set the glass down and grabbed her fork, using it to push calamari around her plate.

"I've tried, but I can't do that anymore."

Alex raised her eyes from the plate and stared at me.

"Staying out of it hasn't done any good." I reached across the table and squeezed her arm. "I've seen the problems, babe. I want to help."

"I don't know what you're talking about." She looked back down.

"I saw the flirtation with Steve Richards..."

"You didn't see anything like that," Alex interrupted.

I put my hand up. "Don't. You certainly don't have to tell me anything you don't want to, but please don't lie to me. I know what I saw." I looked down at my own plate. "I heard you and Will arguing on the dock after the Fourth of July party."

"You eavesdropped? On our private conversation?" She tossed her fork down. It clattered on the table.

"It's not like that. It was late. I was picking up trash. I had no idea you and Will were even on the dock, and when I did recognize you, I left. I didn't try to listen."

"You just listened until you decided we're having problems?"

"I heard enough, Alex. And before we go any further I want to tell you a few things that you may not remember or even have known about."

"Say whatever it is that's on your mind and get it over with." She slumped against the back of the booth, like a disgruntled teenager.

"I don't know what happened with Steve and I don't know what's going on with Will, but I do know that your mother and your grandmother had a hell of a lot of problems in their lives because of marital troubles and sex. And most of it didn't have to happen." I stared out the darkened window. "Do you remember how beautiful Grandma CiCi was?"

Alex nodded.

"Beautiful, smart, great career. But she had to have a man in her life. If he could fog a damn mirror, he qualified for her bed."

Then Alex gave me the eye-roll. "I really don't want to hear this."

"I think you need to hear it. Somehow, in spite of everything your grandmother had going for her, when it came to men, she had no self-confidence. Daddy adored her, but CiCi Dolan couldn't function in a mature relationship, rooted in real life. She clung to her beauty like a lifeline and when some new man showered her with compliments, she ate it up. Her sexual relationships had to be new and exciting. She never learned to be a grownup, Alex. She behaved like a sixteen-year-old right up until the day she died. And the sad part is that no one, except maybe your granddaddy, saw the insecurity in her. They only saw the town tramp."

My eyes filled with tears. "It didn't have to be that way. If only she had gotten help. Every good intention she ever had evaporated when she got drunk."

Alex's eyes softened a little. "Mom, what's your point?"

I ignored the question. "Then when your daddy and I split up and my drinking got so bad..." I tore at the napkin on my lap, unable to look Alex in the face. "I let things get bad, especially for you. I shouldn't have stayed in the marriage as long as I did. And I shouldn't have drowned in the booze." I shook my head, trying to fling away the images that had sprung up. "Those years are a blur. I did a lot of things I'm not proud of. You were the most important thing in my life, but I tried to find happiness in a bottle or a man. It didn't work." I looked up at Alex. "It still won't." I choked back tears. "I know you had to live with Daddy and Nora Jean's problems, too. All the same crap. I'm so sorry, Alex. For all of it." I leaned across the table. "It wasn't until I got sober and left that behind me that I found Russ and God and peace. I want that for you. I don't want you to make the same mistakes."

"Your grandmother used to say, 'Olivia, the secret to life is knowing when to hang on and when to let go.' Alex, only you know if your marriage is worth saving. If it is, fight for it. If it isn't, then move on. I'll be there for you, whatever you decide." My voice cracked. "Just don't let it destroy you the way your grandmother and I did."

Alex had begun the evening with an angry scowl. At some point, she evolved to resentful and then, mildly interested. By the time I finished speaking, her chin quivered and she rubbed at her temples like a headache had formed behind her eyes.

"Will cheated on me," she said so quietly that I thought I didn't hear her right. But the pain in her eyes left no doubt of what she had said.

"I can't forgive him. I don't want to be around him." The catch in her voice hinted at her despair. "And I don't want him to touch me." Tears flowed down her cheeks. "But I love him, Mom. I still love him. And the kids need him. I don't know what to do."

I got up and moved to her side of the booth. When I put my arm around her shoulder, she leaned into me like she used to as a child. "When?"

"Over a year ago. He says it was a mistake. That it only lasted a few weeks. I don't care if it only happened once. How can I ever trust him again?"

I rubbed her back and pulled her closer. "I'm so sorry. I should have been there for you."

"Don't do that, Mom. Don't feel guilty for my problems." Alex swiped her hands across her face and snorted through a muffled sob. "I was so ashamed. I didn't want anyone to know." She pulled away and grabbed my arm. "Oh, God. No one else knows, right? I couldn't handle that."

I shook my head. "I don't think anyone knows. Do you and the kids want to stay with Russ and me for a while until you can figure things out?"

"No. If I did that, the kids would know something was wrong. I don't want to do that to them."

My eyes widened. "You think they don't already know? You knew something was wrong with Sonny and me. You thought you could fix it. You knew something was wrong with Daddy and Nora Jean. Alex, Garrett and Darcy must suspect that something is very wrong. And they're kids. They probably think that somehow it's their fault."

Alex buried her face in her hands. "They probably do know. I've screwed everything up."

"You didn't screw anything up, babe. You're just hanging on to your marriage. Is that what you want?"

"I don't know."

"Would you consider counseling? Not marriage counseling. Just for you. To figure out what it is that you do want."

"I do need to talk to somebody. I can't keep going on like this." She turned in the booth to hug me. She clung to my neck while I rubbed her back.

"Lord, please help my little girl. Heal her hurt. Light her path. Give her strength and wisdom."

I hadn't realized that I'd spoken out loud until Alex whispered, "Thank you."

Maybe she really is different from us, Momma,

Livvy

P.S. After a couple of months of individual counseling, Will and Alex started going to marriage counseling. I see improvement. Slow, but better. Neither of them wants to let go of the other. They're hanging on.

December 5, 2011
8:00 AM

Dear Mom,

WILL AND I had been bickering for weeks. Nothing important, just stuff. "You forgot to get the ice cream I asked for." "You left the back door unlocked last night." "Could you, just for once, fix the kids breakfast?"

Anyway, I left the dealership early one day and picked up a bottle of wine to surprise Will at work. Lord, did I ever.

I walked into his office and found some tacky bitch I'd never seen before sitting on his lap, nibbling his ear while his hand wandered under her blouse. My feet rooted into the carpet. I didn't want to see any more, but couldn't look away. My cheeks flamed so hot that my blush should have melted. Tears welled and I fought the urge to vomit.

Will jumped up, dumping the tacky bitch to the floor. He stared at me, glanced down at her and looked back at me.

"Hey," she whined. "That hurt."

Her nasally voice grated on my nerves and brought me to life. I snatched her purse from the credenza next to me. "That's nothing compared to how bad it'll hurt when I shove this so far up your ass that you'll be puking credit cards for a week."

She pulled herself off the floor, marched right up to me, grabbed her handbag and headed for the door. Then she spun around and said, "In case you have any doubt, Will Crenshaw, you will no longer be doing my taxes." She slammed the door behind her.

Will still hadn't moved. I'm not sure he had taken a breath since I'd walked in.

"So, you do her taxes, and she does you?" I held up the wine bottle by the neck and brought it down on the edge of the credenza. The glass shattered and flew everywhere. Wine flowed over the wood and the books on the shelves until it puddled on the floor.

I backed toward the door. Will held out his hand. "I screwed up, Alex. I'm sorry. Please let me explain."

When I got to the parking lot, I started my car and knew I shouldn't be driving. Will ran out behind me so I threw the stick in gear and burned rubber as I drove away.

I don't want to remember that pain, Mom, but I can't forget it either. Once in a great while it still hangs over me like a damp, cold fog.

But you know what's funny? When you caught Dad, you set fire to a trashcan. When I caught Will, I "wined" his accounting books to death. Fire and water, so to speak.

We make a formidable tag-team, Mom.

Alex

Dear Momma,

FOR YEARS, I suspected that I had a crazed, vengeful, eighty-year-old stalker. What the heck happened to mellowing with age?

After Wilbur Walker's bizarre display at my retirement party, he taunted Delores a time or two, but I didn't actually have a run-in until a few months ago.

A spotty drizzle had been coming down all day making it feel far colder than the forty degrees the weatherman predicted. I stopped at the post office, dashed inside, and when I stepped back out, I saw him standing at the row of newspaper vending machines near the curb. Wilbur stood in a small patch of grass under a tree. He wore a wide brimmed hat, but no raincoat. Water droplets coated his sweatshirt and shimmered like little sequins. He stared at me as I walked out the double doors and raised his hand like he might wave. Instead, he formed a gun with his hand, aimed it at me and pulled the make-believe trigger. He smiled and lowered his arm to his side.

One glance at my car and I realized that I had to walk right past WWII to get to it.

That cantankerous old man's smile broadened and that pissed me off. I decided I wouldn't let him frighten me, at least not any more that he already had. I took a deep breath and marched toward my car, ignoring Wilbur until I opened the driver's side door. I tossed my purse inside and turned around to face him. His smile had vanished and while I couldn't see his deranged eyes under the brim of his hat, I felt the fury emanating from them.

"Have a nice day, Wilbur," I said.

When I slid into the seat and closed the door, I reached up and locked it before I even put the key in the ignition.

After that incident, I thought I caught glimpses of him everywhere, at the gas station or the grocery store, driving past my house. Then, nothing. If Wilbur Walker wanted to terrorize me, he couldn't have done it more thoroughly with a bomb. And he'd done it with only a few well-timed visits. I pulled a muscle in my neck from looking over my shoulder all the time. I'd feel a whisper behind my ear and spin around. I checked the back seat of my car before I opened the door. I couldn't shake the feeling that he watched me from the shadows. Not until I read the short article in the local section of the newspaper.

> *Monday, February 11, 2008, Wilbur Walker II was found dead in his home in Rocky Point. Walker, 79, lived alone and had apparently been dead for some time. His neighbor contacted the Sheriff's Department after she noticed a putrid odor and suspected something might be wrong. Autopsy results are pending, however, no foul play is suspected. Several people living near him said they felt terrible that no one had noticed sooner, but Walker liked his privacy and shunned most contact with others.*
>
> *Wilbur Walker II is survived by a son, Jackson Walker of Raleigh, who had no comment on the death of his father. Walker will be interred at Greenlawn Cemetery, Friday, February 22, 2008 at 10 in the morning.*

When I finished the article, my head said I should dance a jig that that evil man was gone, but my heart hurt that anyone, even WWII, would end up so horribly alone. Booze and vengeance had destroyed too many people in my life.

At ten o'clock on February 22, I stood several sections away from the casket carrying Wilbur Walker II. My need to be there made no sense, even to me, so I explained it to no one and just showed up. Clearly, I had been the only person to follow that impulse. The other two people in attendance had been paid to be there to lower the plain, unadorned casket into the ground. I pulled my coat tight against the wind gusts and walked closer.

"He kin to you?" one of the workers asked.

"No. I worked with him many years ago."

He shook his head. "Can't remember the last time we did this with nobody here. He must not have been from around here, huh?"

I shrugged. A tiny part of me felt pity for Wilbur Walker II, but mostly I hurt for his family. What a terrible thing it must be to think so little of your father or grandfather, brother or cousin that you couldn't set the resentment aside for the man's funeral.

Steps Four through Ten of Alcoholics Anonymous are devoted to searching ourselves for wrong-doing, making amends and living our lives a better way. Those steps taught me to ask for forgiveness. But somehow, in recent years, God kept putting me in situations that forced me to learn to forgive. I had no flowers to put on Wilbur's grave, so I lowered my head and prayed. I asked God to help me let go of the anger I held toward him for so long and to finally be able to forgive the man.

Maybe I'm getting there, Momma.

August 12, 2008
Happy Birthday

Dear Momma,

DELORES RETIRED. After all those years of making the dealership function with some semblance of organization, she decided that she needed time. Time with children, grandchildren and friends. Time to travel, read, sleep. Truthfully, I think she just didn't want to be there anymore without Daddy.

She talked to the attorney about turning her share of the dealership over to me, but I said no. "Daddy gave you a life stake in the dealership, so if you want to retire, we'll look over the books and make you an offer to buy you out. You helped build the business, and you earn the buyout."

Russ laughed. "No point arguing with her, Delores. The woman's stubborn, especially when she's right."

We made an offer. Delores accepted and set out to embrace her new life.

And I set out to embrace mine, full control of, and responsibility for, the dealership. For years, I wondered what would happen to the place if Daddy weren't there. Delores stepped in and made it look seamless. I hope I'll do the same. And since they both taught me everything they knew and left me with the model for how to do it, deep down, I knew I can.

I love you, Momma,

Livvy

Dear Momma,

GARRETT TURNED eleven in June, and the last guest hadn't left his party before he spun me around until we stood back to back so his father could measure Garrett's height against mine.

Will held his hand to the middle of the back of my head. Garrett pulled out from under his father's palm to see for himself.

"Only two or three more inches and you'll tower over your grandma."

Garrett pumped his fist in the air. "Yeah!"

"Tower over me is a little bit of a stretch." I turned to Garrett and held my thumb and forefinger a little ways apart. "Two or three more inches and you might break even with me. But it'll take a lot more than that to count as towering."

"Don't take it personally, Mom," Alex said. "They've driven me crazy with that every day for the last month. And every day they try to tell me Garrett has grown another inch and is putting me in his shadow." She shook her head. "Not yet, he's not."

Will elbowed his son. "They're just jealous." His eyes twinkled. "Because they're short."

Alex and I sputtered. Garrett laughed. "I'm getting taller and you guys are shrinking."

I glanced at Alex and wondered if the same thoughts flashed through her mind that filled mine. Eleven years ago, when Garrett came into the world, none of us knew if he could survive the day. When he made it through surgery, we wondered if he would be sickly and frail. I prayed for his life. It didn't occur to me to ask for that life to be normal and yet, God gave Garrett a complete healing. He gave Garrett a miraculous gift that blessed us all.

Over the years, I'd watched him be a full participant in school, church and at home. He ran, played soccer, mowed the lawn, teased his sister and laughed like he never had a worry in the world. And then I realized that he never did have a worry. All the rest of us carried that burden. Garrett saw only a small stretched out faded scar on his chest. He used to ask his mother about it, but didn't even do that anymore. When I saw that same scar, it reminded me that every single one of us balanced on the razor thin edge of our fragile lives with possibilities or limitations waiting for us to slip in one direction or the other.

Darcy watched her brother check his birthday height against everyone in the room and shook her head. "How can he be taller today than he was yesterday?"

I hugged her close. "Birthday magic, I suppose."

Sweet Darcy never faced the health issues of her older brother and yet, I saw her as a beautiful crystal vase with the potential for chipping or cracking at any moment. After the unthinkable happened in our family, I never took health or time for granted again.

December 5, 2011
12:00 PM

Dear Mom,

I REMEMBER that birthday. Garrett obsessed about his height every moment of every day, and I began to stop obsessing about the problems in my marriage. Hope blossomed as my despair faded.

When I finished your letter, I wanted to feel the same joy we all experienced that day. I kissed your cheek. You didn't respond. No moan, no sigh, no movement. So I talked. I wanted to believe that you listened.

"I didn't think things would ever be really good between us again. I was wrong." I grinned. "We saw a counselor for months. I didn't want to be there and I let everybody know it. I didn't speak unless it was to tell Will what a jackass he was. He was ashamed and felt guilty, but that didn't stop him from being upset with me for being angry with him. It became our private dance. Anger for anger. Sarcastic potshot for sarcastic potshot. I couldn't see a way through it. But then the counselor asked us one question. 'Do you want to be right or do you want to be happy?' His question made no sense to me. I knew I was damn well right and I deserved to be happy, too. I knew Will was screwed-up six ways to Sunday and should be miserable trying to make me happy."

I threw back my head and laughed. Still you didn't move.

"Sounds like a marriage made in adultery hell, doesn't it?" I shook my head. "It took weeks, but that simple question ate at me until I realized that my strutting around beating my chest and whining about how I deserved to be happy was one of the very things keeping me unhappy. That's when I looked at Garrett and Darcy and saw how our bickering affected them. They had pulled away from us, become more timid and withdrawn every day. I guess I would've too, to stay out of the line of fire."

I stared out the window of your hospital room. "I didn't want to do that to my children anymore. I didn't want to do that to myself anymore. I finally saw how not forgiving Will hurt me as much as it did him. And then, I woke up one morning, watched Will help Darcy brush her hair and thought, *I still love him and that's all that matters.*

"Mom, I couldn't have done it without you and Russ. You showed me what love's supposed to be. You showed me that we all make mistakes, but we don't have to keep making them. You showed me that I can't fix the past, but I can sure as hell change the future.

"Thank you."

August 12, 2009
Happy Birthday

Dear Momma,

O N JUNE 5, Russ drove me to Wilmington Surge-Care for a routine colonoscopy. The anesthesia left me groggy and I remember very little of what the doctor told us afterward. Words and phrases, foggy fragments. "Tumor." "Cancer." "Surgery."

I slept the afternoon away, drugged and dreamless. When I look back on it, I'm grateful that I heard my cancer news under the influence of heavy-duty meds. Russ took the brunt of the sucker punch and had to relay the information to me when I came around.

I remember the look on your face when your doctor said you had cancer. Now, I'll remember the fear in my husband's eyes when he told me about mine.

I woke up hours later, muddled and confused. The word "tumor" rang in my ears, but since I couldn't even remember putting my clothes back on when the nurse cleared me to leave, I thought I had to be imagining it. Maybe I'd had a nightmare.

Before I'd climbed in bed, I'd thrown on one of Russ's soft, worn, over-sized T-shirts. I still had it on when I stumbled out to the family room, but I'd slipped my favorite threadbare robe over it. The television set in the corner yammered a low background noise though no one watched it. I saw Russ through the sliding glass doors. He sat in a chair on the deck with his back to me. I slid the doors open and stepped outside, squinting in the summer sun.

Russ jumped up. "Are you okay? How are you feeling?" He pulled out the chair at the table next to him. "Can I get you something to drink?"

I knew then that it hadn't been a nightmare. I had heard the word "cancer." So had my husband.

"I don't remember much," I said. "How bad is it?"

Russ stared out at the Intracoastal Waterway watching it shimmer like a liquid gemstone. "We have an appointment with the doctor first thing in the morning. He'll tell us more then."

I cinched my bathrobe tight at my waist and sat down. "I need to know what you know, babe," I said softly. "Now."

Russ closed his eyes, sat back down and took a deep breath before he spoke. "You have colon cancer," he said. "There's a tumor." His voice cracked. "You need surgery, as soon as possible."

"How big is the tumor?"

"I'm sure he'll go over all of that with us in the morning. He called it 'good-sized.'"

I leaned back in my chair and played with the robe sash. "Good-sized tumor." I wanted to laugh, but what came out sounded more like a whimper. "Does that mean good, as in small enough to deal with or good, as in, 'Holy Crap! Get a load of that thing!'?"

"Please, don't, Livvy," Russ said. He grabbed my hand and rubbed it between his palms.

"Don't what? Laugh? Cry? Pitch a fit? Tell my doctor he should never again use the words good and tumor in the same sentence because it doesn't make fucking sense?" I felt my eyes get wider and wider. I wanted to cry, but tears wouldn't come. My dry, wide-eyed rant must have made me look like a lunatic. I thought about how much the anesthesia after-effects and severe bedhead added to my new, going-off-the-deep-end appearance and I burst out laughing. Which turned, as quick as it had come, to hysterical sobs. Tears soaked my cheeks until I looked like I'd been standing in a rainstorm. Snot ran like water from my nose to my upper lip, and I struggled to breathe. I jerked my hand away from Russ's and doubled over in my chair. Bile rose in my throat and I feared I might vomit right there in my lap. I heard noises coming from my throat but couldn't recognize them as belonging to me.

Russ jumped up from his chair and knelt beside me. He pulled me so tight to his chest that I felt his heart hammering in time with mine. "We're going to get through this," he whispered into my hair. He kissed the top of my head over and over again. "You're going to get through this and I'm going to walk with you every step of the way." He lifted my chin until our eyes met and he looked straight into my splotchy tear-stained, snot-covered face. And in that moment, love filled his eyes to overflowing and he made me believe him. We would make it through this.

The next morning my doctor told us little more than he had the day before. He had, however, already scheduled an appointment with the surgeon for the same afternoon. The hair on the back of my neck stood straight up and fear raced down my spine. Scheduling the surgeon told me more than he could have explained in an hour-long lecture. I needed an emergency appointment with the surgeon to have my "good-sized" tumor removed as quickly as possible.

"How big is it?" I asked.

The doctor pulled out a flip chart from his desk drawer. "Colon cancer is one of those rare cancers where the size of the tumor really doesn't mean much in terms of your prognosis." He pointed to one of the diagrams. "The tumor can be large, but as long as it hasn't penetrated through the colon wall, then it's fully encapsulated within the large intestine. If that's the case, then when we remove that section of colon, we also remove the entire cancer." He flipped the page to a new diagram. "The problem comes when the tumor gets through the colon wall. That's how they determine the stage of colon cancer—by how far it's gotten through the colon wall."

I interrupted him. "What about mine?"

"We won't know for sure until after your surgery and the final pathology report comes back."

"You've done this for a long time," I said. "What do you think?"

"We need to get you into surgery."

He lowered his gaze as he laid the flip chart back down. He couldn't look me in the eye, and I thought once again that this doctor told me more with his actions than he did with his words.

Ten days later, the surgeon removed about forty percent of my large intestine. At our first meeting, he had explained his reasoning for the enormous slash-line he described with a quick cutting motion across his own abdomen. "I need to do a large incision so that I can clearly see what's going on in there. If the cancer has spread, I want to get it out while you're on the table."

He needed a course in Remedial Bedside Manners, but everyone assured me of his stellar qualifications. I had my doubts when I woke up from my surgery feeling like I'd been trapped in a malfunctioning magician's box and the idiot had kept on sawing.

I drifted off again and remember nothing after that, for hours, maybe days. I slept. I moaned and complained and prayed. I hit my drug button and slept some more. After about twenty-four hours, the physical therapist showed up and forced me to get out of bed to sit in the chair. After forty-eight hours, they took out my catheter and removed my spinal IV for self-medication. At that same time, they made me start walking down the hall. I'm not sure what moron decided that decreasing the meds and increasing the exercise on the same day sounded like a good idea, but if I could have gotten my hands on him, I would have ripped his ignorant little head off.

Seventy-two hours after surgery, they brought me a bowl of lime Jell-O, and I forgave every medical abuse I'd suffered. I thought I'd died and gone to heaven with my first bite of real food.

For five days, I drifted in and out of a fog of sleep, pain and drugs. As long as I sat up or lay flat, I didn't experience double-me-over agony. Just an endless, irritating ache. But getting up or down brought tears to my eyes. And sitting or standing too long left me white-knuckled.

In fairness to my surgeon, I should explain that on the afternoon of Day Five, when he marched in like he'd been sent directly from God's office to my hospital room, I had already exceeded my maximum sitting up limit by about fifteen minutes. The clear thinking that had finally emerged from the muddle earlier that morning melted as the pain intensified.

The surgeon stepped over to the hand sanitizer dispenser hanging on the wall near the door and held his palms under it until the perfect serving size dribbled over his fingers. He rubbed it in, snatched my chart from its holder and flipped it open.

He hadn't said, "Good afternoon, Olivia," "How are you feeling, Olivia?" or "Kiss my butt, Olivia." Not one word passed his lips as I clutched the arms of my chair like the safety bar on the Thunder Road roller coaster. I needed my miracle pain relief button to ease myself into oblivion.

Russ sat in the corner. He said nothing while he watched the doctor's every move.

After the surgeon gave a quick glance at the notations on my chart, he slapped it closed and dropped it back into its slot. He leaned against the wall with his arms folded across his chest.

"We got the final pathology report back. The good news is that the lymph nodes are clear. The bad news is that your tumor had ruptured the colon wall. I've scheduled you for an MRI before your release. I'm also referring you to an oncologist."

He dropped his hands to his sides and moved toward the door like he might get away without having to actually listen to me or answer my questions. The surgeon god speaks, the peon listens, the surgeon god goes on about his important business. Clearly, the surgeon god had not anticipated the pain-addled patient on the verge of a total meltdown.

"Whoa," I said. "I have questions."

He turned back to me. His puzzled eyes said, "You're questioning me?" His furrowed brow added, "I'm a busy man. Don't waste my time."

Russ stood up, walked around the bed and parked himself directly behind my chair. I understood his unspoken message. *I've got your back and I have questions for the good doctor, too.* I love my husband more than I could ever say, but never more than right then.

"The tumor ruptured the colon wall," I said. "What stage of cancer does that mean I have?"

"Your oncologist will discuss all of that with you. He'll need the results of the MRI in addition to the pathology report to make his diagnosis. The tumor itself was about a centimeter through the wall. Enough to make us cautious, but not panicked. Nothing to cause any alarm."

"Nothing to cause any alarm?" I sounded high-pitched and shrill. "You mean no more alarming than colon cancer, right? No more alarming than a tumor growing right through my large intestine, right? No more alarming than thinking this shit might be spreading, right?" Now, I sounded fully outraged. I pointed at him, and my finger shook. "Doctor, you might deal with this every day, but I don't!" I thumped that same finger on my chest. "I don't have surgery or cancer every day! I'm not scared half out of my mind every day! And the very damn least that you can do is act like you have the time and the inclination to answer every question I have during one of the most God-awful times of my life!" I paused for a breath.

The surgeon stepped back, but a hint of compassion flickered in his eyes. "I didn't mean to be brusque. It's just that I have other patients and I try to keep to a tight schedule."

"Do I look like I give a rat's ass about your schedule?" I felt Russ's calming hand on my shoulder, but it only made me bolder. "I want to know what stage of cancer I have. I want to know if it has spread in my body. I want to know when this damn pain will get better. I want to know when I can go home. I want to know if I'll live to see my grandchildren grow up." My voice cracked. "I want to know if I'm going to die." Russ fingers tightened their grip. "I need you to tell me those things, doctor." I inhaled and bit my upper lip. "Please," I whispered.

The surgeon god stepped closer. His tone softened. "The oncologist will be able to tell you the stage of your cancer at your first appointment. The MRI will give us more information, but right now it's impossible to say whether or not it has spread. I can tell you that there are no large tumors and no visible damage to other organs. The pain will improve in a few days, but you won't be back to normal for several weeks. You will probably be released to go home tomorrow after your MRI and no, you're not going to die."

My heart pounded in my chest so loud I could barely hear him. My mouth dried up when he said, "You're not going to die." I wanted to say, "Thank you," but couldn't form the words.

Russ asked, "Will we get the MRI results tomorrow?"

The surgeon shook his head. "Not for a couple of days. I'll go over the results with you at Olivia's check-up. Call my office and schedule an appointment for next week."

"Is there anything we need to know about taking care of Livvy?"

"The nurse will give you written instructions for her home care and go over it with you."

The surgeon god tone returned. Busy man, nurse takes care of trivialities, blah, blah, blah. Everything about the man annoyed me.

At the top of his irritating quirks—he assigned ownership of this damn cancer to me. "Your cancer," he said repeatedly. Like I ordered it from the menu. "Your salad will be right out." He made it sound like my decision, my choice, my possession. I called it "the damn cancer." An entity that invaded me, attacked me. He called it mine and I resented the hell out of him for that.

Momma, I saw your fear and pain way back then and I understood it to a degree because I had my own fear of losing you and my own pain, watching you go through the damn disease.

I understand a great deal more now, Momma,

December 5, 2011
5:00 PM

Dear Mom,

YOUR BATHROBE. The one you wore after your colonoscopy. The same one you asked me to retrieve from your closet only a few days ago. The one that led to discovering the hatbox. The robe that jump-started my journey through your letters. The one that lies over your frail shoulders now.

I reached across the bed and rubbed the sleeve of your favorite worn threadbare robe. Your eyelids fluttered. "Mom?" I asked.

Russ had been dozing on the other side of your bed. He shivered when I spoke. "Livvy?" He jumped up and looked into your face, hoping to spend just one more moment with you, awake and responsive. But you didn't wake or speak or even open your eyes. Russ looked at me through his tears.

"I'm sorry," I explained. "I touched her and she moved like she might be waking up."

I looked at you, Mom, and felt the same panic bubbling up in me that I saw chiseled into Russ's face. I need you to wake up. I need you to look at me. I need you to talk to me, just one more time. Russ and I both need that. Please, Mom.

I love you,

P.S. You asked your surgeon if you would live to see your grandchildren grow up. He said yes. You asked him if the cancer would kill you. He said no. He lied.

Dear Momma,

I FELT like a big-ass crybaby when I came home from the hospital. Then I started chemotherapy and realized that I had yet to face the worst.

At first, I didn't notice much of a reaction and I hoped to be one of the lucky ones showing minimal side effects. The gut-twisting bouts of nausea and vomiting changed everything. The cancer-killing poison damaged my taste buds and destroyed my appetite.

After that came the Great Follicle Release. I found clumps of hair on my pillow. Water streaming from the showerhead sent the hair from my head floating to my feet. Chemo had weakened every cell in my body until they said, "The hell with it" and stopped doing their jobs. In the end, I had only wisps of thin, limp hair so scattered on my head that hunks of scalp the size of a saucer shone through for the world to see. I learned the hard way that I could let it all hang out at home, but needed to wear a scarf in public, always. The gawking stares or averted eyes reminded me that everyone could see the damage that cancer had done. It frightened them.

I ventured to the grocery store one afternoon bareheaded. Since chemo left me super-sensitive to cold, I enjoyed the tingle of spring warmth on my scalp while I crossed the parking lot. I lifted my face to the sky for a little love-hug from God. Then I noticed a teenage girl staring at me as she got into her car. She wrinkled her nose and turned away. My hand flew to my hair and I patted a strand or two of my female comb-over into place. I considered going home for a scarf, but decided people needed a hefty dose of cancer reality that morning.

Before I'd snagged a grocery cart, a woman I'd known at the plant ran over and threw her arms around me. "You look wonderful," she gushed. "How are you feeling?" During our entire conversation, she kept her eyes trained on my face like a couple of laser beams. I never saw her hazard a glance at my hair. Though if I had eyes in the back of my head I felt certain I'd have seen her stare as I walked down the first aisle.

Over the next half hour, I rushed through the store, picking up everything on my list. Strangers passed me like they hadn't noticed anyone near them. Not one other person greeted me or smiled. So much for their dose of reality. Seemed they'd given it to me instead.

I went home and stared at myself in the bathroom mirror. I cringed. I saw blotchy cheeks and scraggly hair. My eyebrows and eyelashes had long since given up their fight for life and fallen off. My skin looked gray and the blush I had added that morning to give my face a touch of color made me look like an overly made-up corpse. I hardly noticed my tears when they started.

I reached for Russ's shaving cream and pushed the button until it filled my palm enough to lather my head. Then I picked up his razor, took a deep breath and dragged the single-edge blade across my skull. When I finished, I used the hand towel to wipe away the dregs of hair and foam.

Two rounds of chemo down, four to go. It didn't sound like a lot, but when I saw what two sessions had done to me already, I couldn't imagine the devastation the rest would bring. I could only hope that the damn disease had suffered worse destruction than my poor body.

My family has stood by me and loved me no matter how I look or feel. My mood swings and bitchiness never phase them. They cry when I cry and laugh when I laugh. Even my grandchildren don surgical masks and sit by my bed when I'm too weak to get up. If I survive this cancer and treatment, it will be on the shoulders of everyone around me.

I'm tired, Momma,

December 5, 2011
9:00 PM

Dear Mom,

I CAN'T remember when I last slept. I must doze from time to time, but it doesn't feel like it. I sit by your bed, read your letters to Grandma CiCi and stare at you. Russ hasn't moved either except to straighten your sheets or brush your hair back from your face. You don't respond. Not to his touch or to our voices.

I'm not ready to lose you, but after everything you've been through I am ready to let you go. Your body can't take much more. Neither can my heart. I wiped away a tear.

Russ looked over at me. "Are you all right, Alex?"

I nodded and pointed to the hatbox.

"Your mom's letters? They're getting to you?" He looked at the envelopes. "You know, she never let me read them, never even told me what she wrote about. On Mother's Day and CiCi's birthday, Livvy disappeared to write. I swear when she came back, she'd be energized, happier. I didn't understand it, but it meant so much to her that I never questioned it."

"You and Mom always fit together, like you were meant to be," I said. "You give each other the space to be yourselves and end up stronger as a couple because of it."

"You and Will have a lot of that, too. The hard knocks only bring you closer."

"I hope so." I choked on a sob. "Do you want to read them?" I held up an envelope. "She talks about things that happened, her feelings and doubts. It's like reading her life story. Sometimes she makes me laugh and sometimes her words slice me open. They physically hurt me."

"Maybe someday." He shook his head. "Not yet."

"I wish I'd read them years ago, when I could have talked to her about them."

"Livvy wasn't sure she ever wanted you to see those. She thought you wouldn't accept her if you knew her wounds and warts."

The trickle of tears became a torrent. "The truth is that they made me love her more. They made me see the woman, not just my mom. And I may never get the chance to tell her that."

Russ walked over to my chair and put his hand on my shoulder. "You just told her, Alex."

Dear Momma,

WHEN I divorced Sonny, I thought things couldn't get worse. When I got sober, I believed I'd hit rock bottom. When you and Daddy died, my world collapsed under the weight of my grief. Then chemotherapy took me lower physically, mentally and emotionally than I thought possible.

I could barely lift my head from my pillow. Nausea gagged me and if I managed to get food down, it tore the sores in my mouth to pieces on its way back up. Isolation tested my sanity as my chemo-damaged immune system struggled for balance. My weight plummeted and muscles atrophied. On my best days, I hoped to sleep until I woke healthy. On my worst, I prayed for God to take me. I no longer knew which would be worse, death by cancer or by chemo.

About a month after my final round of intravenous hell, I woke up hungry and ate a piece of toast. A minor miracle. Every day after that, I felt invigorated, stronger.

I looked in the mirror. Fuzzy wisps of new hair growth dotted my head. Hints of color splotched my cheeks. I returned to work a few hours a day. My mind functioned again, though at first everything seemed muddled. But I smiled and laughed and looked forward to each day.

The one thing I hadn't allowed back into my life drove Russ crazy. He'd been patient and understanding through the surgery, chemo and aftereffects of both. Now that his wife had rejoined the living, he couldn't grasp why I had no desire for romance, no interest in sex.

We hadn't argued in years, but chronic horniness could make even a saintly man ornery. Our record fell apart a few weeks ago when Russ and I quarreled from dinner to bedtime and about the time I lay my head on the pillow, he started in again.

"Livvy, you've recovered from the surgery and chemo. Your energy is back and you're functioning again. I've heard all your excuses for not wanting to make love with me." He leaned up on his elbow and stared at me in the dark. "But they don't wash with me. The only thing that makes any sense is that you've lost interest in me. Is that it?"

"No! Of course not. I've tried to explain this to you a dozen times."

"Then try again."

I stared up at the ceiling. "You've seen me at my worst. You can't still be attracted to me. How could that even be possible?" I fought the catch in my throat. I had cried enough over the cancer and didn't want to do it anymore. "You've seen me for months with constant diarrhea and vomiting. You've seen the ribs protruding and the scar screaming out for you to notice it." I shuddered at the thought of what I'd just seen of myself in the bathroom mirror a few moments before. "I look like a bald, emaciated Holocaust survivor. There's nothing sexy about that." I felt damaged and shriveled. Ugly. The catch in my voice strengthened to a choked sob.

Russ rolled onto his side and pulled me close. "Listen to me, Livvy. I love you. I miss you. I want you." His arms tightened around me. "You are the sexiest woman I've ever known, before, during and after chemo. Just let me prove it to you." He kissed my forehead.

"Not yet. Please."

Russ rolled away from me. I let my tears fall.

On a sweltering Saturday morning in July, my husband decided he'd had enough. A thunderstorm popped up and lightening lit the sky. Heavy raindrops splattered on the deck.

We watched from the sliding glass doors in the family room. Russ kissed my cheek.

I leaned into him, glancing down at my pajamas. "I think I need a shower and real clothes."

Russ picked up his coffee mug from the side table and walked to the kitchen. My stomach tightened as I watched him walk away and I wondered if we could ever be pre-cancer Russ and Livvy again. I missed my husband but had no clue what to do to get him back.

I walked into the bathroom and turned on the shower. By the time I stepped out of my clothes, steam filled the room and fogged the mirror. Within moments, the hot spray turned my skin pink. I washed my hair and lathered up a floral scented salt scrub on my skin. All my sexual tension crystallized and slid over my body with the soapy water to swirl down the drain. I closed my eyes and relaxed, from my fingers and feet, through my limbs, all the way to the knot in my gut.

After I shut off the water, I did a quick pat down before I wrapped a towel around my head and another around my body. When I pulled the shower curtain back, my breath caught in my throat at the sight of Russ leaning against the closed bathroom door, his arms folded across his chest. He wore a pale blue shirt with the sleeves rolled up almost to his elbows. The shirt tucked into his faded Levi jeans accented his still trim waist and muscular thighs. Through the steamy fog, I saw the look on his face. Panic swelled in my chest. My discomfort might have been mingled with lust, but it had been so long that I didn't know if I'd recognize it any more.

I stepped over the rim of the tub onto the bath mat. Russ didn't move. He never took his eyes off my face. I licked my lips, but couldn't muster up enough saliva to swallow.

"I've always loved the way you smell when you get out of the shower," Russ said.

He took a step closer and brushed his fingers across my cheek. My skin tingled. I stepped back only for the bathtub to stop me from going any further. He moved closer.

"And the way you look. Your pink cheeks." He glanced down at my chest. "The way your nipples get so hard the towel can't hide them."

He grasped the towel between his fingers. I put my hands over his. "Please, don't."

He looked back up to my eyes, never moving his fingers from the towel. With one quick tug, he pulled the ends apart and let it fall to the floor.

My already pink cheeks darkened with embarrassment.

"I love you, Livvy. I love everything about you."

Russ leaned closer and kissed my tears as they slipped down my face. "I love the way you think that after all these years a damn disease could keep me from wanting you." He kissed me, parting my lips with his tongue, teasing it across my teeth and deep into my mouth. The feel of his lips pressed to mine lingered even after he pulled away. "No disease could ever do that."

He kissed my neck and boney shoulders. He lowered his head and nuzzled first one breast and then the other. He dropped lower until he knelt in front of me on the hard tile. He ran his fingers over the nine-inch scar that still looked neon red against my pasty-pale skin. "I love your scar."

I choked back a sob and he looked up into my face.

"It reminds me that I almost lost you. The surgery that gave it to you saved your life. It's the reason you're still here where I can still touch you…" He ran one finger the entire length of the scar and sent shivers up my spine. "And kiss you…" His lips touched me half a dozen times from one end of the wound to the other and my shivers formed a single, tingling tremor in the pit of my stomach. He stood and tilted my chin until I had to look up at him. "I'm grateful for everything you went through because it means you're still here, and I can still make love to you."

Russ opened the door behind him, picked me up and carried me to our bed. He laid me down as gently as he would a sleeping child before he unbuttoned his shirt and let it drop. I reached out to unzip his pants and he stepped out of them. He lay beside me, propped up on one arm. With the other, he unwrapped the towel from my head and ran his fingers through my spikey, wet hair. He kissed my forehead, my cheeks, my nose and my lips.

I matched him kiss for kiss and wondered how I had ever managed to go through so many months without his passion. My fingers played across his chest and shoulders. He grabbed my hands and put them to his lips, kissing each fingertip as though he couldn't get enough, kissing the inside of each wrist and up my arms. I buried my face in his neck and inhaled the masculine scent of him. Fresh-mown grass after a spring rain mingled with a hint of toothpaste, motor oil and chocolate. Russ had always reeked of sex to me and that morning it rolled off him in almost visible waves, and I breathed it in like oxygen. I needed it to come back to life.

And he did bring me back to life that day, in every sense of the word. Every nerve in my body screamed for release. The shame and embarrassment I felt earlier vanished in the afterglow. Russ made me feel sexy and loved, desirable and desired. He showed me that not everything we had walked through together had dampened anything between us. It enhanced it.

By the time we climaxed, a sheen of sweat glistened over our bodies. We fell back against the pillows, and a grin spread across Russ's face. "I knew we hadn't lost it," he said.

"I knew you hadn't, but I had doubts about me."

Russ rolled over and kissed me again. "Look at that storm." He pointed out the huge picture window in our bedroom that framed the waterway beyond it.

The rain pounded and the thunder rumbled over the churning waterway. "Imagine the past year tied to a boulder and tossed into that water. It's gone, Livvy. We have a fresh start." He looked at me. "You're cancer free and we have the rest of our lives in front of us." He touched his lips to mine in a tender, gentle kiss. "Let's not waste a single moment of it."

Life is good, Momma.

December 5, 2011
10:00 PM

Dear Mom,

I PUT your last letter down more than once. Reading it made me antsy and uneasy, like I'd accidently picked up your diary, flipped the page and intruded on your most erotic entry.

Do kids, even grown kids, ever feel comfortable seeing their parents as sexual beings? Seeing Grandma CiCi that way bothered you. And I remember, as a kid, being grossed out when you and Russ kissed or held hands. Later, it seemed so natural that I seldom noticed.

You haven't moved in hours. Your sleep seems so deep, yet your chest rises and falls in short, shallow bursts. I'm almost afraid to look away, for fear I'll miss your last breath. Russ and I both look for any flicker of awareness even though we know there is almost no hope of that. You're dying right in front of us and there's nothing we can do. The lights in the room seem dimmer, colors more muted. Even Russ's complexion has paled.

We're fading with you.

Dear Momma,

RUSS AND I declared a cancer-free Christmas. We wanted no mention of illness or treatment, the months of hell the family went through or even my newly grown, funky hair. We spent the entire month of December decorating, baking, shopping and wrapping. I can't remember ever being so happy.

Russ hung the outdoor lights and arranged an inflatable Santa and his reindeer all around the front yard. He even snuck in a Grinch that waved to people from behind an azalea bush. I put up two trees indoors and bought a dozen poinsettias that I scattered around the house. I displayed the hand-carved wooden nativity scene on the mantle. By Christmas Eve, we had everything ready early, so we snuggled in the swing on the front porch, waiting for Alex, Will and the kids.

Russ pulled me close and kissed the top of my head. "Doesn't get any better than this."

"Mmm," I mumbled.

Car lights beamed down the driveway. Will, Alex, Garrett and Darcy threw open their doors and jumped out. Garrett and Darcy wrapped their arms around Christmas offerings that shimmered with way too much scotch tape.

"Merry Christmas, Grandma and Grandpa," they yelled as they ran up the steps. "We brought presents!"

"I see that," I said. "Should we go put them under the tree?"

Garrett and Darcy glanced at each other. "We want you to open your presents now," Garrett answered.

Will and Alex came up the steps carrying a stack of packages. "They came up with the idea for your gifts on their own. It's pretty important to them, Mom."

"Yeah. Besides, you need them before dinner," Darcy said.

Russ grabbed my hand. "Then let's open a couple of presents."

Alex arranged the new gifts under the tree. Thirteen-year-old Garrett and ten-year-old Darcy continued clutching their treasures to their chests. Russ and I sat on the couch.

Garrett coughed. "May I have your attention, please?"

Will and Alex took their seats. We all sat a little straighter and waited for him to speak again.

"Darcy and I talked about what to get for you and Grandpa. We wanted it to be something that told you both..." He blushed and dug the toe of his tennis shoe in the carpet.

"We wanted you to know how much we love you," Darcy finished for him.

Garrett nodded and handed us the smallest of the packages he held. "Open this one first. It's for both of you."

I took the gift from him, and Russ and I both tore the paper and ribbon off to reveal a wooden picture frame that said "Family Time—The Best Time." It held two pictures. The first looked like it had been taken a couple of years earlier. All six of us clustered together on the dock admiring the fish Garrett held up by the line he'd used to catch it. We all grinned and pointed at his trophy.

I didn't think it could be possible for us to look any happier. Until I saw the second picture. I sat up in bed, leaning against a mountain of pillows. Garrett and Darcy sat on either side of me holding up the books they'd been reading to me. Will, Alex and Russ surrounded us. My scalp gleamed in the photo like I'd polished it, but my eyes sparkled and our smiles glowed.

At the time, I thought I looked like a Halloween ghoul set on the front porch to frighten trick-or-treaters away. But when I looked again, I saw something different. I saw a fighter, a woman who loved her family so much that she would walk through hell to stay with them. And I saw the family that loved her enough to hold her up while she did it.

Before I could swipe away the first tear, Darcy said, "Open the next ones."

She and Garrett handed each of us another gift. Russ and I opened them at the same time. "Now I see why we needed these before dinner," Russ said. We both held up aprons, the kind that slip over your neck and tie in the back. As we read the slogans written on each one, Russ's tears matched mine.

"Put them on," Garrett ordered.

We slid the fabric loops over our heads. An arrow pointed up to our faces. Beneath it, mine said, "My Grandma Is My Hero." Russ's made the same claim about Grandpa.

Garrett stepped behind me to tie the strings. When he finished he hugged me and squeezed tight. "I love you so much, Grandma."

Life gets better every day, Momma,

Livvy

December 6, 2011
1:30 AM

Dear Mom,

$\mathcal{I}$ SEE last Christmas so clearly. Garrett and Darcy scoured every photograph I had to find the perfect pictures. Nothing less would do. And those cheesy aprons – they hunted for those, too, ordering them only when they'd found exactly what they wanted.

Mom, we haven't had enough Christmases and birthdays and ordinary days. I want time. It's such a precious thing, and I feel like I've wasted too much of it.

They say your life flashes through your mind when you're drowning. I feel like that's happening to me, like I'm going under with you. And you know what's running through my head? Every argument, every disagreement, every spat we ever had. I remember rolling my eyes at you, and you getting so angry about it. I remember telling you I hated you. I remember telling you to mind your own business, to stop telling me what to do and trying to control my life. I remember you telling me you had cancer. I remember praying for hours during your surgery. I remember holding your hair while you heaved after the first few chemo sessions. Then I remember toward the end of those treatments, how you longed to have your hair back, even if it got in the way. I remember thinking you'd never get better and then you did. And I felt hope that you would beat this damn disease.

I want those memories to leave me alone, but they won't let go. They won't make way for the happy ones. Smiles and laughter won't come. I pray that they do again one day, but for now, joy has taken a back seat to the illness.

I know that it's time. I know you can't hold on any longer, and I don't want you to try. I can't bear it. I'm ready, if you could just give me one more moment.

I hope you know how much I love you, how much you've meant to me, to my children and to my life. You showed me how to love and live, grow and change. You showed me how to be strong and happy. You showed me failure and success, frailty and faith.

I need you to know that I want to be just like you when I grow up, Mom.

Alex

Dear Momma,

T HE STIFLING summer felt unusually hot to me. Any time I got up the courage to venture outside, a haze of humidity met me at the door. I might as well have spent the entire month of July living in a steamy bathroom. I wanted to do nothing more physically taxing than watch television from my favorite spot on the couch. But I agreed to a family cookout for Independence Day.

The weatherman predicted that day to be a carbon copy of each one for the month leading up to it and every foreseeable day afterward. By eight o'clock, the temperature had already climbed to eighty-five degrees with ninety-five percent humidity. Not one cloud offered respite from the sun's glare and no hint of breeze dried the perspiration that started within seconds of stepping outside. Most days, this kind of heat brought on brief afternoon thunderstorms. They lasted long enough to wet everything down, send a thick layer of muggy mist rising from the ground and reduce the temperature for about ten minutes before the increased humidity made it feel even worse. But on that day, even the storms avoided the coastline around Wilmington.

Russ, Will and Brody grilled steaks and hamburgers, complaining about the heat the whole time. Alex, Gina and I sat under umbrellas on the deck. Garrett, Darcy and Mia lounged on the dock in their swimsuits. Their teasing banter quickly turned to quarrelling that we heard from across the lawn.

"When did they start bickering like that?" I asked.

"The same time Garrett started teasing Darcy about having a boyfriend," Alex answered.

My mouth formed a silent "Oh." "So, what do we know about the boyfriend?" I asked.

"His family just moved in down the street. Seems like a nice kid. His name's Conner. Garrett overheard Darcy tell one of her friends that she thinks he's cute and he hasn't stopped ribbing her about it since."

"No wonder she's so mad at him." I chuckled. "Do you remember how you were at that age, Alex? Hormones raging. Mood swings worse than my menopause."

She cut her eyes in my direction. "You're exaggerating."

"No, she isn't," Gina said with the authority of experience. "I remember it well."

Gina and I laughed. Alex folded her arms across her chest. "Ganging up on me won't work."

"Sure it will." Gina nodded her head. "Give you a little reality check."

"At the time, you acted like your life was a high level national security secret. Everything was on a need-to-know basis and Russ and I didn't need to know." I looked across the table at her. "If you'd had a sibling, I bet it would have been even worse." My gaze turned to the dock. "I'm sure Darcy feels the same way, just like every teenage girl before her."

Alex sighed. "I'll talk to Garrett and get him to ease up."

"Good plan, Mom," Gina agreed.

By the time we ate steak and potato salad, hauled the dirty dishes into the kitchen and waved good-bye to the Waters family, I felt like I had been chewed up and spit out.

Alex noticed it first. "Mom, are you all right? You look really pale."

"I'm so darn tired. The heat this year is really getting to me."

"Go lie down," Alex ordered. "We can take care of this mess." She waved her arm around the room and pointed Garrett and Darcy toward the kitchen.

I couldn't find the energy to argue with her.

Alex waited while I changed into my pajamas and tucked me into bed.

"I think I like this," I said.

"Don't get used to it." She smiled. "Get some sleep, Mom."

Alex closed the bedroom door behind her and I lay in the dark feeling once again like the luckiest woman on the planet.

Livvy

Obituary

Olivia Marie Dolan Abbott Montgomery

Olivia Marie Dolan Abbott Montgomery, 65, of Wilmington, N.C., died Monday, December 6, 2011, at the Lower Cape Fear Hospice and Life Care Center after a courageous battle with cancer.

Olivia was born in Wilmington, N.C. on November 15, 1947. She was preceded in death by her mother, Cecilia Cathleen Hewett Dolan and her father, Luther Alan Dolan.

She graduated from New Hanover High School and retired from Cape Fear Textiles. She was co-owner of the Dolan Ford Dealership and an active member of Fountain of Grace Methodist Church. She loved life, her family, her church, her friends, her home and her business. She was a constant source of inspiration to those who knew her. Olivia Montgomery was loved deeply and will be missed by many.

She is survived by her husband, Russell Dwayne Montgomery, her daughter, Alexandra Madison Dolan Crenshaw, son-in-law, William Jeffrey Crenshaw and two grandchildren, Garrett William Crenshaw and Darcy Cathleen Crenshaw.

A celebration of her life will be held at Fountain of Grace Methodist Church on South College Road at 11 in the morning on Monday, December 10, 2012.

In lieu of flowers, the family requests donations to Cape Fear Hospice, Fountain of Grace Church or The American Cancer Society.

May 13, 2012
Happy Mother's Day

Dear Mom,

YOU COMPLAINED about last summer's triple digit heat and sweltering humidity. You said it exhausted and drained you. You spent more time indoors than I ever remember you being willing to do. And you didn't stick your toes in the sand at Wrightsville Beach all season, not once. I look back on it now and I don't understand how I missed the red flags. We all did. Sometimes I wondered if you missed the signs, too, or if you somehow knew what it meant and what the future held. By September, we knew the cause of your weakness and fatigue. The real culprit, your cancer, had come back, with a vengeance.

You had been healthy for so many months that the weight of dread hanging over me since the day of your diagnosis had finally lifted. You beat the damn disease and said, "Good riddance," while you watched it shrink in the rearview mirror.

So, it blindsided Will and me when you and Russ told us. I see that moment etched in my mind like the old tintype photo you had of Granddaddy's parents. Except that stark faded black-and-white image leaves a trail of scars behind every time it shows up. And it always ends the same way. You look at Will and me and say, "I saw the doctor yesterday. The cancer is back." I feel my tears fall and I hear my heart shatter like a dropped crystal goblet. I see your hand reach out to cover mine, but I can't feel your touch through the tingling numbness. And I want to feel it. I long to feel it. I miss the way your hugs and your touch comforted me.

Some images of you bloom in joyful hues. I see the blue of the sky and the Intracoastal Waterway behind you while you read in your favorite chair on the dock. I see the pink and white azaleas in the background while you hide brightly painted Easter eggs in the yard. I see you covered in sage green drips when you helped me paint my kitchen.

But the memories of the day you told me the news and many of the days that followed leave no joy in their wake. You've been gone five months and the flashbacks to that time still bowl me over in tsunami waves. They crash through my mind with searing pain.

I want to do more than hit the pause button in my head. I want to erase the memory tape completely. I want to turn back the clock and stop you from telling me that the cancer had returned. As soon as you say, "I saw my doctor today," I want to say, "Stop right there. I don't want to hear any more. If you tell me, it becomes real. If it becomes real, you'll die. And, if you die, I have to deal with it for the rest of my life. So, don't tell me. Please. Don't tell me."

But it's too late to stop you. You did tell me. I knew. You died. My life will never be the same. I look in the mirror and see Alex reflected back at me. Long brown hair, brown eyes, oval face, high cheekbones. My mascara's in place, lipstick's applied and the tiny, faded scar on my cheek from the tricycle accident decades ago still flares red when I perspire. But I also see more crow's feet around the eyes and the full lips that used to grin at the slightest provocation tug downward at the corners, looking more sad than sensual. I suspect the changes will become more pronounced every day.

The doctors offered chemo and promised you a few extra months. You decided to spend whatever time you had left coping with only one demon ravaging your body instead of two. None of us questioned your decision. You had to be the one to make that choice. Now, I wonder if you might still be here if you had flipped the coin the other way. But at what price would I have you in my life today? Would you be in pain, suffering, sick, bed-ridden? Flashbacks of your last weeks haunt me. They overwhelm the years of vibrant life that came before. You made the right decision for you. You probably made the right decision for all of us, though none of the rest of us would have had the courage to make it.

Russ never left you. He drove you to doctor's appointments, cried with you after every diagnosis and held your hand through each procedure. He prepared your meals and spoonfed you on the days you couldn't lift your own fork. He walked you to the bathroom, washed your hair and helped you dress, as gently as if you have been a china doll. He juiced fruits and vegetables and lifted you from the pillow so you could swallow. He lay in your bed with you at night, though he slept little, listening for the slightest indication that you might need him. Russ promised you that you wouldn't be alone at the end. He kept that promise.

Hours before you died, you opened your eyes, looked around the room and I swear, you actually saw each one of us before you said, "I love you all so much. Please take care of each other." I stood on one side of your bed, and when you turned to me to speak, I leaned as close as possible. Then you took Russ's hand and said, "Pray with me." He did exactly as you asked, though I have no idea how he could through his tears. As he spoke, you calmed and closed your eyes. You never opened them again.

I read your letters to Grandma Cici during the last days of your life. Your voice echoed in every word. By the time I read your final words, I knew that, somehow, I had to give your eulogy. Russ agreed.

When I walked to the lectern in the front of the church, my hands shook so badly that I feared I might drop my notes. My legs felt like rubber bands and my voice quivered. I took a deep breath and looked out at the church pews filled with people who loved and missed you. I looked at Russ, Delores, Will and Gina. I saw Garrett keeping his arm around his sister while she wiped at her tears. I saw love in every face and felt strengthened by it.

"I always knew that my mother was strong and resourceful and loving, but the last several months of her life, I learned how truly remarkable she really was." I took a deep breath while I struggled to control my emotions.

"In her youth, Mom had a rebellious streak that got her in a lot of trouble. She married young, had her only child young and dealt with the death of her own mother young. All those things brought her to her knees for a while. They changed her, dampened her spirit. She grieved those losses and came through them even stronger, more of a hellion. She fought with her father and her husband. She partied. She divorced. She hit bottom and arrived at Alcoholics Anonymous to get sober. My mother overcame odds and obstacles in her life. I stand in awe of that.

"You know, Mom got sober at a time when drunken young women were seen as shameful and trashy. I've got news for you. What Olivia Montgomery did, in standing up and admitting her alcoholism, required more courage than I will probably ever have. She took responsibility for her choices, changed her life and showed me what it meant to be a strong woman.

"She fell in love again and her marriage to Russ became a real example to me. They taught me patience and compromise and devotion. Mom built not just one career, but two. And the whole time she loved her family with a ferocity I've never seen before, but I'm so grateful to have been the recipient of. Somewhere along the line, she found God. And like everything else she did, she embraced Him and felt embraced by Him. She didn't preach her faith. She lived it.

"We watched Mom fight her cancer with everything she had in her, but in the end, in those last days, I knew that she couldn't hold on much longer. Still, I wanted her to try. I sat by her bed and begged her not to leave me. I'm embarrassed to tell you that now because it makes me sound like such a coward in the face of my mother's bravery.

The day she died, she took my hand and repeated something that I had only heard from her a few months before. But hearing it again that day, in her raspy whisper, through her dry, cracked lips, I really heard her. I finally understood.

"She said, 'Alex, the secret to life is knowing when to hang on and when to let go.'

"Mom looked up at me with such palpable pain in her eyes. I ached for her.

"She added, 'Hang on to your family. But it's time to let me go. I want you to find the joy in your life again and treasure it. The Bible says, "This, too, shall pass." It took me the longest time to understand that meant the good and the bad. Everything changes. Everything is fleeting, so hang on to the good for as long as you can grip it. And let go of the bad. Clinging to it wastes such precious time.'

"When Mom finished speaking, I knew she couldn't suffer any more and I couldn't watch it. I kissed her cheek and held her hand while Russ prayed with her. When he finished speaking, I whispered in her ear, 'I promise we'll be okay. You taught us how to love and how to be strong. You can let go now, Mom.'

"She closed her eyes and later, when her breathing stopped, I still held her hand. I'll never stop missing her. I'll never stop loving her. But all her life, Mom had been laying the groundwork to teach me how to let her go."

I looked up over the heads of hundreds of mourners and spoke only to you. "I love you past the sky, Mom. I always will."

CPSIA information can be obtained at www.ICGtesting.com
Printed in the USA
LVOW10s1947190715

446788LV00003B/5/P

mL   1-14